Readers everywhere rave about Roxanne Henke's
Coming Home to Brewster series...

Here's what they say about *After Anne*, Book #1

From California: "A dear friend gave me *After Anne* several weeks ago....Your book was awesome and should be sold with a box of Kléenex!"

From North Carolina: "I felt as though the characters were my best friends. The last time I cried this much was when I read James Patterson's *Suzanne's Diary for Nicholas.*"

From Oregon: "I could hardly put the book down. Oprah should know about this!"

From Christianbooks.com: "*After Anne* is probably my favorite [book of the year]. This moving story of an unlikely friendship between two women will have you laughing and crying and longing for a relationship like theirs."

From an Amazon.com reader: "I don't know how I got this copy of *After Anne* but however I got it, I am so glad I read it!...It's just beautifully written—and so true.... It is one of the must-reads for the coming year if not tomorrow."

From North Dakota: "We read *After Anne* for our book club in our MOPS (Mothers of Preschoolers) group in Fargo and all fell in love with it. We all kept saying even if you cannot make it to book club this is a book you have to read."

And Book #2, *Finding Ruth*

From Virginia: "I read *Finding Ruth* after I finished *After Anne,* and I thought this book couldn't be as good...but sure enough you did it again! You are my favorite author."

From California: "I just finished reading the last page of *Finding Ruth*....The tears went down my cheeks as I read it....But what kept me so on the edge...was your showing me Brewster town. I could see everyone, even their laugh lines."

From Kentucky: "Your book couldn't have come to me at a better time. I struggle with contentment or lack of. Thank you for a touching story that fit quite nicely into my life. I was moved by it....If I had my way, your book would be topping all the best-seller lists."

From Indiana: "I chose your book from the new fiction section at our public library without realizing it was a Christian book....I could hardly bear to put it down."

And Book #3, *Becoming Olivia*

From Indiana: "I've been burning up the e-mail lines telling anyone who will listen that your books are required reading. Please hurry with number 4!"

From North Carolina: "Just finished *Becoming Olivia*—loved it!...Your Christian insight and faith shine through as realistic and practical without coming off 'preachy.'"

From South Dakota: "I could not put it down! I could relate to so many of the things Olivia went through, especially the struggle with depression and anxiety....*Becoming Olivia* was the first of your books that I have read, and I look forward to reading the others. Thank you!"

From Ohio: I've just read *Becoming Olivia* and am so moved. There are many words to describe the book, but none seem adequate enough."

Via e-mail: "I am a voracious reader and many authors have touched me, moved me and changed me, but you are the first one I've written to. I needed you to know how important your writing is to people like me. Thank you."

"I just finished *Becoming Olivia* and had to write and tell you how much I loved it. I have read all three of your books...but *Becoming Olivia* especially spoke to me....I know that this had to have been a difficult book for you to write, but you did a superb job, as always."

"[*Becoming Olivia*] is amazing for its healing powers....I'm going to use the book in my clinical practice to give to patients who know they don't feel right but don't think it's bad enough to be classified as depression. Thanks for telling the story so beautifully."

And about Book #4, *Always Jan*

From Dorothy: "I just finished reading *Always Jan,* and, like your other books, I loved it....God has truly given you a beautiful talent...one which I pray you will continue to use so that we can share in His goodness and mercy through your stories."

From Ellen: "I just finished *Always Jan* and hated leaving Brewster as I read the last page....I absolutely loved this series....I want to go to Brewster and see these wonderful people. I want to go to Pumpkin Fest. I want to visit Aunt Ida. I want to buy her house. I want my life to be transformed like Jan's and Kenny's, and I want to be a friend like Libby."

From Nancy: "I just finished your book, and man! This is your best work yet!"

From a housewife and mother in Indiana: "I just finished reading the fourth book in the Brewster series. Wow! What a read....Life can sure be difficult at times, and a good, uplifting, honest book is a treasure."

ROXANNE HENKE

HARVEST HOUSE PUBLISHERS

EUGENE, OREGON

Unless otherwise indicated, all Scripture quotations are taken from *The Living Bible,* Copyright ©1971. Used by permission of Tyndale House Publishers, Inc., Wheaton, IL 60189 USA. All rights reserved.

Verses marked MSG are taken from The Message. Copyright © by Eugene H. Peterson 1993, 1994, 1995, 1996, 2000, 2001, 2002. Used by permission of NavPress Publishing Group.

Cover by Koechel Peterson & Associates, Inc., Minneapolis, Minnesota

Roxanne Sayler Henke: Published in association with the literary agency of Janet Kobobel Grant, Books & Such, 4788 Carissa Avenue, Santa Rosa, California 95405

This is a work of fiction. Names, characters, places, and incidents are products of the author's imagination or are used fictitiously. Any resemblance to actual persons, living or dead, or to events or locales, is entirely coincidental.

WITH LOVE, LIBBY

Copyright © 2006 by Roxanne Henke
Published by Harvest House Publishers
Eugene, Oregon 97402
www.harvesthousepublishers.com

Library of Congress Cataloging-in-Publication Data
Henke, Roxanne, 1953–
    With love, Libby / Roxanne Henke.
        p. cm. — (Coming home to Brewster ; bk. 5)
    ISBN-13: 978-0-7369-1197-9 (pbk.)
    ISBN-10: 0-7369-1197-9
    1. Women—Fiction. 2. North Dakota—Fiction. 3. Self-realization—
    Fiction. I. Title.
    PS3608.E55W58 2006
    813'. 6—dc22   2005018229

All rights reserved. No part of this publication may be reproduced, stored in a retrieval system, or transmitted in any form or by any means—electronic, mechanical, digital, photocopy, recording, or any other—except for brief quotations in printed reviews, without the prior permission of the publisher.

Printed in the United States of America

06 07 08 09 10 11 12 13 14 / BC-MS / 10 9 8 7 6 5 4 3 2 1

A Note from Roxy

With Love, Libby is the final book in the Coming Home to Brewster series. *Sigh.* It's been hard saying good-bye to old friends. I want to thank my readers who love these characters as much as I do. Thank you for reading these books...and for writing to me. Thank you for your letters and for so generously sharing the many ways the books in this series have touched your lives.

As always, many "Thanks" go to my family and friends. Thank you for giving me the time and space to write, and also for knowing sometimes I need a break. Your love, laughter, and support mean the world.

A big "Thanks" to Bon Wickenheiser for sharing her dream of serving others for so many years...and for letting me use her idea here. I owe you lunch!

It would be hard to imagine writing these books without the never-failing support of my wonderful editor, Nick Harrison. He's a gem more precious than gold!

Thanks to my agent, Janet Grant, and the stellar folks at Harvest House. You make the way smooth and the journey pleasant indeed.

And, finally, to my husband, Lorren, and my daughters, Rachael and Tegan. Thank you for sharing my dream. It's thrice the thrill because I get to live it with you!

Oh, and I can't forget Gunner, my faithful canine companion who makes sure I don't ever sit at my computer for *too* long. Thank you...I think.

This is what God said: Before I shaped you in the womb, I knew all about you. Before you saw the light of day I had holy plans for you.

Jeremiah 1:4-5 MSG

This book is for my daughters,
Rachael and Tegan.
God had holy plans for me, indeed!

Prologue

Libby's letter...

Why had I thought this would be so easy? I stared at the blank page, took a deep breath, put my pen to the paper.

Dear Anne,

I rested the end of the silver pen on my bottom lip and stared at the words. I read the two words over...*Dear Anne...Dear Anne...* I hadn't expected to get writer's block *now*. Not after two simple words. Not after several hundred thousand words.

Dear Anne, I put the pen to the paper. I'd learned it was best to just write. Not over-analyze. Not try and *think* my way through. Just write.

My pen hovered above the page. What should I say?

Pretend you're talking to her. Pretend she's sitting next to you.

I took a sip of coffee, took a quick breath as if I were going to speak. I started writing. *Where should I start? Anne, do you know that if it hadn't been for you, I wouldn't be sitting here next to...* I looked at the ream of white paper sitting on the desk by my elbow. Over four hundred pages filled with words. My words. Double-spaced. Telling the story—mine and Anne's.

If it hadn't been for you—A familiar lump pushed its way into my throat. I closed my eyes. This was silly. I had no reason to cry now.

Did she know? Did *I* really know?

7

A single tear made its way down my cheek. I smiled as I brushed it away with my fingertips. I could almost hear Anne laughing with me. "Just tell me the story," she'd say. "You're a writer. Start at the beginning. Once upon a time…"

A soft breath of laughter blew through my lips. Heavens, I didn't need to go back *that* far! I glanced again at the sheaf of paper at my elbow. Those pages held our story. What they didn't tell was what happened next. The part Anne hadn't lived to see but had been part of all the same.

In those pages I'd already told the story of a dream that appeared impossible. Of a friendship that seemed unlikely. Of a life gone too soon. Now I would tell the rest of the story. About a friendship that didn't die with the friend. About a dream that did come true.

So…okay…I would start there. At the end. The end that was really a beginning.

"The End" that was only a beginning...

Libby

"Mom?" Emily's voice crackled over the phone line. "Are you there?" Her voice faded. "I have to talk to yo—u. Wa—it—a—"

I rolled my eyes, certain that someday in my lifetime we'd laugh about the "olden days" of cell phone technology. I tossed my car keys on top of the fridge and shrugged out of my coat. Considering the fact I hadn't known Emily was going to call, I'd timed my trip home from the post office perfectly.

"Mom? Hang on. I'm alm—ost out—" The line went dead.

I knew enough to wait. We'd been through this drill often enough. Emily would call back as soon as she found a spot on campus where she'd have at least two bars on her cell screen. Bob and I had given her the phone as a going-off-to-college gift. Our not-so-subtle way of letting her know we weren't quite ready to empty our nest. While I waited for her to call back, I sifted through the mail. The usual stack of catalogs. You'd think Christmas was just around the corner the way my mailbox was filling up these days. I glanced at the calendar. October. Well then, it *was* just around the corner. At least for folks like me who lived miles from the nearest mall and relied on the Postal Service and UPS as a substitute Santa to deliver gifts to my doorstep. I set the catalogs aside. I'd page through them tonight while Bob slept through the History Channel.

The electric bill. Three pleas for money. The first two I tossed into the garbage, the other I'd think about. With Brian in grad school and Emily starting her third year of college, even a banker's family had to live on a budget. I scanned a postcard from Elizabeth's store at the Carlton mall; their fall merchandise was on sale. I tossed that, too. Old news. My friend Jan had given me the head's-up a week ago. One more business-sized envelope. My name and address neatly typed. No other flashy words calling for my attention. First class postage. Hmmm…No return address on the front. I flipped the envelope over. My eyes took in the return address as the phone rang again.

Pearce and Sutton Publishing House.

My heart took a familiar leap then sank. I was pretty sure I knew what was in this envelope. It could wait until I talked to Emily. Bad news can always wait.

Vicky

"I'll be with you in a minute." I caught Jim Magner's eye at the cash register at the same time I refilled Kenny Pearson's coffee cup. Jim nodded as he rolled a toothpick out of the holder on the counter. Usually he simply left enough change lying by the till to cover his coffee. He must want something more today.

I emptied the decaf coffee into my husband's cup, pouring regular into my brother-in-law's mug.

"Want me to ring up Jim?" Dave, my husband dipped his head toward the door.

"That'd be great." I leaned over the table into the booth and topped off Dan Jordan's cup as Dave slid out and headed to the till.

Paul Bennett, my brother-in-law, looked at his watch. "I can't figure out why Ruthie isn't here yet. She was getting the girls ready for daycare when I left for work this morning."

Automatically my eyes grazed the clock on the café wall. It was nearly ten in the morning, a good forty-five minutes later than my sister, Ruthie, usually arrived. She was my partner-in-hamburgers, as we liked to joke about our joint venture in Victoria's Café. *Vicky's* to everyone in Brewster. After all her years working in the time-sensitive radio business, I could usually set my watch by Ruthie. "Do you think we should—"

Just then the swinging door from the kitchen of the café swung open, and Ruthie hurried toward the coffeemaker. I watched as her eyes expertly surveyed the busy tables, noting the empty decaf pot in my left hand and the cups that needed filling all around. She dumped the grounds from the filter and got a new pot brewing as if she'd been doing this as many years as I had. She grabbed the backup pot of coffee off the top warmer and began making her way around the tables as if she hadn't missed a beat this morning.

"*Later...*" she mouthed in explanation to me.

"How about one of those Long Johns?" Kenny turned my attention back to business. It was no secret he had a weakness for the deep-fried rolls with maple frosting that were one of our specialties.

"You're in luck," I said. "There's one left." Funny how I kept a running total of the number of rolls I baked early each morning. A dozen and a half. Eighteen Long Johns five mornings a week. An even two-dozen on Saturdays. I didn't even want to do the math on how many of those rolls I'd baked in the almost twenty years I'd been working in this café. It wouldn't be hard to figure out the exact count of pie slices either. I baked five pies every morning. Cut them into eighths as the soup broth simmered, just minutes before the first customer walked through the door at six-thirty in the morning. Marv Bender. I could set my watch by him, too. He needed a Long John and two cups of coffee before starting his school bus route each morning. What would he do if Vicky's just wasn't open one morning? What would half the town do?

I shook my head. No use to think about things that weren't going to happen. I lifted the rectangular roll onto a plate and carried it to Kenny. Obviously his two-week flirtation with the Atkins diet was history. He picked up the roll with his thick fingers and took a big bite. "Ahhh," he said, pushing the pastry into the side of his mouth. "Life is too short not to enjoy your baking, Vicky."

I left Kenny to his chomping and surveyed the café. It looked as if Ruthie had things under control. The almost-full house was buzzing. Spoons clinked stirring coffee; cups clattered as they were lifted and put down. Jim Magner was out the door, and Dave was slipping back into place to finish his half-hour coffee break from his insurance business. Make that forty-five minute break if it was a typical day. But, then, when wasn't it a typical day?

I slipped through the swinging door into the calm of the kitchen and simply stood there. Chicken broth simmered on the stovetop. If it was Tuesday, this was chicken noodle soup day. Tomorrow it would be vegetable soup. Thursday chili. Friday knoepfla soup.

Suddenly I felt like screaming. Like throwing off my apron and running out the back door with my arms flailing in the air. I could imagine the chilly October wind tugging at my hair, tossing it every which way. I'd look like a crazy woman. What would people in Brewster make of that? What would they do if I did something so unexpected? If, for instance, I made chicken soup on Friday?

Get a grip, Vicky. Chicken soup means Tuesday.

I shook my head, trying to clear these goofy thoughts. I knew I'd never do any such thing. Ruthie's late arrival had simply thrown off my routine. Even I knew I was a creature of habit, and it was my habit to stick to my schedule. I grabbed a bag of carrots from the fridge and picked up the peeler. By ten-thirty they'd be sliced and diced and simmering next to the onions, celery, and chicken in the soup broth. One thing I didn't like in Vicky's *famous* homemade chicken soup was over-cooked carrots.

As I peeled and then diced the carrots, I planned my day. Not that it took much planning. Every one of my days was pretty much the same. About the only thing that changed was the lunch special, depending on the day of the week.

Whoop-dee-doo. My daughter, Angie's, over-used understatement was working its way into my vocabulary.

Like it or not, by the end of this school year my well-regulated life would have to change. Angie was a senior, and by this time next year she'd be off to college.

At the thought, I felt the now-familiar racing beat in my chest. Most of the moms of seniors I knew were viewing graduation with a mix of dread and excitement. I pretended I was wishing Angie had another year or two to spend at home, but inside I was doing nothing but cheering the fact that she was going to get to do something I never had—go to college.

I lifted the cutting board and pushed the finely diced carrots into the simmering broth. I wasn't going to have to do any pushing to get Angie out the door. She was as ready to spread her wings as I was to watch her do it. She could live the life I'd never had a chance at.

College? What would I be doing if I'd gone to college? I opened the fridge and pulled out the large can of ketchup. It was best to start the lunch rush with all the red squeeze bottles filled to the brim. I'd be frying burgers within the hour, and there'd be no time for details like that then. As I guided the thick tomato concoction into the bottles, I knew one thing for sure: If I'd gone to college, I wouldn't be standing in this over-heated kitchen.

Vicky, why are you thinking like this? You know you love running this café. You love the customers. You love feeding them good, home-cooked food. What's with you today?

What *was* with me today?

It's only natural. Angie will be leaving home in just a few short months. You're worried things are going to change. They will, but change can be good.

No, change isn't good.

It can be if you give it a chance.

But what if I didn't want to? *What if...* I clamped my eyes shut. Tight. I didn't want to think about the "what ifs." I'd learned a long time ago that if I stuck to what was familiar, life was easier. I opened my eyes. *Shoot!* I'd dripped ketchup all over the counter.

See what happens when you think too much? When you break your routine?

I grabbed a paper towel and wiped up the mess, vowing to keep my eyes open while I finished this task.

You can still remember that day…even with your eyes open.

I poured ketchup, trying not to think about what I knew I couldn't help thinking of. *That day.* There was no rhyme or reason, but try as I might, about three times a year I couldn't help but remember…everything. Why now? Why today? Why fight it? Another thing I'd learned was that it was best to let the memories play out. Only then could I put them away.

I lined up ten ketchup bottles as if they were red-coated soldiers getting ready to ward off an enemy. I carefully tilted the ketchup can and let the deep red liquid flow with my thoughts.

I'd been a junior in high school *that day.* Almost a year younger to the day than Angie was now. When I thought of that time through the filtered eyes of motherhood, I saw anew how young I'd been. I'd been in Home Economics class—last period. They still called it that back then. Not "Home Living" or "Life Skills."

My mom knocked softly on the Home Ec room door, opening it a few inches and motioning with her finger for me to come near. I remember feeling embarrassed. I mean, after all, I was a *junior,* what could my mom possibly have to tell me that was so important she'd have to pull me out of class? Didn't I already know *everything?* We were making quick bread that day. Funny how dumb things like that stay in a person's mind. I put down the big spoon I'd been using to scoop flour and hurried to the door. The faster I talked to Mom, the quicker she'd leave.

I stepped out into the hall, closing the classroom door behind me. "What?" There was no reason for me to have an attitude, but I did. I could feel my eyebrows pulling together.

Mom reached up and gently pushed the left side of my hair behind my ear. I shook her hand away with a flick of my head. She smiled as if she didn't feel the irritation in my movement. At least that's the way I like to remember it.

"Dad and I decided to drive over to Carlton for dinner tonight. It's our anniversary." She said it as if she hadn't expected me to remember…and I hadn't.

Suddenly I felt bad. I hadn't gotten them a card or anything. Usually Ruthie, my older sister, was the one who thought of those sorts of things. But she was off to college this year. Apparently she'd forgotten, too.

"Oh, Mom, I forgot!" Surely she heard my honest regret. I knew all about important things like anniversaries. I had a boyfriend—Dave Johnson. We'd be marking our six-month "going-steady" anniversary in a little more than a week. He was off to college along with most of Ruthie's class, but he drove home every weekend so we could be together. I'd feel terrible if he forgot our special day. "What are you going to do to celebrate?"

Again she smiled. "Dad actually said he'd take me shopping at the mall. You know how he *loves* tagging along to do that. Must be love, huh?" She looked kind of dreamy-like. "Then we'll probably go to Red Lobster. We don't get much seafood in Brewster."

Red Lobster. Mom's favorite. "Sounds fun." I meant it. "I have to work at the café tonight. What time do you think you'll get home?"

"Oh, it shouldn't be too late. It's a work day tomorrow for both of us." My dad was a pharmacist and owned Brewster Drug. Mom worked for him part-time. "You'll be okay until we get home?"

"Mo-*om*." I rolled my eyes.

"I know. I know. You're growing up too fast." She brushed my cheek with her fingertips. "Love you."

Little did we know just how fast I was going to have to grow up.

I'd fallen asleep on the couch. Some infomercial had taken the place of the movie I'd been watching. Why hadn't Mom woke me up and told me to get to bed? She never let me sleep all night on the couch on a school night. Why was the doorbell ringing? What time was it? Why wasn't Dad answering the door?

I stumbled to the door, rubbing my eyes, straightening my sweater, not thinking what might be standing on the other side this late at night.

"Vicky." It was Eddie, Brewster's cop. *What is he doing here?* "Are you alone?"

"Uh, I think so." I looked over my shoulder as if there just might be a crowd behind me. "I fell asleep. My mom and dad went to—Are supposed to—" It was then the awful news began to take shape…began to turn from an interrupted dream into a nightmare.

Eddie stepped into the house. He put one beefy hand on my shoulder. In a voice so thick it brought instant tears to my eyes, he said, "I need to tell you some bad news."

The next three days were a blur of images. Big old Eddie wrapping me in his arms after he told me about the car accident. Ruthie coming home from college in the middle of the week. Casseroles and date bars filling up the kitchen fridge and counter…food I had no appetite to eat. A funeral I step-walked through. Relatives I hardly knew trying to plan what to do with me now that Mom and Dad were gone. Ruthie announcing to everyone that she would be moving home to live with me until I graduated. All I'd felt at her announcement was relief. Nothing would change…even though everything had.

I sighed and set the ketchup can on the counter. I'd been sixteen then. Twenty-three years later not much had changed. I'd married my boyfriend, good-old, same-old Dave. I'd worked in this café the night my parents were killed, and here I was, still standing in the kitchen filling ketchup bottles. Only now I owned the place. This café had been my refuge back then—and in some ways it still was.

What would you be doing if that day hadn't happened?

Ah. The question. The possibilities. The very things I tried not to think about more and more these days. What was the use in dreaming of something that couldn't happen? I loved Dave, Angie, and my son, Sam. Was it possible Sam was a freshman already? I wouldn't trade one minute of my life with my family. Or when it came right down to it, this café. Then why did I feel so restless?

Maybe you need a change?

That wasn't possible. Dave had his insurance business. I had the café to run.

Remember that idea you've been toying with, dreaming about? What if…

I could hardly find enough help to run the café the way it was. I could never start another business.

Ruthie could run this place with her eyes shut. Angie, too.

That's my point. Angie will be going to college next fall.

Well then, what if you took a class? You could drive to Carlton for a night class one night a week. Ruthie would love to give you that chance. Dave, too.

Do I dare? I'd often wondered what I would have chosen if I'd had the chance to go to college. Taking a class wouldn't change much of anything, except for helping me to get out of my rut. *Maybe I could—*

"Coffee crowd's gone. I suppose we'd better get baking after lunch." Ruthie pushed through the swinging door into the kitchen of the café, brushing her hands against the front of her black skirt as if she was already dusting flour away. "Pumpkin Fest will be here in what? Three weeks. We'd better get a start on putting pumpkin pies in the freezer."

"Pumpkin Fest? Already?" I could feel my jaw drop as the thought of Brewster's national holiday hit me. It seemed to roll around faster and faster every year. It meant baking fifty or more pumpkin pies. Breaking eggs, mixing spices, mashing cooked pumpkin until even my skin felt orange. Setting up a booth at the old high school gym. Recruiting extra help. Hauling coffee pots and pies. Paper plates and cups. Don't forget the forks. Napkins, too. Manning the booth until clean-up after midnight. Then back at the café to bake Long Johns by five-thirty the next morning. Suddenly it seemed as if all I'd done my whole life was wear this apron and stand in this kitchen.

With the back of my hand I pushed my bangs away from my forehead. "There's got to be more to life than this."

Ruthie took a step toward me. "Are you okay? I thought you loved Pumpkin Fest."

Picking up the ketchup can I nodded. "I'm fine. Just tired." The bubble of an idea of that college class I'd just thought of taking expanded as if a gust of wind had lifted it high. I needed to do *something* to get out of this rut. Did I dare grab on to it? Maybe after Pumpkin Fest I'd take a day off. Ruthie could handle the café for a day. I'd drive to the college over in Carlton, pick up a catalog, talk to a professor. One class. I'd start with that.

As if I'd already registered I felt a lift to my shoulders. I could do this. I could.

Ruthie grabbed a dishcloth and quickly wiped the rims of the plastic ketchup containers I'd been filling, turning the pointed caps on tight. "Sorry I was late this morning."

I waited for her to go on, to explain. Silence. It wasn't like Ruthie to leave me guessing. We were sisters. Something *more* after all we'd been through together. Often she didn't have to tell me things…I…*we*…simply *knew*. She'd probably overslept. Or one of the girls spilled apple juice as they were leaving the house. Maybe the daycare sitter was chatty this morning. No matter. I'd fill the silence. Tell her about my idea of taking a college course. She could dream along with me.

I lifted my eyes, ready to share my brave resolve. I smiled at Ruthie. She smiled back. It was then I *knew*. The words that came out of my mouth didn't surprise her, but they did surprise me. "You're pregnant."

She nodded as I watched my little bubble rise up…high… higher… and then burst.

Libby

I stuck my thumb under the flap of the envelope, already suspecting what I'd read inside. This wasn't the first rejection letter I'd received. You'd think I'd have learned to deal with them by now. I hadn't.

I'd purposely set the letter aside after Emily and I had finally connected again by phone. She was in her usual early-in-the-semester funk, wondering why she'd signed up for the classes she had, already "angsting" over the several term papers that were assigned for the end of the term. As I did every semester, I reminded her that the key word was "end" of the semester. Somehow she seemed to think she had to get all of the course work done *now*. After she'd calmed down a bit the conversation took another familiar turn.

"Mom, it's Mike."

I could tell by the tone of her voice where this was going. I propped my unopened letter next to my coffeepot, as if I'd forget it if it wasn't in plain sight. Ha. Then I held the phone close to my ear as I poured myself a cup of coffee. From experience I knew this might take a while. "Um hmm," I murmured as I took a sip and sat down at the kitchen table.

"He wants to get back together again."

Oh, that familiar dance. They'd gone off to the same college after being high school sweethearts. That had lasted one semester. Then they'd both agreed they were young, needed to meet other people, make sure they weren't missing out on…well…

something. In the meantime, Emily had casually dated a string of boys. Erics and Ryans. Names that all started sounding as alike as their personalities. At first the boyfriend-of-the-moment would be *so cute* or *to-die-for* or *hot*. Within the month Emily would lose interest and move on. In-between there was Mike. Every now and then I'd get a frantic phone call. Emily had spotted Mike on campus with another girl. I could tell by her jumbled conversation that as hard as she was trying to pretend it didn't matter, it did.

"And?" I asked now. I was secretly hoping they would get back together, but I knew that decision wasn't up to me. I'd imagined Mike as my son-in-law more than one sleepless night. He was good for Emily. He settled her drama-queen tendencies, he remembered little things like her addiction to gummy bears, he was funny and smart, he was a hard worker, and he had a strong faith. What mother wouldn't love a guy like that? What girl wouldn't?

Maybe Emily.

"I don't know. He's just so...so..."

"Nice?" I prompted.

"Yes! He's too nice."

I was glad this conversation was taking place over the phone so Emily couldn't see me roll my eyes. I'd heard this complaint before, and for the life of me I didn't understand what could be *bad* about too nice. But I knew enough to keep my mouth shut and simply listen.

"Whatever I want to do is *great!* If I said, 'Let's take knitting lessons together,' Mike would go buy yarn. If I say, 'I'm hungry,' he's already turning the car into a drive-through restaurant. I want someone who...who... Oh, Mom, I don't know *what* I want!"

Now there was something I could empathize with. I well remembered the tug of emotions that threaded my earlier years.

The longing to do *something,* be *somebody,* wondering what on earth I'd been put here for. I still wondered that now.

I glanced again at the unopened envelope sitting on my counter. *Hope-in-the-mail* I called the query letters I sent to publishers. I thought I knew what I wanted…to get the book I'd written published. But lately I was beginning to wonder if God had some other plan for me. Pounding on closed doors didn't seem like much of a God-inspired plan.

It would hardly help to tell Emily that she might be struggling with her same angst twenty-five years from now. I breathed a quick prayer: *Lord, give me wisdom. Help me encourage her, not discourage her.*

"Emily." My voice held a calm I hoped would reach her. "You're twenty years old. You don't have to decide your future today. You have time."

I could hear her deep sigh through the phone. "Yeah, I know. But Mike wants an answer. And I don't know what to say."

"Tell him you're not ready to make that kind of promise."

"But, Mom," her voice cracked, "what if he goes and finds someone else?"

I rubbed at the back of my neck. "Well…then…" I prayed for an answer. "I guess if you feel like that, maybe it should tell you something."

"Like *what?*" I could hear frustration building.

Didn't she have girlfriends to help her untangle this mess of emotions? "Like maybe you care about him more than you're willing to admit." Was that really the case or was I just hoping it was so? I wasn't so sure I was any surer about this than Emily. But it wouldn't do any good to tell her that. I only hoped the advice I'd given would help her think clearly.

Goodness knew I could use some encouragement myself. Who would be my cheerleader when I opened the envelope sitting by my coffeepot? The letter I was certain held another rejection. Did Emily have any clue that she wasn't the only woman in our family whose future was undecided?

"But, Mom," Emily turned my thoughts back to her looming problem, "how do I know Mike's the one for me?"

Ah, so that's what it boiled down to. I knew she wouldn't like my answer, but I said it anyway. "When you find the right person, when the time is right, you just *know*."

"*Mom!* That's not an answer. I'll just *know*. Yeah, right."

"Trust me on this, Emily. You will."

Silence.

I could feel her shutting down. Turning me off. Tuning me out. She had a habit of doing that when she didn't like what was being said. Emily liked her advice in black and white, but love didn't quite come that way. It was the best I could do under the circumstances. "You'll know." I repeated. "Keep praying about it."

"Oh, hi!" I could hear Emily speak away from the phone for a second, and then she spoke to me. "Mom, Sara's here. We're going to walk to class together. Gotta go. Bye. Love you."

Just like that her life-altering questions were forgotten. "Love you, too." She was gone. Off to her life. Even though she had more or less blown off my advice, I knew Emily well enough to know she'd be thinking about it. Give careful consideration to what I'd said…even if she'd never admit it to me.

Ah, well, I had a life to live, too. A house to clean. A column to write. I'd best get at it. I pushed my chair away from the kitchen table and hung up the phone.

The neon-white letter on the counter screamed at me. *Open me!*

Pointedly I reached around the envelope and pulled the coffeepot from behind it, topping off my cup. I wasn't in the mood to read bad news. I'd give myself a pep-talk while I tried to write my column. I'd read the letter later. In the meantime I could pretend there was good news inside.

⌣

Bob was in the recliner next to the couch. His eyelids fluttered open and closed as if a toddler was playing with a garage door opener. Sleep would win this battle soon. I pulled the stack of mail-order catalogs onto my lap, putting the letter that had waited impatiently for me all day on top of the pile. Now was as good a time as any.

As I picked it up I silently congratulated myself on my restraint. I'd had a productive day in spite of what I knew was waiting. I'd written my bi-monthly column for the *Brewster Banner,* the house was dusted and vacuumed, and I'd even had time to meet my friend Jan Jordan for coffee at Vicky's Café. I looked at the envelope. Why ruin things now? Maybe I should just leave it until tomorrow. No, that would just make tomorrow gloomy. Might as well open it, read the bad news, then sleep it off.

I felt the familiar pit in my stomach as I slit the flap of the envelope with my thumb and pulled the cream-colored paper from the envelope. At least they'd bothered to print the letter on company stationary. Nice letterhead. Some of the rejections I'd opened looked as if they hired third-graders to do the typing on bargain-basement paper.

It didn't take but a glance to know what it said:

Dear Writer, Thank you for submitting your manuscript to us. Unfortunately...

Blah, blah blah. I didn't need to read the rest of the words to know what they said. They weren't interested. They recently published something similar. They received many fine manuscripts and couldn't publish them all. They were sure I'd find an appropriate market, but they weren't it.

My eyes scanned the neatly typed words, not reading them, simply trying to come to terms with another rejection. Why, when I *knew* the news this letter held, did it still sting so much?

Oh, Lord, what is it You want me to do? I thought You wanted me to write this book. If that's not it then show me what is!

I let the letter fall to my lap. It had taken me one year to write my book. One year when I didn't know if anyone but me would ever read the story of my friendship with Anne. I'd been convinced this was the work God wanted me to do. To share my story of friendship with others. In a book. In the book I called *After Anne.* Could I have been so wrong?

There were so many times over that year of writing when my conviction wavered. When I pulled words out from under my fingernails, one-by-one with bent tweezers. When I'd turned down invitations for coffee with Katie Jeffries so I'd have time to write. When I brought notepaper to Emily's volleyball games in case inspiration happened to strike. Midnights when I should have been sleeping and instead scribbled notes to myself. Had all that time been a waste?

Nothing I do is ever wasted. I have a plan for you...

If that's true then why don't You tell me what it is? What purpose does it serve to keep me in the dark? To have me question and doubt? To...

Because it keeps you turning to Me.

He had me there.

I have a plan...

Well, I could use a little encouragement.

My hands fingered the letter in my lap. I hadn't finished scanning it before my discouragement had taken over. Now my eyes read the name scrawled at the bottom of the letter. Pam somebody. Did she know she'd stomped on my dream? Did this *Pam* sit behind her big, important desk in New York signing form letters that brought disillusionment to a doorstep, giggling with glee over the devastation she was creating? For not the first time I wondered if she, or any editor, even read what I sent. Had she simply tossed my pages into the recycling bin without glancing at my carefully crafted words? The words I'd cried and prayed over? I guessed I would never know.

The bottom third of the letter was tilted upward. I pushed the paper down, and it was then I noticed a postscript. Tiny black, block letters so neatly printed they could have been mistaken for typewritten. I pulled the letter close, then held it back a bit. The day was soon coming when reading glasses would be a semi-permanent fixture on my face. The small words swam into focus.

This is very interesting, and I urge you to continue.

I could use a little encouragement. Here it was.

I ran my finger over the ink as if I could somehow absorb this small bit of silent applause. *I urge you to continue.*

Five words that may not have been much of an effort for Pam to write, but they meant the world to me. She had read my manuscript. She had liked it. She wanted me to keep on trying to get it published.

I smiled to myself as I folded the letter and slipped it back into the envelope. Maybe my time hadn't been wasted. Maybe God really did have a plan. Tomorrow I would page through my *Writer's Market* and find another publisher that might be interested in my story. Living in rural North Dakota, I had no other hope of contacts with publishers than through the good old U.S. Postal Service.

Feeling more content than I had all day, I sifted through the catalogs on my lap one by one, folding down a page here and there to remind me of items that might make good Christmas gifts. I shifted the second-to-last catalog to my side, ready to open the cover of the last one. A stiff, folded brochure lay on top. I picked it up, surprised I hadn't thrown it along with the other junk mail I'd tossed earlier. I couldn't help but see the large-print enticements on the outside of the pamphlet: *Get your book published! Network with editors and agents! Attend our 24th annual writer's conference.*

My heart did a quick flip in my chest. How had these people gotten my address? How did they know this was exactly what I needed? How did—

I have a plan.

Oh.

I opened the brochure, carefully reading the detailed schedule of events as my heart pounded in my chest. Classes in writing. In sending out queries. What editors were looking for in a first manuscript. It was as if a postal-fairy had read my mind and dropped this leaflet into my mailbox. Could I really do this?

Yes, I could.

A snore from Bob brought me to my senses. Where was the conference? I scanned the page, looking for a return address. California. My heart sank into my stomach. Yeah, right. As if I'd be packing a bag and heading *that* far away all by myself.

I looked over at Bob. Maybe if I woke him up and talked it over with him he'd help me sort things out. Could I go? Should I go? Did I dare? I didn't need to ask Bob to know what he'd say: "If you think it will help you get published, do it." Then he'd say, "How much is it?" Good old Bob. Always the banker, even when he was asleep.

But it wouldn't hurt to dream. I reached to the end table and picked up the silver pen my friend Anne had given me before she died. The pen she'd meant for me to write my first novel with. I smiled as I read the inscription she'd had engraved: Write on...

I would. I'd follow her instructions. I'd fill out this registration form while I simply tried out the idea in my mind.

I filled in the blanks. Easy enough. There was no test. No special qualifications required to attend.

I urge you to continue.

I could do this. I got up from the couch and carried the form into the kitchen. There I cut carefully around the dotted lines. I grabbed my checkbook from my purse and filled in the amount for the full registration. I wiped my sweaty palm on my leg as I grabbed an envelope out of a drawer and addressed it. Then I folded my check inside the registration form and tucked both into the envelope. A stamp in the corner and I was done. I looked to either side of me as if I'd done something wrong.

Or right.

This didn't feel right...it felt scary. My heart pounded, my ears filled with a weird, cold echo. *You can't do this. It's too far away. Who said you were a writer, anyway? What business do you have going—*

STOP!

I filled my lungs with a deep breath as I reminded myself of the technique I'd learned to bring a halt to the negative thoughts that sometimes threatened to overwhelm me. The battle I'd had with depression was never completely behind me, but I'd learned I could manage my way around those old habits.

I would do this. I propped the letter against the coffeepot. I'd mail it first thing in the morning.

If I didn't chicken out during the night.

Vicky

"I'll have two pieces of *apple* pie and two cups of coffee." Kenny Pearson bobbed his head in time to the lively accordion music coming from the three-piece band on the stage of the gym.

"Ha-ha," I said picking two slices of pumpkin pie out of the three dozen polka-dotting the table and handing them to Kenny. I must have heard that old apple-pie joke at least a hundred times since I'd started serving pumpkin pie at Pumpkin Fest. I handed the ten dollar bill he'd given me to Angie, who was my banker for the night. "Thanks," I said as I motioned Kenny and his wife, Diane, to the end of the table where Ruthie's mother-in-law was manning the coffeepot.

Diane pointed to her young daughter, Paige, balanced on her hip. "We're going to share," she mouthed to me as if I was thinking they should have purchased three pieces of pie instead of two. I couldn't help but glance at her tummy. Talk around the café said Diane was expecting…again. I didn't envy her. I doubted Paige was out of diapers yet, and this would be Diane and Kenny's fourth child. I was glad I was done with those baby days. I just wished I had something to look forward to that was nearly as exciting.

I smiled at Diane and nodded, automatically surveying the table, mentally counting the number of pieces on the table and the number of pies that were uncut in the old gymnasium kitchen. This late in the evening there weren't too many left. If tradition held, I'd be out of pie long before the folks in Brewster had eaten their fill. I'd already tucked away two slices for my husband and I to share when all was done. It was our tradition to eat those last two pieces together. After all, Dave had proposed over pumpkin pie at Pumpkin Fest. That had been a long time ago. We'd been much too young to know what we were getting in to, but we'd done okay. I smiled at the memory, but reminiscing wasn't going to sell pie.

Out of habit I wiped my hands against the apron I was wearing. "Who's next?" I looked at the long line of people waiting for pie. There was a gap in the line, and I waited while Mrs. Kuntz fumbled in her purse, no doubt searching for loose change to pay for her dessert. As I waited I pushed my hands into the small of my back, stretching against the slight pressure. Oh did that feel good.

How long had I been doing this? Five hours already tonight, but it had to be close to twenty-five years total, considering I'd helped at the café since high school. There had to be more to life than this, didn't there?

Out of the corner of my eye I could see Angie counting out change into Kenny's outstretched hand. "There you go," she said, her voice sounding so much like mine it was spooky. "How's Paige tonight?" She reached across the table and pretended to tickle the little girl as she giggled and squirmed away from her finger. "Are you having fun?" Paige buried her big brown eyes into her mother's shoulder, shyly peeking back at Angie.

Angie had a knack with kids. Whenever a small child was in the café I had to remind Angie to keep watch on her tables. More than likely she'd be crossed-legged on the floor entertaining the child as the parents enjoyed a meal. As I watched Diane encourage Paige to answer Angie's question, I remembered that old saying, "It takes a village to raise a child." Well, if there was one thing I loved about this town it was that we looked after each other, quirks and all.

"I'd like one slice of pie, please." Mrs. Kuntz had shuffled up to the table. "And one cup of coffee. Please." Speaking of quirks.... She held out her hand which was filled with loose change.

"Why don't you give those to my daughter, Angie," I told her, not wanting to take the chance of spilling all those coins on top of the pie slices below.

"Here, let me help you." Angie stepped near and held her cupped hands under Mrs. Kuntz's, catching the coins as Mrs. Kuntz tipped her hand. Without counting the coins, Angie sorted them into the change box as she chattered. "Did you make any pickles this summer? Do you remember when Steph and I used to come to your house and you'd let us sit on your back steps and give us each one of those big dill pickles you make?"

"And the juice would run down your arms, and then you'd ask if you could run through the sprinkler to clean off." Mrs. Kuntz filled in the blanks.

"You never did let us."

"I was afraid what your mama would say about you coming home looking like a wet dog." Mrs. Kuntz laughed at the memory along with Angie. "Did you know that?" She turned to me.

"I can't say I did." I was holding a small paper plate with her slice of pie, wondering how Angie had grown up so fast. It seemed just a blink ago when she'd asked to be my helper at Pumpkin Fest. Back when she could barely peek her eyes above the edge of the table. She had been the "Official Napkin Passer-Outer." A title she created for herself. Now she could run the whole booth by herself if she had to.

Mrs. Kuntz pushed her beige handbag into the crook of her elbow and reached a shaky hand toward the pie.

"I can carry that for you." Angie intercepted the pie. "I'll get your coffee. Why don't you go find a space to sit on the bleachers and I'll bring it over to you."

"That would be very kind of you." She caught my eye before she turned. "You have a good daughter there."

"I know," I replied. A space in my chest filled as I watched

Angie pick up a Styrofoam cup of coffee and walk patiently behind the shuffling Mrs. Kuntz. I was certainly going to miss Angie when she went off to college next fall.

Even if my plans to take a class had fallen through, I was willing to put my dreams on the back burner if it would help Angie achieve hers. Speaking of which, I needed to remind Angie to start filling out those college application forms. We'd toured three colleges over the summer—two in North Dakota, one in Minnesota. Dave would have driven halfway across the country if his daughter had wanted to see a school on either coast, but Angie hadn't wanted to venture too far from home. There was a small part of me that was glad she wanted to stick close, but another part, a bigger part, wished she would go somewhere I'd never glimpsed. Do things and see places I'd never had the chance to. What would my life have been like if I had the opportunities Angie had?

You could have gone to college. Ruthie pleaded with you to go. Money wasn't a factor. Your folks left a life insurance policy that would have allowed you to go to any school you wanted.

But I didn't want to go anywhere. Not back then. All I'd wanted was to stay where life felt secure. Well, as secure as it could feel without my parents. Somehow I knew the people in Brewster would keep watch out for me. I'd married Dave Johnson, a local kid just like me, two years after high school. I worked in the café those two years, learning the ropes, waiting for Dave to finish college. With the money my parents had left we'd put a good down payment on a house and used the rest of the money to buy the café. I shook my head now, amazed at how young I'd been when I took over the restaurant. What had made me think I could make a go of it? Had I given any thought at all to what I was giving up by tying myself down to a business? To a husband. To a life that had been routine. If I'd wanted security, I'd gotten it. In spades. My life had been good, but I wanted more for Angie. So much more.

I had a feeling the guy who was walking up behind her now had a lot to do with her self-imposed college boundaries. Mark Hoffman had been her boyfriend since she'd been a sophomore. He was a year older than her, a freshman at college in Carlton this fall. A freshman who drove back to Brewster every weekend, so far, to spend time with Angie. I wasn't so sure I liked the arrangement. Mark should be using this time to spread his wings, not fly back to this familiar nest every Friday night. On the other hand, I knew Angie would be heartbroken if he decided the girls at college looked better than she did. What was a mother to hope for?

They were too young to be too serious. The natural course of things would play this hand out. Mark and Angie would slowly drift apart. Mark's attention would turn to his classes, his new friends, and his new life at college. Angie would start dreaming about her own new life that would start less than a year from now. She'd get accepted to college and be put in touch with her new roommate. They'd start deciding what color their bedspreads would be and who would bring a stereo. She'd soon realize there were other guys on the planet besides Mark.

Not that I didn't like Mark. He came from a decent family. He was polite and personable and treated Angie well. But he seemed a little too...too...What was the word I was looking for? Predictable. If I was being honest, he seemed a little...boring. As if driving back to Brewster each weekend was the highlight of his week. As if the world held nothing of interest outside Brewster's city limits. Of course I'd never tell Angie that. She'd find out there were more exciting guys than Mark, more exciting places than Brewster, soon enough.

I might not have had a chance to explore the world, but my daughter would.

Angie

"Hey, Ang, did you send off your application, yet?" My best friend since first grade, Julie Anderson, opened her locker, which was right next to mine. She bent at the waist to look inside at the mirror that was stuck to the inside of the door, fluffing her hair as she talked. "Just think, this time next year we'll be rooming together at UND." She turned her head, looking at her profile. Her eyes caught mine. "Aren't you excited?"

"Mmm hmm," I said, ducking behind my locker door, pretending to search for something. Suddenly I was being squeezed between the door and the junk inside my locker. I pushed at the metal door with my elbow. "What are you *doing?*" I said, standing up straight, pushing against the pressure. Julie was leaning against my door with her shoulder. I ducked from behind the door and slammed it shut, sending Julie onto one foot, trying to catch her balance.

"What's up with you lately?" By the way she asked, I knew Julie wasn't just ticked about me almost knocking her over with the locker door deal.

I opened my locker again using the door as a divider. "What?" I said, bending at the knees and pretending to search for something in the bottom of my locker. "You started it." I was also pretending I didn't understand her question.

She waited until I found what I'd faked I was digging for and stood up. I tucked an old issue of *People* magazine into my folder. An issue with Britney Spears on the cover with someone

I didn't even recognize. How old-news was *that?* I hoped Julie hadn't copped a glimpse; she'd know for sure I was trying to hide something. I turned to head to class.

"So," Julie said, stepping directly in front of me, "what gives?"

"Nothing," I said, dancing around her.

Without missing a beat she fell into step beside me. "You expect me to believe that? I may be blonde, but I'm not stupid." She nodded at several underclassmen who walked by. "You haven't sent in the application yet, have you?"

Okay, that much I could admit. "No, I haven't."

"Ang, come on. You know how long we've planned this! We've talked about going to UND and rooming together since what? Seventh grade? I mean, I'm not worried that you won't get accepted. But if you don't get your housing application in soon, the dorms are going to fill and we might not get put together."

"I know. I'm sorry." I really was sorry. Just not for the reason she thought.

"Promise me you'll send it in tonight?"

I stopped at the classroom door. Once we stepped inside there would be too many classmates around to continue our conversation. I bit at the side of my lip, stalling for an answer. I didn't want to lie. "It's just that my mom was so busy with Pumpkin Fest I didn't want to bug her about writing out a check for the room deposit, you know?"

"Well, Pumpkin Fest is over now. Send it in tonight. Okay?" Julie put one Skechered-foot forward, then pulled it back. "You haven't changed your mind about UND have you?"

Ah, saved by the bell. "Talk to you after class." I hurried to my seat. Mrs. Koenig, our English Lit teacher was a bear if anyone was tardy. I threw my Lit book on the desktop then pushed myself into the seat. I pulled my notebook out of my folder, a pen from my purse, and tucked the rest of my stuff on the wire shelf under my seat. Thank goodness the bell had rung. I still didn't know how I was going to explain my decision to Julie...much less my folks. The longer I could put it off the better.

Or worse.

Mrs. Koenig started lecturing, her voice a monotonous drone as she repeated the same stuff she'd said yesterday about the sheltered author who'd written the story we'd been assigned to read. I opened my literature book, hoping to lose myself in an old-fashioned world of proper ladies who had nothing better to trouble their minds than wondering if the butler had pressed a suitable gown for the evening ball. Why couldn't I have been born in England?

Get real, Angie. High school seniors in England don't live like that anymore.

Okay, so then why couldn't I have been born a century *earlier*? In England?

With your family genealogy you would be slaving away in the kitchen of the manor, not attending the parties.

I could have worked my way *out* of the kitchen. Caught the eye of a baron's son. Scandalized all of society when we ran off together...

Kind of like you're planning to do now?

Mark and I are *not* planning on running off together. Besides, this daydreaming was supposed to keep my mind *off* of my troubles, not bring them right back at me.

No matter when you live or where you live, there are always troubles. You need to learn from them. Grow from them.

But no one will understand.

I will.

I felt a soft poke at my right elbow. I knew better than to turn around while Mrs. Koenig was talking. I dipped my head, glancing behind me under the veil of my long hair. Jason Erbele was holding a white, folded note between his fingers near my elbow. I reached my left hand around my stomach, pretending I had an itch I couldn't reach. I held out two fingers and Jason slipped the note between them. *Good job.* I slid my hand to my lap and held still as Mrs. Koenig's eyes swept my direction, then moved on. Safe.

Slowly I unfolded the note, quickly recognizing Julie's handwriting.

Is it because of Mark?

All I had to do was turn my head slightly and nod. Julie would understand. She wouldn't like it, but she'd know that because my boyfriend was going to school in Carlton, well, that's where I would be going too. But with that nod I couldn't explain the fact that Mark had offered to transfer to UND if I wanted to go there. That all he cared about was being with me. It didn't matter which school he went to…*we* went to.

I folded the note and tucked it between the pages of my Lit book. Then I slid my hand to the edge of the desk and wavered my fingers in the air. Julie would know I was "talking" to her. She'd know I didn't have a one-word answer for her. It wasn't as simple as "yes" or "no."

I slid my hand back and rested my chin in the cup of my palm. Why couldn't I just say, "Yes, it's because of Mark?" That would be the easy way out. Sure Julie would be bummed that all our sleep-over dreams weren't going to happen as we'd planned. She might be a little hurt that I'd chosen Mark over her. She didn't have a boyfriend, so she didn't always understand when I wanted to spend time with him over my girlfriends. But she always forgave me. I knew, if I had the words to explain, she'd understand.

But that was the problem. I didn't have the words. Not to

explain to Julie. To my folks. Or even to myself. It was much easier to let everyone think I was being pokey about sending in my application and debating about which college to choose, rather than try to explain why I didn't want to go to college at all.

Libby

"Do you want a receipt?" Dale Herr, Brewster's postmaster, carefully eyed the address on my manila envelope. You'd think after all the manuscripts I'd sent out this past year his curiosity would have died by now. No such luck. "Taking another shot at this, I see."

I ignored his comment. "Yes, I would like a receipt," I said, trying to sound nonchalant. As if my entire life's dream wasn't inside this plain-looking packet.

I waited while the receipt printed. *What do you need a receipt for? It's not as if you have any writing income. You're not going to be deducting this on any tax forms. You're—* STOP!

I'd gotten very good at cutting off those sorts of endless mind games but less adept at overcoming the discouragement I was beginning to feel. What if this publisher wasn't interested in my book? I was running out of places to send it. Then what?

Dale handed me my receipt and put his hand on my envelope. "Want me to—"

"No," I interrupted. "Thanks." I wasn't about to let him take over my traditional mailing ritual. I slid the first fifty pages of my manuscript from under his hand and walked out into the deserted lobby of the post office. I paused as I inserted the manila envelope into the mail slot and said a silent prayer. *Please let them want to publish this.*

Oh pitiful. I pulled the envelope back out and held it between my fingers. It was too late to change any of the words inside. I didn't have a clue who in their office in Colorado would be reading this. If anyone would read it. I didn't know if they'd be having a bad day the afternoon my dream arrived. Whether they'd have already read a hundred manuscripts that day or none. Suddenly I wanted to take my words and run. Hide them in my desk drawer where they'd be safe. Where I knew no one would read them…or reject them. I had absolutely no control over this process at all.

But I do.

I took a deep breath. Did my story mean anything to anyone besides me? If I didn't mail this, I'd never know. There would never be a chance for anyone to read my story. To know Anne the way I had. To know the way her friendship had changed me. Changed my life.

I put the envelope partially in the slot for a second time, then paused. *Go with these words.* There, that was better. I heard the satisfying sound of my manuscript falling into the bin. Hope-in-the-mail. Again.

I turned. "Oh!" Dave Johnson, Vicky-from-the-café's husband, was standing quietly behind me, holding some letters in his hand. "I'm sorry. You startled me. You must want to mail something and here I've been… Oh goodness, let me get out of your way." I was babbling, feeling suddenly silly for acting as if this mail slot was for me alone.

He smiled and stepped around me, dropping his letters into the slot. "I'm in no hurry. You looked like you were debating whether to mail that or not." He nodded toward the now-empty slit. "Don't worry, if you would have stood there too much longer I would have nudged your arm." He paused, then laughed. "Or pinched you so you would have been forced to drop it in."

"So either way it would have gone into the mail?"

"Yep." He jangled the change in his pocket. "Brewster could

use an author living here. It would give us a sort of *up-town* sound."

I could feel myself flushing. How did he know what I'd just mailed? Had Dale, the postmaster, been blabbing? There must be some sort of law against telling people what patrons were putting in the mail.

As if he'd read my mind, Dave answered. "I talked to Bob the other day. He said you'd finished writing that book you've been working on. Said now you were working on getting it published." As he turned to leave, Dave reached out and patted my shoulder. "Good for you. I hope it works out."

Well, I did, too. But I wasn't so sure I wanted the whole town knowing about it. What if those words never saw the light of day? What would people think then?

I had a good mind to march on over to the bank and tell Bob what I thought of his advertising. I stopped short. Even after several years, I still had to remind myself that Bob didn't work at the Brewster bank anymore. He was over in the Carlton office, forty miles away. Today that was a good thing...for Bob. Especially since I could still feel my blood boiling. What right did he have to share my private dream with Dave Johnson? With anyone for that matter? For all I knew, Dave would bring it up during coffee time at the café and pretty soon I'd have people asking, "Where can I find that book of yours?"

Nowhere. That's where.

Once again I felt the familiar tug of despair. What if all my work, all my dreaming, ended up being for nothing? If it wasn't writing God wanted me to do, what was it? If it *was* writing, I sure wished He'd get on the stick and show me.

I'd been so sure that once the kids had both left home I'd be well on my way to a writing career. Goodness, I certainly had the time. And the inclination. And now a book I'd written. What I didn't have was a publisher.

Oh, but you have plenty of rejections.

Ouch.

Maybe you should be doing something else.

There had to be something better than this. Better than feeling dejected every time I didn't hear back from a publisher immediately. Better than feeling rejected when I did. Not to mention having half the town watch me wallow in it all. Maybe I should give it up.

But what about that writer's conference you registered for?

Oh, heavens! Not that again. I hurried out of the post office and into my car. Even the cold, late-November breeze couldn't stop the heat I felt just remembering that fiasco...

"I mailed that letter you had sitting out this morning." Without a clue about the Pandora's Box he had just opened with his sentence, Bob sat down for what was supposed to be a pleasant dinner after a hard day at work.

"You what?" I set down the bowl of lettuce salad I'd been holding. Hard. Too hard. Shredded carrots and dressing-coated lettuce popped over the side of the dish.

"I mailed that letter you had sitting out." Innocently he scooped dressing-glazed lettuce onto his plate.

Hadn't he heard my tone? Hadn't he seen the lettuce fly? How could he sound so clueless?

"I didn't want that letter mailed." It would be hard to eat anything with my teeth clenched the way they were.

"But it was where you always leave the mail..." I could tell by the way Bob's words trailed off he was beginning to get it. "It had a stamp on it." His final defense, and a good one under normal circumstances. Unfortunately for Bob, this wasn't normal.

"I didn't want that mailed." My voice cracked. Emotion I didn't completely understand filled my throat. "I wasn't going to send it." I pushed my chair away from the table. I was going to have to cry before I could eat.

"*Sorry.*" One confused-sounding word from Bob followed me to the bedroom.

I sat on the edge of our bed and pressed my hands against my face. What was I going to do now? I didn't want to go to that writer's conference. It was too far. It cost too much. It wouldn't help me get published anyway. I threw myself backward on the bed, shutting out any light with an arm across my eyes...much like the way I'd spent most of last night.

I'd started out the night tossing and turning in bed with that signed, sealed, and stamped letter glowing in my mind like a beacon. The thought of *doing something* about my writing was so exciting sleep was nowhere to be found. *Just think...California! Me. At a writer's conference!*

I might start feeling like a *real* writer. Maybe after that, when people asked what I did, I could say the words "I'm a writer," with confidence, not as if they were a question I was still trying to answer.

As the midnight-minutes ticked by, and then the hours, the shining beacon turned into a searchlight. A piercing, soul-searching, blinding light. *What was I thinking? California? Good grief, what had ever made me think I would pack a suitcase and go to California? By myself? For my writing? My nonexistent writing career? I was just a small-town, middle-aged woman pursuing an impossible fantasy.*

That piddly, twice-a-month column I wrote for the *Brewster Banner* would be the laughing stock of a conference like that. Only *real* writers attended those kinds of events. Not someone like me.

I'd made up my mind around three o'clock that I would tear up the letter, that silly idea, in the morning. Finally, with that decided, I feel into a deep, dreamless sleep. Bob was gone by the time I glanced at the clock and realized I'd overslept. Not that I had anything pressing to jump out of bed for. Not like the days when I was on a mission to finish writing my novel.

I felt a small stab of disappointment as I slid my legs out from under the covers. At least when I was writing, I had something to *do*. A purpose that made me want to get out of bed. Even if writing was one of the hardest things I'd ever done, it was also the most satisfying.

Then I remembered my sleepless hours. The reality those night-time hours had made me face. I would never be a writer. Not a *real* writer. I was living in the middle of North Dakota, not New York. And we weren't going to be moving anytime soon.

As I got dressed and walked out to the kitchen to get my morning coffee brewing, I knew I was going to have to make peace with the idea that my dream had been just that…a dream. Writing my column, serving on the local library board, delivering Meals on Wheels now and then would have to be enough.

I didn't notice the letter was missing until I started spooning fragrant coffee grounds into the filter.

Where was it? I looked around, certain the white envelope had fallen to the floor and somehow gotten kicked under the stove. It was only after getting a yardstick and sweeping beneath the oven, then pulling out the bottom drawer and brushing the dusty floor with a flashlight, that it dawned on me the letter really wasn't under there.

It briefly crossed my mind that Bob might have taken it. But as forgetful as he'd been lately, I highly doubted that option. Just the day before I'd asked him to carry out the trash on his way to work. The garbage that was already bagged and sitting by the door. He'd had to step *around* it to get outside without it, and yet somehow he managed to do just that. No, Bob hadn't taken my envelope.

After searching high and low while my coffee brewed, I half-convinced myself I'd gotten up in the middle of the night and thrown it away...even though a glance in the garbage can told me that hadn't happened. I didn't have any other logical explanation. Then again, things disappeared around this house all the time... one sock, Bob's reading glasses, another sock, a recipe I'd cut from a magazine. Who knew where those things went? They were either lost for good or would turn up sometime. No matter about that lost registration. I hadn't planned to go anyway.

I'd taken my cup of coffee and gone to my desk, determined to write my *Wry Eye* column for the *Banner* and title it: *Going... Going...Gone.*

I'd pretty much put the whole incident out of my mind until that night at dinner, when Bob opened his mouth. Registering for a writer's conference in California? What had I been thinking?

Obviously, I hadn't been.

In the two weeks since my sleepless night and Bob's fateful dinner-time announcement, I'd been thinking about nothing else. One minute I'd pick up the phone, ready to call the conference and tell them to refund my money and tear up my registration. But the thought of trying to explain the *why* behind my cancellation had me hanging up the phone, determined to act like the adult I was. I'd simply not show up.

Oh yeah, *adult.*

Come to think of it, sitting outside the post office in my cold car and reliving the event wasn't very adult either. I shook the memory from my head, started the car, and pressed my hands to the steering wheel, I looked over my shoulder and pulled out from the curb. Where should I go? There was nothing vital for me to do at home. I'd gone grocery shopping yesterday. The whole day loomed ahead, an empty slate. For a moment I felt an all-too-familiar-panic pound in my chest. The dark days of my depression weren't that far behind. I well-remembered the emptiness of those days. Days I didn't want to repeat. I needed to be busy with something…but what?

Write.

I already had. Nothing would come of it. I needed something more. I drove slowly, aimlessly, through the streets of Brewster.

Write.

"Good, Lord!" I said in frustration. Only after I'd said the words did I realize they were a prayer. I continued driving, muttering to God. "If you want me to write, then *do* something about it!" I pushed down my blinker and made a hard left. "I've been writing my whole life in some way or another. What's come of it? Huh?" I waited, then answered for Him, "Nothing! That's what. *Nothing!*" I tapped at the brake, slowing to let old Mr. Ost drive through the intersection without looking, as usual. "How about this? How about if I take all those rejection letters I've been getting as a sign? I get it, God. I'm not supposed to write, am I?" I felt hot tears fill my eyes. If I wasn't a writer, what was I? I talked past the lump in my throat. "Why would You give me this desire and not have a purpose for it? I don't understand. Do You really want me to give it up? *Do You?*"

No answer. No sound except for frozen pebbles of snow knocking against the side of my car.

"Okay then," my voice was a choked sob. "I'll give up writing. If that's what You want. I'll give it up." I quit talking out loud and finished what I had to say with my heart. *"But then show me what You want me to do because I don't have a clue."*

I punched at my blinker and took a hard right onto the highway that would lead me away from Brewster. I batted away my tears with the back of my hand and pressed on the gas pedal as if I could drive away from my misery. Drive far away from my dream.

If only it were that easy.

Vicky

The café door opened and a cold gust of wind blew Olivia Marsden inside. Even though there wasn't but a dusting of snow on the ground this late in the year, she lightly stomped her feet on the mat inside the door before climbing the three small steps that led to the level of the cafe. I liked that she did that. I could use all the help I could get keeping this place clean.

As I made my rounds, refilling coffee cups, I could see the heads of the men in the morning coffee crowd briefly glance as Olivia greeted a few people then walked to a booth and sat by herself. It didn't take long for my coffee guys to turn back to their usual loud guff.

What wasn't usual was to see Olivia in the café by herself. Under any circumstances, she didn't come in often. She was too young to be a part of the older, widowed women who met here most mornings for toast and coffee. And even if she might have joined them today, she was too late. That group had come and gone. Maybe she was waiting for a friend to show up? When Olivia did stop for coffee it was almost always with her friend Jan Jordan or some gal from Carlton. I was sure someone would show up in a minute.

I grabbed a mug and carried it to her booth. "Coffee while you wait?"

Olivia looked up at me, dabbing at the corners of her eyes with her gloved fingers. "This wind must have blown some sand into my eyes." She pulled off her gloves and grabbed a paper napkin from the small dispenser on the table and patted at her eyes. "Sorry. Who knows what this has done to my mascara."

"You look fine," I said. Fine for someone who looked like they'd been crying. But she didn't need to hear that. What she needed was coffee and, maybe, some company. I hoped her friend would show up soon. "Would you like some coffee while you wait?"

"Sure." Olivia watched as I filled the creamy white mug with hot coffee. "That smells good," she said. "Thanks."

"I'll be back," I said as Ruthie called from the kitchen. "I've got an order up."

I pushed with the back of my shoulder through the swinging door leading into the kitchen, twirling myself into the room as I'd done thousands of times. *How many more times will I do this in my life?*

"Are you busy out there?" Ruthie placed a plate holding two over-easy eggs, bacon, and wheat toast into my hand.

"No." I shook my head, trying to erase the sudden image I had of thousands of fried eggs on thousands of plates. "The coffee guys are starting to leave. Olivia Marsden just walked in. I think she's waiting for someone else. And," I held up the plate, "once Dan Jordan eats this I'll be back to help you get ready for lunch. How many hamburgers do you think we'll fry today?"

"You okay?" Ruthie tilted her head and narrowed her eyes at me. My sister could always see right through me.

"I'm fine." I sighed. Even I could hear the monotony in my voice. I lifted the plate. "Gotta get this out while it's hot."

"Say your verse," Ruthie called after me.

My verse. Right. I'd been saying *my verse* like a mantra for years, but these past weeks it was as though the words were doughnuts with sugar left out. There wasn't much good in them. Automatically I ran through the words: *"I have learned wherever I am to be content."*

Content. Sure. There was a big difference between contentment and complacency. The fact was, while my life was fine, I was
bored. I'd been serving bacon and eggs, or some version of it, for
well over twenty years. Just once I wished someone would come
in and order...oh, I don't know...spinach soufflé. Of course I'd
have to say we didn't have that...but still, it would be something
different.

"Here's your eggs." I placed Dan's plate in front of him. Quickly
I surveyed the empty coffee cups of the other businessmen sitting
at Dan's booth and the tables nearby. "I'll get all of you some
more coffee."

A chorus of "No, gotta get back to work" greeted my offer.
Chairs pushed back and loose change and dollar bills were put
on the table. As full as the café had been a minute ago, except for
Dan and Olivia, it was now empty.

"Well, I'm sure *you* want more coffee," I said to Dan.

"That'd be good," he said, reaching for the salt and pepper.

I made a detour past Olivia's table, topped her cup, then went
to fill Dan's. I emptied the pot into his cup. "There you go. Enjoy
your breakfast."

"Jan's working in Carlton today," Dan explained before I
could turn away. "Thought I'd have a late breakfast and count
it as lunch, too. Say, if you have a minute, I'd like to talk to you
about something." He eyed the almost empty café, then nodded
to the vacant side of the booth across from him.

I'd had years of reading people as they ate their meals. Some
people didn't mind eating alone. Salesmen and women did that
sort of thing every day. Some people went out of their way on a
drive across the state to seek out local cafes and check out what
was homemade. Then there were others who hated to take even
a bite by themselves. They'd lose themselves in a newspaper or
strike up a conversation just to bide time until they had their

meal eaten. Funny, though, Dan didn't seem like either of those types. I had a hunch he'd purposely planned a late breakfast today because of whatever it was he had to say.

Not much went on around here that I couldn't predict. This was different. And wasn't that exactly what I'd been wanting?

I glanced at Olivia who seemed to be lost in thought. The way the wind was picking up outside, I doubted our lunch business would be booming today. I held up the empty coffeepot. "Let me get a new pot started. Then I'll have a minute." No doubt about it, I was curious.

Both eggs were already gone and Dan was spreading jelly on his toast when I slid into the booth across from him. I'd wished I'd thought to grab a snack for myself. Breakfast for me had happened almost five hours ago, and I'd been on my feet ever since. It felt good to sit. I leaned back, determined to enjoy this rare break. "How's business on your end of town?"

Dan laughed, catching the joke right away. His *end of town* was across the street from the café, just past the beauty shop.

"Business is good. I'll get busy with end-of-the-year tax business soon." He took a bite of toast, eating half a slice in one chomp, finishing it off in another. No wonder men finished eating so much faster than women. My morning coffee-and-toast women could make their toast last for forty-five minutes. He swallowed, then added, "I'll have a little breather, and then I'll get busy with April tax season. Between taxes and real estate it's always something."

"Ain't that the truth." I purposely used poor grammar, turning it into a joke. Anything less and even Dan Jordan might pick up on this funk I was in.

He picked up a slice of bacon with his fingers and took a bite, chewing slowly. I was beginning to wonder why he'd asked me to join him if he didn't have anything to talk about. Maybe I should just let him eat. I glanced over at Olivia. She seemed to be doing fine with her cup of coffee, and it sure did feel good to sit here and just let my heart beat. Not doing anything for once. Just sitting.

The radio I always had on when the café was open played softly in the background. I could hear the wind howling outside as the café furnace kicked in. I felt the long-time, business-neighbor connection between Dan and me settle between us. He'd talk when he was ready. Until then I could relax.

Eventually he wiped his mouth with a napkin and started talking. "Do you remember some time ago—gosh, I'd guess it would be close to three, four years ago, you came into my real estate office and said you might be interested in buying a small place to open some other sort of business?"

At his words my heart took up a new sort of thumping. How could he possibly remember that?

You never forgot.

No, but it wasn't his dream.

Dan couldn't possibly know all the nights I'd lain in bed, wondering if this dream of mine would ever have a chance of coming true. As I listened to Angie and her friends talk about pursuing their dreams of going off to college, my dream seemed to get further and further away. I couldn't see a way it could ever happen, but I had to know what Dan had in mind. "Yes?" I said. The one word was a question. A *big* question.

He glanced quickly from side-to-side, pushed his plate to the edge of the table and leaned forward. "You've got to promise not to say anything about this yet because it's not a done deal. But I couldn't help but think this might be the perfect place for your idea."

The fact he remembered pushed a lump into my throat. I leaned forward, too. I found myself almost mouthing, "*Tell me.*"

His voice was low. "Kenny Pearson stopped in yesterday and

mentioned his aunt's house might be on the market soon." Dan sat back a little. "You know Ida had that bad fall on Halloween and she's not doing so great."

I nodded. Ida Bauer had helped me serve pie at Pumpkin Fest for the past umpteen years and helped me out at the till many times over the years when I was short of help. And that was *after* she'd taught me to make pie crust as good as she made it… without a recipe. I'd been to see her in the hospital once since her fall, and Kenny kept me posted on her health when he stopped in for coffee most mornings. But Ida not doing *that* good? Bad enough to make her move out of her precious home? That feisty woman was as independent as they come.

I'd only gotten a peek inside her house one time when I'd stopped to drop off her paycheck. Almost all of my visiting with Ida had taken place right here in the café. If she wasn't helping me, she stopped in to have coffee. I'd missed her this past month. But the quick peek I'd gotten inside her house that one time had stayed with me.

"She's selling her house? For sure?"

Dan moved his finger in a "no" maneuver. "Not for sure. At least not yet. But the family is thinking about it. Would you still be interested?"

Would I?

It would be perfect.

I closed my eyes and filled my lungs with the coffee-scented air of the café. All it would take was a small space. I didn't need much room. Just a few tables with thick tablecloths. Some unmatched chairs painted in creamy white. A kitchen. I'd worry about the other stuff later.

You mean dream about it. All this is is a dream, you know.

But did it have to be just a dream? Maybe…just maybe…

I opened my eyes. I wondered if Dan could hear my heart pounding. "I'd like to see it."

Dan laughed. "Well, that's good. Except you can't. It's not for sale. Not yet. But I wanted to check with you just in case."

"Why now?" I asked. It suddenly occurred to me there had been scores of houses for sale in Brewster over the past four years.

Dan shrugged one shoulder. "I don't know," he said sounding as baffled as me. "You just came to mind."

"I supposed I should mention this to Dave."

Dan slid to the edge of the booth, pulling his wallet from his back pocket. "You've got plenty of time. Who knows? Maybe Ida will pull out of this."

I felt as if he'd thrown a bucket of cold water on my dream. But then again, I could hardly wish anything bad on Ida. I wasn't sure what to hope for, but I could already feel my mind running ahead of me at a hundred miles an hour. *A couple big mirrors with unique frames to hang on the walls. White votive candles for the tables. Oh, and silverware. I'll need silverware. And advertising to start…*

"So," Dan said, handing me a five-dollar bill, "I'll keep you posted." He pulled out a dollar bill and nodded toward the booth on the opposite wall. "Get Libby's coffee today, too."

Oh goodness, I'd forgotten all about Olivia Marsden. "Thanks," I called to Dan as I hurried to pick up the pot of freshly brewed coffee. I wouldn't have *any* customers at my new little café if I ruined my reputation for good service at this one.

"Your friend must be running late," I said as I refilled Olivia's empty cup. "Or are you early?"

Olivia swept one hand over her ear, pushing her hair behind it. "Oh, I'm not—I mean, I wasn't waiting for anyone. I was just…"

She paused, looking down into her cup. "I needed to get out of the house. One of those days, you know?" Her eyes met mine.

"Do I ever." I rested the coffeepot on her table. "Only with me, I don't need to get out of the house. I need a break from this café."

If you need a break, why are you thinking of starting another café?

I was already wondering the same thing. *Lord, help me make sense of this.*

She took a sip from her mug. "I hope you don't mind if I sit here for a bit."

One side of my mouth turned up. "That's what we're here for."

Slowly Olivia looked around the empty café, then outside. The gray clouds threatened snow. "It's cozy in here, isn't it?"

I simply smiled. *Just wait until you see my new place!*

"You can tell when someone is doing what they love. You can…" She paused, searching for a word. "…*feel* it."

I wasn't sure what to say to that. Five minutes ago I'd been wondering if all I'd ever be doing the rest of my life was frying hamburgers and pouring coffee, and now I was dreaming about doing even more of it. Not that I'd serve something as simple as hamburgers at my new place.

"Are you ever looking for a writing project?" Before I knew I'd asked, the words were out of my mouth. Everyone in town knew Olivia was a writer. Her column in the *Brewster Banner* was the best part of the paper twice a month. And just the other day, Dave had mentioned that he'd heard Olivia had written a book. Even so, in all my dreaming, I'd never dreamed of asking her for this. I was jumping ahead of myself big time. I could feel heat rise into my neck. If I was lucky, maybe she hadn't heard me.

Her head tilted. "What did you have in mind?"

Yeah, what did I have in mind?

You know.

Actually I did. Even if I didn't start the specialty café I'd dreamed about for years, I had another idea I'd batted around just as long. Maybe this was nuts, but I needed something to make my days not so routine. I set down the coffeepot and perched myself on the opposite edge of the booth. I was as nervous as if I were asking for money. I licked my lips and bit the inside of my cheek. I might as well get it over with. Tell her my idea. Let her say no. Be done with it. I'd be no further behind than I was right now.

I took a deep breath. "People are always asking me for my pumpkin pie recipe. For the ingredients in the salad dressings I make. I've thought for a long time that it might be interesting to do a recipe book. But I—"

Olivia opened her mouth. I quickly held up my hand stopping whatever she might be thinking of saying. I wanted to get it all out. Then she could turn me down.

I pushed the words from my mouth, thinking if I said them fast enough she'd at least hear me out. "But I don't want to do just a plain old cookbook. I want it to be something special. To have—to be…"

That was as far as I'd gotten in my late-night dreaming. A recipe book that wasn't one. Some big idea. I stopped talking. Olivia didn't even have to comment on my non idea. I reached for the coffeepot, trying to avoid looking at her. I couldn't believe I'd just asked the banker's wife to write a recipe book with me. What had possessed me? Her coffee was already paid for. Maybe if I hurried back into the kitchen with Ruthie, Olivia would slip out of the café and I could be mortified without her watching.

I was beginning to stand when I felt a light touch on my arm. As hard as I tried I couldn't help but look at her. Just as I thought, she was almost laughing. Her eyes were crinkled and she was shaking her head as if she couldn't believe my stupidity.

"I'm sorry," I said quickly standing. "I know you have—"

"Please sit down." She picked up her mug and took a sip. "Let's talk about this."

I sat.

Her voice was soft as she gazed into her cup. "Do you know why I came in here this morning?"

I'd thought she was meeting a friend, but she'd said she wasn't. "You said you needed to get out of the house." I tilted my head. "We all need a change some days." She had no idea how much I meant that.

"Exactly." She looked up at me and smiled. "I think this might be just the change I need. Will you give me some time to brainstorm ideas?"

"Will I? *Will I!*" I was laughing now. What would *some time* be when I'd been brainstorming for *years?* "Of course!" I felt like shaking her hand. Or hugging her.

"No fair having so much fun without me." Ruthie was standing by our table, one hand on a hip, grinning as if she were in on the conversation. "It's not nearly as much fun back in the kitchen, you know."

I jumped to my feet, looking first at Ruthie, then at Olivia. "I know. I've got to get back to work."

Olivia slipped out of the booth. "We'll talk soon. Should we wait until after the holidays?"

I'd completely forgotten about all the Christmas banquets the café would be serving starting in just over a week, not to mention the turkey-and-trimmings buffet we'd be serving for Thanksgiving this Thursday. *When would I have time to even think about a recipe book?* But then, it never had taken any effort to *dream.* "For sure," I said, feeling the sudden added pressure of the holidays. Even so, I couldn't quit smiling.

Olivia reached into her coat pocket and pulled out two dollar bills.

I held up one palm. "No, no, coffee's on me. Well, actually, it's on Dan Jordan. He paid for it before he left."

"My, my," Olivia said, laying one of the bills on the table before she turned to go, an over-sized tip for a cup of coffee. "This day is getting better by the minute."

A bubble of bliss danced in my chest as I cleared Dan's breakfast plate and silverware, removed his coffee mug, then wiped off the table, brushing toast crumbs into my hand and then into the garbage. I moved to Olivia's table, and my good mood moved with me. I lifted her coffee cup, noticing the faint lipstick stain along the rim as I wiped her table with my damp cloth. Funny how having something new, something to plan for, made such a change in this cloudy day.

I'd just gotten the café cleaned when the front door blew open and four of the guys from the implement shop stepped inside, stomping their heavy boots on the entry mat.

"Hey, guys," I called out as usual, "four specials with coffee?"

"Same as always," John said as they settled themselves around a table.

But the funny part was, as I walked back to the kitchen to give Ruthie their order, it didn't seem like same-as-always. It felt as though it was somehow brand-new.

Libby

"Mom! I'm home!" Emily pushed a bulging duffle bag through the kitchen door with her foot. She didn't even give me time to let her know I was standing at the counter three feet away before she yelled again. "Mom!"

"Emily," I said, trying to keep my voice calm. "I'm here." I put down my spatula and went to hug her. She greeted me by turning back into the garage and lifted an overflowing laundry basket into my arms. "Hold this," she said. "It's my dirty laundry." As if I couldn't smell.

I stepped over Emily's duffle bag, carried the basket into our small laundry room behind the door, and started separating whites from darks. Best get this done so I wouldn't have to step around dirty clothes all of Christmas vacation. Knowing Emily, she'd leave the pile until the night before she had to return to school and then, instead of having some last-minute time together, she'd be burning the midnight laundry soap.

"I can do that, Mom." Emily squeezed around me and yanked a pair of jeans from the basket, a tumble of panties, socks, and sweatshirts fell to the floor.

I bent to pick them up. *If she was going to do it, why didn't she do her laundry* before *she came home?* STOP! I wasn't going to go there. I was going to be happy Emily was home safely. *Thank You, Lord, for travel mercies.* There.

I put down the dirty sweatshirt in my hand and opened my arms. "How about that hug I didn't get yet?"

Emily grinned and folded me in her arms, along with a rumpled T-shirt. "Mmm," she murmured, her head against my neck, "it's good to be home."

"It's good to have you here." I gave her a big squeeze. "How about if you do this and I'll go finish that batch of cookies I was mixing up?"

"Molasses crinkles?"

"How'd you guess?"

"It must be all that college education you're paying for."

I threw a sock at her and walked back into the kitchen. Already I could feel the kids-home-for-the-holidays vibe in the air. Even though both Brian and Emily had said they wouldn't make it home until after supper, I'd been glancing out the window most of the afternoon waiting for them to arrive. Being greeted with an overflowing laundry basket wasn't exactly the way I'd imagined Emily's homecoming, but I shouldn't have been surprised. Brian was on his way home from grad school in Minneapolis, and I had no doubt he would head straight for the chocolate chip cookies right after he hugged me. I just hoped he'd done his laundry before he left the city. It seemed as if both my *kids* reverted to kid-dom when they walked through the kitchen door.

I set the oven temperature to 350 degrees. I scraped the side of the bowl with the spatula. Turning the mixer on low one more time, I watched as the thick brown dough wound around the beaters. A bit like I felt these days. As if I were being turned in directions I hadn't quite planned. How quickly things could change in a few short weeks!

It wasn't hard to remember a month ago, that gloomy day I'd stopped in Vicky Johnson's café to drown my writing sorrows in a cup of coffee…or two. I'd more-or-less decided to quit writing that morning. You'd think I would have been happy after making the decision to rise up out of the heap of rejection and start doing something worthwhile with my time. Instead, after mailing my last manuscript, I found myself driving out of town, tears streaming down my cheeks, crying as if my best friend, Anne, was riding beside me. I had spoken to her aloud, my voice cracking... "Why can't you be here now? I need you. I need to talk to you. Why did you have to die?"

I could almost hear her logical response. *"If I hadn't died, you wouldn't have written your book. You wouldn't have just sent it off in the mail.*

I spoke into the air as if she could hear. "A lot of good that's gonna do."

Remember the "What if...?" game?

I couldn't hold back my teary-eyed smile. How could I forget that silly game of Anne's? The game where she always got me to tell her something I'd never told a soul...until her. "What if...?" she'd say, and then follow it up with some outlandish question. Something like, "What if you could do anything in the world? What would you do?" It was as if she already knew. She just wanted me to say it out loud.

Writing a book was your dream. When I asked, you told me your wildest dream was to write a book. Now you've done it.

She had me there. But still...I'd rather have her.

Would you? Would you rather have a friend than have a story to write?

That stopped me. I weighed my desire to write with my desire to have Anne back. What would I choose if I could?

I slowed the car and turned onto a gravel road. Frozen stones crunched under the tires as tears came hot and fast. As much as I wanted to write, as much as I felt I'd been put on this earth for just that purpose, I had to pick Anne. I wanted her friendship. Someone to laugh with. And cry with. Someone to go shopping with who wasn't afraid to tell me I looked not-so-great in purple.

I wanted someone who understood me. Someone who *knew* me like she did.

I know you.

I know. But sometimes I just want a friend with skin on.

I could almost hear God laugh. Somehow it always seemed when I started talking to Anne, I ended up talking to Him.

You might not have Me, either, if it hadn't been for Anne.

I know that. But why do I still miss her so much sometimes? I pulled into an approach and shifted into park, letting my tears flow freely. *I can't keep doing this, Lord. Sending out my manuscript, getting nothing but rejection back. Feeling as if I'm in this all alone. Is there any purpose to my life at all? If You want me to keep doing this, I need some...some...something!* I jabbed the heel of my hand into the steering wheel. The horn honked, a staccato jab into the empty countryside as if in harmony with my discord. *Something!*

Coffee.

Coffee? Coffee! That wasn't what I meant. I need some...some...*sign,* some encouragement. I've had three cups of coffee already this morning. I need a bathroom, not more coffee!

Disgusted with my wallowing and more than a little annoyed with God, I shifted into reverse and headed back to town. Back to my life as "just a housewife." Some women flourished in that role. Why couldn't I? For me it just wasn't enough. But what would be?

How I ended up at Vicky's Café was still a mystery. In all the years I'd lived in Brewster, I'd seldom been to the café by myself. And certainly not indulging in self-pity...wondering what my purpose was if it wasn't to write.

And then there she was, Vicky Johnson, asking me, Olivia Marsden, if I wanted to write.

I smiled into the cookie dough. It looked as if I would be

writing for at least a little while more. A recipe book wasn't quite what I had in mind when I asked God what He expected of me, but who was I to argue?

The ideas that had been brewing in my mind about this new project had even taken a bit of the sting out of the most recent rejection letter. As much as my paltry, track-keeping system, the one I kept in my sieve-like brain, could keep count, the only query I had out was the one I'd mailed the day I'd stopped by Vicky's. If that one came back with a "no thanks" written on it, well, I was out of options. A recipe book might be the extent of my personal library. *Please, Lord, let it be more.*

For busy December, anyway, the only option I had was the just-a-housewife one. Other than writing my columns for the *Banner* and our annual Christmas letter, I hadn't had time to whine about my nonwriting career all month. In the business of shopping, wrapping, decorating, and baking, I'd been blessedly free from that monkey-on-my-back all month. I scooped a tiny pat of molasses-flavored dough from the side of the bowl with my little finger and licked it off. *Why'd I do that?* I don't even like uncooked cookie dough. Oh well, it just goes to show that even when we don't like something, sometimes we do it anyway…for instance, inviting Brian's new girlfriend to spend Christmas Day with us. Another twist that had surprised me this past month.

It wasn't that I didn't like Katie; it was that I hadn't met her yet. I couldn't help but think it might be a little awkward on Christmas morning watching Brian and Emily open their Santa-stocking gifts while we were all in our pajamas, knowing some *stranger* would be knocking on our door sometime mid-morning. Of course the thought of what this young woman might think of a mother who still gave her twenty-five-year-old son a stocking filled with Santa gifts had crossed my mind one…*or ten*…times in the two weeks since Brian had called. But what could I say? As if Brian was in the kitchen with me, I could repeat the words of that phone call…

"Hello?"

"Mo-om?" His strong tenor voice strung out the word.

I could tell the minute I picked up the phone that Brian wanted something. Something important. "Hell*o-oh*," I said for the second time, stalling a bit. I had a feeling whatever he was going to ask was going to upset my tradition-filled Christmas cart.

"Oh, yeah." I could hear him chuckle. "Hello, Mom."

"You're wondering what to get me for Christmas?"

"Well, yeah, but—"

If he was going to tell me he wasn't coming home for Christmas I didn't want to hear the "but" part. Not yet. Not ever. I jumped in like an elf on speed. "I'd like a decent kitchen knife. The few I have are as old as my marriage to your dad. And, oh goodness, you get to shop at the Mall of America, there's all kinds of fun stuff there." I was babbling. Why? My question didn't stop me. "I could use a new winter scarf. Don't even think about getting cashmere. It's too expensive, and it makes me itch. Blue would be nice. Black is always—"

"Mom, I'll figure something out. Kate is going shopping with me this weekend."

Oh. There was the "but." She had a name. Kate.

Somehow, I knew it. Not her name, but that this was going to involve a girl. Well, young *woman*. Better be politically correct about this.

For a split second I thought about acting as though I hadn't heard. But that was a cliché I didn't want to dance around. Might as well get right to her. "Katie, hmm?"

"*Kate*," Brian repeated, more emotion in those four letters than I would have guessed possible.

But then *love* was a four-letter word, too. My heart did a funny twist that had me pressing my fingertips to my breastbone. Brian and I had been through a lot together when he was younger and experimenting with who he would become. I had no trouble imagining him as the elementary school principal he planned on being soon. I knew my son. I *felt* what he didn't say in that one word. *Kate.* It had to happen sometime. But now? At Christmas?

He's twenty-five.

Old enough. He'd be done with grad school this spring. Frankly, I was surprised Brian had waited this long to fall in love...if that's what this was. He was the kind of young man who had seemed destined for a committed relationship early on. We'd had more girl "friends" through this house than I could count. He seemed more *settled* when he had a girlfriend. Maybe that's why Bob had told Brian often enough—Emily, too—that they'd be better off waiting until they were through with college before they got married. Bob pointed out the fact they could stay on our health insurance policy as long as they were in school and *not* married. Ever the banker, Bob didn't fail to point out the bottom line: "That's a big savings."

As if *love* cared about money. I doubted an insurance policy was the reason Brian hadn't found the right young woman yet. But he sure had followed his dad's advice. He'd had several somewhat serious girlfriends over the past years. Two, at least, I could have imagined as my daughter-in-law. If this Katie—Kate—was what she sounded like, I'd be shopping for a beige dress soon...and trying to keep my mouth shut. Isn't that what mothers-of-the-groom were bred to do?

Aren't you getting a little ahead of yourself?

I gave my head a small shake, reminding myself to get back to reality. I was already planning a wedding when Brian had simply told me her name. I should know by now that my habit of extrapolating ordinary events to an extreme conclusion usually left me…wrong. From the way Brian sounded, this time I hoped I was right. Broken hearts weren't my specialty.

"So is it okay if Kate spends Christmas Day with us?"

I had a million questions. Where is she from? How did you two meet? Is she as special as you're making her sound? But I knew they'd all get answered on Christmas Day.

The preheat buzzer on the oven sounded, bringing me back to my kitchen and my cookies.

I'd meet the girl of Brian's dreams in two days.

⁓

"Thanks, Santa!" Emily grinned, holding up the Aveda body cream Santa-mom had splurged on. She continued riffling through the large red stocking as if she were two instead of twenty. "Ah-ha! I knew it had to be in there somewhere." She held up her annual new toothbrush. This year's was pink.

"Here's mine." Brian held up a blue one. His gaze danced nervously toward the window. The same direction mine had been floating all morning.

I leaned back into the couch next to Bob and sipped my coffee. It was amusing to watch my two now-grown children marvel over the shampoo and bath soap that now filled their Christmas socks instead of toys and candy. We'd all broken tradition this morning by getting dressed before the Christmas-morning stocking ritual. It seemed Kate was already changing our lives.

I'd get to meet her soon enough. She was due to arrive from somewhere in Minnesota before lunch. Another tradition that was broken…the brunch I usually served after we slept in and opened the stocking gifts. Kate couldn't make it here until almost noon. I looked outside again, wondering if her mother was worrying about her daughter driving alone in the blustery weather that had arrived overnight.

It had been a wonderful Christmas so far. Brian and Emily had developed a brother–sister friendship that went past the tortured-teasing of their early years. They laughed and joked, but also talked, as if they truly appreciated each other. They had both grown into adults Bob and I could be proud of.

I looked at the Christmas tree, its multicolored lights twinkling amid the ornaments I had collected over the years. In addition to souvenirs from our travels and gifts from friends, I'd also added an ornament each year for the kids. One for Brian...usually sports related. And one for Emily...something sparkly and "girly." They each knew someday those ornaments would be theirs. For their own Christmas trees. This morning the day I would need to pack up some of those ornaments seemed all too near.

There were reminders of my kids growing up at every turn this season. Last night we'd attended the annual Christmas program at church together. Brian and Emily had long out-grown their parts in the service. We watched as the bath-robed shepherds, the four-year-olds on all fours bleating like lambs, and the miniature Mary and Joseph carrying the doll that was baby Jesus, worked an annual lump into each of our throats. By the time the youth group surrounded the congregation for the candle-lighting ceremony, even Bob was blinking as if he'd been in a sandstorm.

I couldn't help but remember another Christmas Eve. The year Anne died. Her funeral had been in that very church, that very afternoon. Christmas Eve. It had been that evening, when I'd been trying to run from my grief, I'd dragged my family to a church service in Carlton. A service so similar to the one we'd just witnessed in Brewster it was uncanny. A service that changed my life and brought me to God. "Joy to the World" was surely written for me that night ten years ago.

Could it really be ten years since Anne had died? It didn't seem possible. Sometimes it still felt like yesterday. But then, all I had to do was take one look at Emily and see how my ten year old, the little girl who'd played the fancy version of "Jesus Loves Me" by heart at Anne's funeral, was now a twenty-year-old young woman. A young woman who looked as if she, too, might have something called *love* in her future.

"Hey, Em." Mike Anderson had wasted no time finding Emily in the crowded foyer of the church last night.

"Mike!" Emily threw one arm around him in an exuberant hug. "Merry Christmas!"

I couldn't help but notice the way both of Mike's arms wanted to curl around Emily. I stood to the side and shamelessly eavesdropped.

"You look amazing." That from Mike.

Emily seemed to ignore his comment, but I could tell by the flip of her long hair and the way one hand smoothed her cranberry-colored silk skirt, she'd heard every word. "When'd you get home?"

I was wondering, too. In fact, I'd half-expected they would share the drive home from the college they both attended. Or at the very least, Mike would call Emily the second he got to town. Apparently I'd been waiting for the phone to ring more than Emily. I leaned closer, but missed his answer completely when my friend Jan Jordan sidled between us and wished me Merry Christmas.

The crowd in the foyer had dwindled by the time Bob had visited with half the men in attendance. It was fun to see Brian reconnecting with old high school friends who were home for the holidays, too. I could tell by the look on Bob's and Brian's faces that they loved being with people almost as much as I preferred being at home with a good book. I caught Bob's attention with a lift of my chin and he walked over.

I buttoned the top button of my coat. "It's probably time for us to get home and have some of Grandma's Green Punch and then open our gifts. It's getting late." The green punch was his grandma's recipe...and also his favorite holiday treat. I knew the sherbet-laced punch would get him moving the direction I wanted to go. *Home.*

"You ready, Brian?" Bob turned to his son who now bested him by an inch.

"Yeah. Where's Emily?"

My radar had kept them on my Mom-screen. Mike and Emily had moved to a corner near the coatrack. Their heads were bent close as if they hadn't talked in ages. Mike's shoulder turned and bumped against Emily's much the way I'd seen in *National Geographic* documentaries of dolphins doing a ritual courting dance. I could only hope.

That had been last night, and I was positive Mike would call Emily sometime today. Surely the choreography I'd seen in the church was leading to something. At least I hoped it was. I had liked that young man since he'd become Emily's friend in elementary school. I liked him even more now. How could I *not* like someone who was as enthralled with my daughter as I was?

"She's here!" Brian was on his feet and race-walking for the door before I'd even realized the doorbell had rung. But, then again, maybe it hadn't. Brian had been keeping a detective-like eye on the street since he'd opened his eyes this morning. He must have seen her car drive up.

Okay. I stood. Licked my lips. Smoothed my dark gray sweater and knit slacks. Adjusted the crystal snowflake broach I'd pinned to my collar. This was it. If everything Brian had told me about

Kate over the past two days was any indication, I was about to meet my future daughter-in-law.

I let Brian take the lead. Gave him time to greet Kate by himself. After I heard their hellos and imagined a silent hug, I motioned to Bob and Emily with a wiggle of my fingers that we should join them at the front door.

"This must be Katie," I said as I rounded the corner, suddenly unsure if I should hug this stranger or shake hands.

She solved the problem by quickly sticking out her right hand. "Mrs. Marsden," she said, her voice cool…nervous.

I was tempted to glance over my shoulder to see if my mother-in-law had appeared behind me. The last person to call me Mrs. Marsden had been a bellman at a fancy hotel Bob and I had stayed at during a banker's convention last June. That man had held out his hand in a similar manner, only he was expecting a tip. I doubted the propriety of palming five bucks into Katie's outstretched hand and then expecting her to leave. Instead I acted like the mom I knew Brian expected me to be and put my hand in hers, moving my left hand to cup hers in both of mine. "Katie," I said, "it's so nice to meet you."

"It's not Katie. It's Kate." Her first words corrected me.

Okay.

I forced myself to keep smiling. "Sorry. Kate. I have a good friend named Katie, and I guess it just slipped out. Merry Christmas." I pumped her hand, then released it and stepped back as Brian introduced her to Bob and Emily.

Katie. *Kate,* I reminded myself, trying not to stare while I gathered my first impressions.

Light brown hair, slightly wavy and long, pushed behind one ear, which held a small, gold, hoop earring. I sized her up against Brian. Five-six, if I had to guess. Slender in a healthy sort of way. I didn't know if the kids still called the way she dressed "preppy," but that was the way I would describe her dressy black slacks and cable-knit red sweater with a white shirt peeking out from collar and cuffs. Tailored.

Or uptight.

I shushed myself. She reminded me of someone...and it certainly wasn't my friend Katie from Carlton. I just couldn't place who it was. "Should we go sit in the living room?" I suggested as the awkward introductions were over. "Katie. *Kate!*" I quickly corrected. "Would you like something to drink? I've got coffee made. Or Brian and Emily are having some Chai Tea mix I have. Would you like some of that?"

"Coffee. Thank you." She smiled politely at me and then followed Brian into the living room.

I was glad for the excuse to go into the kitchen. Coffee. One point in her favor. Not that I was keeping score. As I reached for a mug, then the coffeepot, I realized Bob and I had almost emptied the whole pot while we'd watched the kids rifle through their Santa gifts. Good. Having to make a new pot would give me a chance to stay in the kitchen a little bit longer. Give me time to sort through the unsettled emotions that were twirling through my mind.

She reminds me of someone. I couldn't get the thought out of my mind. Who was it? If I could just think who it was I could start to compare and contrast what it was about her that seemed so familiar.

"*So-ooo?*" Emily's loud whisper just about caused me to drop the glass container where I kept the coffee grounds.

"*Emily!*" I loud-whispered back. "*Shhushh! She'll hear you.*"

Emily waved her hand through the air. "The only person she's interested in hearing is Brian." She rolled her eyes. "He's giving her the play-by-play of what he's done since he left Minneapolis three days ago. As if anyone cares."

I bit the insides of my cheeks, suppressing a smile. It sounded as if Katie might be in an unwitting competition for Emily's brother's attention.

"So-ooo…" Emily stood so close she was practically touching me. "What do you think of her?"

Just as when Brian had told me about Katie in the first place, I wanted to dance around the question. This time I did. "Oh, Emily," I said, scooping coffee grounds into the filter, "I haven't said more than two sentences to her. I need a little more time than that to get an impression."

Emily leaned her backside against the counter. "I don't like her."

"Emily!" I cringed, realizing I'd spoken too loud. I lowered my voice. "You haven't even given her a chance."

With the confidence of youth, Emily crossed her arms over her chest. "I don't have to. She's not even that cute."

"Emily." My tone held a warning. "You should know better than to judge people by how they look. It's what's on the inside that counts. You know that."

She grabbed a molasses crinkle off the plate of cookies I had ready to serve for dessert after lunch and broke off a bite. "Even if she was cute, I still wouldn't like her."

"You need to give her a chance."

The same way you did when you first met Anne? Or…didn't.

Inwardly I cringed again. It wasn't hard to remember the instant dislike I'd taken to Anne the first time we met. Even now, ten years later, I felt humiliated at the way I'd judged her so quickly…and so wrongly. Thank goodness God intervened. If I'd had my way, Anne and I would have never become best friends. At the thought, a quick line of goose bumps marched down my back. I didn't want to contemplate for one second what my life would have been like these past years if I hadn't met Anne.

"We need to give Katie a chance," I said as I waited for Katie's coffee mug to fill directly from the coffee maker.

We?

I picked up the plate of cookies and handed them to Emily. "Why don't you take these into the living room?" So what if we had dessert before lunch. It was Christmas, after all, and it looked as if more than one of us could use a little sweetening.

Quickly I substituted Katie's mug with the coffeepot and followed Emily into the other room. Katie was telling Brian and Bob what her family had done to celebrate the holidays. I watched as she reached over and rested her hand on Brian's knee...as if she was claiming her property.

Get it off! I bit back the words, forced a smile, and handed Katie her mug of coffee. There was more than one way to get her polished little fingernails off my son.

I eased myself into a chair and told myself the same thing I'd told Emily. *You need to give her a chance.*

As Katie sipped her coffee and chattered away, I racked my brain trying to think who she reminded me of. For the life of me, I couldn't place her. The only thing I knew for sure was that I didn't like her.

Angie

"Here's to my college girl!" My mom slid into the booth across from me and clinked her glass of Diet Coke against mine. She took a big swallow and then pointed to the huge bouquet of fresh daisies sitting in a vase by the café cash register. "For you," she said, grinning. "Dad bought them."

Only in summer did Mom occasionally have real flowers in the café. Flowers she went out in our backyard and picked herself. Real live flowers in Vicky's Café in *January* must have been the talk of the morning coffee hour. I was sure the supper crowd, who would be marching in any second, would have plenty to say, too. I had no doubt most of Brewster knew by now that I'd been accepted to UND next fall.

I pushed the last bite of hamburger into my mouth, took a sip of Diet Coke, then pointedly looked at the clock. Five minutes to five meant the early supper eaters would be here soon. Thank goodness. It was hard pretending I was excited about going off to college when I wasn't. I slipped to the edge of the booth. "I'd better start getting the dinner salads ready." Mom sat back in the booth with a satisfied smile on her face.

Before heading into the kitchen I scooped some more ice into my glass and topped off my Diet Coke at the fountain dispenser. I wished everyone would get off my back about this college business. Of course it might be more incentive for them to quit bugging me if they knew I didn't plan on going. But I still hadn't figured out how I was going to break the news.

I let Mom continue her fantasy—planning my life for me—and walked back into the kitchen. I washed my hands, then pulled ten fake-wood salad bowls down from a shelf and lined them up on the island counter in the middle of the café kitchen. From the fridge I took out prechopped lettuce, tomato chunks, and shredded carrots.

Almost every night after school this was my routine. As soon as the final bell rang I'd head home, change clothes, and then drive to the café to help my mom or Aunt Ruthie with the supper hour, which really was two hours, sometimes more. First I'd grab a Diet Coke, then I'd pick something off the menu for my own supper, usually a hamburger. The café was always slow between four and five, a perfect time for Mom and me to play catch-up while I grabbed a bite before getting to work. Some nights Mom would leave around five and go home to have dinner with Dad and Sam, leaving Ruthie and me in charge. Other nights Ruthie would go home early and Dad and Sam would come eat at the café.

Some of my friends thought it was weird for our family to eat most of our meals at the restaurant, but I'd grown up eating here, so it didn't feel odd to me at all. The café was like a second home. Sometimes, on a cold night like tonight, it was my favorite place in the world. I loved the steamy warmth of the kitchen. The smell of roast beef in the oven. The cold feel of the fresh lettuce and tomatoes in my hands. My reliable routine. It made me feel safe and secure. Why should I go off to college when I was already doing what I loved?

It's because you're chicken.

I wrinkled my nose at the thought. So what if the thought of going off to college made me feel scared? I'd done lots of things that made me terrified. Like standing in front of my speech class in tenth grade and giving a speech against abortion. Or last year when I yelled at the senior guys who were bullying that kind-of-weird kid who'd just moved to Brewster and was a freshman. They could have told me to shut up and blown me off, instead they actually listened and quit it. Just because I was scared to go to college didn't mean I wouldn't…if I really wanted to. The thing was…I didn't. Want to, that is.

The letter had arrived yesterday. It had been propped up against a candle in the middle of our kitchen table so that it was the first thing I saw when I got home after school. The return address left no doubt it was from the only college I'd applied to. I was just glad Mom had left it on the table instead of showing up at school and making an announcement over the loudspeaker. As if getting into college in North Dakota was a big deal. Anyone who placed well on the ACT test and still graduated from high school could get accepted into college in this state, even without the more-than-decent score of twenty-six I'd gotten on the test. Good enough to qualify for scholarships. Even if I wouldn't be needing any, I felt proud of that.

I looked at the envelope, the new centerpiece on our kitchen table. Just because my mom had never gone to college, she thought I should be doing back flips because I was getting to go. She'd been watching the mailbox ever since she made sure I mailed my application in late November. I couldn't forget the way she'd hovered over me.

"Are you sure you don't want to apply to a couple other schools?" Mom had asked as I was tucking the check for the application fee into the envelope. It wouldn't have surprised me if she'd licked the envelope for me, too. As it was, she'd hung over my shoulder as I filled out the form as if she'd taken cheating lessons from a really bad teacher. Subtle she wasn't.

Well, here was the letter my Mom had been waiting for. The letter I dreaded. I'd let my backpack drop to the floor and stared at the white envelope. I knew Dad always dropped off the morning mail at the café when he stopped in the café for coffee. Mom usually gave me any mail that was for me when I went into the café for work after school. I knew she must have made a special trip home from the café just to make sure I'd get the "good news" first thing. The way she'd positioned the envelope "just so" on the table, it was obvious she knew what was inside.

So did I.

My best friend, Julie, had received her acceptance and roommate assignment—me—two days ago. All she talked about these days, all anyone in my class talked about was "Next year. Next year." They didn't really mean "next" year, what they meant was next fall. *This* fall. It seemed as if every single one of my twenty-three classmates couldn't wait to move away from Brewster. Well, all except for Jason Erbele. Everyone knew all he planned to do was stay home and help his dad on the farm.

Kind of like you wanting to stay home and help your mom at the café?

It was sort of the same, but different. Everyone knew Jason wasn't that smart. Even the school counselor wasn't pushing him to apply to schools. He was lucky his dad had a big farm and needed the help. Even so, I'd heard more than one of my classmates trash-talking Jason. Calling him "too stupid to go to college" behind his back. I wasn't sure what they'd say about me when they found out I wouldn't be going either.

I wasn't stupid. You couldn't call being on the honor roll every nine weeks since seventh grade stupid. Sometimes I thought it was my classmates who were dumb. I mean, they talked about being open-minded and about wanting to ditch this small town and go somewhere bigger. Somewhere more exciting. But most of the time they tried so hard to be open-minded they were closed-minded. What was so bad about liking where you were? They acted like staying in Brewster would be some kind of crime.

I'd always loved Brewster. And I love the café. Sure, sometimes when I was younger I complained about having to work there so much. But deep down I'd always been happiest when I was helping in the kitchen or kibitzing with some of the old men who hung out at the café for coffee at night before we closed. Was there something wrong with knowing what you wanted to do in life even when you are young?

It sure seemed like it. The couple times I dared say something like "I'd love to work in the café the rest of my life" I'd barely have the sentence out of my mouth and my mom would be interrupting, saying something like, "No you don't. You want to get out in the world. There are all sorts of careers you don't even know about." Then she'd smile at me in this condescending way, as if she knew me so much better than I did.

Well, I knew one thing—it would be a complete waste of money to send me to college when I didn't want to go. The problem was, I hadn't figured out how to quit jumping through the hoops that were leading me there.

Like this application letter sitting on the table. It wasn't as if I hadn't known this was coming. I picked up the letter, wishing there were some way I could make it disappear.

I was glad I was home alone. My brother, Sam, was at basketball practice. Dad was still at his insurance business. Mom was at the café, the same place I'd be heading to help with the supper shift as soon as I changed clothes.

After I opened the letter.

I slid my thumb under the corner flap and pushed along the edge, jagged rips outlining my thoughts.

I wish I could be excited about this.

I don't want to go.

How am I going to tell my parents?

How am I going to tell Julie?

And how will I ever tell Mark? Especially now when he's already applied for a transfer to UND.

"Let the dinner hour begin." Mom pushed through the swinging door leading into the café kitchen and headed to the grill, pulling my thoughts from last-night's acceptance letter back to the present. On her way past me she reached out and cupped my cheek with her hand. "I wish I could be in your shoes. I am so excited for you! And proud of you!"

I dipped my head away from her hand. I hated the way I could feel my cheeks getting red. I only hoped Mom thought it was because I was excited about getting my acceptance letter—not because I was still trying to figure out a way to get out of going to college.

Two-at-a-time I put the filled salad bowls onto the shelf in the fridge, enjoying the wave of cool air on my warm face. I had the beginning of a plan that would make it okay for me to stay in Brewster, but for someone who'd gotten a twenty-six on her ACT test, it didn't take much planning to know most everyone else would think it was plain old stupid.

Especially Mark…and I needed his help the most.

Vicky

"What do you think? Didn't I tell you it was interesting?" Dan Jordon waved one arm around Ida Bauer's quaint living room.

I wrapped my arms around myself, not sure if the goose bumps running up my arms were from the near-frigid air in the barely heated house or from the vision I suddenly had of the potential this place had.

I'd driven past the house thousands of times in the years I'd lived in Brewster, never once pegging this as the place my long-time dream might come true. But ever since Dan had mentioned the house might be coming up for sale, I'd craned my neck each time I crept by, trying to imagine just what was inside the small, yellow stucco framework.

Dan had cornered me at coffee time at the café this morning with a nod of his head. We'd stood near the cash register as if he was simply paying for his coffee and the sweet roll he'd eaten. Instead of pulling out his wallet, he'd reached into his pocket and held out his open palm.

"It's official," he said, his voice low, a faded-gold house key laying in his palm as if it were some sort of secret treasure.

My eyes darted to the side, then to his. "Ida's?"

"Um hmm," he confirmed. "I haven't put the sign out yet. Thought I'd give you first chance." He paused while he shuffled one foot against the floor mat lying in front of the cash register counter and stuck the key back into his pocket. He looked directly at me. "I'll level with you, Vicky. I don't expect a *run* on this house.

It's small. Most young families now days want something bigger to start. And it needs some work. Especially the kitchen. But it's something special inside, and I've got an older couple from near Flanders who are interested in moving into Brewster from the farm. I don't think the house they're living in now is much of anything so they might jump at this." Once again his eyes locked on mine. "You interested?"

Interested? Oh my! I could feel my heart thumping against my breastbone. That word didn't begin to describe my feelings about this dream. But for as many nights as I'd tossed and turned trying to figure out a way to make it come true, I hadn't come up with any idea that was even close to a possibility. I looked at Dan and shook my head, then found myself nodding instead.

"No? Yes?" Dan was chuckling, nodding his head in the same crazy circle mine was bobbing. "It doesn't cost anything to look. What's a good time for you?"

"Today?" My eyes widened. I felt as if I'd been holding onto the reins of a gentle work horse who suddenly decided to run in the Kentucky Derby. I was being pulled into a race I hadn't planned on running.

Dan nodded. "Later this afternoon work for you? I could meet you over there."

A thousand answers rushed through my brain. None of them were "*Sure!*" but that's what I said. "Four-fifteen?"

"Done." Dan laid two dollars and some change on the counter as if he had no idea what I'd just agreed to do.

The minutes of the day ticked by as though a turtle had taken over the inner workings of the Coca-Cola clock hanging on the café wall. My hands served food, my mouth joshed with customers, but my mind was somewhere else. Dave had been easy to fool at lunch time.

"You okay?" he asked when I set a piece of banana cream pie

in front of him. His favorite was pumpkin, and he apparently knew there were four pieces left in the glass case.

I simply smiled and walked to the pie case and exchanged the slices, all the while debating whether I should ask Dave to meet me at Ida's house with Dan. He'd know a lot more to ask about the soundness of the house than I would. But then what good would it do to add Dave's "no" to the one I'd been practicing all morning? As I placed his pumpkin pie on the table in front of him, I decided it was best to keep this little dream to myself.

Ruthie had been harder to dupe. I should have known.

Dan hadn't been out of the café more than twenty minutes when Ruthie called me back into the kitchen with a *ding!* of the "Order Up" bell. I knew there weren't any orders pending. The morning coffee drinkers had finished their mid-morning snacks. Lunch orders were a good hour away. After making a last round of the café with the coffeepots, Ruthie had gone back to the kitchen to fry up the spiced-hamburger we'd be using for the taco salad special at noon. The sound of that bell was a signal she wanted to tell me something.

She didn't waste any time. "So just say it." She pushed sizzling meat around the grill, chopping it into fine pieces with the edge of a metal spatula. Her apron formed a cute little tent over the bulge that was the baby growing in her stomach. Almost six-months along, her morning sickness thankfully gone, Ruthie hadn't missed a day of work since early October.

"Say what?" I didn't have a clue what she was getting at. She couldn't have possibly overheard Dan and me talking. And I knew she couldn't read my mind. Then again...

"You're in a *zone.*" Ruthie said, pushing the fried meat to one side of the grill and adding another batch in its place. "What's up?"

"*Nothing?*" I said, my voice rising like an adolescent boy going through puberty.

She held the spatula aloft and pointed it at me. "And I'm supposed to believe you? I know you better than that. What was Dan Jordan talking to you about?"

Good grief. Ruthie should rename herself Nancy Drew…or Snoopy. But then, since when did we have secrets from each other? After our parents died, Ruthie had moved home from college and become my best friend and confidant. Not to mention the mother I no longer had. I'd confided my dream of having a specialty café to her years ago…

"Someday I'm going to own my own café," I had said as we lay together in our parents' big bed, the television flickering some late-night movie. It was after midnight and one of those nights, not too long after the funeral, when neither of us could sleep. We often found ourselves under those cozy covers as if somehow cotton sheets and a comforter could replace what we were missing.

"What kind of café?" Ruthie asked, turning down the sound, going along with my dream. That's about all the both of us had to live on back then…dreams.

"Oh," I said, turning to face her, propping my cheek on my hand. "It's going to be different. I'm going to decorate it so that it has *atmosphere,* and I'm going to serve something new almost every day. You know, try new recipes out of magazines."

Ruthie rolled her eyes and turned the sound on the TV back up. "Then you'd better plan on moving out of Brewster. These old German farmers won't eat that kind of stuff."

I remember turning onto my back, sorry I'd shared my fantasy with her. Just because Ruthie didn't like living in Brewster she thought I shouldn't either. But I loved this little town, the way the people here made me feel safe. Back then I didn't see why a café like the one I dreamed about wouldn't be possible right here.

What I hadn't known then was the reality of running a business. How hard it was to find reliable help. How many hours it would take to run a business…that is, the time in *addition* to the hours the front door was open. Ordering food. Preparing schedules. Keeping the books. Getting deposits ready for the bank. Making sure there was change in the till. Cleaning and more.

I learned in a hurry that owning a café was a *lot* different than simply working at one. It was baptism-by-experience, sink-or-swim, when I purchased the café from the couple I'd worked for all through high school. It was the money I inherited from my parents' life insurance that made my naïve dream possible, but it was pure grit and stubbornness that had let me make a *go* of Vicky's. That and the support of the people in Brewster. The people who kept coming back to the café even when my pie crust was as tough as a bad steak, and they'd probably eaten that before they ordered the pie.

Ida Bauer had volunteered to teach me how to make pies, and I was in no position to turn down her offer. And now here I was, standing in her small living room, seeing all over again just how impossible my original dream was.

I turned to Dan. "You're right, it is interesting." I didn't say, "*But…*" Not yet. I at least wanted to see the rest of the house first. Pretend for just a few more minutes that my dream wasn't dead.

Dan waved his arm around the quaint living room. "You'd want to replace the carpet. Or…" He walked to a corner of the room and tried to lift an edge of the carpet. "I wouldn't doubt there are hardwood floors under here. Pretty standard for the time this house was built."

As if this house were food, I could feel myself salivating. Hardwood floors. Those had been part of my dream.

"And just look at these walls. Can you believe someone hasn't painted over them in all these years?" Dan did a slow circle of the room, pointing out what I'd noticed on my first envious glance around the room.

The walls were an old-gold, textured in a way I'd only seen in design magazines I rarely had a chance to page through. They appeared mottled in a way only someone who knew what they were doing could make work. Along the edges, where the walls met the ceiling, there was a dusty-brown vine trailing along the ceiling line, cascading down the corners of the room, sprouting faded-green leaves that reminded me of somewhere exotic. Italy? France? Anywhere but Brewster, North Dakota. There were two bronze-like sconces on one wall, with candle-like bulbs in each socket. In the middle of the room hung a small crystal chandelier.

It was hard to imagine my plain-spoken friend Ida Bauer living in such elegant quarters.

"It's... It's..." I searched for the word.

"Something." Dan spoke for me.

"Yes." I realized I was holding my breath. This was the *atmosphere* I had dreamed about but hadn't known to imagine. It was perfect. That was the word. *Perfect.*

"Want to see the rest of the house?"

I didn't need to. This was more than enough. But why not see the rest of it? If I wasn't going to have any of it, I might as well see it all. Give me something to dream about when I went back to my same-old, same-old.

I followed Dan down the short hall. The floor plan was predictable, but what was inside the rooms wasn't. One small bedroom had the same sort of rag-painted look to the textured walls as the living room, only these walls were a cocoa-colored hue. Light enough to not be oppressive, dark enough to make me feel wrapped in marshmallow-topped hot chocolate. There was a small, nondescript bathroom that separated a second bedroom, the *master* bedroom, if rooms back then were called that. It was a nice-sized room where I could easily imagine three or four square tables filled with chattering women. Again the texture of the walls was what amazed me, as if an ancient architect had designed these surfaces to match my dream.

Who knows that I didn't?

Once again chills ran down my arms as I reached out and ran my hand over the uneven surface. "Harvest Moon" was the phrase I would use to describe the burnt orange shade of the room. A late October moon rising slowly above the North Dakota plain, even if it was late February. If a simple color could evoke such a feeling, what would this whole house do if I were to turn my dream into reality?

I was speechless, trying to hold back from blurting, "I'll take it." There were a million reasons why this house would never be mine, but right now I didn't want to say even one of them. However, I couldn't help but *think* them as I peered into the second bathroom that appeared to be added on to the bedroom as an after-thought. I followed Dan to the opposite end of the house, to the kitchen.

Time was only the first reason. How would I *ever* have time to do the planning and work it would take to turn this house into the specialty café I envisioned? The answer was clear. I wouldn't.

Then there was the issue of finding help. Ruthie being pregnant was one factor. Angie off to college was another. Those two had been my second and third set of hands the past several years, and most of the time three sets of hands weren't enough for *one* place.

Then there was money. The café had been profitable, mostly because I'd started out with no debt...thanks to my parents' life insurance...and because we'd worked hard. Dave and I at the beginning. The kids as they could help out according to their ages. In addition, Dave's insurance business had grown over the years and afforded us a nice life...when we weren't working, that is. But with college expenses coming up for Angie, and Sam soon to follow, plus the fact that Dave and I hoped to retire at some time while we were still young enough, and healthy enough, to enjoy those years, well...I wasn't so sure Dave would be nuts about spending our nest egg on my dream.

The problem was, I was going to have to find the letters that would form the word "No" when with all my heart I wanted to shout, "Yes!"

I almost collided with Dan's back as he stopped short in front of me at the entrance to the kitchen. He turned sideways, half-in, half-out of the doorway. "Okay, now," he warned, "I already told you, the kitchen needs work. Ida's nephew, Kenny, knows that and it's priced accordingly. So keep that in mind." He stepped back and let me go first.

I stood in the doorway and surveyed the room. Here was the first logical reason I'd found to walk away from this dream. The kitchen was painted stark white, almost as if they'd used up the prism of colors in the other rooms of the house. Old-fashioned metal cabinets hung on the walls above a gray-speckled linoleum-looking countertop trimmed with a brushed-metal edging. Whoever had designed the rest of the house must have used up all their ideas by the time it came to this sorry room. I stepped onto the well-used flooring, something beige that looked as if Ida had scrubbed the living daylights out of it. No doubt on her hands and knees.

There wasn't much to look at. The cupboards and countertops had been cleared. Any cheery knickknacks or even a bright cookie jar were long gone. There was a four-burner stove that could have qualified for museum status, an empty fridge, white of course, door propped open, with rounded-edges I hadn't seen since I was a kid, and yellowed-porcelain double sinks with a faint rust stain near the drain, where apparently water had dripped for much too long. A rectangular wooden table surrounded by four wooden chairs filled the rest of the space, the only warmth, if you could call it that, in the room. No wonder Ida had been so quick to offer her help at the café; this room seemed an awfully lonely place to spend much time.

"There's a basement," Dan was saying, an obvious attempt to divert my attention from this calamity. "And a single-car garage." He motioned me to the window. "If you can see past the snow, you can tell there is a great backyard back there. Lots of mature trees. Kenny tells me there's a garden in the far corner, and all kinds of perennials that will bloom through the summer." He kept up the real-estate patter as if his chattering might convince me to overlook the kitchen.

I took one more look around the barren kitchen. It would be easy to say no if the rest of the house matched this room. But all it took was a blink for me to recall the vision I had when I walked through the other rooms in the house. I wanted this house. Badly.

It might be old, but it's clean.

I forced myself to stare once more at the stove, the ancient fridge, and the time-worn sink.

Porcelain can be scrubbed. And if the stove and fridge work...

I felt as if I might cry. I opened my mouth to say "I can't," but no sound came out.

"Think about it," Dan said, leading the way to the front door where we'd come in. "You don't have to decide right away. I probably won't put the 'For Sale' sign in the yard for awhile. Ground's frozen, you know. It'll be listed in the paper next week."

I nodded, the lump in my throat making speech impossible as we stepped out into a knife-like February wind. Night came early this time of year; it was almost pitch-dark outside. Sort of like my heart was feeling right now. I pulled my fleece scarf tighter around my neck and hurried to my car. I needed to get back to the café. If luck was with me, Angie would already be at work and Ruthie would be on her way home for the evening. I wouldn't be forced to dash my dream out loud. At least not tonight. As usual, there were no secrets between Ruthie and me. She'd weaseled it out of me in no time that Dan wanted to show me Ida Bauer's house. Ruthie's only comment had been, "Go for it."

She'd always been there for me. She'd given up her dream of going to college to come back and stay with me after our parents died. After I graduated from high school she'd encouraged me to go to college. When I told her I wanted to stay in Brewster, marry Dave after he finished college, and buy the café, she stayed with me until it happened. Ruthie had given up her dream of leaving Brewster so I could follow my dream and stay here. It seemed selfish of me to even consider the idea of dragging Ruthie along with my hare-brained scheme. She spent enough time at the café the way it was. She had a growing family and possibly some dreams of her own.

And then there was Angie. I knew she didn't mind helping me at the café, and she was great with the customers and just as adept in the kitchen. I had no doubt she would end up doing something food and people related someday…just not in Brewster. She needed to go to college. She needed to explore the world and follow *her* dreams…not mine.

Even the recipe book project I'd pinned my hopes on a couple months ago seemed to have fizzled into nothing. I hadn't seen Olivia Marsden in the café since that gloomy day, and I was too embarrassed to call her about an idea she probably dismissed the minute she gave it some thought.

I pulled the car into the graveled alley behind the café. Just as I'd hoped, Ruthie's car was gone. Angie's was there. My precious daughter, holding down the fort while her mother was chasing an elusive rainbow.

A deep sigh escaped my lips. No more. No more daydreaming. This was my life. Being a wife to Dave. Raising our two kids as best I knew how. Running Brewster's only café. Some people would say all that was more than enough.

Not you?

I blinked against the stinging in my eyes. *Is it wrong to want something more?*

Before I shaped you in the womb, I knew all about you. Before you saw the light of day, I had holy plans for you.

Holy plans. *Ha!* The familiar Bible verse wasn't a comfort tonight. There had been a time when my work felt as if it was some sort of ministry. Feeding the folks of Brewster, listening to their joys and heartaches, even cleaning up after they left. There had been a time when I'd felt pleasure in all of it. Where had that feeling gone?

I stared out the windshield at the one small window lit up from the inside of the café kitchen. There was nothing but darkness surrounding it. A thumbnail of light, barely able to hold its own against the pressing winter night.

I put my hand on the car door latch, bracing myself for the blast of wind I could hear howling inches away. There didn't seem to be much I could do about the bleakness I was feeling but put one foot in front of the other and carry on. There was no law that said I couldn't keep *thinking* about that intimate restaurant of my dreams. But that's what it would have to stay…a dream.

What other choice did I have?

Libby

The first six weeks of the New Year had been a blur. There was no question, from now on I would be getting a flu shot every fall. It didn't take a detective to figure out I'd picked up my flu bug at the New Year's Eve party Jan Jordan had hosted. Who knew that virus would keep the party going in my body for almost a month?

I hadn't wanted to go in the first place. The forced-merriment of that particular holiday had never appealed to me. I'd rather stay home and *read-in* the New Year. But try telling that to Jan.

"Libby, you *have* to come!" She'd stopped over the day after Christmas to drop off a gift and stayed to have coffee and help make a dent in the dozens of cookies I had left. Usually when Jan and I got together, we both had all sorts of news to share, but that day I had too much inside of me bursting to get out. I was glad Jan was willing to let me climb on my soapbox and preach away.

I had just waved good-bye to Brian's girlfriend, Katie, hoping she wouldn't tip the tray of cookies I'd sent home for her folks as she and Brian walked to her car, arms entwined like Creeping Jenny. She said she needed to get back to Minnesota early to see some visiting relatives. I had a sneaking hunch she was as anxious to end this strained visit as I was. For Brian's sake, we had both done our best to keep our polite masks in place. It felt good to finally let my smile-muscles relax. Ho-ho-ho it wasn't.

I watched as Brian poked his head in through the open car door to give Kate's neck one last nuzzle. Had Bob and I *ever* been that affectionate? If we had been, I certainly couldn't remember. And I knew we would have *never* kissed in front of the Christmas tree with his parents sitting right there. I usually didn't feel as if I was nearing fifty, but this time when my kids were home it was clear a new generation was in the making.

Another reason, I guess, why I still didn't understand Emily's attitude toward Mike. In my day, if a young man was *that* nice and *that* attentive, I was sure I would have returned his interest. But then I hadn't grown up with near the confidence about making it through life without a man at my side as Emily and her friends had. She seemed to take independence for granted. I just hoped she wasn't over-confident. Sometimes having someone at your side was kind of nice.

Poor Mike. The guy couldn't make his intentions any more transparent, and yet Emily acted as if he was nothing but an after thought. My heart still did a slow clench when I remembered him standing on our doorstep Christmas afternoon, a red-wrapped package in his two gloved hands.

"Is Emily here?" he asked, his eyes darting over my shoulder, trying to spot the person he had really come to see.

"Come in," I said, stepping back so he could come inside where it was warm. "Merry Christmas."

"Oh, yeah, Merry Christmas!" He laughed. "Is Emily around?"

"Hey, Mike." Emily poked her head around the corner and lifted her hand in a casual wave. "What's up?"

He glanced at me and then at the gift in his hands.

I could take a hint. "Would you like some hot chocolate, Mike?" I didn't wait to hear his answer. As if I were reading from a script I added, "I'll go in the kitchen and make some for you." Exit, stage right.

I wished the next scene of this play would read: *Mother eaves-drops near door.* That part I could play without practice. I wanted nothing more than to hang near the doorway, curious as to what Mike would say. And what Emily would say back. Young love was intoxicating to watch, and I liked it better from a front-row seat…not my cheap seat in the kitchen. Familiar Mike was a refreshing change from the strained conversation we'd struggled to make with Katie the past twenty-four hours. Emily had to be as glad to see Mike as I was.

I didn't even have time to wonder what was happening out in the entryway when Emily dashed into the kitchen, her voice low and filled with drama. "Mom! Mike's got a gift for me! What should I do? I didn't get him anything!"

Pure panic caused my mind to tumble through quick possibilities. Did Bob have an unopened bottle of cologne upstairs? Was there a CD we hadn't taken the shrink-wrap off of under the tree? How would I get it? How would I wrap it without Mike knowing about his makeshift gift?

As quickly as I discarded the possibilities, my panic was replaced with a stab of anger. "Emily, how could you *not* know Mike would give you a gift?"

"Mom!" I could hear the defensiveness in her tone. "We're just *friends*. When will you *get* that?"

"Well, even *just friends* exchange Christmas gifts." My heart suddenly ached for the eager young man who stood around the corner, just a few feet away, oblivious to my daughter's calloused heart. A heavy silence blanketed the space between Emily and me as we stared each other down.

Emily blinked first, rolling her eyes dramatically and sighing, "So what should I do?" She had her hands on her hips. As if this was my problem to solve.

I turned to the counter. "I suppose you'll have to tell him you didn't get him a gift." A heavy pillow of ache pressed against my chest.

"Mo-*om!*"

How could a college junior sound so much like a three year old? I couldn't give her a time-out, but I sure felt like it. I turned and held out my empty hands, trying to keep my irritation with her and my sorrow for Mike out of my voice. "Emily, I can't manufacture a gift out of thin air. If you didn't buy him anything, you can't give him anything. All you can do is go out there and accept his gift graciously. Say, 'Thank you,' nicely. Don't make excuses." Since when had I become Miss Manners?

She turned on one heel. "Fine."

Suddenly I was glad I didn't have a ticket of admission to the drama that was about to take place in my foyer. I didn't have to watch, only had to imagine Mike's eager expression as he handed Emily his carefully wrapped gift. Only had to imagine the way his heart would hurt when he realized Emily had nothing for him. Only had to imagine his brave, it-doesn't-matter smile. If Mike didn't cry over this, I might do it for him.

Suddenly I was disappointed in both my kids. Emily for treating Mike's emotions so indifferently. Brian for falling in love with Little Miss Priss, an uptight girl with a personality to match.

Olivia, stop it. You can't live your children's lives for them. They need to discover My plan for them all by themselves. Let them go.... Easier said than done. I swallowed the silent sob that worked its way into my throat. Why did parenting have to be so hard sometimes?

It wasn't too hard, after confessing all that had happened in our house over Christmas to Jan, to agree to attend her New Year's Eve party. A night out might be good for me. I could quit thinking about the people I *wished* my kids would be for at least a few hours.

"Happy New Year!" Gary, my friend Connie's flirtatious husband, grabbed me in a bear hug as I walked into Jan's living room. Before I could gather my senses he pulled back and smacked me on the lips, then turned away and coughed loudly into his hand. "I think I'm getting a cold," he muttered between hacks.

Oh great. It wasn't even close to midnight. The mystery novel I had left lying open on my bed called my name. Loudly. Jan owed me big time.

My eyes searched the room for Bob, spotting him already deep in conversation with Dan Jordan. Maybe if I stuck close to Bob I could avoid any more unwelcome New Year's kisses. I didn't miss the glare Connie shot my way as I started to cross the room. I wasn't sure if her glare was directed at me or at her boisterous husband. I wondered if she'd feel any better if I told her I was tempted to run into the bathroom and wash her spouse's germs off my lips. I pressed my lips together, determined *not* to lick them until I found a napkin and discreetly wiped them off.

I poured myself a glass of punch and then pretended to be interested in the stock market fluctuations Bob and Dan seemed fascinated by. It was easy to smile and nod, tilt my head one way, then another, as they threw the conversation back and forth. In the meantime I was free to let my mind wander.

Brian had left to head back to the twin cities—and his work on his thesis—two days ago. I'd managed to tango around his subtle inquiries about what I'd thought of Katie by saying, "She's certainly got a certain something about her." He smiled and left it at that. Thank goodness he wasn't as direct about these sorts of things as Emily. She would have cornered me naked in the shower and grilled me like a terrorist.

Emily, too, had gone back to Fargo to hang out with her

college friends for New Year's Eve. I'd harbored a certain hope that she and Mike would spend the evening together in Brewster but, as far as I could snoop, no such luck.

Maybe my New Year's resolution would have to be to let Emily decide who her boyfriend would be.

Or Me.

God knew. I'd been praying about Mike and Emily for ages. Maybe it was time to put Him in charge of this project instead of me. Look where my prayers for Brian had gotten me.

"Earth to Olivia." Jan was waving a manicured hand in front of my face. "Come on. The men are being boring tonight." She pulled me by one arm over to the sofa. "Some of us gals are going to play the Alphabet game."

Oh great. Games. My *favorite*. How much longer until I could go home and read? I snuck a glance at my watch.

Think of something worse...

Out of the blue, another old game Anne and I used to play popped into my mind. I couldn't help but smile, remembering. We'd used that silly, simple phrase to get us past whatever new obstacle a doctor had thrown in her path. No matter what her latest diagnoses had been, we'd always managed to come up with something worse. Good grief, there were all kinds of worse things than being with good friends on New Year's Eve and being forced to play the Alphabet game. I could almost hear Anne's clear laughter. Okay, I'd quit my bellyaching and have fun.

I looked around the room at the friends sitting near me. A couple of them I had known most of my life. I hadn't known Jan anywhere near that long, but she was my best friend here. I'd learned that Jan's fun-loving personality was a good balance for my introvert tendencies. I would have fun tonight for Jan's sake.

And Anne's.

I pressed my lips together, trying to hide the sudden trembling that threatened to turn into tears. Now *that* would put a damper on things. Sitting here, among these people, I couldn't help but remember that it was Anne who had opened me up to true friendship in the first place. If it hadn't been for her, I doubted I would have been invited to this party, and really, as much as I thought I wanted to be home reading...I could do that on any of the 364 nights that were ahead.

"Okay." Jan clapped her hands together once. "Let's start with something simple. Get our brains in gear."

Oh, Jan! I pressed my lips together to keep from laughing... or gagging. I constantly marveled at the way Jan could find fun in the most mundane things. She seemed to barrel through life, taking life one second at a time. Not thinking ahead. Not wishing she was somewhere else...*like in bed reading*. On the other hand, I spent most of my time, even at a New Year's party, trying to find a deeper meaning and purpose to everything.

So what gives yours meaning?

Oh goodness, couldn't I get away from those thoughts for just this one night? I crossed my legs, hoping the women around me would soon agree on a topic and get this game started.

Oh, so now you do want to play?

Anything to quit agonizing over what I was supposed to do with my life. I could hardly chide Emily about sticking to a college major, when here I was, nearing fifty and still wondering, "What will I be when I grow up?"

Deep in my heart the answer came easily. *A writer.* But I'd done my part. I'd written a book. I'd sent it off to a publishing house...hous*es*. If no one wanted it, I had no idea what God wanted me to do next.

"Are we ready?" Was that me, urging this group to get the show on the road? Maybe this year would be different after all.

"Libby's right," Jan said. "Let's go. At this rate it'll be midnight before we get started. Since it's my party, I'll pick the topic. Women's names. Libby, you go first. Say a name that starts with 'A.'"

A no-brainer. "Anne."

It always came back to Anne.

$$\sim$$

New Year's morning I woke up with a scratchy throat I immediately blamed on Gary's unwelcomed greeting. I gargled with warm salt water, popped a couple aspirin and a Vitamin C tablet, then curled up on the couch with the mystery novel I was hoping to finish over the course of the day. Bob hauled in some firewood from the backyard and built a roaring fire a Boy Scout would earn a badge for. He sat in his recliner staring at the flames for a bit, then walked into the kitchen. I could hear the fridge door open, then shut. Open. Shut. I knew what was coming next.

"Would you mind if I ran over to Carlton for a bit? I've got end-of-the-year stuff stacked on my desk. I can get a lot done when no one's at the bank interrupting me."

I opened my mouth to answer but was cut off by a deep cough. "No-o," I hacked. "Go ahead. I don't think—" I stopped to cough again. "I'm not going to be much company today."

"Thanks." He bent to kiss me, then thought better of it and squeezed my shoulder instead. "Maybe you should take something for that."

"Already di—" A spasm of air cut off my words. I waved Bob out the door. Then I proceeded to sniff, cough, and drag through the next six weeks.

$$\sim$$

I slipped my cotton-socked feet into my snow boots, pulled

on my below-the-knee, down-filled coat, tied a thick scarf around my neck and snuggled a fleece headband over my ears. I pulled the hood of my coat up over it all. Two below zero or not, I planned to get some fresh air.

I took one last breath of furnace-warmed air, and stepped outside into a crisp breeze. Ahhhh, did that feel good. It had been almost six weeks, two trips to see Dr. West, and three prescriptions ago since I'd left the house for anything but a doctor appointment or groceries. What had started out as a winter cold turned into bronchitis, then walking pneumonia. I'd never been so sick in my life. After my second round of antibiotics, Dr. West had given me a shot and some pills for my cough that made me understand why some people got hooked on drugs. When a person felt as lousy as I had, for as long as I had, I was willing to do anything to find some relief. I was also tempted to send my medical bills to Gary.

I started down the sidewalk, heading into the wind. I was glad the wind would be at my back on the trip home. I never had as much enthusiasm for cold weather at the end of a walk as I did at the beginning. This morning I planned to stop at Vicky's Café for coffee and, hopefully, a quick talk with her about the recipe book she'd mentioned ages ago. She must have thought I'd fallen off the face of the earth since I hadn't gotten back to her about it in all these weeks. I wasn't looking forward to confessing to her that I hadn't come up with a single good "hook" to make her idea more than just a plain-old recipe book. I didn't know if she'd buy my excuse, but I was convinced all that coughing had destroyed my brain cells.

I stopped at the end of the walk and stared across the street. Since when had Ida Bauer's house gone up for sale? Unless that sign had been stuck in the snow this morning, it was more evidence that my mind was deteriorating. Certainly I would have seen the sign on my many glances out my living room window each day. I wondered what my old neighbor thought of the idea of selling her house. She'd lived across the street from me for as many years as we'd lived in our house. I'd visited with her in her small room at the retirement home several times in the months since her fall. I hadn't been about to stop by and see her recently and risk passing on whatever it was I had. I'd felt as if I might die from my wracking cough. I was positive an older person would succumb for sure.

I promised myself I'd stop and see Ida very soon, but I had a feeling my trudge through the snow to Vicky's and then to get the mail would be all I could handle today. I was still feeling a little weak from all the lying around I'd done. And if I didn't need stamps to mail our monthly bills, I wouldn't even be stopping by the post office. My mind had been mush most of the first two months of the New Year. Still, somehow, I'd managed to write two columns for the *Banner*, but that was the extent of my productivity. The only good news was that I'd hardly had the gumption to think about my nonexistent writing career and what I would do with my life instead of writing.

Unfortunately, unless something brilliant popped into my head in the next couple of minutes, it looked as if this recipe-writing project would be as successful as my novel. My unpublished novel.

As I pulled open the door to the café, Vicky caught my eye and raised one of the coffeepots in her hand in greeting. It was impossible to miss the glimmer of anticipation I saw in the lift of her eyebrows when she spotted me. I lifted a gloved hand and looked away. As I stomped my boots on the entry mat I cringed inside, knowing I'd be sending that gleam down the drain in just minutes.

"Hey! Good to see you!" Vicky wasted no time in getting a

mug of piping hot coffee in front of me. "Happy belated New Year."

She stood there, coffeepots in hand, as if waiting for me to spill my good-idea beans onto the table, just like that. As if I *had* good-idea beans. I wrapped my hands around the warm mug and leaned over to breathe in the warm mist. "I've been *so* sick." I wanted to get that out of the way right away. "This is the first time I've been out of the house for anything other than necessity since January first."

The smile fell from Vicky's face. "Are you okay now?"

I tilted my head from side to side. "I think I'll live. Finally. There were a couple weeks when I wasn't so sure." I gave her a lopsided smile, letting her know it maybe wasn't quite as bad as I was making it sound. I turned my head and quickly scanned the almost-full café. "I was hoping to talk to you about that…that… *project* you mentioned. I didn't think the café would be this busy this late in the morning."

Vicky looked over her shoulder and then back at me. "Most of these guys will be out of here in ten minutes. Coffee break is going a little longer this morning. Some days are like that. Sometimes they get on a political topic and everyone has to throw in their opinion. Today they started trying to reconstruct Brewster. Trying to remember what buildings used to house what businesses. What used to be on the empty lots on Main Street. About the only thing I learned is that this building has always held a café of some sort." She shot me a grin. "Don't worry, they've just about talked themselves out."

The sound of chairs being pushed away from the tables underscored her prediction.

"You know these people pretty well." I took a sip of coffee, an idea beginning to brew in my mind.

Vicky rolled her eyes. "You wouldn't believe how well I know some of these people. Let me go ring them up, then I'll be back. Ruthie's in the kitchen. I'll have her keep an eye on things so you and I can talk."

I was grateful for the extra time to think. I knew I wouldn't have near the time I needed to flesh out my idea, but at least I'd have something to offer Vicky besides nada.

"It's not much," I started as Vicky slid into the booth across from me. She'd brought two warm cinnamon rolls with her and set one in front of me. After barely tasting food the past two months, the gooey fragrance of sugar, cinnamon, and warm yeast bread sent my appetite into overdrive. I picked up my fork and cut off a good-sized bite. It was surprising the way a simple idea could perk up my appetite. "Give me a minute," I said, motioning with my fork to my full mouth. I'd yell at my kids for being so impolite, but after so many weeks of not really eating, I was suddenly starving.

Vicky cut into her own roll, seeming to completely understand my need to scarf down this sweet treat. Not only did it taste heavenly, it also bought me a couple more minutes to think.

"Wow!" I pushed my empty plate to the edge of the table. "No wonder this place is always full in the morning. I'd like the recipe for those rolls."

Vicky burst out laughing and leaned toward me. "See? That's why I want to do a recipe book. People are always asking for my recipes."

"Need a refill?" Ruthie, Vicky's sister, had her timing as perfected as Vicky. I couldn't help but notice she was many months pregnant. I really had been out of the loop. But now didn't seem like the time to comment on it. She filled our cups, removed our plates, then left us alone.

"Here's what I'm thinking." I set my elbows on the table and leaned forward. First of all, I had to be honest with her. "When I came here this morning, I was going to tell you I simply couldn't think of a hook for this book you want to do. I've had several months to think about it, but there was absolutely nothing that grabbed me that would make this book different." I sat back and wrapped my hands around my coffee mug, watching as Vicky's slight smile faded. She took a slow swallow of coffee and waited for me to continue. "But then…" I held up one finger. "Just a few minutes ago, you talked about those coffee-men reminiscing about what Brewster *used* to be like." Once again I leaned forward. "Now keep in mind, I haven't had more than a few minutes to think about this. But…what if we somehow tied the history of Brewster into a recipe book?"

Vicky was quiet. I could almost see her mind at work, tumbling the idea around as quickly as I had. One side of her mouth turned up. "I think I like it."

My smile matched hers. "So do I."

She pushed her coffee cup across the table until it clinked against mine. "Here's to a recipe book."

I picked up my mug and lifted it toward Vicky. "I'll drink to that."

⌒

I hardly noticed the cold wind as I made my way from the café to the post office one block away. The warm blanket of a good idea kept my mind off the swirling snow at my feet.

I pulled a curl of mail from the postal box, quickly shuffling through the catalogs and junk mail to see if there was anything important. Ever since the advent of e-mail, much of the thrill of a trip to the post office had gone by the wayside. There had been a day when a personal card or hand-written letter would grace my mailbox…an unexpected surprise among mundane mail. Today, as usual, there was nothing exciting.

The *ding!* of the here's-a-customer bell sounded as I pushed open the door leading into the post office service area. The postmaster, Dale Herr, slowly pushed back his chair and got up to wait on me. If he had looked any more annoyed by my interruption I'd have warned him, as I used to do to my kids when they were having a crabby day, that if he wasn't careful his face might freeze like that. I highly doubted Dale would start laughing the way Brian and Emily used to.

"I need a roll of stamps." I would get this over as fast as possible and put him out of his misery. I placed my check on the counter. "Please."

He glanced at the amount on my check and then yanked open a drawer and pulled out a roll of flag-draped stamps, pushing them my way. He sure wouldn't win any Employee-of-the-Month awards. I pocketed the stamps, picked up my mail, and turned to go.

"Ever hear anything about your book?"

Now he wanted to chat? About my book? About my mail? There had to be a regulation about this sort of thing, but Dale probably followed that rule as rigidly as he did the one about cheerful customer service. Just when I was finally feeling good about the idea of the recipe book, he had to go and burst my writing bubble. That should teach me to get my hopes up about anything to do with writing.

Not that it was his business, but I wasn't about to be as rude to him as he'd been to me. I'd answer his question, but I couldn't bring myself to look his way. I glanced down at the stack of mail in my arms, knowing full well if I heard anything about my book it would be in the form of another rejection letter. Dale would probably know before I did. I shook my head, mumbled "no," then stepped out into the dismal, frigid day.

A cocoon of cold air seemed to hang around me after my trudge home from the post office. Or maybe it was my tainted mood that made me feel so chilly. I tossed the routine mail on the kitchen counter, slipped out of my snow boots and into my flats, hung up my coat, then went to check e-mail. If I was lucky, maybe Emily or Brian had a minute to spare out of their busy lives and sent me a note.

No luck. Not even a message from my friend Katie who lived in Carlton. I could usually count on at least one quick note a day from her. Oh well, the day wasn't over yet. She was probably substitute teaching today. I quickly jotted her a couple paragraphs and then deleted an automatic message from Amazon, letting me know a book similar to one I'd previously purchased was being released. The message only served as a reminder of just how *many* books were published each year...none of them mine.

As the Amazon reminder disappeared from my inbox a new message arrived, bearing a name I didn't recognize. I wasn't one to surf the web much. Other than Amazon, I hadn't given my e-mail address to many companies or even friends. When other people complained about all the spam they received, I thanked my lucky keyboard that almost all of the e-mails I received were from people I knew. I swiveled my mouse to move the cursor to the new message. I hesitated. Maybe I should simply delete it. I'd never yet had a computer virus, why start now?

The longer I stared at the name, J. Koller, the more it seemed somehow familiar. I took a chance and left-clicked, opening the message. At first glance I saw nothing more than the full name: Joan Koller. It was on my second glance, when I took in the heading under the e-mail address that my heart started pounding. Koller Literary Agency. The agent I'd sent my manuscript to so long ago I'd forgotten.

This couldn't be. I'd never had an e-mail response to anything I'd sent out. Only letters in the mail. Rejections letters. Impersonal rejection letters.

I saw my name. *Olivia.* Quickly I closed my eyes. I wanted to savor this moment. No matter what this message said, there was a person in-the-business just a mouse click away. I'd never been this close to an actual person who could offer a professional opinion on my writing. I tried to imagine what this Joan-person looked like. If she liked my writing, she'd have to be beautiful. If not, well... I could feel my hand growing damp as it rested on the curved plastic.

I'd have to open my eyes sometime. Have to scroll through the words no matter what they said. Maybe this was just a quicker way to reject manuscripts. It would certainly save time and postage.

An evil thought flicked through my brain. Dale Herr better watch it. If he wasn't careful, he might be out of a job as Head Postmaster and Snoop. With that small thought to bolster my confidence, I opened my eyes to take a peek at my computer screen. Through my eyelashes I read the first sentence.

> I was enthralled with the sample chapters of your novel *After Anne.*

Enthralled!

I opened my eyelids all the way, my grin as big as my eyes. I knew exactly where Joan Koller had come up with that particular word...from my manuscript. It was a word I had one of my characters use.

She'd read my manuscript! She'd actually read it and was *enthralled!*

A gaggle of geese ran down my arms and my spine. A cluster of butterflies took wing inside my stomach. *She'd read my words!*

I should probably read the rest of hers...

Please send the full manuscript as soon as possible. I greatly anticipate reading the rest of this intriguing story.

Warmest regards,
Joan Koller
Literary Agent

I wasn't the kind of person who talked to herself out loud, but this deserved something. *"Hoo-hoo!"* I shouted to no one but myself.

I read the e-mail again. Then one more time. I went into the kitchen, started a pot of coffee, and read the e-mail four more times while it brewed. I poured myself a cup, then went back to check. The words were still there.

I grinned at the computer screen as if it were Joan herself. "Thank you, Ms. Koller," I said, lifting my cup and taking a sip. It was hard to swallow with such a big smile on my face, but somehow I managed. I walked through my house, repeating the memorized e-mail to myself. *Please send the full manuscript. Please send the full manuscript. As soon as possible.* The winter sun glanced off the snowbanks outside in a way that made them glitter as if they'd been sprinkled with fairy dust. Even my old knickknacks looked new. Life was very good. Very good indeed.

I set my half-full cup next to my computer and walked to my favorite chair in the living room. I didn't sit down. Instead I got on my knees. I had a few more "thank Yous" to say to someone else.

Libby's letter

Oh, Anne. I could hardly believe it. If you would have been here I would have called you in an instant.

Once again, I rested the silver pen she'd given me against my chin. I couldn't help but smile as I imagined what Anne would say to my news.

I could almost hear her voice over the phone, "*I knew it! I knew it!*" Then she'd shriek and I'd scream along with her.

Better yet, I would have printed out the e-mail and raced to your house. That way I would have been able to see your face as you read the magic words: Enthralled. Send it as soon as possible.

She would have stared at the words and then at me. Her eyes wide. Her mouth open. My jaw would have been open, too. Wide and beaming. I would have slowly nodded along as she grasped the meaning of the letter.

You would have known how long I waited for those words. For that bit of confirmation.

She would have held that precious piece of paper in both hands for a moment. Then she would have let go of one side and thrown her arms around me in a joyous bear hug, crumpling the paper against my back in a way that would only serve to remind me later of how we'd celebrated. She'd squeal into my ear the same way I would shout into hers. She would start bouncing, jostling in counterpoint to my leaden-with-shock feet.

I want to jump with you, Anne. Scream with you. You gave me this story. You told me to write it. You knew. You knew all along the power friendship had to change my life.

You should've been here to share this with me.

A familiar thickening filled my throat as I set the pen aside. This was enough for now. I wanted to remember this part a little while longer. This good part.

Little did I know just how much I would need the confidence Anne had in me. How much I'd need God. There was more. So much more.

I'd thought this was it. My ticket.

Finally.

But my story, *our* story, wasn't anywhere near over...

Angie

"So what color bedspreads should we get?" Julie rested her hand on a lavender chenille spread in Target, making her choice clear.

I closed my eyes instead of rolling them. Julie knew I didn't like anything even close to the color purple. Or pink, for that matter, her second favorite color. As it was I was feeling ambushed. We'd driven to Carlton to look for Valentine presents. Well, at least I was looking for a gift for Mark. Julie was trying to decide if she should get something for Eric, a senior from Flanders she'd gone out with three times. I felt sorry for her that she didn't have a boyfriend like I did. At least I knew what I'd be doing for Valentine's Day. Well, Valentine's night, anyway. First of all I'd be helping my mom at the café. She always had a special dinner that night, with carnations and candles on the tables. The lights of the café would be turned down low and people would talk in sort of quiet voices. Not like they did on normal nights in the café. It would be kind of romantic. As dreamy as any place in Brewster on Valentine's night.

My mom let me skip work at the café after school today so Julie and I could make this quick trip. As much as I loved living in Brewster, even I had to admit that sometimes in the winter it could feel a little claustrophobic. If the wind was blowing, the snow could stick to the highway in a way that made driving scary. Today the roads were clear and dry.

I wished Julie would get off this college-on-the-brain thing she'd had all year, so far. I'd been tempted more than once to yell at her, "Shut up! I'm not going!" But I knew there would be too many questions to answer and when she finally believed me that I really wasn't going to college with her, she might get mad and drop me all together. I didn't want to ruin both of our senior years with us not being friends.

Besides, so far the plan I had to get out of going to college hadn't worked. I was counting on Valentine's night to seal the deal. If only I could find the perfect gift for Mark. Plan the perfect night. I'd tried once already, on New Year's night, but the night didn't work out quite like I'd hoped...

"Happy New Year." I had put my arms around Mark and kissed him. This was Plan B. We were in his car, parked on the side of a gravel road outside of Brewster. We'd been at a party at Susie Welk's house, but it had been kind of boring, people trying to *act* like they were having fun instead of really having a good time. I'd been hoping this party would put Mark in a good mood. Let him see all the good friends we had here in Brewster. Remind him that his life at college wasn't everything, and that living in a small town was something special. Instead, even I was wishing we were somewhere else. My high school friends were acting...well, like high school kids. Juvenile. I had to show Mark that I was grown up. That we were both grown up enough to do what I was planning.

That's when I suggested we go someplace and have our own private New Year's party. I'd spent many nights in my bedroom dreaming of a marriage proposal. Somehow I always imagined us in a fancy café in Carlton. But when I was with Mark, anywhere could seem romantic. Even a cold winter night with the wind pushing snow across the windshield of the car. The heater was turned on high, but we still had to snuggle to stay totally warm. That was okay with me.

This wouldn't be the first time we'd talked about the idea of getting married. We'd joked around about it a lot. But this time I wouldn't be joking.

I leaned my head against Mark's chest and cuddled close. Maybe being in a cold car on the side of the road wasn't so bad. I lifted my head and looked up at him. The dim dashboard lights made him look extra cute. I hoped I looked the same to him. Especially tonight. I smiled, then unzipped his coat and tucked my head back against his warm shirt. I had something to say, but I didn't dare say it while I was looking at him.

"I'm cold." I rubbed my cheek into his shirt. I waited while he squeezed me close and laid his head against the top of mine. *Okay. Now.* "I wish we were…married." There, I'd said it. "Then we could be at home together not…here." I shivered again.

"I'll keep you warm." Mark rapidly rubbed his hand up and down my arm.

That wasn't what I had in mind. I was going to have to say it a different way. I gathered my courage. "Do you think we should get *married?*" I didn't like one bit the way my voice sounded as it rose at the end…like I was a kid.

You are.

I clamped my teeth together. Just because I was seventeen, eighteen in a couple months, didn't mean I wasn't old enough to think like an adult. I knew exactly what I wanted out of life. Love. A husband. Kids.

What about My plan for you?

This *is* God's plan for me. I took a deep breath and said it again. "Do you think we should get married?" There. That was more like it.

Mark's pause was two seconds too long. My heart pounded in my ears. What if he'd changed his mind? I'd feel *so*…incredibly stupid. Then what would I do? "I love—"

"Sure," Mark interrupted, shifting a little bit against the seat of the car. "After we finish college and I have a good job."

This wasn't going the way I'd planned. I lifted my head and looked into his eyes, pushing my lower lip out just a bit, blinking my eyes as if I might cry. It wasn't fake. If he didn't go along with my idea, I just might. "I don't want to wait that long. I love you too much."

With a warm hand, Mark pushed my head back against his chest. "I love you, too, Angie." He squeezed me again. "But I'm gonna need a job before we can get married. We'd never be able to afford health insurance or car insurance. And I like to eat."

"See?" I said, pulling away and sitting up. "That's why it'd be perfect for us to stay in Brewster. I'd work at the café, and we could eat there. And my dad sells insurance so I'm sure he'd give us a deal."

You don't know a thing about insurance. And...eating all your meals at the café? Oh sure, that sounds really mature. Your mom can cook for both of you.

I was suddenly glad it was dark so Mark couldn't see the way my cheeks were turning red. "We don't need to have college degrees to live in Brewster."

"My folks would kill me if I dropped out of college." He ran a hand through his hair.

"Well, lots of people are married and still go to college." I crossed my arms over my chest. "I could work in the café, and you could drive to Carlton for school. It's not *that* far. And you could—"

Mark pushed himself up straight against the car seat. "I already applied for a transfer to UND so I could be there with you this fall."

"You can transfer *back?*" I hated when I sounded as if I didn't know what I was talking about.

You don't.

I slumped down into the seat. "Mark," I said, real tears pushing into my throat, "I don't want to go to college." There. I'd finally said it. "I'm tired of school. There's nothing I really want to be, anyway, except a wife and a mom." I looked at him as two fat tears crawled down either side of my face. Perfect. He hated it when I cried.

He reached out and pulled me into his arms. "Don't cry, Ang. We're going to be together at college next fall."

"But I don't want to go to college." I was crying for real now. "I want to be married."

"Ang." Mark rubbed my back through my coat. "It'll be okay. You'll like college. I'll be there." He pulled back and held my face between his hands. "I love you. We're going to be together always." He tipped his head and touched my forehead with his. He pulled back to look into my eyes. "Okay?"

It wasn't okay. It wasn't one bit okay. I didn't want to be with him at college. I wanted to be with him in Brewster. In a house of our own. Getting on with *life*. College would be nothing but a waste of time. I just wanted to start my life with Mark. Didn't he want the same thing?

"Angie...hello-*oh*." Julie was standing next to a purple plastic wastepaper can in Target, waving her hand in front of my face.

I had no idea how we'd gotten from bedspreads to trash cans, but I did know how New Year's night had ended. For a second I was tempted to tell Julie. Maybe then, for five minutes, she'd be speechless and I wouldn't have to listen to her jabbering on and on about *college*.

But I couldn't tell. Mark and I promised we'd never tell a soul what happened that night.

But I knew something even Mark didn't...it had all been part of my back-up plan.

Vicky

"Okay, I think everything's ready." I nodded at Ruthie as she dimmed the café lights. I put my hands on my hips and gave the café a quick once-over with my eyes. The tables were covered with thick, white, cloth-like paper. Red paper napkins were folded at each place setting. Silverware arranged just so. Sparkling glassware. Red and white carnations stood at attention in the middle of each table. Small white votive candles would soon cast a golden glow over each table. "Oh! The music!"

Ruthie had read my mind. The loud trill of piano music blasted through the cafe. "Ooops!" She quickly cranked the volume knob to low. "That's better." She worked to stand up, her rounded stomach barely missing the basket of white silk peonies I had arranged near the CD player I'd brought to the café for Valentine's night. She rubbed her protruding stomach. "This little guy is busy tonight. Too bad he can't use all that energy to help us wait on tables."

"He?" I teased. Paul and Ruthie already had two little girls. It was no secret both of them were hoping for a boy this time around. Their *last* time around according to Ruthie. They had thought their family was complete with Naomi and Rebecca. Now they seemed to think the power of positive thinking would make this last child of theirs a son.

"Yes, a *he!*" Ruthie's eyes twinkled as she shared a smile with me. She pressed her hands against the small of her back and leaned into them. "Thanks for letting me man the kitchen tonight. My hips have been so stiff with this pregnancy. Must be my age. I don't think I'd have a prayer of keeping up with the rest of you tonight." She turned toward the kitchen. "Better get the water boiling for the linguine. What time is our first reservation?"

I looked at the clock on the wall. "Fifteen minutes." It would all start at five o'clock. The café doors had been locked at three while Ruthie and I got the tables ready for the night ahead. Dave, Angie, and Sam would be here any second. Angie had even recruited Mark to help out tonight. It would be a busy night, but fun. I only hoped the evening wouldn't be too much of a drain on Ruthie. This pregnancy had slowed her down a bit.

As I began lighting the candles on each table, I realized, not for the first time, how hard it was for me to think of Ruthie as being older than me, even though it was only by two years. I'd gotten married and had kids early in life. Ruthie had waited until just a few years ago to start her family. Here was my daughter, Angie, graduating from high school, and Ruthie was still adding to her family. I was happy for Ruthie, but I certainly didn't envy her. Having a newborn along with a four and three year old…well, I got tired just thinking about it. I knew Ruthie's time at the café would soon be at a premium.

I unlocked the front door and then straightened a fork. I moved a water glass an inch to the left…and moved it back. People better start coming soon or I'd go nuts. Waiting was not my strong point. I'd rather be busy.

I stood in the doorway and looked over the quiet café. It was nice. Cozy. Much different than the usual brown Formica tabletops with black napkin holders and salt and pepper shakers as centerpieces. In my mind I couldn't help but imagine what this night might look like if I had Ida Bauer's house as my backdrop. The folks in Brewster would drop their jaws if they could see what I was visualizing. Crisp white cloth tablecloths and napkins.

Heavy, old silverware I'd collected from garage sales. Each place set with a different pattern of antique china. Tall, stemmed wine glasses and water goblets. A place card with fancy writing marking each diner's special seat. If only—

"We're here!" I could hear Dave and Sam, Angie and Mark stomping their way into the kitchen through the rear entrance of the café, chasing away my fanciful dreams. Tonight would hold no surprises for the folks of Brewster. Vicky's Café was as special as it was going to get.

The front door of the café opened and a cold gust of wind pushed three widowed ladies from Brewster inside for their Valentine's dinner together.

Let the night begin...

"You holding up?" I grabbed two filled plates off the counter and paused for just a second to hear Ruthie's reply.

"Hangin' in there." She brushed at the side of her kitchen-warmed cheek with the back of her hand. "How's it going out there?"

"Full house," I said. "If everyone would make reservations it would be easier to plan. We've got Emil Wahl and his wife staring down the Hadley's for the next table." I lifted the plates. "Better get these out there."

With my shoulder I pushed through the swinging door leading into the café, side-stepping Angie as she pushed through the other door on her way to get her order. We didn't need to say anything, we'd been working in tandem all night. We'd done this dance together many a time.

Mark, on the other hand, had a few steps to learn. After he bumped into me and almost spilled a plate of deep fried shrimp and mashed potatoes and gravy on Hertha Krein, I watched as he stuck his thumb into the potatoes as he set the plate on the table. I silently prayed he wouldn't stick the thumb in his mouth and lick it off. Give him one point for grabbing a napkin and wiping it off.

Mark reminded me a lot of Dave back in our younger years. He wasn't naturally built for the finesse of twisting his way around café tables filled with people. It took some practice to maneuver around chairs that might suddenly be tilted back just as you were walking by with plates full of food. It hadn't taken Dave long to realize he was a better insurance agent than table waiter. But like Dave, I had to give Mark credit for pitching in to help.

Whoa! I found myself reaching into the air as if to catch Mark as he stumbled over Ella Just's purse lying on the floor. Sam saw it, too, and got the giggles, laughing over his shoulder long enough to miss the movement as Marv Bender stuck his foot out of the booth, ready to pay for his meal. Sam did a fine job of tripping himself, spilling water all over Marv's red-plaid flannel shirt. It was Mark's turn to laugh.

I hurried over with a towel, dabbing at Marv, offering him a free caramel roll when he stopped in for coffee on Monday. Thank goodness it was just water...and that Marv had a sense of humor.

"Throw in a Long John, and I'll let Sam spill something else on me," Marv said as I followed him and his wife to the cash register.

I wasn't getting much done in-between quietly trying to run interference for Sam and Mark. I decided to put us all out of our misery. It was time for the captain of this team to do a little shuffling. It didn't take long to set up my defense. Dave was an old hand at waiting tables on Valentine's night. So was Angie. I didn't need to drill them on anything. Sam, on the other hand, was much quicker on a basketball court than he was on a café floor. I wasn't sure who would be our second casualty...Sam, Mark, or an unsuspecting customer.

"Sam," I pointed, "you fill water glasses. Keep the coffee brewing and man the cash register." I'd had him filling water glasses at the café since he was old enough to reach the spigot. And one of his favorite tasks as he'd been growing up was to measure coffee grounds into the filters, stacking them as if they were wooden blocks.

"Mark, you pour coffee. Keep the cups full. When a table opens, bus it and put a new tablecloth and napkins on. Silverware and water glasses." I darted my eyes between Sam and Mark. "And watch your feet."

Sam smirked. Mark nodded sharply, as if he'd enlisted in the army. He took orders well, turning almost immediately to clear off a table. I hoped he didn't regret Angie's offer to have him help out tonight. We'd done this as a family more times than I could count. I knew from experience the night would fly by, and soon we'd be gathered in the empty café—empty except for us—tired, hungry, and ready to compare notes about the quirky customers we'd waited on.

Out of the corner of my eye, I noticed Angie playfully bump her shoulder against Mark as she passed him with a full tray of water glasses on her way to a new table. *Be careful.* Mark had the presence of mind not to bump her back. He simply winked at her in a way that made my heart skip a beat. A look like *that* was what Valentine's Day was all about.

Be careful! I found myself thinking again. Only this time, in a whole different way. There was something about Angie and Mark's body language that made me take a second look. Now that I was watching, it was hard *not* to see the side-long glances they were exchanging. As if they shared a secret from everyone else in the crowded room.

I stopped by the various tables, asking how their meals were or if they needed anything else before I brought them their free dessert. Angel food cake topped with whipped cream and strawberries. My mind was on automatic when it came to running the restaurant. Good thing, because I was suddenly having a hard time thinking of anything else but the way Mark and Angie were gazing at each other.

As I headed to the side counter to top four slices of angel food cake with topping and fruit, I couldn't help but remember those heady days when Dave and I were falling in love. I had been in high school, just like Angie. Too young to know that young love could easily trap me into choices I was too naïve to care about.

Oh, I wouldn't change a minute of my marriage to Dave, except to have waited a few years longer to say our vows. Lately, I wondered, maybe if I'd waited, if I'd had a chance to go to college and see a bit of the world beyond the city limits of Brewster, maybe now I would be content simply running Vicky's Café. Maybe I wouldn't have this constant urge to do something more. I wouldn't have to spend so much time dreaming because I would have had an opportunity to *live* out my dreams.

That was one of the reasons I was so excited for Angie. The whole world was in front of her. Every dream was still a possibility. College. New friends. A career. Then marriage and a family. She had so many more options than what I'd limited myself to.

As I placed the colorful desserts in front of my customers, I realized I was going to have to make a point of talking to Angie about being careful where her relationship with Mark was heading. Mark was a great guy. He'd make someone a wonderful husband someday. Maybe even for Angie. But there was a universe out there she needed to explore first.

I never had the chance. I would make sure my daughter did.

Libby

"I'm going to miss having you live across the street." I leaned forward and rubbed my hand against Ida's papery arm.

"Acht." Ida waved one hand through the air, then let it come to rest on the back of my hand. She looked at the pink flower design on the lap of her dress for a bit, then shook her head. "It vass time."

I could hear a squeaky cart being rolled down the hall of the Brewster retirement home. I'd driven my friend Jan Jordan here for her therapy appointment and stopped in to see Ida while I waited. Jan wasn't one bit happy about the treatments she needed to take to regain muscle control in her face after her bout of Bell's palsy. In fact, she'd put up such a fuss her husband, Dan, had enlisted my help to get her to her first appointment...

"Olivia? This is Dan Jordan. I need to ask a big favor of you."

Well, he certainly wasn't using this phone call to beat around the bush. Other than the times we got together as couples, Jan hosting one of her many parties, I'd rarely talked one-on-one with Dan. "O-*kay?*"

He cleared his throat. "Jan got the card you sent. Thanks." He paused. I could almost see him shuffling his feet, deciding what to say next. "Um, when I told you about her...her..." He coughed. "Her Bell's palsy, I thought she would be getting better by now. But—I'm sorry she won't talk to you when you call. She's being so stubborn. It's almost as if she's given up hope."

Ah, I knew what that was like. My bout with depression had taken me through a valley so deep there was a time when there was no hope in my life either. My advantage was that I knew that was false thinking. "What can I do to help?"

A deep sigh came through the phone line. "I can't get her to go to the therapy appointments she's supposed to be taking to get better. I thought maybe if *you* would drop by the house and take her. I mean, with me she just keeps saying she won't go, but if you'd just show up and—well, maybe it would shock her into going...or something." His voice faded as if he'd lost hope, too.

Dan thought he might be imposing on me; little did he know how grateful I was for something to do. Something besides sitting around my house and not writing. "Tell me the day and time. I'll be there."

I felt a little bit like a traitor, showing up on her doorstep that first morning. Dan had told me he would at least mention to Jan that I'd be coming. We were both hoping she'd at least be up and dressed. I'd half-expected a phone call from her telling me she wasn't feeling well...something. Either that or she simply wouldn't answer the doorbell.

To my surprise, she did, standing in the doorway with her head cocked at an odd angle, trying to hide the half of her face she thought I couldn't bear to glimpse. After having been through my own depression, I already knew the pain *inside* Jan was much worse than any wound she wore on the outside. I took her in my arms and wrapped her in a big hug. And that was that. She seemed to know I somehow understood what she was going through.

Since that day, I'd driven Jan to a couple more appointments, using my waiting time to visit some of the residents who lived in the home. People I knew from living in Brewster all my life. My old neighbor, Ida, was my favorite stop. I could tell by Ida's tone today that she might be fighting this change in her life as much as Jan.

I squeezed her hand. "Change is never easy, is it?"

Ida's eyes grew watery. "The Biple says der iss a time for efferyting. But I don't remepber Gott saying anyting about haffing to moff out uff my house."

I could see the twinkle behind her tears and felt a tightening in my own throat. I hoped I'd have half the gumption Ida did when I'm her age. "Well, it sure seems strange not to see your kitchen light on in the morning when I look across the street."

She waved her hand in reply. "How iss the kidts? I vasn't home at Christmastime to see them vhen they vere home. I missed dat dish uff cookies they alvays dropped off at my house."

A quick stab of guilt dashed through me. Ever since the kids were small I'd had them deliver a Christmas plate of baked goods to Ida across the street. It had never occurred to me to have them stop by the retirement home during their few days at home.

You are so forgetful. How could you let an old woman—
STOP!

I wasn't going to let my mind go there. My battle with negative thoughts and depression was one I wasn't going to lose. I quickly countered. "I'm sorry, Ida. The kids were home for such a short time and it was so quiet across the street, I guess I thought you might be visiting relatives. I didn't know you were living here at Christmastime."

"Yah. Even I tought I vouldt be coming home shtill at Christmas. I vass so sickly I vass vishing Gott vouldt take me home. But I guess He's shtill got plans for me." She was quiet, then added, "I chust vish I knew vhat dey vere." Ida's gaze drifted toward the window of her small room. Her view of the outside world was limited to a leafless tree and the parking lot near the entrance of the building.

I was having a hard time thinking of something encouraging to say, especially since my thoughts lately were so similar to hers.

What kind of plans did God have for me? Was I going to grow old still wondering what my purpose on earth was?

A blanket of quiet thought covered our silence. I'd meant my visit to cheer her up, not suffocate both of us. I wallowed in these same thoughts enough during my long days at home. I wasn't going to let my despair cloud Ida's day. Pointedly I looked at my watch. "Jan should be done with her appointment any second. It'll be lunch time soon. How about if I wheel you to the dining room? You can watch the birds in the atrium until it's time to eat."

"Dat vouldt be nice."

As I pushed Ida down the long corridor, I couldn't help but think of Ida's question. What was the purpose of all these frail people? Some in wheelchairs like Ida. Some inching their way with walkers in the same direction we were going. Was this my fate? Would I simply live out my empty days in Brewster and someday end up here?

I gave my head a shake. *No! Quit it!* I wanted to do so much more with the years I had left, but it was hard to imagine what that might be when I lived in a little town in the middle of nowhere. My parenting days were done. I had the small hope of Joan Koller taking on my manuscript and turning it into a book. But if that didn't pan out...what was left?

"Shtop me ovffer der." Ida pointed to her right. "Put me by Vilma. At least she's not deaf so's ve can talk to each udder."

I parked Ida by her friend, gave her a quick hug, and then went into the lobby area of the home to wait for Jan. Settling myself in a chair, I pulled a small paperback book from my purse and opened it to the page I had marked. Try as I might, I couldn't get the light mystery to chase away my train of thought. I pretended to read as my mind chewed over the past few weeks.

After the e-mail from Joan Koller, the agent who was *enthralled* by the beginning of my novel, I'd floated on a cloud, a light and fluffy cloud, all the way to the post office. I'd printed my manuscript out that same afternoon. It didn't need even one comma changed before I sent my words off. I'd worked on editing my story since the day I'd finished writing it, well over a year ago. Even Dale Herr's nosy inquiry as he weighed the package, "So, giving it the full shot this time, huh?" couldn't dampen my spirits. Finally I was on my way to being a writer.

That had been weeks ago. Week one I sat down at my computer, determined to get started on a second book. Surely they'd want me to write more than *one* book. At night, while Bob slept in front of the History Channel, I planned what I'd wear on Oprah. During the second week of waiting, I made a trip to Carlton to have lunch with my friend Katie Jeffries. When we made our usual swing through Barnes and Noble, I didn't tell her the reason I lingered so long in front of the Women's Fiction section, the section where authors with a last name starting with "M" were shelved. I was scouting out the exact spot where my book would stand. When I hadn't heard anything by the end of that second week, doubts crept in. Joan Koller had loved the first 50 pages of my story, maybe she'd hated the other 320 and couldn't think of anything to say. The outfit I'd planned to wear on TV suddenly seemed too frumpy to wear out of my house, much less in Chicago. The words of my second book came slower and slower and finally dried up altogether.

It occurred to me late one night that really, I was no further along to getting my book published than I had been three weeks ago. I was still an unpublished writer.

What about your newspaper column?

That didn't count. I didn't want to write a newspaper column. I wanted to write a book.

You have written a book.

But it doesn't mean anything if it doesn't get published.

All that hard work and you're discounting it? You wrote a book. At least you can quit dreaming about doing that. You wrote it. It was your dream, and you did it.

True, but with that thought, another followed. *It isn't enough.* Sure, I'd dreamed of writing a novel, but now that I'd done it that long-held dream had suddenly changed. As if it were a carrot on a string, it had moved just beyond my reach. The brass ring on my carousel of dreams eluded my grasp. There was still something more out there that I hadn't known I wanted…*needed*…until now.

I needed this book to get *published*. To have the validation from someone that my writing was worth reading. That my story would have meaning to someone besides me.

Lord, please see to it that my book gets published.

It was a prayer I prayed again and again. It seemed selfish somehow, and yet the Bible said to *ask* for what we wanted. Well, this was what I wanted.

Did you hear that, Lord?

As usual, there was no answer.

⟡

"Hey, Mom." It was Brian on the other end of the line.

I checked my watch as I slipped out of my coat. It was odd for him to be calling in the middle of the day. Between his teaching assistantship in grad school and the time he spent in the library working on his thesis, his days were busy. Not to mention his part-time job and the time he spent with Katie.

Not anything like my drawn-out days at home. Even though I did volunteer work around town, Meals on Wheels only took an hour of my time, one week every few months. I helped out serving lunch at a funeral now and then at church, and served on the local library board, as well. But now that the kids were out of high school and I didn't have their activities to attend—or bake brownies for—there wasn't enough to keep me busy. I was thankful Brewster didn't have the social problems of the bigger cities, but I knew living in a larger town would give me many more volunteer options. As it was, even something as simple as an unexpected phone call was a highlight in my day.

Kind of pathetic when you think about it.

"Hi!" I said, pushing aside the negative thought. I was happy to talk to my kids anytime. "How's school?" I hadn't talked to Brian much since the Christmas break. His schedule was so packed I usually let him make phone calls home when he had time to talk. Tucking the phone under my chin, I hung my coat in the closet, pulled out a kitchen chair with my foot, and sat down, letting my gaze drift outside as I listened to Brian catch me up with his hectic life.

A bright, mid-March sun beat against the snow. I watched as small circles of glimmering water dripped from the eaves. After my gloomy line of thinking all morning, it was refreshing to watch Mother Nature at work, starting to melt away the ice of winter. Spring was on the way. Maybe there was hope for my dreams in the whole scheme of things.

"...and so I think I'll be spending Easter break with Kate and her family."

Hope? Uh, then again, maybe not.

I didn't like the feeling of my heart in my stomach, but I sat up straight and tried to sound like a supportive mother should. I knew the psychology...the harder a mother tried to discourage a relationship between her son and his girlfriend, the more she would be pushing her wonderful son and his aloof girlfriend to bond together. Well, if that was the case, I'd make sure and do the opposite.

"I'm sure Katie's parents will love having the two of you at their house for Easter." Why, I sounded just like June Cleaver. Ward would be so proud of me. Bob, too, for that matter. He didn't share my unfounded dislike of Katie, a dislike I still couldn't pin down.

If matchmaking were left up to Bob, the only qualification Katie would need would be a love of the Vikings and the Twins, Brian's favorite sports teams. I hoped for a bit more for my son. "We'll miss having you home," I added. I hoped he didn't hear the emphasis on the word "you." I'd miss Brian, but not Miss Priss.

"How is Katie?" I asked, trying to be polite, hoping to hear in Brian's voice that his infatuation with this girl had waned.

"Kate's great, Mom. Just great. She said to say hello, by the way."

I fake smiled into the phone, glad Brian couldn't see me. Glad no one could see me. I was acting no better than an infant. "Greet her from me, too." I sounded much nicer than I felt.

I hung up the phone, my mood no better than when I'd answered it. I wanted the best for Brian…and *Kate* wasn't it.

You need to pray.

I already knew that, but every time I tried, I found myself asking that Brian would find someone…well, *better.* I was ashamed to even think it. I'd taught my children to view everyone as being as good inside as they were. So why was I having so much trouble thinking of this Katie as "good enough" for Brian?

Okay, so that was it. I didn't want someone "good enough." Those words made the person sound as if she didn't quite measure up. I wanted someone *special.* Not someone I had to force myself to like. Not someone uptight like Katie. I wanted more for Brian.

And for you?

Hard as it was to admit, there was that, too. I wanted a

daughter-in-law I could love like my own kids. If only I could figure out what it was that made her seem so familiar, maybe I could get to work on changing my attitude.

I remembered a boy in my first-grade class named Percy. He was an obnoxious kid who pulled my ponytail and yanked my stocking cap off my head during recess any chance he got. He moved before the end of the year—a good thing or I might have strangled him with my winter scarf. I'd certainly thought about it enough as he continually kicked the back of my desk with his dirty tennis shoe. I'd almost forgotten about him until my freshman year at college, when I shared a biology lab with, guess who? Percy. My old resentment was right there, trying to convince myself he was the same annoying kid I remembered. It took half a semester for me to realize he'd morphed into a good-looking college freshman. Funny and much smarter than me when it came to Biology 101.

Unfortunately, I didn't think I was going to have twelve years to let my feelings for Katie mellow a bit.

Lord, change my heart toward her. Let me see her with Your eyes, not mine. There, that was good. But then I couldn't help but add, *Or else help Brian see her the way I do.*

Okay. I'd better just stop. I repeated the first part of the prayer as I walked to my computer. Maybe if I said it enough, I'd come to truly see Katie with different eyes. Goodness knew, mine weren't seeing much.

I sat down at my desk, pulling my chair in close, slamming my knee against the edge of the knee space. "Ouch!" Talk about not seeing much. I watched as two foot-high stacks of mail tumbled off the edge of my desk onto the floor, spreading across my carpet, looking like a very poorly organized coffee table…on the floor.

I heaved a sigh, then slid off the chair and sat crossed-legged on the floor. I'd been putting this off long enough. Guess what I'd be doing the rest of the day? Sorting through the mail that had accumulated over the weeks when I'd been ill.

Usually the mail at home was my job. Bob always complained he had his desk piled high at work, but during the time I'd been sick I simply couldn't drag myself out of the house every day to go to the post office to pick up the mail. Bob had to step in. His method was to stop by the post office every couple days, shuffle through the first-class mail on his way to the car, pull out any bills, then set the rest of it on the corner of my desk for me to deal with later.

Well, it was later.

I leaned forward and started sorting. Oh, my *More* magazine. That would have been good to page through when I was feeling so lousy. I set it behind me. The magazine and a cup of coffee would be my reward when I got through this jumbled pile.

It was easy to pull out the many catalogs and create a stack all their own. As I pulled and piled, I remembered a national banking convention Bob and I had attended in Denver. During the cocktail hour I'd struck up a conversation with a woman from Washington, D.C. She asked where I was from.

"North Dakota," I said, taking a small sip of my Chardonnay, waiting for what I was sure was coming next. She didn't disappoint.

"I've never met anyone from North Dakota," she replied, matching my sip.

"I guess you can't say that anymore." I smiled.

The remark took a few seconds to register. "I guess you're right. Cute jacket," she countered. "Where did you get it?"

Trying to remember, I looked at the gossamer sleeve, flecked with silver metallic thread, then at her. "This? I got it from a catalog."

Her eyebrows rose. Then she laughed in that big-city way some people have when they think they have one up on you. "I always wondered what sort of people shopped out of catalogs." She lifted her glass and gave me a once-over as she swallowed.

She might have meant it as a put-down, but it struck me as hilarious. I held out both arms so she could get a better look and then said, "That *sort of people* would be me."

Too funny. I put three more catalogs on my growing pile. That's what we get for living so far from an urban center…catalog shopping. I wasn't about to give mine up. Mrs. D.C. would have to wear out her Jimmy Choo's shopping for her clothes. I could buy mine from my living room couch.

Next I gathered the junk mail into my hands as if it were a deck of oversized playing cards. I tapped the edges against the floor, straightening the corners with my fingers so I could easily page through the many envelopes. My back was starting to feel the strain of sitting on the floor with no support to lean against, so I moved into the kitchen. Besides, mundane tasks always went better with coffee. I needed to brew a pot anyway. My mail pile was whittled down, and my *More* magazine was waiting.

As I waited for the water to turn into coffee, I stood at the counter and flipped through the many envelopes. Normally I gave the pleas for money at least a cursory glance. There was no way I could begin to help all the organizations who had my name on their list, but I somehow felt guilty if I didn't at least slit open the envelope and glimpse at the work they were trying to do. Maybe my *awareness* would be a compensation of some sort.

I thumbed through the thick wad of mail in my hand, suddenly feeling overwhelmed by the sheer volume of mail and need in this world. I'd written out several donation checks at Christmastime, not to mention our monthly giving to the church. This was one time all those organizations would have to do without my help. I moved to the garbage can and started flipping envelopes off the top of the stack into the trash, my feelings of guilt growing more calloused with each toss. At this rate I'd be sitting on the couch with my coffee and magazine within the minute.

Maybe ten more envelopes to go. I listened as the coffee maker gurgled through the last drops of water. I couldn't wait to hit the couch with my stack of catalogs and magazines. World Vision. Maybe next month. Red Cross. Toss. Writer's conference info. Trash.

Wait! I felt my heart somewhere in my throat as I quickly bent to retrieve the first-class letter from the garbage can. The writer's conference. How could I have forgotten? I set the remaining mail on the counter, grabbed a paring knife, and slit open the white envelope. I didn't want to open the trifolded letter. My fingers fumbled with the simple creases as a light film of sweat glazed my hands. I forced my eyelids to stay open, marched my eyes across the words:

> Dear Conference Attendee,
>
> We're pleased you will be joining us for the twenty-fourth annual Writer's Conference at our retreat site in California...

The only trouble was, I wouldn't be joining them. A glance at the calendar near the phone told me what I already knew.

The conference started today.

Without me.

Angie

As I shouldered my way into the café kitchen, my mom flipped two hamburgers, quickly buttered the buns and placed them cut-side-down on the edge of the grill, then lowered the french fry basket into the hot grease. "Angie, I asked you to take that apple pie out and put it in the display case. I don't want to ask again. If people don't see it, it won't sell and by tomorrow the crust will be soggy." She shook the fry basket with one hand and pressed on the hamburgers with the back of a spatula with another. Just because she never had anything on her mind besides the café didn't mean everyone else's life was as simple as hers.

Like mine, for instance. Making sure my back was to her I rolled my eyes as I picked up the pie. I'd come into the kitchen to grab three salads out of the fridge, but if Mom wanted the pie tended to before her customers, fine.

I marched back into the café, carrying the pie. Ruthie had left at five, leaving Mom and me to close up tonight. Usually Tuesday evenings were slow. Not tonight. I put the pie in the case. *Are you happy, now?*

"More coffee, Angie?" Jim Magner held up his empty cup.

As if he hadn't already had five cups. I grabbed the pot and filled his cup to the brim, secretly hoping he'd get a caffeine buzz and lay awake all night.

"Could we get some coffee, too?" It was the table of people who were still waiting for their salads.

Couldn't they see I only had two hands? And there were five

tables full of people? I felt like screaming, *"Get your own coffee!"* Instead I grabbed three mugs in one hand and the coffeepot in the other, stood by their table, and started pouring. As the third cup was nearly full, Mrs. Mindt piped up, "Oh, I'll need decaf. I can't drink regular coffee this time of night. The other night at bridge club I accidentally drank a cup of regular coffee and I didn't get to sleep until four in the morning."

As if I cared. Without saying a word I left the table and came back with a new mug and the decaf pot. "I'll get your salads." I forced the words from between my clenched teeth and headed for the kitchen. I could see the Magners slipping out of their booth and heading toward the cash register. I hadn't even given them their check, yet.

"More ketchup!" Jerrod Braun, an elementary kid, shouted at me with his mouth full of hamburger. Gross.

"Say please." His mom offered me a condescending smile, as if I should have known he'd use three-fourths of a bottle all by himself.

I pushed the swinging door leading into the kitchen too hard. It banged loudly against the wall and then bounced back, hitting me on my right arm. Even the door was having a bad day.

My mom's head shot up from the two orders of hamburgers and fries she was plating. "Be careful," she said, her voice sharp. "We've got customers out there."

"As if I don't know that?" I stood stock still in the middle of the kitchen, trying to remember what I'd come for. My head was spinning. Ketchup? Salads? More coffee? Someone needed to pay for their meal? What should I do first? Argh. I felt like tugging at my hair, instead I blurted, "Sometimes I hate this place."

"And sometimes I do, too." Unlike me, my mom's voice was soft. "But luckily the feeling usually passes quickly." She grabbed six slices of dill pickles and arranged three by each of the hamburgers. "Just remember to try and be content in all things." She lifted the plates. "I'll take these out for you. Which table?"

I looked at my shoes. "The Vetters."

"Just think," she said, pausing for a moment with her back against the swinging door, "in a few months you won't have to work here anymore." She pressed her lips together into a thin smile. "Vicky's Café will just be a line on your resume when you get to college. Someday you'll look back on these days and laugh."

She pushed her way into the main part of the café and left me standing alone in the hot, humid, and too-quiet kitchen. I could hear muted voices drift through the wooden swinging door. As usual, Mom was in her element, visiting with the customers, asking if their food was all right, if they needed more water or coffee. Most nights I could handle the supper crowds as effortlessly as she could. But it had been a bad day. Make that a bad two weeks. A muffled burst of laughter floated under the door into the kitchen. I certainly didn't feel like doing any laughing.

Try and be content in all things? I felt my eyeballs flutter back into my head. *Lame.* Let Mom try being content if her boyfriend hadn't called her in more than two weeks.

He's waiting for you to call him. To tell him that you—

No! I wasn't going to think about it. There was no way I could sit down and cry now. The café was full of people, and Mom would be calling me to help any second. I yanked open the fridge and pulled out the salads, sticking my head into the cold air. I took a deep breath. Then another. I had to calm down. Maybe he tried. Maybe Mark's cell phone had died. Maybe he'd gone over his minutes for this month.

He could have e-mailed.

Yeah. I know.

He said he didn't want to talk to you until—

I closed the fridge door and tried to breathe normal. It wasn't easy when I couldn't help but remember the sixteen long days since I'd last talked to him.

Prom was a week from now. I had no idea if I should be ironing my dress or checking what was on TV that night. I blew at a strand of hair that fell over my face. Who would think after being exclusive with Mark for two years, that now I didn't even know if I had a date for the prom?

Don't you think you have bigger worries than that?

Well, sure. What would Julie and all my other classmates say if I suddenly told them I wasn't going to our senior prom? Totally busted. They'd know Mark had—

No. I wasn't going to think about that. Mark hadn't broken up with me. Not even close. He'd just said he didn't want to talk about getting married anymore. Not right now. He needed time to think.

Think. That's all I'd been doing. I wasn't going to go to college and that was all there was to it. And now—

You have to talk to—

I know. But I couldn't. I just couldn't.

Mom poked her head into the kitchen. "Angie, could you bring out the salads for the Woehls?" Her voice held an edge.

Salads. If only all I had to worry about were salads. I balanced two salads along my arm and picked up the third one in my other hand. Maybe if I stayed busy I wouldn't have to think about—

You have to talk to Mark first. You could drive to Carlton. Show up at his apartment. He'd listen if you were standing right there.

I'd ask Mom if I could go to Carlton after school tomorrow to shop for a shawl to go with my prom dress. It was Ruthie's night to close the café, and I could bribe Sam into coming in after track practice to help out. Mom was looking forward to my last prom more than I was. She'd let me go. I only hoped she wouldn't invite herself along. That would ruin everything.

Everything might already be ruined.

Vicky

Remember, try and be content in all things. I wasn't sure if I was saying those words to remind Angie…or myself. I picked up the two plates of hamburgers and fries and carried them out of the kitchen and into the busy café. Angie could use a few seconds to herself, and I could do with getting out of the kitchen for a bit.

I delivered the meals, found the slip for the Magners' roast beef combos and rang them up. I grabbed the coffeepots and started making my rounds.

It was no secret Angie was having a bad day. She'd let me know first thing when she walked into work after school.

"Mrs. Koenig is so psycho." Angie dropped her backpack by the back door of the café and slipped out of her coat, hanging it on a peg by the door. "Now she tells us she expects a ten-page paper on our favorite English poet before prom." Angie walked to the fridge and snatched a Diet Coke. Before she opened it, she dramatically waved one hand through the air. "What if I don't *have* a favorite English poet? Ten pages. Sheesh. I can't wait to be done with school." She popped the top and took a long drink.

I worked at sucking in my smile. Senioritis. A classic case. She'd been acting like this off and on the whole month of April. In fact, I was surprised it hadn't shown up sooner. As Angie carried on, I busied myself measuring oil and vinegar and adding sugar and spices to the homemade salad dressing I was making. One of my signature recipes. I turned on the blender and watched as the jumble of ingredients twined into something I was known for.

Bavarian Dressing. *Yippee.* If I didn't break out of this rut soon, I was going to be as psycho as Angie said her teacher was.

I turned off the blender and started pouring the mixture into a glass quart jar. I had a case of senioritis myself. I was just as anxious to see Angie go off and follow her dreams as she was. The prom was next weekend; three weeks later, graduation. After the summer, college. I would have the vicarious pleasure of watching my daughter spread her wings.

Even though Olivia Marsden had stopped in the café a few times to discuss the recipe book we were trying to collaborate on, she hadn't come up with any more of a hook than tying it into the history of Brewster. Which, we both agreed, was sounding about as exciting as watching paint dry.

"We can't just list things that happened in certain years and then tack on a recipe." Olivia hooked her hair behind her right ear, stating out loud what I'd been thinking.

"So…" I said, taking a deep breath, "any ideas?"

Olivia ran her tongue over her lips as if trying to drum up something brilliant quick-like. She shook her head. "I went to the library and spent some time looking at the old issues of the *Brewster Banner,* trying to come up with something, you know…*different.*" She lifted her palm as if it weighed nothing. "I'll keep thinking," she said as she left the café that day, sounding as discouraged about this project as I was becoming.

Most every night I tossed in bed, trying to twist the images of Ida Bauer's house-transformed-into-dream-café out of my mind. Instead of planning the way I'd redesign the rooms as a restaurant, I forced myself to plan Angie's graduation reception.

There would be no standard cocktail wieners smothered in BBQ sauce at our party. I planned to make miniature meatballs slow-simmered in a Merlot sauce. Tiny finger sandwiches filled with a mixture of cream cheese and chopped olives. Maybe I'd add some walnuts, too. And for dessert we wouldn't be having a boring sheet cake decorated with "Happy Graduation" in blue frosting. I planned to make small cream puffs, fill them with homemade vanilla pudding, and stack them high. Then higher. As a finale I would drizzle homemade hot fudge sauce over it all.

I turned over in bed. Come to think of it, those same scrumptious tidbits would make great menu items in my new café. I punched at the pillow and turned over—again. It always came back to my dream. There were a million reasons why I should quit thinking about the idea; a million more why I couldn't.

I'd even dragged Dave into my angst in the middle of one sleepless night.

"Good grief, settle down," Dave said, turning on his side and pulling the covers back his way.

I glanced at the clock. 3:07. Four minutes had passed since I'd last looked. "I can't sleep." I flopped my arms out from under the covers and laid them across my chest. "Are you tired?" Dumb question at this time of night…er, morning.

"Um hmm." Dave was already halfway back to dreamland.

"Did I tell you about Ida Bauer's house?" I knew darn well I hadn't, but my ideas were thumping around inside my head in a way I knew would never allow me to get to sleep until I said something.

"No." His voice was sleepy as he turned onto his other side. At least now he was facing me. "What about it?"

"I looked at it."

"Is it nice?" He might as well have patted my hand and said, "Go to sleep."

He wasn't getting this at all. I could tell he was trying harder to not completely wake up than he was trying to carry on this conversation.

"Yes, it's nice. Dan Jordan took me through." I sighed loud

enough so Dave would know something was up. "A few months ago. He thought I might want to buy it."

Dave rearranged his pillows and turned onto his back, half sitting against the headboard. I had his attention now. "*Buy* it? Why would you want to buy Ida Bauer's house?"

How could Dan remember my dream and not Dave? It was late. I was already over tired. Now this. A clump of tears crowded my eyes. I pushed myself up against the headboard, too. I'd rather have tears run down my cheeks instead of falling into my ears. To answer his question I lifted my hands from my lap, then let them drop. How could I begin to tell him? It wasn't just the house. It was my life. I couldn't help it. I sniffed loudly.

Dan reached out an arm. "Come here." He pulled me to his chest, stroking my arm as I sobbed out my story. Making hamburgers and fries until my skin smelled like McDonald's. My longing to do something different. Try new recipes. Host fancy parties.

"Why can't you just change the menu at Vicky's? Or redecorate?"

I'd thought about all that. "But it wouldn't be the same. Vicky's has been a café in Brewster, not always by that name, for close to seventy years. There's a place for a hometown café on Main Street. A coffee spot and hamburger joint. A meeting place like *Cheers.* A place where everybody knows your name. I don't want to take that away from our town. I just want something...*more.*" I leaned over to the nightstand and grabbed two tissues, dabbing at my eyes, blowing my nose. "Is that so wrong?"

"No, it's not wrong..."

I could tell there was a "but" coming. I didn't want to hear it. I already knew all the arguments. The time it would take. How to find help. Not to mention the money. I knew it was an impossible dream. "It's late," I said, scooting over to my side of the bed. "Let's try and get some sleep." I slid deep into the covers, turning my back to Dave, pulling the blankets up near my ears.

I lay awake, watching as the moonlight and wind touched the trees outside and quick-stepped a shadow-dance against the curtains. Now that I'd said the words, said them out loud, I knew just how intangible my dream was. It would vanish in the light of day. I needed to put the filmy thoughts out of my mind and concentrate on what I *could* do. Run the café I had. But it was hard to quit dreaming when I'd been imagining it most of my life.

Please, Lord, You know this dream of mine. If there's any way...

Just as my eyes finally began to close, I felt Dave's palm touch my back. He let it rest there as we both fell asleep, silent support for a dying dream.

Back to reality. I turned the lid onto the quart jar and began measuring ingredients for my homemade Thousand Island dressing, shaking my head, clearing the cobwebs from my memory. At least one of my dreams would soon be coming true. Angie would get to explore the world beyond Brewster in a way I never did. *You go, girl!* I found myself silently cheering, using a phrase I'd only heard on TV. Folks in Brewster didn't talk like that. But I could think it.

I imagined Angie walking across the high school stage, taking her diploma in her hand, and then stepping off the stage as if it were a map, entering a whole new world. *You go, my girl!*

Out of the corner of my eye I watched as Angie stacked the clean dishes she pulled from the counter-level dishwasher, readying them for the dinner hour. She'd been doing the job since she'd been tall enough to reach the counter...longer actually. I had a vision of a tiny Angie dragging one of the chairs from the café tables, fumbling it through the kitchen door, and pushing it close enough to the counter so she could climb up and "help Mommy."

It was memories of little things like that, that started me blinking, setting me off on one of my rare moments. Times when I dreaded the fact she was leaving. Wondering how our house and how the café would ever be the same without her. I shed a few tears when no one was looking, marveling at how fast her school days had gone. Surprised that the nervous little girl I'd taken to kindergarten was now ready to go off on her own.

Angie had caught me crying once, a month ago. I'd been sprawled face-down on my bed, crying into a pillow to muffle my sobs, the thought of our house without Angie too empty to bear silently.

"Mom!" she'd called, barging into my bedroom without knocking. "I need some money for senior—" She stopped. Her voice changed instantly. "What's *wrong?*"

I could feel the bed sink as she sat down beside me. As I'd done hundreds of times over the years, she reached out and started rubbing her hand in small circles around my back. Comforting. Consoling. Her tender touch set off a new round of blubbering emotion.

"Are you sick?" She sounded worried.

I hiccupped. "No."

"Is Dad?"

This was silly. I shook my head and wiped my face against the pillowcase. I could be crying for a real reason, illness for instance, not about the fact that my daughter was doing exactly what I'd raised her to do…going out into the world, getting an education, preparing for a career. It was all part of God's plan.

But still, it hurt. "I'm just going to miss you." My voice sounded as if I'd been inhaling helium. I turned and propped myself on an elbow, laughing at how over-blown my emotions were.

Angie didn't crack a smile. She looked at Mark's high school class ring on her finger. She opened her mouth as if to say something. Then she closed it.

I understood. Our roles had been reversed. I was the one who had always consoled her. I squeezed her hand. She didn't need to say anything; caring was enough.

Oh my, where had my mind been? I looked around the café. No one was trying to catch my eye. Everyone seemed to be taken care of. There were soft murmurs combined with the sounds of silverware against plates. I took a quick look at the clock. It felt as if I'd been lost in thought for days. In reality, only minutes had passed. Angie was still in the kitchen. The Wetzels were sliding out of their booth, ready to pay for their meatloaf dinners. I headed to the cash register.

There were only three more tables of people left. By the time they were done eating it would almost be time to lock up for the night. I doubted anyone else would wander in for an early-evening cup of coffee on a rainy night like tonight. As it was, I was thankful for the rain. I'd seen May Firsts in North Dakota when it had snowed.

I rang up Frank Wetzel's order. "That'll be twelve forty-four." I waited while he pulled a wallet from his back pocket and fingered through the bills for a ten and two ones, then dug in his pocket for change. It looked like Angie wouldn't be getting a tip from this table. One more thing to add to her bad day list.

I could see the Brauns finishing up at their table. Only two tables left to clear. As soon as Peggy Braun paid, I would tell Angie she could head home. An early night to bed might do her some good. I waited at the cash register as Peggy and her son got ready to leave. On slow nights I often closed up the café by myself, letting Angie get an early start on whatever homework she might have. Tonight had started out busy, but it looked to settle down just as fast. I would get these dishes going through the dishwasher, then wipe down the tables and vacuum the floor. Ruthie could put the clean dishes away in the morning. It might take me another fifteen minutes to get the bank deposit ready, and then I'd be heading home for a good night's sleep, too.

I rang up Peggy's order and walked back and poked my head into the kitchen. Angie was leaning over the island, her head in her arms. She reminded me of an ostrich, as if burying her head would make this day go away. "Angie, go ahead and go home. I can finish up here."

She didn't stand. Instead she turned her head my way. "Are you sure?"

Had she been crying? Her day must have been *really* bad. This wasn't the time or place to get into it, I'd talk to her about whatever it was tomorrow. "I'm sure." I'd long ago learned there was nothing like a good night's sleep to cure whatever ailed you. Everything always looked better in the morning. I only hoped one night's sleep would do the trick.

∽

I counted out twenty-five ones and paper clipped them together. Then I sorted out one hundred in twenties. I would need quarters, dimes, nickels, and pennies from the bank tomorrow. I stacked the checks and started entering them in my deposit book. One of these days I was going to have to join the millennium and start accepting credit cards, but so far I'd rarely been stuck with a bad check. People were honest around here.

I put the readied deposit in the bank bag and tucked it under the M&M's in the glass case under the cash register. Okay, so it wasn't Fort Knox, but this was Brewster. I gave the café one last once-over. It was ready for business tomorrow. The only thing different about tomorrow would be the date on the calendar. I walked toward the swinging doors that led into the kitchen and turned off the lights in the main part of the café.

With my shoulder I pushed my way into the kitchen, then checked to make sure the grill was turned off. Oh, I needed to turn down the heat for the night, too. Just as I reached for the thermostat, the furnace kicked in, along with the large café fridge. The lights flickered and I flinched. There was a creak from the basement, a sound I'd heard hundreds of times as the furnace went to work, but tonight it creeped me out. My cozy little café suddenly seemed a little eerie. I needed that good night's sleep as much as Angie.

I slipped into my coat and was just reaching for the light switch when the phone rang. I jumped again. Good grief, this was ridiculous! I practically lived in this kitchen. There was nothing to be afraid of. The phone rang a second time. I was tempted to ignore it. After all, I was on my way home and this had to be Dave. Often when I was closing the café alone, he called to check to make sure everything was okay. Years ago he'd even insisted we think up a code word, just in case things weren't okay. I told him he watched way too many *Miami Vice* reruns. He insisted.

"It has to be something that sounds logical from your end of the phone, but that I'll know right away something's wrong."

I rolled my eyes.

"You'll thank me some day," he said. Then he scratched his head. "Well, let's hope you never have to. Chicken fried steak."

"What?"

"Chicken fried steak," he repeated. "See, here's what I'm thinking. If someone, say a burglar, snuck into the café and surprised you just as you were leaving, and then the phone rang and you said, 'That's my husband calling to check on me.' And then the guy got worried that I'd call the cops if you didn't answer, so he'd say, 'Answer it,' and then—"

"Dave," I was trying to be patient with his off-the-wall storytelling. "I don't even make chicken fried steak."

He grinned. "That's the beauty of my plan." He rubbed his hands together like a diabolical fiend. "So, you pick up the phone and you say to me, 'Chicken fried steak,' and then you hang up and tell the guy, "Someone wanted to know what the special was tomorrow. It's perfect."

"Fine," I said, unable to hide my cynical smile any longer. "Chicken fried steak."

That had been years ago. I doubted Dave even remembered the silly phrase, but just thinking about his worries was beginning to spook me more.

The phone rang a third time. I looked over my shoulder then reached for the receiver. "I'm on my way home," I said without waiting to hear Dave's hello.

"Mrs. Johnson?"

Oh, great. This wasn't Dave. Now I felt stupid. "Sorry," I mumbled, wondering why a telemarketer would be calling so late. I wondered if his call was even legal these days. "This is a business place," I said, wanting only to hang up and get home. "We're closed for the night."

"Uh, Mrs. Johnson? Vicky? This is Mark. Uh, is Angie there?"

Weird relief flooded through me. It wasn't a stranger. Only Angie's boyfriend. I laughed softly. "Oh, Mark," I said, scrunching the phone between my jaw and my shoulder while buttoning my coat. "You must have dialed the wrong number. This is the café. Angie went home over an hour ago. I'm heading out right now. Try her there."

He cleared his throat. "Uh, actually, I wanted to talk to you." I could hear him take a deep breath and blow it out. "Has Angie talked to you about..." He paused too long. "...anything?"

My fingers were clammy as I transferred the receiver into my hand. His obvious nervousness had transferred to me. I racked my brain. Other than the paper she needed to write for English Lit she hadn't said much tonight. And certainly Mark wouldn't be calling me about Angie's English paper.

I closed my eyes as a reason for his tenseness occurred to me. I hoped he didn't want to propose to Angie as a graduation gift and was seeking my permission. It didn't surprise me that Mark would call me before Dave. My husband could be intimidating when it came to his "little" girl. But even I wouldn't allow this.

I opened my eyes and stared into the darkened café. *Marriage.* Great idea...lousy timing. Maybe in four more years I'd consider it. But for now, Angie was going to college...without a wedding ring on her finger. She had a life to live before she'd be ready for marriage. I was going to have to gently put the kibosh on his grand plan.

"So, uh..." Again, he cleared his throat. "She didn't say anything to you?"

"No?" I'd let my questioning tone lead him on while I concocted an impromptu speech about young love and taking time to live a little and getting an education before taking that big step.

"So. Umm." Once again he blew into the receiver.

He should be nervous. He had to know Dave and I wouldn't be in favor of Angie getting married. She'd turn eighteen in two weeks. Much too young for what he had in mind. I'd set him straight as soon as he got up the courage to say the words.

"Um, I don't know quite how to say this. But... umm...Angie's scared to tell you, but I told her you have to know. She...um..." He coughed once, then blurted, "She thinks she's pregnant."

The kitchen spun around me as Mark's words took hold.

It couldn't be.

⤙

I didn't remember hanging up, sinking onto my butt on the floor, or curling my knees to my chest and rocking as if I were in shock. The next thing I remembered was the phone ringing again. And again. Slowly, as if I'd been wounded, I pushed myself to my knees and lifted the receiver off the wall. I didn't say anything. I wasn't sure I could. I simply held it to my ear.

"Vicky? It's late. Are you coming home?"

I somehow mustered the strength to say the only three words that mattered. "Chicken fried steak."

Libby

"Life is good. Life is goo-ood." I did a little shoulder shimmy in front of my computer screen. Never in my life had a rejection felt so good. I sat back in my chair and read the e-mail from the Joan Koller Literary Agency, again.

> Dear Olivia—Forgive my tardiness in replying to you. I have deliberated long and hard about my response and find I have good news and bad. First the bad.

It was almost as if I was reading the note for the first time. My heart started thumping and my hands grew sweaty, even though I knew every word that lay ahead. I gripped my coffee cup and read on...

> While I absolutely loved your manuscript, *After Anne,* unfortunately I find myself unable to take on any more clients due to previous commitments.

The first time I'd read that sentence my heart dropped as if it had suddenly been cast in concrete. This time I knew what lay ahead. I picked up my special silver pen and jiggled it between my fingers as if I were a majorette leading a celebration. Well, in a way I was. I grinned and read on...

> The good news is that I plan to send your manuscript on to an editor/friend of mine at Prism Publishing

Company. I strongly feel that your novel has great
potential, and I will send it along with my highest
recommendation.

Highest recommendation. Wow! I sat back in my chair and
beamed at the screen. I wouldn't even have to give an agent a per-
centage of my advance or royalties. Life was good!

I reached for the phone. I would call my friend, Jan, and
share this news. Maybe she could meet me for lunch at Vicky's
to celebrate. My treat. I dialed her number and waited while the
phone rang. Lately Jan had become my biggest cheerleader. There
weren't too many people who were interested in hearing about
my writing angst but, surprisingly, since her bout with Bell's
palsy, my chatter-box friend had turned into a wonderful listener.
I'd given her a copy of my manuscript to read, handing it over
as if it were a child…my first-born child. Those words were my
heart on a page. The story of my friendship with Anne and the
countless ways she'd changed my life. I had no idea if anyone else
would *feel* this story as deeply as I did. Jan had. Big time.

"You *have* to get this published," she said, putting the bulky
manuscript into my hands as gently as possible for a ream of
paper so thick. There were tears in the corners of her eyes.

Looking at Jan, remembering the story I'd written, I felt a
stinging in my eyes, too. She hugged me tight, pressing the pages
of my story of friendship tight between us. She released me,
moving her hands to my shoulders, stepping back and peering
into my eyes. "Thank you," she said, "for-r writing this."

Her words were a vote of confidence back when I was running
out of that very thing.

The answering machine picked up. Shoot. Oh well, it was still
early. "Jan, this is Libby. I've got some good news I want to share.
Can you do lunch? Call me."

My balloon of good news was bursting to be told. I shouldn't have left that message with Jan. I could've called Katie Jeffries in Carlton and driven there for lunch with her. With my luck, she'd be subbing today.

What about Bob?

Well, it would be nice to say "I told you so."

That's not nice.

No, but neither was the way he'd acted when I'd confessed I missed the writer's conference...

He'd taken off his reading glasses which didn't bode well. "You mean you sent in the *full* registration and then completely forgot about it?"

"Remember," I tried to explain, "I had bronchitis for so long after New Year's and then it turned into *pneumonia*." He couldn't very well argue with pneumonia, could he?

Oh yes he could. "Why didn't you just send in a down payment?" He was waving his right hand in the air, a gesture I knew meant he was getting worked up. "Who sends in a *full* registration months in advance? And then forgets about it?"

They say "confession is good for the soul," but Bob wasn't acting much like a benevolent listener. Time for some comic relief. I raised my palm like a shy first grader. "That would be me." I ducked my head, apologetically.

I could see the tug of a smile working at the corner of his mouth. He put his reading glasses back on and reached for the newspaper. "Well, you did call and ask for a refund, didn't you?"

Oh, boy. "I'm going to do that first thing in the morning." *If I can get up the nerve.* "Think about it, though..." There was another way around this and I hurried to point it out. "That agent has my manuscript now. Once she makes an offer to represent me, all the elbow rubbing I would have done at that conference would be worth diddly. It would have been money down the drain anyway."

He put the newspaper back in his lap. Why didn't I know by now I should just keep my mouth shut? He took off his glasses. "I don't want to be the bearer of bad news, but you haven't heard from that agent since…when was it you sent her your manuscript?"

I did the math. "Early February," I said into my lap.

"And it's the end of April now." He lifted the paper.

"It's not unusual to wait that long for a response." I didn't sound convincing even to myself, even though from all the reading I'd done about the publishing business, I knew what'd I'd said was true. But I had to admit, if this Joan Koller had been *that* enthralled with my writing, it seems I would have heard from her by now. "Sometimes it takes longer."

Bob dipped his chin and simply looked at me over the top of his glasses. Point made.

It had been a sleepless night as I tossed and turned, mentally preparing one speech, then another. I had a hard time returning a carton of spoiled milk to the grocery store. Asking for several hundred dollars back for my conference registration when it had been my stupidity that had lost it…well, give me spoiled milk any day.

Groveling didn't seem appropriate. I mean, even if I lost the registration money, Bob and I would still have food on the table. Our bills would all get paid. But I remembered the early days of our marriage, when several hundred dollars was a fortune we couldn't afford to lose. Then we would have gone hungry. I was just going to have to bite the bullet and make the phone call. I was a woman of words, hopefully I'd chose the right ones when I needed them.

"Hi-iiii! How are *you* today?" A cheerleader. I sounded like a ditzy cheerleader. Hyped up on sugar. I sucked in a calming breath and tried again. "My name is Libby… Olivia Marsden." I paused, waiting for the woman on the other end of the line to start laughing hysterically in recognition.

"Yes." She didn't laugh, but it didn't sound as if she was having a bad day.

I took it as a good sign. At least my name wasn't on the tip of her brain. "I'm calling about the…the writer's conference."

"I'm sorry," she said, her voice professionally cool. "It's already begun and registration was full weeks ago. I can put you on the list to receive next year's brochure." I could almost see her picking up a pen to write down my address. Ms. Efficient.

She couldn't be all that efficient. After all, it was *not* true the conference was full. I wasn't there.

She said registration was full. Quit trying to nit-pick your way out of this.

I took a fortifying breath and started my spiel. "I registered for the conference a long time ago and then I got sick right after the New Year and well, one thing led to another and I ended up with pneumonia." Suddenly I was wishing for my cough back. It would make this story a lot more effective. I cleared my throat as if I possibly had some lingering effects of my illness. It was met with silence. Okey dokey. "Anyway, as I said, one thing led to another and I…well…the mail piled up and…"

Through the phone line I could hear a pen methodically tapping against something. Or maybe it was her long, talon-like fingernails preparing to scratch my argument to pieces. Then again, maybe she was totally bored and was multitasking on her computer until I ran out of steam.

Heck with this. "Okay. Here's the deal. I forgot."

"You *forgot?*" She sounded genuinely surprised. "I don't think anyone has ever done that before."

Give me one point for honesty, another for originality. "So can I get my money back?"

There was a long pause. Her practiced tone was back in place. "Unfortunately, I am not authorized to give refunds once the conference has started."

"You can't give me *any* money back?" Bob was going to have a field day with me. Groveling might be an option in a minute. I opened my mouth to begin my verbal crawl—

"Let me check with my supervisor."

While I waited, I wondered if complimenting her on the hold music would endear her to my cause.

A new woman's voice came on the line. "Mrs. Marsden, I understand we have a bit of a dilemma."

We. I liked that. It wasn't *all* my fault. "Yes, we do."

"We've never quite had this situation before, but here's what I'm prepared to do. Our policy is not to issue full refunds less than one week before the conference begins. What I can do is refund half of your money or we can defer your full registration and you can attend next year's conference already paid up. You would be getting a savings as we anticipate the registration fee will go up next year. What do you think?"

What did I think? I think I wanted my money back. Not half of it. All of it. But there was something even more important to consider. What would Bob think? Knowing how his banker-mind worked I knew he'd vote for me to get my money's worth.

"I guess I'll sign up for next year's conference." I cleared my throat and picked up a pen. "Can you give me the dates?" I guess I knew what I'd be doing next year in April.

Oh, by then this convention will seem like small potatoes. After all, your book might be hitting the shelves about that time. You'll be busy with book signings. Maybe a book tour. If you have to cancel

*you can donate your registration to someone needing financial
assistance. Bob would agree to that.*

My calendar didn't extend to next year, so I wrote the dates on
a sticky note and stuck it on December. The hot pink note would
serve as an early-bird reminder when I transferred birthdays to
my new calendar.

Jan never did call back that morning. I ended up having a
rather pathetic little celebration all by myself. Somehow the
occasion seemed to call for chocolate. I did my best to savor the
lone survivor from a Christmas box of a Whitman's Sampler.
Then I sat back to wait for the phone call—at least I assumed
it would be a phone call—that would send me on my path to
publication.

It didn't come.

Life went on.

⌇

"Are you ready?" Bob was standing by the bathroom door,
jingling the change in his pocket. A habit he knew set my teeth
on edge.

He was lucky I was brushing mine and couldn't snap at him to
cease and desist. I spit into the sink. "As soon as I rinse."

He shot his arm out of his cuff and looked at his watch. "We're
going to have to sit in the bleachers."

"We always sit in the bleachers," I reminded him as I quickly
smoothed lipstick on my lips. "The only times we haven't were
when Brian and Emily were the graduates. You can see better
from there anyway."

⌇

"Not so fast." I followed Bob to the top row of the Brewster

High School bleachers. Not easy to do in two-inch heels. For not wanting to sit in the bleachers, he sure was going for the gusto. "High enough?" I asked as he settled himself against the concrete block wall of the gym.

"At least we have a backrest." He crossed his arms over his chest and surveyed the crowd. The gym was almost full, and it was still a good fifteen minutes before the high school graduation ceremony would begin.

Carefully, I balanced my purse on the metal footrest between the bleachers and the floor far below, then I, too, started looking for familiar faces. It seemed all of Brewster was here. Hardly a surprise considering half the people in town were related to each other and the rest of us, the ones without relatives here, had known most of the graduates since they were born.

Now that Brian and Emily were gone from home, Bob and I had been tempted to skip out on the graduation event from year-to-year. Between the nervous, air-filled voices of the high school choir, the long-winded speakers, and the lengthy video production that included photos of all the graduates from their baby photos to senior photos, the wooden bleachers could get awfully uncomfortable. But every year a few graduation announcements would trickle in, reminding us that just because our kids were past this milestone, many of our friends' children weren't.

This year it was the Brewster bank staff. At least two of Bob's employees at the Brewster location had graduates. Which meant we'd not only be sitting through the graduation ceremony, we'd also be dropping in at several open houses. Well, open garages, anyway. It never ceased to boggle my sensibilities that people thought it was appropriate to entertain in a garage when they had a perfectly good house just behind the garage door. I leaned over and looked in my purse. Good. I had remembered the cards with checks tucked inside.

There was a high-pitched squeal of a microphone being turned on. Then the high school band played a loud, off-key tuning note that gradually moved on-key. The music instructor raised his arms and another group of graduates were on their way to life beyond these walls.

I watched as the graduates slow-stepped their way through the gymnasium. It wasn't hard to remember Brian's and then, four years later, Emily's walk through this mass of people. They had both been so ready to graduate, chomping at the bit to see what life had in store for them. I was sure these graduates were feeling the same anticipation.

It was hard to believe Brian would soon be searching for a job as an elementary school principal. Brian. My little boy. Well, not so little anymore. He now topped Bob's six-foot-one height. I wouldn't admit it to anyone, but I had a secret hope that Brian would get offered a job far from Minneapolis, where he'd been attending graduate school.

Don't you mean far from Katie?

That was why I wouldn't admit it to anyone. I knew the cliché "absence makes the heart grow fonder," but in reality I knew it usually turned into "out of sight, out of mind."

Brian's conversations all spring had been sprinkled with her name. He'd called home on Easter Day, while visiting Katie's folks, to tell me her parents had lived in Brewster for a short time when they were first married. He was wondering if I remembered them?

No, thank goodness. That's all we'd need...a connection. Something else to draw Brian and Katie closer. *Kate.* Oooo, why couldn't I remember to call her that? I was sure she was a nice-enough young woman. For someone else's son. Even through the phone line and Brian's rose-colored filter, there was something about her I didn't like.

What? Name one thing.

I shifted in my bleacher seat. Okay. I didn't like the way she wore her hair. It was too long.

How petty can you get? Most of the college kids wear their hair long. Even Emily.

I squirmed again. Well then, I didn't like the way she talked. Or, rather, *didn't* talk. The way she'd answer a question and no more. Trying to carry on a conversation with her was like trying to pull words out of a Barbie doll. It wasn't natural.

She's young. Give her a break. She was nervous.

Another thing I didn't like was—

Aren't you avoiding the fact that no one is going to be good enough for your son?

I folded my hands and squeezed them together in my lap. I never thought I'd be the kind of mom who grew possessive of her grown son. I'd never been one to try to live my life through my kids. I was the first person to encourage them to do things on their own. The sooner they were self-sufficient, the more time I would have to concentrate on my writing. But here I was with all the time in the world to write, and I found myself searching for distraction. Trying to micromanage Brian's love life by wishing it away. Obsessing over a young woman I hardly knew. Instead I should be proud of the fine way he treated Katie. How warmly he spoke of her. I should trust his judgment—

And Mine?

I dipped my head and stared at my folded hands. As the kids would say…*busted*. I'd been praying for my future kids-in-law for years. Who was I to say this Katie wasn't exactly who God had in mind for Brian?

I sat up straight. I'd take a lesson from these graduates. I'd use tonight to make a brand-new start. No more meddling, even by osmosis, in my children's personal lives. I'd trust God to be in charge. I'd even do my best to listen to the speaker, although from the looks of him as he approached the podium, I might have better luck swearing off coffee for a day.

As the speaker lived up to his looks I reached over and slipped the graduation program from Bob's hand. After this presenter there would be talks from the salutatorian and valedictorian. The high school choir would sing another number. Then we'd be favored with the graduation baby-photo video. Finally the graduates would get their diplomas. I had no doubt they were as anxious to fast-forward through this night as I was.

There was nothing better to do than to read, one-by-one, the names of each of the graduates. Aaron Ammon. Our pastor's son. I'd have to try and remember to bring a card to church with me on Sunday. Julie Anderson. Candace Benson. Jon Bettenhausen.

Wait a minute. My eyes jumped back two names. Julie Anderson? Wasn't that Mike's sister? Mike Anderson. Emily's boyfr—*friend*. He had to be here. I craned my neck, methodically looking at the backs of heads in the section of the gym reserved for families of the graduates. Ah, there he was. Well, the back of his blond head, anyway. I felt a slow smile creep onto my face. Now there was a young man I could accept as a son-in-law. Why couldn't Emily see how perfect he was for her?

Stop it!

Hardly ten minutes had passed since I'd vowed to quit meddling in my kids' future. And here I was, at it already. But was it so wrong? All I wanted was for them to be happy. For them to find someone they loved and, hopefully, I would, too. To get married. Have a job they enjoyed. A family. To love life.

Isn't that what all mothers want for their children?

With misty eyes I watched the photo-video, marveling at

how so many toothless first-graders could so quickly grow into young adults old enough to vote. To move away from home and begin a new stage of their lives. It was exciting and scary all at the same time. I wondered if these young people were aware of the disappointments and heartaches that lay ahead…or if tonight they only felt the excitement of the unknown world that was just a piece of paper away.

As the superintendent asked the twenty-some graduates to rise, I felt a swell of longing for my children. Oh, to have them here. To hold them close for just a moment. But there was no turning back the clock. I was sure the moms and dads sitting in the folding chairs on the gym floor knew that fact all too well.

I watched as the graduates began a one-by-one parade across the stage. A handshake, a turn of a tassel and they were grinning. I doubted they noticed the tissues being pressed against tears in the parents' section.

It didn't surprise me when Julie Anderson's name was called and Mike gave her a one-person standing ovation. It was as if he knew we could all use a laugh. The crowd chuckled as he called out, "Way to go, baby sister." Who didn't love this kid?

Well, Emily, for one…

"Oh, Mom, I met the *cutest* guy in my sociology class." Her breathless phone call on Sunday was fresh in my mind. "I noticed him the first day of the semester, but Sara told me she thought he was exclusive with someone so I didn't try and find out who he was."

It didn't matter that I didn't know who Sara was or that I wasn't completely sure what "exclusive" meant these days. All I knew for sure was that his name wasn't Mike Anderson.

"And then after class on Friday he asked if I wanted to do something that night. Sara about died! *I* about died!"

I was going to have to quit watching *Oprah*. Just last week I'd seen a show about dating. About how to know when a guy was, or wasn't, "all that into you." From what I remembered, getting asked out an a Friday afternoon to do something Friday night, well…maybe things hadn't changed so much since my dating days. Half the fun of having a date Friday night was looking forward to it all week. Wasn't it?

"So," I said, trying to sound nonchalant, "did you have fun?"

There was the slightest of hesitations then, "Oh, yeah!"

Emily always had been my drama queen. It was hard to know if she really had a great time or if she was trying to convince herself she had.

"He's *so* cute. And funny."

So was Mike. "Have you bumped into Mike lately?"

"Mo-om, aren't you even going to ask his name?"

Had she purposely gone deaf? I didn't care about some stranger's name.

"It's Brad."

There wasn't much to tell about a guy she'd only gone out with once. The conversation soon turned to her plans for the summer. She'd stayed in Fargo last summer to work. She'd be doing the same this summer. Brad was going to be there, too. *Wasn't that cool?*

When had both of my children grown up enough to make their own decisions? When had they stopped asking me to help them decide things? Two more milestones that wouldn't make it into their baby books.

I followed along in the graduation program as each name was called. In turn, each graduate walked across the stage. Some scurried as if they wanted to move things along, get this over with, and get on with life. Others sauntered across the stage as if this was their final, crowning achievement, and they were going to milk it for all it was worth.

"Angela Johnson. Honor student." The principal was now to the middle of the list.

I'd forgotten Angie Johnson was graduating this year. No wonder Vicky had seemed distracted when I'd stopped in the café a few weeks ago to talk about the recipe project. I well remembered those last few months of having a senior in high school. It was a busy time. A time a mom wanted to savor. There was Snow Week and Awards Night. Graduation announcements to address and mail. Senior Skip Day and the prom. I should have known Vicky had more on her mind than our no-rush venture.

Angie Johnson walked across the stage toward the school-board president. Unlike a few minutes before when Julie Anderson crossed the stage, there was no sound other than the shuffle of programs and a couple people clapping halfheartedly from somewhere on the gym floor. Angie took her diploma in her hand, moved her tassel to the other side of her graduation cap and, without smiling, cast a nervous glance over the audience. She lowered her eyes and carefully made her way down the rickety temporary steps pushed to the front edge of the stage.

I scanned the few bystanders near the front of the stage holding cameras at the ready, trying to spot Vicky. There was no flash as Angie descended the stairs. But these days, that didn't mean much. With the right film a person could take a decent photo without a flash. Maybe she had a friend or relative in charge of taking photos. I was going to have to remember to congratulate Vicky on her graduate the next time I stopped in for coffee.

∿

Bob and I worked our way to the bottom of the bleachers, but the line to congratulate the graduates was already backed up from the school hallway into the gym. Even if we'd planned to bypass the line, we weren't going to be leaving anytime soon. Bob started talking to some men standing near us. I felt a tap on my shoulder.

"Hey, Mrs. Marsden!" Mike Anderson was pushing his hands into the pockets of his black dress slacks.

"Mike! Hi." It wasn't hard to match his grin. I would have liked to hug this lanky friend of Emily's, but I knew what Emily would think of that. I pulled my purse onto my shoulder. "It's good to see you. I saw your sister graduated. What are her plans for next year?"

"She's going over to the enemy," he said, the glint in his eye letting me know Julie wouldn't hear the end of this. "She's going to UND."

"Ahhh." The rivalry between Mike's school, North Dakota State University and the University of North Dakota was known across the region. "You couldn't convince her to follow in her big brother's footsteps?"

He grinned. "I think she was afraid I'd chase all the guys away from her if she was on the same campus as me. Upperclassmen can't wait for the new crop of freshman." He lifted his chin. "I tried to talk Emily into coming home with me this weekend, but she said she had a paper she needed to work on."

The good news was that Mike and Emily had talked. The bad news? I had a hunch her "paper" was a boy named Brad. Time to change the subject. "What are you going to be doing over the summer?" *Please say you're going to be in Fargo...near Emily.*

"I'm going to stay in Fargo. I'll be working and taking a summer class. Want me to say hi to Emily when I go back on Sunday?"

Mike didn't give up easily. Good for him. "Better yet," I said, "give her a hug from me."

Mike took his right hand out of his pocket and lifted it to his forehead, saluting me as if we were collaborating on an important mission. "You got it."

Suddenly I was very glad Bob and I had decided to sit through another long graduation ceremony. If my being here could somehow keep Mike and Emily in touch, I was very glad indeed. Bleacher-butt was a small price to pay for my daughter's happiness.

What about your vow not to interfere?

This wasn't interference. There wasn't a referee in the world who would pull a yellow flag on a mother's instinct about what was best for her daughter.

And what about your son?

Oh, that. There was a fine line between interference and playing fair. I'd play fair, but I never said it might not get rough.

Angie

Did she know?

I leaned forward to accept a hug of congratulations from our neighbor, Joyce Krein, making sure I kept my stomach far away from her too-tight hug. I didn't care how dumb it looked if my backside was sticking out, she wasn't going to satisfy her curiosity by trying to pretend she was happy I was graduating. "Congratulations," she said a bit too loudly in my ear.

That word could cover a lot of things. My graduation. My— No, I wasn't going to think about it tonight. "Thank you," I mumbled, trying hard to smile.

"I'm going to miss having you next door next year."

Maybe she didn't know. It seemed impossible that the Brewster grapevine hadn't reached everyone in town. Especially my nosy next door neighbor. Thank goodness for one small favor. I looked over Mrs. Krein's shoulder to the next person in line. Marv Bender, one of my favorite Saturday morning coffee guys. He winked at me as his eyes met mine. It was pretty cool of him to stand in this long line just to shake my hand.

Does he know?

Marv took my hand, then leaned in and gave me a light, awkward hug. "How's my favorite coffee pourer?" His eyes traveled from my goofy, royal-blue graduation cap all the way down to my shoes as he answered his own question. "All graduated, I see." Had his glance stopped just a little too long in the middle? On my stomach?

I could feel my cheeks burning. Vicky's coffee crowd had to have heard the news. But then again, they probably didn't dare breathe a word of it right in the café. Not when my mom was standing nearby. Or me.

I pressed my glossed lips into what I hoped looked like a smile. This was the graduation day I'd waited for, for over twelve years, and I'd never felt stupider in my life. I glanced to my right, past Marv, at the long line of people that snaked through the school hallway waiting to congratulate my classmates. How many of them knew? How many of them were standing in line just so they could get a close look at me? At my stomach?

As Marv shuffled past I pushed myself up straighter and made sure my graduation gown draped away from my stomach. Not that it was sticking out.

Not yet.

No, not yet. But from the dinking around I'd done on the Internet, I knew what I'd done would start showing all too soon. Then, even the people who were giving the rumor about me the benefit of the doubt would learn that some rumors weren't idle gossip. Some were true. All too true...

"Is it true?"

It had taken a split-second for my mom's words to register. I was lying on my bed, trying to work on the ten-page Lit essay Mrs. Koenig had assigned.

"I asked you if it's true?" Her voice was icy. As cold as the tingle in my arms and head as my blood retreated somewhere I wished I could go. Far away where no one could see me. Or talk to me.

I kept staring at my notebook, but even so I could see as my mom took two steps into my room, then stopped, inches from the side of my bed. My heart was trying to bang itself right out of my chest. I knew exactly what she was asking. Even so I looked up from my notebook and said, "Is what true?"

"Mark called me at the café." She sounded as if someone had wrapped their hands around her throat and was squeezing tight.

Mark had called my mom?

She knows.

The guilt I'd been feeling weighed heavy across the back of my shoulders. I fixed my gaze on the small dot of an "i" in my notebook. There was a small part of me that wanted to jump off my bed and run from the house.

As if you really could run away from what you've already done.

Another part of me felt a tiny lift of relief. My mom would help me through this.

Isn't it a bit late to be wanting your mom? You're going to be a mom. Remember?

All I'd been doing was remembering. Thinking about that first night in January when I'd convinced Mark I was ready to take our relationship further. When I'd accused him of not loving me enough to do what I was asking.

"I do love you," Mark had said, blowing a hard puff of air out of his mouth. "But we can't do this."

"We can," I said, putting my hand on that soft spot of skin below his ear. "We love each other."

I love you more. A voice from somewhere pricked my conscience.

I blinked the thought away. I wasn't going to let some old Sunday school lesson get between Mark and me. We'd been raised in the same Brewster church. Because we were only a year apart we were in the same Sunday school classes and the same youth group. We'd sat through the same discussions—make that *lectures*—about the dangers of teenage intimacy. All our leaders ever talked about was how we were too young to know what love really was.

I wasn't too young. I was going to be eighteen in a few months. Old enough to vote. Old enough to know what love felt like. Old enough to know not everyone had to go to college to have a good life. All I wanted was to get started with *my* life. I didn't want to be in some kind of holding zone. Four years of wasting time until *society* thought I was old enough to get married. Mark was the person I wanted to spend the rest of my life with. Now.

I put my hands on either side of Mark's face. Even in the cool night air of the car, his face felt hot. This wouldn't be so hard. I leaned in and kissed him. I could feel his lips grow soft under mine. I tilted my head, whispering into his ear. "You're the only person I've ever loved."

What about Me?

Well, sure I loved God. But this was different. This was love I could feel.

Don't do this.

But I wanted to. I wanted Mark. I wanted the life we could have if only we could be together always.

I have a plan for you.

I had a plan, too…and tonight was it. God had to know how this kind of love felt. Nothing that felt this good could be wrong.

Gently I pressed my lips against Mark's neck again and again. "I love you so much."

I knew it wasn't that he didn't want to do it. There had been other times when we'd come close to crossing that line, but he'd always been the one to pull away, take the deepest of breaths and say, "We can't do this. Not here. Not like this. I want it to be special. Not until you're ready."

I was ready that New Year's night. Just not in quite the same way Mark had been thinking. I was looking for a way out.

It had been easy after that first time to convince Mark it was okay to keep doing it. Each time it got easier to forget the things I'd learned in Sunday school and youth group about waiting for that one special person. For marriage. Mark was my special person. He was the person I wanted to marry. If everyone thought I was too young to know what I wanted, I'd prove to them I wasn't.

As best I could figure, I got pregnant on Valentine's Day night. Exactly three months before my eighteenth birthday. I missed one period. I didn't tell a soul. Not even Mark. I knew enough to know that girls missed periods all the time for all sorts of dumb reasons. Stress, for instance. And the way everyone was talking about graduation and summer jobs and college...well, it was causing me to stress out, big time.

When the second month passed I started to panic. As much as I'd been thinking a baby would be my way out, it wasn't until being pregnant seemed like an actual possibility that I realized how incredibly brainless I'd been.

And dumb. Stupid. Foolish. Dense. Idiotic. There were all sorts of words to describe how I felt now.

Trapped.

Scared.

Speechless.

Finally I found the words to tell Mark.

"I think I might be pregnant." The words were a whisper, not at all the brave way I'd practiced them in my bedroom mirror. I hung my head and looked at the chipped nail polish on my left thumb. Why wasn't he saying anything?

Out of the corner of my eye, I could see him sitting next to me on the couch in his scummy college apartment in Carlton. His two messy roommates were out, and I hoped they weren't coming back anytime soon. Mark was staring straight ahead at the movie we'd rented. Maybe he hadn't heard me. I took a deep breath. "I—"

"I heard." He ran a hand through his hair once. Then again. He put his arm around me, but before he could pull me close, he lifted his arm off my shoulder and scrubbed at his jaw with his fingers. "Have you told anyone?"

"Just you." This wasn't at all the way I'd imagined this moment. All the times I'd imagined it, we'd been married. Mark already had a good job. We had a beautiful house. We'd been waiting and waiting to have a baby. Our parents would be just as happy to be grandparents as Mark and I would be to have our first child. I would have made a special dinner. Would have had three white candles standing tall in the middle of our kitchen table. One for Mark. One for me. And one, I'd tell him over dessert, "for our baby."

He'd get a big grin on his face and ask, "What did you just say?"

I'd smile back at him just as big and repeat, "For our baby."

Then he'd get up from his chair, walk to my side of the table, pull me to my feet, and squeeze me oh-so-tight. Kiss me. Squeeze me again.

In my imagination there had been no cold pizza sitting in a greasy box. We hadn't been watching the DVD of *Dude, Where's My Car?* for the hundredth time. And there hadn't been any roommates to worry about interrupting what could be the most important conversation of my life. In my imagination, this announcement wouldn't be a conversation, it would simply be a dream come true. Not this nightmare.

Mark put both of his hands on his knees, pushing at them until his elbows looked as if they might pop out of joint. "Are you sure?"

I shrugged one shoulder. "I didn't do a test, but I missed…" I felt a wave of heat rush to my cheeks. How was I supposed to talk to him about my period? About the two months I'd missed? We'd never talked about that kind of stuff before.

If you're old enough to be in this situation, you should be mature enough to talk about it.

Again I looked at my hands. I should have waited to tell Mark. I should have practiced what I was going to say. All of it. I should have taken a test so I'd know for sure before I said anything. But then someone I knew might have seen me buying it. Or, even worse, what if my mom found it at home?

Isn't it a little late to be wondering what your mom will think?

It was a little late for a lot of things. Like wondering what everyone in Brewster would say if I was pregnant. Like going home and trying to find the words to tell my parents. Like what it would be like to work in the café with a stomach that stuck out as if it was a billboard advertising what I'd done. It was too late to think about changing any of those things now. Too late to turn the calendar back to New Year's Eve and stay out of this mess in the first place.

I wanted to throw myself into Mark's arms and have him tell me that everything would be okay. That he'd tell my folks. That we'd get married. That he really did love me. But one look at his ghost-white face told me those weren't the words on the tip of his tongue.

I tilted my chin up and blinked back tears. I was *not* going to cry. If Mark wanted to hug me it wasn't going to be because I forced him to. But if he didn't hug me soon, all on his own, I didn't know what I'd do.

A quick vision of a tired-looking me with stringy hair and dumpy clothes shuffled through my mind. I was holding a dirty rag, wiping off tables at the café, a runny-nosed kid tugging at my pant leg. It didn't take but a second for me to imagine the run-down trailer on the edge of Brewster where I lived alone with this child.

I remembered Rhonda Flynn, a junior this year, who'd gotten pregnant last year when she was a sophomore. I'd whispered along with my friends, wondering what she was going to do. Stay in school? Drop out? We'd guessed at who the father was.

It wasn't hard to picture Rhonda at the Brewster High basketball games. She'd sat through them this past winter, her little boy being passed from classmate to classmate as if he were an oversized toy. It had been fun to hold him, make him smile, and then pass him on. It never dawned on me that for Rhonda, those basketball games were the only break she got. For being an honor student I was sure clueless. Somehow I knew, without saying it out loud, that life as she knew it—as a carefree teenager—was over. Why hadn't I applied any of those same thoughts to me?

I stared down at my hands. At my fingertips that were turning red, then pale white from being clenched so tightly. As if I was trying to hold on to the only certain thing I had left...me.

And Me.

A wash of shame flooded over me. How could I have been so stupid to think that getting Mark to get me pregnant was a way out? Only now could I see what an elaborate game of *Mousetrap* my actions had been. The rush of excitement the first time Mark had noticed me, in a girlfriend kind of way, in the high school gym. The ride home in his fixed-up old car. The way I'd purposely tossed my hair over my shoulder with a flip of my head, copying the move from MTV rock stars. I wanted Mark to think I was sexy. I didn't know those heavy-lidded glances I'd practiced in the bathroom mirror would lead to this. A trap of my own making.

Mark picked up the remote from the arm of the couch and pushed the mute button. "Before we do anything, we're gonna have to find out for sure."

I had expected him to say, "We'll get married." His real words felt like a slap. I guessed this was what reality felt like. Nothing at all like my romantic fantasies. If only I had realized that two months ago.

It didn't take long to drive from Mark's apartment in Carlton to the K-Mart near the highway. What took longer was getting the nerve to go inside, into the bright lights that wouldn't hide what we were doing. We picked up a bag of M&M's. A pair of flannel gym trunks. A home pregnancy test. The candy and gym trunks were camouflage until we got to the checkout counter.

The clerk ran the M&M's over the scanner, picked up the gym trunks. "Did you find everything you were looking for—"

One glance was all it took to know she'd figured things out. I looked away, through the big, glass windows, to where I'd soon be. Out in the dark where this mess belonged.

⁓

Mark stood behind me in the bathroom, reading the directions over my shoulder. "At least it won't take long."

I wanted to say, *"Depending on the results it could take the rest of our lives,"* but all I could do was swallow hard and stare at the thick stick in my hand. How could something that looked not much different from a Popsicle stick predict my future? I looked at Mark in the mirror. *Our* future. At least I *hoped* it was still *"our."*

He stared back at me. In the harsh glare of the bathroom light, we both looked older. Seventeen and just-turned nineteen weren't supposed to look like this. "You need to leave." I wasn't about to go to the bathroom in front of him.

It's a little late for modesty now.

Even so, I needed to keep the little bit I had. I closed the bathroom door behind Mark and prayed. *Oh, Lord, please don't let this happen. Please.*

Again, it was too late. I knew what I'd done was much too late to undo. I should have been praying harder a long time ago. For something totally different. Even I wasn't too dumb to know this wasn't God's plan for me. But it was the plan I had now.

As I put the cap on the stick to wait for the results, I could hear loud voices coming into Mark's apartment. His roommates were home. I rolled my eyes in the privacy of the bathroom. What was I supposed to do with the empty home-test box? I couldn't simply toss it in the garbage can. What about the test itself? I wasn't about to walk out and twirl it around like a short baton. I could feel tears clogging my throat. This wasn't how any of this was supposed to go.

If we were married, in a home of our own, old enough to be ready for this, the night would be special. Instead it was humiliating. I flattened the cardboard box and tucked it in the folds of a dingy towel I grabbed off the shower rod. I'd hand it to Mark and let him figure out what to do with it. The test stick I tucked deep into the pocket of my jeans. Whatever the results were, they'd have to wait. I only wished I could do away with my regret as easily.

"It's true!" My best friend, Julie Anderson, spun me around from behind into a bear hug. Somehow she'd slipped from her place in the graduation congratulations line and snuck up behind me. "We're done. We're graduated!" She bounced on her toes as she did a quick happy-dance in her new graduation shoes.

The outside part of me, the part of me other people could see, laughed at her silly dance. Inside I felt like a total phony. For all the years I'd looked forward to this day, suddenly I didn't want to be graduating. I wanted everything to go back to the way it had been for the past twelve years. A routine I was familiar with.

Wake up, get ready for school, see my friends, go to work, do homework. At the time all those things had felt confining, as if they were holding me back from the life I was supposed to have. Well, if *this* was it, I wanted it all back. I hadn't known how reliable and comforting and worry-free that routine was until I was facing a life without it.

Julie didn't miss the high-falseness of my laugh. "Sorry," she said, scrunching her eyebrows and grimacing. "I forgot." She scooted back to her spot near the head of the alphabetical line. She knew exactly why I wasn't dancing along with her. I had no doubt she remembered the day I'd told her my news as clearly as I did...

"No!" Julie's eyes were wide. Her mouth hung open.

I bit at the inside of my cheek. Besides Mark, and my parents, Julie was the only person who knew. I nodded slowly at her. "It's true."

Why did those two dumb words keep coming up? What was happening to me sure didn't feel true. Instead it felt as if I was watching a cheesy movie about someone else's life. This was not a script I would have chosen for myself. And I certainly wasn't made to play this part...unwed mother. Two more words that sounded as if they belonged to anyone else but me.

"Did you tell your parents?"

Slowly I nodded.

"*What* did they say?"

Tears crowded my eyes as I looked down at Julie's pink-plaid bedspread. There was no way I would tell Julie what my parents had said.

I closed my eyes tightly, determined to keep my memories of that night hidden away. Forever.

Tonight, again, I tried to blink away the memory. I was determined to get through this graduation night without crying....at least not where anyone could see.

"Congratulations." A lady from my church tucked a graduation card into my hand.

Where had I been? As hard as I was trying to keep from remembering, my mind kept going back there. *You're here. Right here. It's your graduation night.*

I fake smiled at the next person in line. A cluster of strangers politely nodded their congratulations to me as they filed past. No doubt they were related to one of my classmates. My heart did a funny dip inside my chest. I'd forgotten all about my own group of relatives here tonight. My dad's two sisters and their families had planned to be here. Did they know? Had my mom or dad clued them in? They hadn't gone through the line yet. Or maybe they'd skipped it altogether, not knowing what to say to me. Embarrassed to be related to someone so stupid.

My Aunt Ruthie would have gone ahead to the café. It was closed tonight for a private party—mine. She would be there, starting the coffeepots. Heating the tiny hotdogs in BBQ sauce. Putting out the sheet cake Mom had ordered from Mrs. Wentz. Getting ready to pretend we were celebrating something.

I turned my eyes from the strangers in front of me and took a quick, brave glance down the line. There weren't many people left in line. My classmates near the head of the line were beginning to remove their goofy square hats. Where were my folks? They knew most of my classmates. Surely they'd want to go through the line and congratulate some of them.

But then they'd have to go past you.

Maybe Dad was talking with someone. Maybe my mom had gone to the bathroom and was standing in there visiting. It didn't surprise me that my brother didn't come through the line. Sam would give me his congratulations at the café, *after* he'd stuffed his mouth with miniature wieners and cake. I'd be lucky if he'd swallow before he said, "Way to go, Sis." If I knew my brother, he was already at the café telling Ruthie he was the "Official Graduation Food Taster." Of all the people in my family, Sam was the only person I knew who wouldn't judge me for what I'd done.

My forgiveness is waiting for you. Ask.

I gulped away the lump in my throat. I couldn't ask for forgiveness. In order to do that I'd have to admit what I'd done. Face the fact that I'd gone against everything I'd been raised to believe. That I'd let my parents down, big time.

Just then I caught a glimpse of the black pantsuit my mom was wearing. Maybe they'd simply waited until the line had gone down. I saw my dad put his hand on the small part of my mom's back, near her waist. She started toward the line, then paused. She turned to look up at my dad. I could see his mouth move. Mom shook her head. She pulled a tissue from her pocket and dabbed at one eye. She glanced through the crowd until her eyes stopped on me. It was as though everything else in the school hallway froze. Only my mom and I were real, standing eye-to-eye, heart-to-heart.

Hers was breaking.

So was mine.

I couldn't stand to see the hurt in her eyes. I looked away, and the next time I looked back they were gone.

I would not cry. Not here. Not now. Not ever if I could help it. If I started crying now I might not stop.

Suddenly I wished I could close my eyes and make myself disappear. Or at the very least make everything go back to the way it used to be. Back to a time when college was an option. Back to when my dad still thought of me as his little girl and my mom didn't get tears in her eyes most every time she looked at me. When she could stand to look at me, that is.

The congratulations line was fizzling out. The out-of-town strangers in front of me were visiting among themselves, leaving me with nothing to do but stare at the gold honor student tassel hanging from my graduation cap.

Stupid. Stupid. Stupid. How could I be so stupid?

I clenched my teeth together. Tight. I wouldn't cry. Not even if everyone would think I was crying because I was sad to leave my classmates, happy to be done with high school. All of that was true, and none of it was. I wasn't sure about anything anymore.

I lifted my chin, swallowing the lump that had clogged my throat. There was nothing to do but get through tonight. Shake hands. Hug. Fake smile. Go to my reception at the café and pretend I was happy. Tomorrow all the pretending would be over.

Tomorrow would be the first day of what was going to be the rest of my stupid life.

Vicky

"How does it feel to have your oldest daughter all graduated?" Holding her plastic punch cup off to the side, Brenda Erbele, my husband's secretary, gave me a quick hug.

I lifted my hands and passed her a lopsided smile. "Who knows? I don't think it's quite registered yet." Brenda didn't need to know I was talking about a whole lot more than the graduation ceremony we'd just sat through. Unless she *knew* more than she was letting on.

So far we'd kept things a secret, telling only Ruthie and her husband, Paul. And our son, Sam. I'd wanted to keep this announcement from him as long as possible. Taking into account the fact that he was a sophomore, and the girls who had been calling him this past school year, I wanted to keep any kind of baby stuff out of his head. But the tension around our house and at the café felt like a military zone on alert. There was no hiding when the enemy, Angie, walked among us. We swore all of them to secrecy for now. But between Angie's doctor visit and her test at the Brewster clinic, it wouldn't surprise me one bit if the news had started making the rounds of Brewster. Some news was juicy enough to break confidentiality rules.

Angie wouldn't be the first Brewster teen who had gotten pregnant. I knew exactly what folks around here would be saying. *Did you hear about Angie Johnson? I always thought she was such a nice girl. Who'd have ever thought something like this would happen to someone like her? And an honor student. You'd think she'd be smart enough to know better. Wonder if she'll keep it? Her poor parents…can you imagine how they must be feeling?*

Unfortunately, I could imagine all too well.

There had been lots of rumored pregnancies in Brewster over the years, and I had a way of dealing with that kind of talk at the café. "Time will tell," I'd always say. And it always did. Sometimes a baby would show up months later, oftentimes none did. I had no doubt the Brewster rumor mill would soon begin to chalk off the months until the latest rumor proved true.

Embarrassment mixed with anger did a slow boil beneath the v-neck of the black pantsuit I was wearing. It hadn't escaped my notice, when I'd slipped into my clothes for this evening, that black was the color of mourning. Mourning was an apt word to describe how I'd been feeling ever since I'd learned the words Angie's boyfriend had stammered out over the phone were true. I was grieving the death of my daughter as I knew her. Carefree and innocent were two words I could no longer use to describe her.

Oh, I knew soon enough I would have stopped thinking of her in those terms. After all, she had turned eighteen a week ago. Two weeks *after* we'd found out she was pregnant. Eighteen was the legal age. Old enough to do lots of things it was hard to imagine my little girl doing. Smoking. Voting. Joining the service. Signing a loan. Getting married. But instead of a gradual shift in the way I thought of my daughter, I'd had the rug yanked out from under me.

I'd almost forgotten about Brenda as she leaned toward me and lowered her voice. "I noticed Dave moved the senior photo he had of Angie on his desk. Things like this are hard on men, too." She pressed her lipsticked lips into a sympathetic smile. "They just don't like to admit it."

What was she talking about? Had she heard the rumor? Had

Dave slipped up and told her at work? Or was she simply talking about Angie graduating?

"Every time I ask him where Angie will be going to college, he lifts his hand and says, 'Can't talk about that now.' It's *so* cute the way he gets choked up about his daughter leaving home." Brenda sipped her punch. "Has Angie decided where she'll go, yet?"

Let Brenda think I was being cute, too. I blinked at the instant tears that stung my eyes, held up my hand and said, "Can't talk about that now."

Brenda laughed. "You two love your daughter so much." She put one hand on my arm. "Take it from the voice of experience. It's good for kids to get away from home. They need to grow up and learn to make decisions for themselves."

I coughed as if I'd swallowed wrong. There was Angie's problem in a nutshell. She'd made a decision for herself all right, she just wasn't grown up enough to handle it. "Excuse me, Brenda," I said, smiling with thin lips. "I need to go check on something in the kitchen." I didn't really. Ruthie had said she and Paul would handle everything tonight. What I needed was to get away from this farce of a celebration. I turned toward the kitchen and a pair of arms wrapped around me.

"Congratulations!" It was Dave's sister, Margo. She and her husband and their two children had driven to Brewster from South Dakota. They'd planned to arrive just in time for the graduation ceremony at the high school gym. It was a long drive. I wondered if they'd made it in time.

I also wondered if she could sense the strain that hung around me like a weird halo. "You're here," I said, forcing a smile onto my face.

"We walked in just as the graduates were walking into the gym. I got a chance to wave at Angie and that was all. I'll bet she's excited tonight. You, too." As usual, Margo was oblivious to my mood. She carried enthusiasm around as if she owned the franchise, spreading it on thick whether you wanted a piece or not. "We didn't go through the reception line at the school. Angie was the only one we knew, and we figured we could see her here." Margo's head bobbed as she looked around. "Where is she? Is she excited?"

"She should be here any second. The kids have to congratulate each other, you know. They're having a group hug right now." I was making things up. Scrambling for words to fill the space between us. Words that didn't have anything to do with how I felt about my daughter. Words that wouldn't give away the fact that I hadn't spoken more than necessary to Angie in three weeks.

A smattering of applause started from near the front door of the café, spreading to the back, near where we were standing. Margo started clapping, too. "There's Angie." She turned her head and beamed at me. "You must be so proud."

Before Margo had a chance to wonder why I wasn't joining in on the impromptu cheering, I said, "That's my cue to go check on the food."

As I turned I felt a hand on my arm, a whisper in my ear. "Are you going to be okay?" It was Ruthie, concern furrowing her forehead. She knew how hard this night was for me. How hard the past weeks had been. I'd told her everything, even how her own nine-month-swollen-belly reminded me of how different the circumstances were between her much-wanted baby and the one *we* were expecting.

I nodded sharply and shook my head, all in one confused motion. "I need—" I dipped my head toward the kitchen. Of all people, she would know the sanctuary that space offered on a night like tonight.

"Go on." She rubbed a hand across my shoulders as I turned. I pushed through the swinging door into the kitchen, hoping with all I had in me that no one else would be there. It would be just like Sam to be in the back, sampling the snacks that hadn't been set out yet. My eyes did a quick review. I was alone.

I stood for a moment, my back to the door, trying to erase the picture in my head. Instinctively, I'd known exactly when Angie was going to open the front door of the café and walk into the gathering. I was her mother. She was part of me.

No! Not anymore! My mind slammed the door on my daughter.

I'd seen her small white car speed past the café windows when I was talking to Brenda. The street outside was already lined with vehicles, everyone already inside waiting for the graduate. I knew Angie would park in back, behind the café where she always parked. When a short minute had passed and she hadn't pushed her way through the kitchen doors, I knew she was walking around the café outside and would be coming in the front doors. She was probably afraid she'd bump into me in the kitchen. Which is exactly why I needed to go there. To avoid bumping into her.

Margo had foiled my plan. I could see the top of Angie's head slowly moving past the lower edge of the café window. She'd be opening the door any second. Even before the clapping started, I knew. As hard as I tried, I couldn't keep my eyes from the door, from the moment I'd imagined so differently from the way it was happening. The door opened. Angie stepped inside. Anyone else would have thought she was looking down, watching her step. I knew she was putting the same sort of smile on her face I'd worn all night. She took one step inside, paused, then raised her chin and quickly climbed the three small steps that led up to the party. It was then, as she raised herself to that last step, grabbed onto the handrail at her side as if she hadn't expected so many people to be here, our eyes met.

For the briefest of moments she held my gaze. Long enough

for me to see a defiant glint in her eye. *I'm not your innocent little girl anymore.*

I narrowed my eyes. *No, you aren't.*

I turned away and took refuge in my kitchen. I walked to the stovetop, automatically picking up a metal spoon and stirring what was bubbling in front of me. The pungent scent of BBQ sauce burned my nose. This ordinary dish wasn't supposed to be on the menu. Not tonight. Maybe for Sam's graduation in two years. BBQ'd cocktail wieners were a *guy* thing. Not my Angie's.

No! Don't think of her like that!

I gave the mixture a solid swirl. I hadn't been able to muster the interest or the energy to carry out the elaborate menu I'd planned for this special night. Well, what was *supposed* to be a special night. Tears pricked at my eyes. I could always tell people I'd been in the back chopping onions. Except I wasn't.

In all things I am content. In all things I am content.

What a lie. The words that had calmed and soothed me through so many of life's bumps weren't a bit of comfort now. I hadn't merely jolted over a pothole. This time I'd driven completely off the road.

How ironic that I'd sought refuge in this kitchen, when this was the room where it all had come crashing down...

Dave hadn't wasted any time getting to the café that night after I'd choked out those three unlikely words: chicken fried steak. He'd remembered our silly code and knew immediately something was wrong. There were times in the days since, I thought most anything would have been better that night than what really happened. If there had been a fire, we could rebuild. If there had been a robbery, well, what was money, really? I could have chopped off a finger in the meat slicer. I could live without a finger. But to have my heart shattered?

I didn't know how to go on.

"What's wrong?" Dave burst into the café. If there had been an armed burglar in the kitchen with me, waiting for him behind the door, Dave would have been toast. As it was, I felt as if I'd been hit across the back of my head with a cast iron skillet. I didn't get up.

I also didn't waste time. "I got a phone call. From Mark. He said Angie thinks she's pregnant."

Dave joined me on the floor. Knees drawn up, elbows on his legs, his head dipped into his hands. He sat like that for a long time. I understood. I'd sat there myself for almost an hour. Finally he raised his head, his eyes covered with a dry, glazed look, as if he'd stared at something awful for much too long.

I knew exactly what he'd seen. Our daughter separated from us in a way that defied explanation. Her future—a future that had been filled with endless possibilities mere minutes ago—was gone, replaced by an image of a face hardened by life. Tired. Harried. Too young to be facing the consequences of what she'd done.

Too late.

"What do we—" We spoke our mutual question together, both of us as out of our element as two parents could be. Normally we would laugh if we'd start talking at the same time. There were no smiles from either of us tonight. I lifted my shoulders and held out my hands. Dave shook his head.

Eventually we got up off the café floor and walked outside to our cars, leaning into each other as if we were the only thing holding each other upright.

I'm here.

I brushed away God's reminder. It didn't feel as if He had any hand in this at all. And if He did, I didn't want to talk to Him. As it was, I couldn't find the words to talk to Dave, much less God.

And if I couldn't find words to say to them, what would I *ever* say to Angie?

Dave and I walked into our family room, a room that hadn't changed an iota in the last ten years but tonight felt as if our furniture belonged to strangers. I could hear music thumping from somewhere upstairs, two discordant beats. Good. That meant Sam was in his room, Angie in hers. Maybe we could spare Sam from knowing about something that might not be true.

A sad, knowing look passed between Dave and me. There was nothing to say. At least not to each other.

As if our shoes had been dipped in lead we climbed the stairs to Angie's room. We stood outside her door for a moment, preparing for the unimaginable. I couldn't help but remember the hand-printed, magic-marker sign Angie had taped to her door the year she was a fourth grader. *My room. My mess. My business.* How Dave and I had chuckled over her statement of independence.

There was nothing to laugh about anymore. If what we were about to question our little girl about was true, we had a mess of grand proportions on our hands. And it would suddenly be *all* our business.

I knocked on Angie's door, then gently turned the knob and let the door swing open. She was lying on her bed, a school notebook between her bent elbows, a teddy bear peaking out from under her arm. I felt a flutter of relief. Certainly anyone old enough to be pregnant wouldn't be doing homework with a stuffed animal under her arm. Angie glanced up and then immediately away and in that instant I knew.

I asked anyway. "Is it true?"

Angie swinging her feet over the side of the bed, her jaw set as if she was expecting a hard right hook. "What if it is?"

Dave stepping into the room. "Angie," he said, the tone in his voice holding a warning. "We need to know."

"I'm almost eighteen. I can do what I want." She was standing now, her teddy bear on his back as if he, too, was bowled over by her words.

"You're not eighteen yet." My words. Harsh and hard. "You still live under our roof." Controlling.

"Then I'll leave!" Angie looked around wildly, as if there might be a packed suitcase she could grab and stomp out from under our rigid thumbs.

I looked around, too, afraid maybe she had one hidden. Fearful, suddenly, that Mark had called her, too. That they'd concocted some crazy plan to run off together. "You will *not* leave this house." My hands were on my hips. It didn't escape my notice that my command was a little too late. A lot too late. If Angie was pregnant no amount of grounding would change things now.

Her eyes were wild. "You're always trying to tell me what to do!"

"What's going on?" Sam was standing in the hall, rubbing one eye as if he, too, was having a hard time believing what he was seeing.

Dave stepped into the hallway and put one arm around Sam's shoulder. "Go back to your room, please," he said. "Your mom and I need to talk to Angie."

Any normal night, any normal fight, Sam would have cracked a joke, lightening whatever tension we felt. Not tonight. It seemed even he could sense this was different. A heavy bass beat thumped as background between the two bedrooms as he walked back to his room. *Danger music,* Angie used to call the ominous beat during the scary part of a children's movie, the part just before the bad guy revealed himself. I wondered just which of us was the villain in this scene. Possibly all of us.

We were silent until we heard the click of Sam's door. I was breathing as if I'd been running from something. Maybe I was. It was time to face it.

"Are you pregnant?"

"What if I am?"

"Then we'll deal with it." This from Dave. "Are you?"

Angie shot me a defiant glance. Then she looked away. She couldn't look at Dave at all. "Maybe. I think so."

My heart did a crazy flip and then fell into a crevasse inside me I didn't know existed. Could it still beat from there? Tears pushed into the back of my throat. "Oh, Angie. No. Please. No."

There was a part of me that knew I should reach out to her. Knew I should cradle her in my arms. Put my hand behind her head and hold it close to my heart. She had to be scared. If I didn't know what to do in this situation, certainly my seventeen-year-old daughter was even more clueless. But there was another part of me that felt a wall spring up, as thick and rigid as prison bars. Sure I could reach through them, try to touch her. But the truth was, I didn't want to.

My tears dried up. "Do you know for sure?"

Angie kicked one of her brown boots against the other. "I took a test."

I could see Dave, standing by Angie's dresser, close his eyes. I couldn't look at him just then. I turned my gaze to her dresser. The top was filled with an assortment of girly things I used to think summed-up my daughter. There were two half-empty perfume bottles. Last year's yearbook from Brewster High. A stack of CDs. Several necklaces were hanging over the edge of her mirror. A bowl of earrings near the left edge. A family picture of us on a rare picnic at Brush Lake, just outside of Brewster, when Angie was about ten. There we were, laughing and squinting into the sun, dripping wet from the dunking we'd taken when the canoe we'd borrowed from Paul Bennett had tipped. Maybe if we'd done more of that sort of thing this wouldn't have happened. How could a child who had most everything she wanted, do this to us?

Dave said the one word I couldn't. "Why?"

As if she had rehearsed the climactic scene in a high school play, words burst from Angie's lips in a screaming rage. "You guys think you can control everything I do!" Her voice rose. "Go to school, Angie! Go to work at the café, Angie! Go to college, Angie!" She held her arms stiff at her sides and yelled, "I am not some stupid robot! I have a mind of my own, and I can do what I want! And I'm not going to college!"

Who was this child? Who did she belong to? We hadn't tried to control her. We'd tried to raise her the best we knew how. All we'd given her was love. Look what we got in return. A flame of anger burned where my heart had once beat. Just as quickly it was doused by my tears. Did she know what this would do to her future? How could she have done this to *us?*

I looked at the daughter I no longer recognized. Her teeth were clenched, her lips in a thin line. I saw nothing of the child I knew in her steely eyes. I felt my gaze harden to match hers. I swiped away the tears on my cheeks with the backs of my hands. I paused and took a deep, shaky breath, knowing full well the words I was about to say were as sharp as any knife in the café kitchen. "If you did this to hurt us...it worked."

There. Let her live with the fact that she'd broken our hearts.

The only problem was, I didn't think she cared. And that hurt even more.

Libby

June. July. August. In large chunks I tore away the pages from my *Farside* desktop daily calendar, the calendar my friend Katie had given me for Christmas eight months ago. She knew the wry humor was right up my alley. Too bad I'd missed so much of it. How could three months pass without me even so much as glancing at the right hand corner of my desk? I tore off the first week of September, vowing to keep current from today on.

The truth was, I'd barely sat at my computer all summer. I'd cranked out my bi-monthly column for the *Brewster Banner* and checked e-mail now and then, but apparently my eyes hadn't strayed far from the blinking cursor in front of my eyes.

I could hardly blame all the summer days I'd frittered away on my depression. I'd spent more time than usual outside, planting flowers and a vegetable garden so small I was glad my old neighbor, Ida, wasn't around to see it. My mini-plot would have sent her into palpitations…of laughter. But I'd taken no small measure of pride when my first tomato appeared on the vine.

In July we spent two weeks in Minnesota at a lake cabin Bob and I rented. Emily and Brian joined us for a long weekend in the middle of the two weeks. Bob spent every afternoon alternately pulling both kids behind the ski boat we also rented. I sat on the deck reading and waving enthusiastically as they sped past the cabin. I was glad to see them having so much fun, and was even happier I didn't have to be in the boat. It wasn't that I didn't like the water…it was hard to read at the speeds they were going. And my idea of a vacation was reading as many books as I could. I'd been afraid Brian would ask to bring Katie along, but he hadn't mentioned it and only called her twice as far as I could tell.

I'd felt so good all summer I'd even contemplated going off my antidepressants. Then I remembered the two other times I'd tried that trick. No, I didn't want to go to that place again.

I looked at the wad of calendar pages I'd thrown away. What did I have to show for all the days I'd just tossed into the garbage?

Nothing. That's what. You're so lazy—
STOP!

I pushed the intrusive thought aside. It wasn't hard to remember Dr. Sullivan's caution during those awful days of my clinical depression. *Depression isn't cured, it's managed.* Now that the fall months were approaching, I felt a familiar tug on my emotions. The depression that stayed at bay over the summer was doing its annual, slow creep into my thoughts. It might be time for me to increase my medication by a few milligrams and get out my special light.

Automatically my glance darted to the doorway that led to the kitchen, the room I'd have to walk through to get to the basement where I kept the clunky light that was part of the "management program" for my depression. When Dr. Sullivan had first suggested using light therapy for depression, I'd laughed.

"Hocus pocus? I thought there was more science to your profession than that."

One side of Dr. Sullivan's mouth turned up. He'd finally learned to recognize when I was teasing. He'd also learned many of my flip quips held deeper questions. "I was skeptical at first, too. But many of my patients find great relief using the special light during the winter months. Seasonal Affective Disorder is a real problem, especially in the northern states like North Dakota. The light helps reset your circadian rhythm each morning and also affects the serotonin levels in your system." He took a breath.

I held up my hand. "Okay, I believe you." I didn't need the science, all I needed was help. This was in the fall, a year *after* my hospitalization for depression, and the dip in my mood scared me into another visit with my psychiatrist. Fortunately, even though Dr. Sullivan had officially retired, he'd come back on staff semi-part-time as long as they allowed him to spend a few months in Arizona with his wife over the winter. Lucky for me he hadn't left yet. I wasn't sure I could muster the confidence to recount my history to someone new.

My change in mood was getting to be a familiar pattern. Each summer I'd start to think I'd put the melancholy behind me... until it showed up in the fall and sat down hard on my chest. It was hard to breathe through the days without being reminded of the weight of emotions that lurked under my skin. The medication I took nightly, the new thought processes I'd learned in therapy, and a healthy lifestyle, including some quality prayer time, usually did the trick. Until old Mother Nature decided to make the days short and dreary.

Dr. Sullivan straightened his tie and picked up his pen. "I can write you a prescription for the light. It's not covered by most insurance policies, but there's a free thirty-day trial period that should give you enough time to assess whether it works for you." He raised his eyebrows in question.

What did I have to lose? If it was hocus pocus I'd find out in a month. If it worked...wow.

Ever since that visit I dragged my light from the basement each fall, usually around the time we changed the clocks, and sat in front of it while I ate my morning cereal, read the newspaper, and had my first cup of coffee for the day. A half-hour each morning until spring. Whatever the special bulbs did, it was enough to take the edge off my depression. Enough to send the clump of tears in the back of my throat packing.

This year the fall melancholy had arrived weeks ahead of schedule. Maybe it had something to do with my unproductive summer. I hadn't written a word on my new manuscript. I'd simply lain-in-wait, hoping to hear from the editor who was supposedly reading *After Anne.*

I hadn't heard a word about the status of my novel, and I wasn't sure what to do about that. I could e-mail Joan and ask if she had, in fact, sent it on. But what if she hadn't? My note would only remind her of her forgetfulness and possibly change her mind about the project all together.

Or maybe she was just being polite. Passing the buck. Maybe she didn't really like your manuscript all that much. Maybe— STOP!

Sheesh, my negative-thought-cheerleader was in fine form this morning. I put my reading glasses on and reached for the *Writer's Market Guide* on the shelf above my computer. I flipped through the pages...M...N...O...P. There it was: Prism Publishing.

I scanned the listing, realizing for the first time I had no idea of the name of the editor who was supposed to be deciding the rest of my life. And even if I did, what would I do about it? I was afraid a phone call asking about the status of my manuscript might ruin any chances I had. Then again, maybe it had gotten stuck on some deep, dark pile of hopeful writers' work and needed my help to jolt it loose. On the other hand...

Oh, give it up. You'll never be a writer, so stop your wishful thinking.

I snapped the *Market Guide* shut and laid it to the side of my keyboard. Taking off my reading glasses, I closed my eyes and rubbed at my temples with my fingertips. I hoped there was a headache brewing. At least then I'd have something to blame this lousy mind-set on.

Who was I fooling? Having my novel published was nothing but a pipe dream. People who lived in remote places like the Brewsters of the world didn't get their work noticed. That editor more than likely took one look at my North Dakota address and ran my manuscript through the shredder.

Laughing maniacally.

Oh, I was in keen shape today. I needed to shake this frame of mind or the entire day might be taken over with my good-for-nothing thinking. Two aspirin would be a start. I pushed myself away from my desk and headed for the kitchen medicine cupboard. Two pills and a swallow of cold coffee. I dumped the rest and refilled my cup. What to do now? I picked up my coffee mug and wandered through the living room. I could dust.

It's not that dirty and what's the use? There's no one but you and Bob to see it.

I ran my hand over the Bible lying on the end table by the couch. There was a veneer of dust across the deep-blue cover. When was the last time I'd sat down and read it? By the looks of it, weeks ago. And that was a generous guess. Last year I'd been faithful about reading through the book in one year. I'd started at the beginning again this past January, but somewhere along the line my schedule had been derailed. The times I'd opened the book over the summer had been spotty, at best. I sat down and pulled the silver-edged book onto my lap. I had nothing better to do.

Great attitude.

Yeah, well, that was exactly the reason I needed to start reading. I flipped through the beginning of the Old Testament to the marker where I'd left off. I was further along than I'd thought. Jeremiah looked to be a little past the middle of my Bible. Once again my rotten frame of mind was clouding my perception.

You'd think after years of this I would learn the symptoms and recognize them before they threatened to undo me.

I took a deep breath determined to concentrate. Frankly, the Old Testament was not my favorite. I found most of it kind of boring. What did all those old laws and kings and genealogy have to do with life today?

Maybe if you studied it more you'd understand more.

Point taken. I turned one thin page. Chapter 29. I'd say a quick prayer. Maybe that would help. *Lord, open my eyes and my heart to Your Word.* There. I was ready to get something out of this.

I started to read. "After Jeconiah the king, the queen-mother, the court officials, the tribal officers, and craftsmen had—" Well, see? This was exactly the problem. Who could make sense of it all?

Keep reading.

But it was so confusing. My head was beginning to throb. There was no purpose in reading something that made no sense. Just like there was no purpose in writing a novel no one wanted to read.

Keep reading.

Another writer had written these words. Had he ever been discouraged? Did he have any idea I would be reading what he'd written thousands of years later? I doubted it. And yet he'd written. I bent my head to the words. The least I could do was honor his diligence at getting his story in print. Besides, I had nothing better to do this morning than plod on.

My subconscious tracked along on a path of its own. *You're just biding time. What are you going to do when you're done reading? Your kids are grown. Gone from home. Bob is busy with his career. And what about you? What's your purpose? Wandering around your neat and clean house? Some purpose. Surely you were meant to do more than this.*

Surely I was. But what? I'd felt so certain it was writing. But when no one wanted what you wrote, then what?

This wasn't my depression talking, these feelings were deep-seated. Even when I wasn't in the throes of depression, I could see clearly…my life was purposeless. My days were empty. Making my bed each morning and putting away the morning paper were hardly a life's calling. What was I meant to do?

I felt a thickening of tears and my throat clogged. I let the tears fall.

"Why, Lord?" There was no one home. I could talk out loud. No one would think I was crazy but me. "Why are You doing this to me? Give me something more to do. I *want* to do more. Why won't You let me?"

There was no sound but my sniffling. I pulled a tissue from the drawer in the end table. I'd learned to keep a stash there during the days I'd spent more time crying than not. It was surprising how often I opened that drawer even now. *Oh Lord, don't let me go back to those days. Give me something meaningful to do.* I blew my nose. *What is it You want me to do?*

Keep reading.

Argh! I already knew what lay on my lap. Some old story about some king and a letter Jeremiah had written to him.

What does any of this have to do with you?

My point exactly.

Keep reading.

I blinked my watery eyes. I wanted to do so much more than simply read some old story. Nothing came to mind. I bent my head over the words, letting my damp eyes skim the paragraphs. "Build homes…" Somehow I knew this wasn't my calling. "Marry and have children…" Been there, done that. "For I know the plans I have for you…"

My eyes stopped. I went back and read the line again: "For I know the plans I have for you..." Plans? For me?

Yes, you.

A shiver traveled from the back of my neck, down my arms. It was as though the words on the page had suddenly been highlighted. "For I know the plans I have for you...plans for good and not for evil, to give you a future and a hope."

Tears of a different sort crowded my eyes. This was exactly what I needed to hear.

I know.

I closed my eyes and savored the message. I had a future. And a hope. He had plans for me.

I do. Just wait.

I ran my fingers over the words. They were my words. Written thousands of years ago just for me. A plan. A future. A hope.

"Thank You, Lord," I whispered.

I was only halfway through the short chapter, and yet it was enough for today. I would cling to these words, to this message. I would claim it as mine. "I know the plans I have for you..."

I didn't know what they were, but God did. All I had to do was wait.

And there was the rub. What was I supposed to do until I found out what those plans were? *Show me.*

Wait.

Sunlight was streaming through my living room window. I hadn't noticed what a beautiful fall day it was until now. I got off the couch, threw on a light jacket, grabbed a broom, and stepped outside. Crisp air bit at my nostrils as I stood on the top step and inhaled deeply. Maybe my purpose for today was to simply appreciate God's creation.

And clean it up. There were cobwebs in the corners of the

front steps. Golden and brown leaves dotted the sidewalk. I lifted the broom and got to work.

It didn't take long to sweep three steps. I started on the sidewalk, occasionally glancing across the street at Ida's empty house. How often, from my living room window, had I watched her sweep her sidewalk? Many a time I'd chuckle and shake my head as she would finish the long stretch of cement and then head out into the street, swiping at the leaves and grime along the curb, bending with a dustpan, over and over, until the street was as clean as I imagined her kitchen floor was.

Time and again I'd chided her in my mind. *Don't you have anything better to do than sweep the street?*

I felt ashamed of the way I'd ridiculed the way she spent her time. Who was I to judge her actions? Today I understood. She'd lived alone most of the years I'd known her. She had to be lonely. Sweeping the curb was a way to spend productive time outside. Maybe talk to a few neighbors in the process. It was good exercise, too. Not to mention that her efforts had given me a meticulous view all these years. And not once had I thanked her.

Her house had sat empty almost a year. The "For Sale" sign tilted as if it were growing weary of its job. Curled leaves and odd pieces of wrappers littered the curb. Ida would be appalled.

I went inside my house. The dustpan was in the pantry closet. Grabbing a folded brown grocery bag from the shelf, I headed outside and across the street. I would do this for Ida. Then I would go visit her. Tell her how much I missed the way she'd kept her property so spotless. Tell her how much I missed her.

Somehow, today this felt like God's plan.

⌒

"L–libby?" Jan Jordan was wheeling Ida past the inside entrance of the nursing home. "I was just tell–lling Ida that I haven't seen yoo–ou in ages."

"Shpeek uff the deffil, vee vass chust talking about you." Ida reached out and took my hand. "Acht, I miss my oldt neighbor."

"Well, I miss you, too. That's why I came to see you." I squeezed her hand. Why hadn't I come here more often? I had a sense this was exactly where I was supposed to be today. I couldn't help but wonder if God hadn't arranged this impromptu meeting. I looked up at Jan. "Are you two off somewhere?"

"No." Jan shook her head. "I just finn–nished polishing Ida's fingernails."

"In the schpaa." Ida held out her pink nails to me as if she were returning from a luxury resort.

"A–aactually," Jan said, "I need to get to my n–next appoint-ment. I was returr–ning Ida to her room. If you wouldn't mind..." She turned the handles of the wheelchair my way and put a hand on my arm. "Ca–all me for coffee soon. Okay?"

As I took the already warm chair handles into my hands, I nodded. "Promise." If a person didn't know about Jan's bout with Bell's palsy, it would be tempting to reach up and try to clean out your ears. Her speech had improved so much since her illness, her pauses and slight slurs were barely noticeable. I was proud of my friend for the way she'd taken that trying time in her life and turned it into something good. Besides her part-time job at Elizabeth's in Carlton, she'd talked the store owner into donating cosmetics to the Brewster Nursing Home so Jan could pamper the female residents one day a week. I only wished I had something so purposeful to do with my time.

As I pushed Ida down the long hallway, we passed several elderly people slumped in wheelchairs, eyeing us as we slowly slid by. I smiled a greeting. Oh my, nothing to do but sit. Their days had to feel twice as long as mine. No sense wishing for something more to do when I should be visiting with Ida. As I pushed the chair, I bent close to her ear. "Do you want to go to your room? Or is there somewhere else you'd rather sit and visit?"

She pointed a wrinkled, polished finger straight ahead. "Let's go to da sunroom. On da endt. It's coseey dere."

"The sunroom it is."

I pushed Ida into the sun-filled room, turning her chair so the sun wasn't in her eyes but would warm her back. I pulled a padded chair near and sat down. Reaching out, I took one of her papery hands into mine. It had been much too long since I'd visited my neighbor. Where should I begin? "I was outside sweeping this morning," I started.

Ida glanced at some leaves drifting down outside. "It's a goodt day for shweeping. Dere's many tings I'dt like to do again." She sighed. "My place must look a sight. My nephew, Kenny, is surely too busy to tink of shweeping my walk."

One corner of my mouth turned up. I felt unexpectedly shy to tell Ida I'd swept her curb clean. *What must the other neighbors have thought?* I gave her hand a light squeeze. "Don't worry about it. I cleaned it up."

"Tank Gott in Himmel, you didn't needt to do dat."

"I know I didn't have to do it. I wanted to." And just like that I realized I had. The act of walking across the street with my broom, of sweeping and bending and cleaning up, knowing I was doing it for my neighbor who couldn't, had added a dimension of meaning to my day I hadn't noticed until now.

Ida squeezed my hand back. "Shpic and shpan neffer lasts long dis time uff year. But I tank you for looking after my place."

A bubble of unexpected joy tickled my throat. I hadn't anticipated that. Not for sweeping. "So," I said, clearing my throat, leaning back in my chair settling in for a chat, "how've you been?"

Ida shook her head slowly as she looked down at her lap.

I braced myself, ready for my sudden good mood to change. I prepared myself to listen to a list of ailments, maybe a complaint about her long days. Some grumbling about how no one visited her often enough or the quality of the meals she was served each day. Unlike me, Ida had a reason to wail. I certainly didn't expect to hear "Bissy!"

"Busy?" I couldn't help but chuckle. Who would think this old woman had a more active life than I did? Maybe if I listened closely I could pick up some pointers to fill my long, boring days. Maybe I could move in with Ida. "What are you so busy with?"

"Acht der liebe." Ida's freshly polished fingers worked at the top button of her soft-pink cardigan sweater. "Effery morning dere iss coffee time in the dining room, and den sometimes I help dem folds the wash rags from the laundry. After lunchtime I go to actiffities, and on Turssday der iss Biple shtudy. Friday iss Binkgo. And den my wisitors." Ida held one curved finger in the air as if counting, "Chan andt Kenny andt Diane. Andt…" She pointed at me. "You." She sighed. "Sometimes I hardtly haff time to rememper vhy I'm here."

I felt an odd tingle in the middle of my chest. Wasn't that the very question I'd wrestled all morning? Trying to find out the *why* of my life?

I was afraid to ask Ida to elaborate. After all, what would an eighty-something woman, a woman who'd spent most of her life on a farm or living alone across the street from me, have in common with me, a lifelong "town gal" and bank president's wife? From her vantage point in the nursing home, my life must appear full to the brim. I had a loving husband, two great kids, and, unlike Ida, two legs and a car that could get me wherever I wanted to go. It would sound like sour grapes for me to bemoan my good fortune. Even so, the emptiness I'd felt most of the morning, echoed. Before I realized I was talking, the words were out of my mouth. "I've been wondering that, too." My sentence sounded incomplete. "I mean, why I'm here." Oh, that sounded even more confusing. "I mean, not *here* in this room. I mean, *here*..." I waved one hand limply around in front of my chest. I hoped she'd get the drift. I wasn't sure I wanted to begin trying to explain the vague emptiness I'd been feeling to my old neighbor. I'd come to cheer her up, not to turn her into a cut-rate psychiatrist.

Ida patted at the tight white curls over one ear. There was a tiny twinkle in her eye. "You and I. Two peass in a podt. Too much time to tink."

It was as if some tightly closed book in my brain slowly opened, revealing a page I hadn't seen before. She'd certainly hit the nail on the head. Too much time...with nothing to do but think about it. I'd never thought of Ida's fate and mine intertwined in quite that way. Somehow I'd always imagined old people in nursing homes as *mindless*. Folks who frittered a day away without thought. Waiting for someone to come get them up. Waiting for the next meal or an unexpected visitor. I never imagined them in the same dilemma I faced...how to make something meaningful out of each day.

I leaned forward. I opened my mouth. Then closed it. Then opened it once more. "So...what do you...?" I couldn't think of how to put my swirling thoughts into words.

Ida's gaze drifted through the sunlit window. "In my day vee didn't haff time to tink on dese tings. We vass too bissy. Vhy, vhen Fredt and I vass on the farm, my days vere shpendt helping witt the chores. I hadt a bic garden. Canned the wegetables. Baked my own brodt. If ve vanted a pie for dessert, I mate the crust. None of dis buying pie crust from the Magner's grocery store." Her shoulders lifted as she chuckled. "I remepber the first time I heardt of store-bought pie crust. I tought, 'Dose vomen's iss too lazy to make dere own.'" She waved a hand through the air. "They didn't know *how*, iss the reason. Can you imachine?"

Actually, I could. The few times I'd attempted to make my own pie crusts had been exercises in frustration. I'd learned Betty Crocker did a fine job. And I didn't mind paying her for it.

Ida smiled at me. "Vhen Fredt and I mooffed to town, it felt like the Life of Reiley. I hadt a vashing machine vhere I didn't haff to push the clothes troogh the wringer. If I gots behindt in my vork, I couldt run to Magner's and pick up some brodt." She cupped a hand near her mouth and leaned toward me. "I effen bought a pie crust once." Her thin lips quivered as she tried to hide a smile. As if she were still keeping the secret from her dead husband.

"Then Fredt died and I hadt even more time on my handts." Her eyes flicked to meet mine and then moved away. It wasn't hard to see the spark of pain that loss had left. "Dat's vhen I started haffing too much time to tink. Acht, the toughts dat vouldt be in my mindt veren't fit for a Lordt's childt. Vhy vass I left here wittout Fredt? Vhy hadt I neffer hadt any childrens? Vhat vass I supposed to do witt my life alone?" Her eyes grew watery. "Too many questions."

Our lives had been so different, and yet were so alike. Even *with* a husband and kids I wondered why I was here. What I was supposed to be doing.

Ida didn't give me time to dwell on our similarities. Her voice cracked now and then as she continued on. "Martha's husbandt died aroundr dat same time. I know now Godt put us together to help us through that time. Martha needed me and I needed her. Vee shtarted meeting for coffee effery day at the café. Andt I can't forget Wicky…"

It took me a second to understand she was talking about

Vicky Johnson, the same "Wicky" I was supposed to be working with on a writing project. The project I'd avoided thinking about all summer. I'd heard the news about her daughter, Angie. I had a feeling a cookbook was on the back burner of Vicky's life right now. But I was curious what Ida had to say about her. I nodded for Ida to go on.

"When she bought da café she askedt me to show her how to makes pies andt bunss andt rolls. She'd lost her mama vhen she vass too young to haff known dese tings. And then I helped her at the Pumpkin Fests, and sometimes at the café I'd take the coffee monies in the mornings vhen she wass too bissy. This wass all vork Godt hadt planned for me. Vork He knew I vouldt needt to keep my mindt from the dark toughts." Ida folded her creased hands in her lap. "Der iss a Biple verse that tells me chust that." Before she took a breath I knew exactly what she would say. "I know da planss I haff for you—"

I chimed in and finished the verse for her. "They are plans for good and not for evil, to give you a future and a hope."

"Goodt." Ida nodded her head as an amen.

I nodded back. Even though I had no specific answers to my questions, I felt at peace. Twice this morning I'd been told I had a future. A hope. I was getting the message. God did have a plan. I just had to wait to find out what it was. I uncrossed my legs and put the palms of my hands in my lap. I'd been here long enough. Ida must be getting tired. And from what she'd told me, after lunch her day would shift into high gear. It was time for me to go. I started to stand.

Ida held up a shiny fingertip. "Der iss one more ting I vant to say to you."

I sat back down.

"Vhen I mooffed here…" She pointed her finger toward the floor. I knew she meant when she'd moved into the nursing home.

"I hadt all the time in the worldt to vonder vhat goodt I vas all offer again." She laid one hand against her cheek. "You might haff heardt about Kenny's bapy?"

I didn't know what had brought about this abrupt change of subject, but I pressed my lips together and nodded my understanding. The whole town knew about Kenny's son who had been born six months ago. About the challenges life would hold for him. Little Freddie. For the first time it dawned on me that Kenny's son had been named after Ida's husband. What a special honor for a special child. And for a special lady. I reached out and took her fingers in mine.

I felt a tremor in Ida's hand as she went on. "Dat little childt needts all the prayer he can get. And who hass more time to pray den me?" Her eyes held a mix of tears and joy. "Godt knew diss all along."

I leaned over and hugged her. How did Ida get so smart? She was right. I had too much time on my hands.

"So, childt." Ida stared at me with glistening eyes. "Vhat iss it Gott is calling you to do?"

Nothing like getting put on the spot. Ida's question was part of the reason I'd come here, but if I knew the answer, I'd be home doing it.

You know the answer.

No, I don't.

You do.

I don't.

You had an answer before the question was asked.

Busted. I did.

Writing.

Yes.

I'd known ever since I was a little girl I was supposed to write.

Now that I was an adult, I still knew it. I just didn't know what I was supposed to do with that desire.

Write.

Easier said than done. What if no one wanted to read what I wrote? What if no one wanted to publish my words?

I've already given you a newspaper column. You are published. Keep writing. I have a plan for you.

"Oliffia?" Ida tapped my knee with her fingers. "I tink I needt to go back to my room before the lunchtime." She looked at me knowingly. As if she'd heard my answer. One eye twitched. I could swear she winked at me. "Andt I'm sure you haff better tings to do den shpendt the morning witt an oldt lady."

Write.

I was getting this message loud and clear. I would take Ida back to her room, and then I would swing by Vicky's Café, maybe have a bite to eat, and after the lunch rush died down, maybe I could corner Vicky and talk about the cookbook project. I didn't have to wait for the whim of some unknown editor to respond to my manuscript. If I was meant to write, *write* I would.

Vicky

Babies. Everywhere I turned, it seemed, there were babies. I was tempted call the census takers and alert them to the population boom in this part of North Dakota.

With a forced smile I set the roast beef combo covered in gravy in front of the hugely pregnant woman sitting in the corner booth. I didn't know her, and I was glad. If she had been a regular customer, I would have felt obligated to talk about her obvious condition. I doubted whether she wanted to hear anything I had to say about pregnancy these days.

"Enjoy your lunch," I said between my clenched teeth, choking on all the things I didn't say. I turned away, thankful the café was full. I wouldn't have to worry about this woman starting a conversation across an empty café about her bulging stomach. I wasn't sure if I could stand one more baby-related conversation.

I grabbed up the coffeepots, grateful to have something to do on this first day of October besides remembering how, if life had gone as I'd planned, Angie would have had a month of college under her belt by now. Instead, belts were a thing of the distant past around her baby-filled belly. I closed my eyes tightly and let myself do a silent, mental scream. It was the only release I would get for the many hours ahead. I forced myself to take a deep breath. Ah, coffee. The fragrant, warm steam momentarily calmed me. I knew it wouldn't last long.

"Coffee? Would you like more coffee?" I went around the

café on autopilot, hoping against hope that none of my regular customers felt the need to inquire about Angie.

"Where's Angie going to college?" If I had a dollar for every time I'd fielded that question over the summer, I could really take the flight to Jamaica I fantasized about. Even though I knew my daily flights were only flights of fancy, an escape mechanism that offered no escape at all, I climbed on board and took them anyway.

Late summer, as Angie's stomach starting making an obvious statement, the college inquiries stopped. I was all too aware of the whispering that had to be going on outside the café, but I had to give my regular customers credit, they were able to drum up enough to talk about during coffee time without my daughter as the main subject. But even when babies weren't being thrust into my face, I was thinking about them.

Even my sister was obsessed. Of course, Ruthie had a right to be. She'd had a baby five months ago, two nights after Angie's graduation reception. The reception I'd managed to get through saying only two words to my oldest child...

"You're done." I hoped anyone within earshot interpreted my thin smile as the look of a mom sad at the thought of her daughter leaving home. In truth, my unplanned words held the bulk of my feelings. Angie was done with high school. Done with any dreams she might have had for the future. Done being my perfect little girl.

Even now, images from the days after Dave and I confronted Angie in her bedroom kept scrolling through my mind. A DVD run amok. There was the scene when Angie jumped off her bed and screamed at us: "We bought a test! Okay? It showed I was—" Even she had a hard time saying the word out loud. She stopped talking and looked at her bare feet.

"It showed *what?*" I was going to *make* her say it. If she thought she was old enough to be pregnant, she'd better start acting like it. "*What?*"

She never looked up. "Preg—*pregnant.*" It was a broken whisper.

Maybe I should have felt compassion for her then. I didn't. All I felt was an obscene rage. I waved an arm through the air. "What were you thinking? Obviously, you weren't! Did you ever—"

Dave, the voice of reason, spoke through my tirade. "We're going to have to make sure. You'll need to go see a doctor."

Of course. In my blind rage I hadn't thought that Angie and Mark's juvenile assessment might be all wrong. I wasn't familiar with home pregnancy tests. Both of my pregnancies had been confirmed by a doctor. For all I knew, the reliability of a drugstore test was as good as a county fair fortune teller.

The next morning Dave went off to work as if our lives were still normal. Angie went off to school with a note saying she would need to be excused for an appointment sometime in the afternoon. I'd be calling the school to let them know when. For the first time in my life I lied to Ruthie, telling her I wasn't feeling well and couldn't make it in to work. Then again, there was no lie in that. Instead of crawling into bed, I dialed the Brewster clinic, setting up an appointment for Angie first thing after lunch, which I already knew I wouldn't be eating. I would use the time to wallow just a bit more in my anger and heartbreak.

Maybe it wasn't just Angie who needed the doctor. But what medicine was there that would begin to mend my broken heart?

Angie walked from school, meeting me in the clinic waiting area. It was ironic that a child old enough to suspect she was pregnant needed her mom along to sign insurance forms and make the co-pay. We waited in silence, arms crossed over our chests. I didn't know why Angie took that pose. I knew I was simply trying to hold myself together.

"Dr. West will see you now." The nurse motioned both of us to follow her into a small exam room and into two side-by-side chairs. Angie and I took up our defensive poses. We both flinched when the exam room door suddenly opened.

"Good morning. Oh, sorry." Dr. West looked at her watch. "I guess it's past that." She closed the door behind her. "Good afternoon, I mean." She smiled.

There was nothing good about it, and here was the one place I didn't need to fake anything. "Afternoon," I muttered, the only thing I could find to agree on.

Dr. West pulled a small stool from under the desk and sat down, opening Angie's half-inch-thick file. That small flip of a page reminded me of the many times I'd sat here with Angie over the years. Holding her tight while she got her baby shots. The way she'd bravely held out her arm and then turned her face to the wall as she got the booster shot she needed to start kindergarten. The time she'd fallen off her bike and needed an X-ray of her arm. The four stitches she'd needed near her hairline when her brother threw a Tonka truck at her… and then screamed at the sight of blood as if *he'd* been the one injured. Brave little Angie had merely whimpered, "It hurts bad." Oh, to have those simple days back again. If only a few stitches could solve this ache. The long-ago words of my mother-in-law echoed: "Little kids, little problems. Big kids, big problems." No kidding.

"What can I do for you today?" Dr. West glanced between Angie and me.

I waited. Angie had gotten herself into this.

Nothing. I cleared my throat and shot Angie a look. She was staring at the beige linoleum on the floor as if she were a hunting dog on point. I cleared my throat again. This was the ultimate definition of a *pregnant* pause.

"My daughter." I leaned my head in Angie's direction, trying to muster the air to force the next words from my mouth. "Thinks she might be…pregnant."

I searched Dr. West's face for judgment. Not a muscle in her face so much as twitched. She simply pressed her lips together and said, "I see." She leaned forward, putting her fingertips on Angie's knee. "Angie? Can you look at me?" Angie didn't move her head, merely lifted her eyes a millimeter. "Is there a possibility that you're pregnant?"

If I hadn't been watching I would have missed it. The smallest of nods ever.

Dr. West sat straight. "Mom, I think it might be best for you to wait outside. I'll examine Angie and then we'll talk."

For the first time ever, I left my daughter alone with a doctor. I paged through old magazines without seeing a word, keeping my head lowered in case any of the other patients in the waiting room decided to ask why I was there. I listened to hacking and coughing around me, wishing with all my might that Angie had what these people did. Anything would be better than what we feared. Then, again, maybe this was all one big false alarm.

"Vicky." The nurse who had been a high school classmate of mine, crooked a finger at me. Did she know why we were here? Did she know the results of Angie's exam?

Please. Please. Lord. Please.

Some prayer. It was all I could manage as I walked the short hall. A grim-faced Dr. West and a red-eyed daughter greeted me. If you could call that a greeting. A pit the size of the Grand Canyon opened inside me. My heart fell in.

In the next scene I was pacing in my kitchen at home. I'd dropped Angie back at school as if she'd been examined for something as basic as a sore throat. I watched as she shuffled along the sidewalk into the school in her blue jeans and sweatshirt. To anyone observing, this was an ordinary day. A mom dropping her daughter off at school. There was nothing special to see. No scar. No medication to take. Only the knowledge that would change our lives forever.

As soon as I got home, I tried calling Dave. His secretary said he had been called to a meeting at the bank, where he served on the board. She offered to take a message. Yeah, right. What kind of paper would you write this news on? What kind of ink would you use? Disappearing?

Permanent.

"No message."

I paced. Turned. Paced some more. Past the stove where I'd simmered noodle soup when Angie had a cold. Past the refrigerator where I kept her favorite after-school snack, blueberry yogurt. I paced past the kitchen table where we'd eaten…how many family meals? Nothing looked the same anymore. I paced. A caged tiger looking for escape.

I was appalled at my thoughts, yet I couldn't stop them. I would drive Angie to Montana where we knew no one. I'd find a doctor who did abortions. No one would have to know—ever.

Mark would know. Angie, too. Dave would. You would.

I would.

I bit off the scream that clamored for release. How could I even consider an abortion for my daughter? It went against everything I believed in.

Do you think it would really solve the problem?

Yes. And that's what I wanted. A solution. I was the *mom.* In the past I'd been able to fix Angie's problems; I could fix this one, too. I wanted it all to be over. Now. We'd put it behind us and move on. Pretend it never happened.

Pretend? This isn't child's play. Pretend means something isn't real. This is.

But I didn't want it to be. I just wanted it to be over. Done. Forgotten.

Think about it, Vicky. No matter what you do, this will never be over. Not in the way you want it to be. You'll never forget. You want it…erased. Life doesn't work that way. You can't run away from it. Or from Me.

But I wanted to. Oh, how I wanted to. I paced some more.

A snippet of a Bible verse I'd memorized years ago wrestled with my whirling thoughts: "You saw me before I was born."

"Arrrrggghh." The sound from my mouth was part scream, part cry. *Before I was born…*

This baby was real, whether I wanted it to be or not. Already God saw this baby as His child.

Just like Angie.

No! I couldn't think of Angie like that. Not after what she'd done to her future. To our family.

Don't you mean to your dreams for her?

I blinked away tears I hadn't known were falling. My dreams for Angie were gone.

Somehow Angie and I had gotten through the summer managing to live in the same house, work in the same café, and hardly speak to each other.

Oh, we played the game around customers. Laughing at their wisecracks but never catching each other's eye. We relayed requests and food orders. When the café was empty and it was time to clean up, Angie wiped tables and vacuumed on one side of the kitchen door, I scraped the grill and mopped the kitchen floor on the other. The jobs got done, but any pleasure I used to take in them was gone.

Poor Ruthie had to bear the brunt of our noncommunication.

"Ruthie," I'd ask when Angie was nearby, "do you think we'll need extra help to cater the Martell wedding next Saturday?"

"Angie," Ruthie would say as if nothing was amiss, "we're going to need you to help out on Saturday."

"Ruthie," Angie would say when she knew darn well I could hear, "tell my mom we need to order more vanilla ice cream. We're almost out."

We were no better than junior high girls playing a verbal game of "I can be more catty than you." I wasn't proud of the way I was acting, but I couldn't bring myself to change. My anger, resentment, and hurt festered in a way that only bolstered my reserve of self-righteousness.

Only once did that reserve crack. The day Olivia Marsden came into the café. Her entrance had been timed perfectly for conversation. If I'd felt like talking. As it was, a before-lunch emptiness filled the café. There was no excusing myself to check on an order back in the kitchen. Ruthie was back there nursing Lily before the lunch rush began. I did my best to stay out of the kitchen while she did that. It wasn't that watching her nurse embarrassed me. No, it only served to remind me of all the ways having a baby *should be*. A baby should be wanted and loved. It should be anticipated, not dreaded. I didn't need that visual reminder five times a day, so I steered clear.

While Ruthie's two oldest daughters spent the day in daycare, over the summer she brought little Lily to the mini-nursery she'd rigged up in a far corner of the kitchen. As I went about my work in the kitchen, out of the corner of my eye I couldn't help but see the many times Angie bent over the playpen to run the back of her index finger across Lily's soft cheek. The tender way she'd cup her palm along the side of the Lily's miniature face. When there was nothing sizzling on the grill, I could hear Lily's quiet coos as Angie bent low and gave her a kiss. When she grew fussy, I could hear as Angie picked her up, held her close, and murmured, "There, there, shh-shh."

Under any other circumstance, I would have measured Angie's actions as a sign of maturity. An indication that she was growing up. Getting ready for the "somedays" that lay ahead in life. As it was, I found myself casting sidelong glances at the same time I rolled my eyes. Sure it was fun to comfort a baby when it wasn't yours. When you could hand it off to the nearest adult the minute cuddling was no longer fun. If Angie thought Lily was a little doll...well, she wasn't the one who walked the floor with her at three in the morning. All she had to do was ask Ruthie if she wanted the *real* story. I highly doubted Angie had a clue what reality held.

Life was simply easier these days if I stayed as far away from babies as possible. I busied myself out in the café, scooping ice into water glasses that would soon be sitting in front of thirsty customers. I was so wrapped up in my self-righteousness that I didn't even hear Olivia Marsden walk in.

"Vicky. Hi!" Olivia stopped when she reached the top of the three steps that led into the café and glanced around the empty space. "I thought for sure this place would be..." She gestured with her hands, lifting them as if sifting through words. "Well... crowded." She slipped out of the light sweater she was wearing and draped it over her shoulders. "This is a nice surprise. I was hoping to talk to you. I thought I'd have to wait until after lunch, but..." She gestured toward a booth as if she were the hostess here. "Do you have a minute?"

"No, I don't." The second the words were out of my mouth I realized how rude they sounded. There was no reason to take my foul feelings out on Olivia. "I'm sorry." I wiped my hands on a towel. "This place is going to fill up within the next ten minutes and I really have to—" What did I have to do? I already had the coffeepots full. Water glasses were at the ready. The broccoli and cauliflower salad-of-the-day was plated on lettuce leaves and in the cooler. Chicken noodle soup filled the warming crock. Roast beef and meatloaf were in the oven. "I guess I do have a minute. Do you want some coffee?"

"Let's talk first." Olivia slipped into the booth. "I know time is short." She put her small purse near the wall then turned to me, folding her hands on top of the table. "I don't know what happened to the summer. I meant to get back to you on this much sooner and then this morning I was visiting with Ida Bauer and something we talked about reminded me that we never did get going on that recipe book idea." She opened her palms and fanned out her fingers. An invitation. "Are you still game?"

I didn't even have to think about my answer. "No." Just like that. My dreams were dead.

"Oh. O–kay." It wasn't hard to read the confusion on Olivia's face. Hadn't she heard about Angie? This town was small. She had to know my life had changed.

I cleared my throat. "Maybe you heard about my daughter?" The defensiveness in my tone was caustic. Drain cleaner was gentler. Olivia didn't deserve this but I couldn't stop myself. "Things have *changed* in our lives." It came out sounding as if it were her fault.

Olivia rubbed the pendant on her necklace as she looked me in the eye. "Yes, I heard." She glanced down at the table, and then right back at me. "It's hard when our dreams for our children don't play out. Or…even our dreams for ourselves." Now she looked away.

What would Olivia Marsden know about dreams? She had the perfect life. Wife of a bank president—

Ruthie's husband is a bank president, and you know her life isn't perfect.

Part of me knew that perfection is never true—even for someone like Olivia. I'd heard, along with the rest of the town, about her struggle with depression. But she'd obviously gotten past that. And now that her kids were grown she could have no idea about the heartbreak of broken dreams. Her kids were both in college, exactly where Angie was *supposed* to be right now. Speaking of which, Angie should be waltzing into the back door of the café right about now.

Somehow Angie had made herself indispensable around the café. Whether I wanted her around or not, she managed to be the extra set of hands we needed most days. Without saying a word to me, she set her own schedule, arriving just as I needed her to cover the lunch rush, cleaning up in the kitchen and getting food ready for the dinner crowd before the three o'clock coffee folks showed up. Ruthie would go home around four, leaving Angie and me to dance around each other until closing.

Angie would pick right up where Ruthie left off. The only difference was her attitude. Where Ruthie was unfailingly cheerful, Angie was Dr. Jekyll and Mr. Hyde. Customers saw one side of her. I saw the other. The defiant set of her jaw was a familiar sight as we bypassed each other in the small confines of the kitchen.

I copied that look now. I didn't need to make excuses to Olivia. The creation of a recipe book had been my idea. I had every right to pull the plug. "Sorry, I don't want to do it anymore."

Olivia fiddled with her earring. She pushed an invisible strand of hair behind one ear. "I know what's going on with Angie is hard, but it might be good to have something else to focus on. I was hoping—"

What did she know about *hope*? About not having any? I opened my mouth as the front door opened and four regulars from the implement dealership walked in. It was just as well. Even though I didn't have a clue what I'd been about to say, I knew it wouldn't have been kind. I slid to the edge of the booth. "That's my cue. Do you want that coffee now?"

Olivia licked her lips, and then slid her arms into her sweater. "Maybe another time." She was blinking fast. I told myself it was lint in her eyes. It had nothing, absolutely nothing, to do with anything I'd said.

I tried to pray as I brought our first lunch order back into the kitchen, ignoring Angie as she hung her purse on a hook inside the door, greeted Ruthie, and then bent to say a whispered hello to the sleeping baby. I prayed for a better attitude toward my daughter. For a better attitude period. For the compassion I'd have for anyone else in this situation. But my prayers got no further than the granite barricade that had become my heart. If Angie thought she was so grown-up, so independent, that she could go and get herself pregnant and ruin any chances she had for a future, well then, let her deal with it by herself. I wanted no part of it…or of her.

Ignoring Angie, I pulled four plates from the shelf and set them on the counter for Ruthie. I thought all my dreams had died when I found out Angie was expecting a baby. Not true. It turned out there were more dreams for her to stomp on. Dreams I didn't even know I had until they were shattered.

I couldn't stay in this kitchen with her and think about these things. With my shoulder I pushed my way through the swinging door into the café. I scooped ice into four glasses, filled each one with pop. Two Cokes, one Mountain Dew, one Diet Coke. I was in no hurry to rush back to the kitchen. I filled each one to the brim.

One day she'd been living at home, the next she dragged several cardboard boxes home and started emptying her dresser. It was late, the café already closed for the night.

"What are you doing?" They were the first semi-civil words

I'd said to her in ages. My heart started an odd thumping as she removed a stack of folded T-shirts from her drawer and placed them in the cardboard box. Next she pulled open her underwear drawer and emptied it beside the T-shirts. This wasn't some overnight sleepover she was packing for. My throat felt weird. Tight with an emotion I couldn't name. I had to cough before I could speak. "Are you going somewhere?"

She didn't answer, just moved to the next drawer and filled another box. The doorbell rang.

"That's Mark," she said, finally looking at me. "Could you let him in?"

I moved to the front door in a sleeplike stumble. It wasn't often our doorbell rang this late in the evening. Dave had muted the television and come to the door, too. From somewhere down the hall I could hear a deep, steady pulse. Sam's stereo was echoing the heavy beat of my heart.

"Mark?" My greeting was a question.

"Hi." He looked nervous as he shifted from foot to foot on the front step, barely glancing at Dave or me. "Is Angie ready?"

"What's going on? Why is Angie packing boxes?" Without planning to, I stepped aside so he could come in. If I'd known what was coming next I might have slammed the door in his face and thrown myself in front of it.

"Umm." He bit at the inside of his cheek, pulled in a deep breath through his mouth, huffed it out. "Angie and I got a place—"

"You what!" There was no way I was going to let her move in with him. Having a baby at her age was bad enough. Living with Mark would only add another layer of complication. "No! I won't allow it." My hands were on my hips, a gunslinger ready for action. It's a good thing there were no guns for this duel. I might have been tempted.

Dave stepped forward. "Mark." His voice was steady. None of the irrational, foot-stomping my tone held. "I don't think this is the best idea for you…or Angie. Why don't you come into the living room and we'll talk."

"Dad." Angie stood at the top of the stairs holding a cardboard box next to her rounded stomach. "There's nothing to talk about. I'm eighteen." She looked straight at me, as if the words that were coming next were meant to stab me alone. "Mark and I got married."

Sometimes in cartoons you see a scene where the image on the screen suddenly starts to crack. Pieces slowly drop away, until the whole, shattered image is left lying at someone's feet. That someone was me.

I didn't realize how often I'd imagined Angie's wedding day until I wasn't there to witness it. Angie and Mark had run off and gotten married sometime in early August. Less than three months after she turned eighteen. If she wanted to make a statement about her independence, she'd done it. Loud and clear.

I couldn't even bring myself to think about the dingy courtroom where they must have said their vows. The "something old" Angie must have worn for her makeshift wedding dress. There would be no giggly shopping trips for the two of us. No wedding cake photos to drool over. No black tuxes for Dave and Sam. No fancy reception to plan. No flowers. No photos in front of the church. None of the things I'd dreamed of without knowing it… until they were no longer possible.

Mark and Angie carried the last of her cardboard boxes from the house while Dave and I stood watch by the door as if we were taking inventory. We were shell-shocked. We followed the two of them halfway down the sidewalk, and then we stood outside in the dark and watched as two sets of taillights trailed off into the night, our sudden son-in-law leading our daughter off to who knew where.

My feet were stuck to the cement. A bowling ball had taken over my stomach. Dave turned and looked back at our house as if he were making sure it was still there. Checking to see if this had really happened. He stared off into the distance where Mark and Angie's cars had been. The night was as silent as if a bomb had exploded and this was the aftermath. All we could do was try to comprehend what was left.

A dog barked from the alley across the street. A cricket chirped near the house. A couple blocks away the deep bass beat of a car stereo grew loud, faded away, somehow pulling us back into the world. Our eyes met. If I looked anything like Dave, we'd both aged ten years in the past hour.

Dave put his hand on the small of my back and turned me toward the house. "Do you know what makes this even worse?"

I had a sudden urge to laugh. There couldn't possibly be anything worse than what we'd just witnessed. Could there?

We scuffed our way toward the open front door. Inanely I wondered how many flies had gotten into the house during this whole drama. Side-by-side Dave and I climbed our four front steps. The same steps that had led our daughter away. How could that be? When we got to the top Dave paused and rubbed his fingertips against his temple. He breathed a slow, heavy sigh. "I wonder if they realize that by getting married Angie's not on our insurance policy anymore. Neither is her baby."

Another bowling ball dropped on top of the one already inside me, weighing me down. There was no way these two young kids could afford insurance. Or qualify for a new policy in Angie's swollen condition. Not to mention the cost of the hospital, even if all went well with delivery.

A scream of anger and frustration fought for release. I

swallowed it back. If I started screaming, the whole neighborhood would know what just happened. I slammed the door instead. The loud thud felt good. I opened it and slammed it again. As I reached for the doorknob a third time Dave put his hand on my arm and turned me into his chest. His warm arms wrapped around me, covering my pain in a thin blanket of shirt sleeves and muscle. I felt his head tilt to lay on mine. It was then the tears came. Filling my eyes, rolling down my face, falling between Dave and me…a slow waterfall.

As I cried into Dave's chest, an idea almost as painful as what had just happened filled my mind. *It might be easier if Angie had died.*

No!

I cried harder only because it somehow seemed true. I didn't ever want to lose my precious daughter and yet, somehow, I already had. If she had died I could take my memories and tuck them away in my heart. Keep them close by and safe. Instead I was left behind with nothing but a gaping heart. A wound that would get scratched open with every thought, every word, every glance.

I couldn't wish Angie dead. I *couldn't.* I hiccuped a sob as I tried to catch my breath, burying my face into Dave's damp shirt. But I could wish I had died.

"Vicky?" Ruthie's voice snapped me back to reality. Somehow I'd ended up back in the café kitchen. She was assembling the four orders I'd brought back earlier. Two roast beef combos. Two meatloaf specials. All with fries. "Could you?" She motioned with her chin. We'd worked together long enough. She didn't need to say more.

I turned to the grill and dipped a basket of fries into hot grease, thawing the frozen potatoes in a sudden immersion of screaming liquid. The sound matched my emotions. Pop. Burst.

Glug. I was drowning and burning and at the mercy of emotions I had no control over any longer.

Give them to Me.

Right. As if. I couldn't do that. If God wanted these jumbled feelings of mine, He was going to have to wrestle me for them. If I gave my resentment and anger to God, what would I have left to hang on to?

"That's four pieces of pie, two coffees, and two glasses of water." Rubbing my tight stomach with one hand, I glanced at the price chart hanging on the wall of the old gymnasium and did the math. Across the room an old man playing an accordion and a just-as-ancient drummer replayed the "Beer Barrel Polka" for the hundredth time tonight. I hoped my baby wouldn't be born loving polka music. That would be the pits. I finished my mental addition. "That'll be nine-fifty."

Kenny Pearson dug into the back pocket of his jeans and pulled out a billfold that looked as old as he was. If anyone ever needed a gift idea for him, here it was. He handed me a ten. "Keep the change."

I gave him a tired smile. It wasn't often that people at Pumpkin Fest, who had to stand in a long line to pick up their pie, left me a tip. "Thanks." I wondered if Kenny knew how badly I needed every penny.

"That's fifty cents you got, right?" Billy, Kenny's oldest son, was quick.

"How old are you?" I asked.

"Seven," he said. "I'm in second grade this year."

I didn't remember being able to subtract numbers like that when I was in second grade. "You must be smart."

He nodded as his dad ruffled his hair. "Takes after his mom."

I was sure Kenny didn't mean anything by his comment, but I could feel myself flush. I hoped my baby wouldn't take after me.

At least not the part about having a baby when he, or she, was eighteen. My due date was next week, and all I could say about it was "stupid." I pressed a hand against my stomach. It wasn't my baby's fault. It was all mine.

Oh, Lord, I am so sorry. Forgive me. Please.

I didn't wait to hear an answer. I wasn't so sure I wanted to hear what God had to say about me these days.

I reached out my finger and tickled the cheek of the newest addition to the Pearson family. "Hey there, Freddie." I didn't have to ask. I knew he was seven months old. His mom, Diane, had him just about the time I found out I was pregnant. It was easy to keep track of his age as I counted off the months of my pregnancy. All I had to do was subtract two to remember his age. My baby would be here any day. But I wasn't going to think about that now. It made me too scared.

Freddie's thick little fingers wrapped around mine and pulled it toward his mouth.

"No, no." I gently pulled my hand away. I didn't think it would be a good idea to put my money-dirty finger into his mouth. "He's cute," I said, smiling at Diane. Even if Freddie did have problems, he was still a doll.

"Thanks," Diane said, juggling Freddie to one hip and more-or-less dragging their youngest daughter, Paige, along with her leg as she moved down the line. "If you see Renae, tell her we're on the bleachers. Eating," she added.

I couldn't imagine what it would be like having four kids. I was scared enough to have one. I'd read all sorts of things about babies on the Internet when I was still living at my parents' house earlier in the summer. Including lots of bad things that could go wrong with a pregnancy. And about birth defects like Freddie's. I laid awake a lot of nights praying none of that stuff would happen to my baby.

Praying was the only option I had. I couldn't afford to go to the doctor for more checkups, and I certainly wasn't asking my mom for help. Ever since I'd moved away from home she'd hardly said three words to me, unless it was to boss me around at the café. But I wasn't counting that.

Then again, I hadn't tried talking to her either. Honestly, I was afraid to. I was afraid she'd tell me I couldn't work at the café anymore, and then what would I do for money? I just kept showing up for work like always, trying to stay off Mom's radar, hoping she'd see how much I helped and let me keep working at least until I had the baby. I didn't have a clue what I'd do after that.

Mark had been home from college over the summer, helping his dad on their farm. He got paid a lot more than I did working at the café, but still, it wasn't near enough for all the things we were going to need.

His folks weren't too happy that he'd decided not to go back to college last month, but it was the only way Mark and I could figure out that we could afford to be together. There was an old house on the farm where his grandparents used to live. It had been sitting empty, used only to put up out-of-state hunters for a few weeks each fall. When Mark asked his dad if we could live there his only comment was, "It needs cleaning."

Water was cheaper than apartment rent. So were mouse traps. I didn't want to think about the scurrying I sometimes heard in the old house late at night. I turned to the next person in line. "How many slices?"

Olivia Marsden smiled at me. "Just two. And two coffees." Her husband, Bob, handed me six dollars.

That was one thing good about working in the café most of my life. I knew almost everyone in town by their first names. Bob and Olivia Marsden looked like they had a perfect life. Mrs. Marsden was so pretty. I bet they never had to worry about mice in their house. I reached into the cash box, pulling out two quarters in change.

Bob Marsden held up his palm. "Keep it."

To him it might have been two measly quarters, and even just a few weeks ago I might not have thought much of it, but Mark and I were quickly learning that even loose change added up to dollars. "Thanks."

As I held the paper plates with pie out to Olivia, I felt my baby do a somersault in my stomach. "Oh–h." I pretended the pie had slipped a little while I tried to stand up straight. There was no way to hide the fact that I was pregnant, but I tried to cover up how embarrassed it made me feel to have people in Brewster eyeing my stomach. Counting on their fingers. Talking about the big mistake I'd made. I knew Olivia Marsden had never done anything so dumb. I handed her their pie, anxious to have someone who looked so perfect move away and quit reminding me how opposite my life was.

Her hand brushed mine as she took the pie. "How are you feeling?"

I couldn't help but look at her. Most folks in the cafe simply pretended they couldn't see I was going to have a baby any day. Her eyes didn't float to my stomach the way most people's did as they talked about everything but my obvious condition. Instead they looked into mine, as if she really wanted to hear the answer.

Why couldn't my mom act like her? Would it kill Mom to ask, just *once*, how I felt?

How do you think she feels?

I didn't have to think about that. I knew. She hated me for what I'd done.

My bottom lip began to tremble. I couldn't cry here. Not at Pumpkin Fest. Not when my mom was standing just a few feet behind me. I wouldn't give her that satisfaction. I sucked in a deep breath and pretended to smile.

How did I feel?

Embarrassed. Scared. Ashamed.

Everyone in town knew what I'd done. Knew I'd slept with Mark. Knew why I wasn't going to college. Knew I was too young to have a baby. But I couldn't say any of those things out loud. "I feel...big." I tried to laugh, but I don't think I fooled Mrs. Marsden.

She leaned close, across the pie-covered table. "Don't worry. I saw the way you were talking to the Pearson kids. I think you're going to be a great mom."

As she started to move down the line I had to look away or I knew I'd burst into tears. "Thanks," I could only whisper.

I felt a nudge against my elbow. "Need more pie?" My Aunt Ruthie was there holding a full tray of sliced pie.

"I need a little break. Is that okay?"

"Sure." She started sliding pie slices onto the table. "I'll stay here until you get back."

I hoped she thought I needed to use the bathroom. Well, I did. But not for the reason she probably thought. I desperately needed to lock myself in a stall and cry for a while.

Three stalls and two were empty. *Thank You.* I closed the door and sat down, my tears not wasting a second in coming. A toilet flushed and I used the noise to draw in a shaky breath. Ever since the awful evening Mom and Dad found out I was pregnant, it seemed like all I'd done was cry...or try not to. Either that or try and feel mad at my parents. I wanted to blame someone for the way things had ended up, but no matter how hard I tried, it always came back to me. I'd screwed my life up all by myself.

A sob pushed its way out of my throat. I coughed, hoping

the person washing her hands thought I had something in my throat.

I did. Tears.

And a big serving of humble pie.

If anyone thought being barely eighteen and pregnant was fun, they should talk to me. The night Mom and Dad found out, all I'd wanted to do was to crawl under the covers of my bed and stay there. First they were mad. Then Mom started crying. Except for sappy movies, Mom hardly ever cried. My dad looked like he wanted to. That was the worst. I could see disappointment in their eyes. It was almost as if they were turning older as they stood in my room. It was easier when they were mad, easier to justify what I'd done.

I thought of running out of the house, but I had nowhere to go. Mark was at college in Carlton, and if I went to one of my friends' houses I would have to explain why I was there. I wasn't ready to tell anyone what had happened.

So I stayed in my room and stuck out my chin. I acted like I knew exactly what I'd done, why I'd done it, and as if I'd be just fine whether they were happy about it or not. Once Mark got home for the summer we'd figure something out.

There wasn't much to figure. Mark asked Dan Jordan, the real estate guy in Brewster, if there were any small houses we could rent. But they were really dumpy and even then the deposits for rent and utilities were more than we had. Not to mention that we didn't have any furniture to put in them. I never knew how much it cost to live in a house. Or just *live* period. Mark's grandparents' old house was our only option. I was suddenly overwhelmed by how much my parents had given me all these years. How much I'd taken for granted. But I couldn't tell them that. The words just wouldn't come out of my throat.

It seemed like all summer all I did was feel embarrassed. My

Aunt Ruthie showed up at the café one day with a big cardboard box. The smell of bacon grease left over from breakfast hung in the air. I was trying hard to clean off the grill without gagging. I hadn't been sick at all in the early part of my pregnancy like some of the websites said I might be, but today the smell was getting to me. Ruthie had the day off, and I didn't dare let my mom see me not feeling good, so every now and then I'd walk to the back door and stick my head outside for some fresh air. I was heading there for a third time when Ruthie walked in. My mom was just coming into the kitchen from the café. She took one look at me, then at Ruthie with her box and backed out.

Ruthie set the box on the floor. "I thought you could use these." She opened the box flaps.

I remembered the cute red maternity top she'd worn just a few months ago. It didn't look nearly as cute when I imagined having to wear it as I waited on customers, advertising to everyone I was going to have a baby. But it was getting too hot to wear the few stretchy sweaters I had and the dress slacks Mom had me wear at the café weren't stretchy at all. I wasn't sure what I was going to do in the next months. Quitting work and hibernating wasn't an option.

Ruthie pulled a pair of black slacks out of the box. As she held them up to me, checking the length, I could feel myself getting hotter than I already was. Ruthie was barely taller than me, but I didn't care, I'd make her old clothes work. It was the only choice I had.

She folded the pants and dropped them into the box as she glanced toward the swinging door leading into the café. "Is your mom coming around at all?"

So Ruthie had noticed the way Mom avoided me. Somehow it made me feel better to know I wasn't imagining the way my mom was acting. I shook my head, then reached out and hugged Aunt Ruthie. "Thanks."

I followed Ruthie outside and put the box in my car so my mom wouldn't ask what was in it, but I had a feeling she already knew.

That had been four months ago. Another wave of tears filled my eyes as I thought of the days that were ahead. I was scared to have this baby. Everything I read said it would hurt. And then I would have to take it home. I didn't know how to take care of a baby. Mark said he'd help, but the person I really wanted to help—my mom—could hardly stand to look at me. I didn't dare ask her to help with a baby she didn't want me to have.

I wiped at my tears with the back of my hand. I needed to get back to the pie tables, but I couldn't go out there until I quit crying. I pulled at some toilet paper and blew my nose. Maybe if I splashed some cold water on my face. I stood up. The muffled music I'd been hearing through the bathroom door suddenly got louder as a group of girls giggled their way into the bathroom. I couldn't let anyone see me. I sat back down. I'd have to wait them out.

"Did you see Angie Johnson? She's *huge!*"

A slow, freezing sensation held me still. This couldn't be happening. Me. In a bathroom stall. Listening to people talk about me. Things like that didn't happen in real life. Only in those dumb junior high teen movies. Only this wasn't dumb, it was mortifying. And it was real.

"She's *not* Angie Johnson. She's Angie *Hoffman* now." The voice was familiar, but I couldn't tell who it belonged to. I could almost see whoever it was put her snotty little face close to the mirror and fake smile.

"She got *married?* No–oo. Really? When?"

"I don't know. That's just what I heard. I think it's kind of dreamy."

"Dreamy? Would you want to be big, fat, and pregnant like her?"

"Well...no."

"Just think, if you had a baby you'd have to get a *babysitter* to go to Homecoming."

There was a burst of high-pitched laughter. "That'd be weird."

"Totally."

"I thought she was always going to youth group at church and stuff."

"Duh. We go to youth group too, and we're not perfect."

More giggles. I could imagine the way they might be pushing at each other with their shoulders. Flinging their long hair away from their faces with a fast shake of their heads. Then, "Look what I've got."

Sudden quiet. A whisper. "Where'd you get that?"

I had no idea what they were looking at. Pot? A condom? Whatever it was I wanted to rush out into the bathroom and shout, "Don't! Don't do it! You have too many other things to do with your lives."

Instead, as I waited for the girls to finish their primping and leave, I stayed in the bathroom stall and sunk my face into my hands. Silent tears streamed down my face. I remembered going over to Julie Anderson's house last month. I helped cram her car full of clothes, her small stereo, a purple bedspread, a tub full of shoes, and a teddy bear she'd had since we were kids.

"Can you believe it? College." She gave me a big hug. "I wish you were going with me."

I wanted to say "I do, too," but I couldn't. I had to make

everyone think I was happy with the stupid decisions I'd made. "Have fun," I said instead. "E-mail me."

"Every day," she promised.

I stood on the sidewalk with her mom and waved at the taillights of her car until Julie turned the corner and said good-bye with a beep of her horn.

That could have been you.

That *should* have been me.

It really didn't matter that Julie didn't e-mail every day. Mark and I couldn't afford to get connected to the Internet anyway. Sometimes when his mom had us over for a meal, I'd get a chance to check my e-mail, but even in the two months since Julie had been gone I could tell things were different. She was changing. I wasn't. Well, certainly not in the same ways she was. She wrote about college classes and sorority rush. Cute guys in the dining center. What did I have to write back about? News flash! Marv Bender ordered a Long John with his coffee yesterday. I didn't know how boring my life was until I read how different Julie's was.

I wanted *her* life, not mine.

You've made your bed, now you're going to have to lie in it. Another thing my mom had said that night she'd found out I was pregnant.

Only now could I understand why my mom had pushed so hard for me to go to college. It wasn't that living in Brewster was bad. It was just that there was so much stuff outside of this little town I would never have a chance to find out for myself.

Mom knew all that already. She'd never left. Her parents had died when she was in high school. She worked in the café. Graduated from high school. Married my dad. Bought the café and worked some more. Then she had me. Sam. And worked. That was her life.

She must have had dreams.

I hung my head. It wasn't hard to see that *I* had been her dream. I was supposed to do all the things she never had a chance to do. Instead she was stuck watching me inch along the same boring path she'd already lived. I had a long way left to crawl. No wonder she'd pushed.

If only I could change things. Turn back the clock. Tell Mom I was sorry. Tell Mark I'd changed my mind about having sex in the first place.

The accusing words of those girls who had been in the bathroom minutes ago slapped me again: "I thought she was always going to youth group at church and stuff."

It was the *and stuff* that had gotten me in trouble. I had gone to youth group. And then I'd gone and done exactly as I pleased. I thought I knew best.

If only I could turn back the clock and tell God I knew I'd let Him down.

You can tell Me. I'm right here.

But I couldn't. I didn't deserve His understanding…or forgiveness, if that was even possible for the mess I'd made of my life. For the way I'd let down my parents. Ruined Mark's life, too. And this baby's.

I felt a sudden cramp. "*Ouch!*" I whispered. I wrapped my arms around my stomach and bent forward. There was strong, steady pressure. Muscles I didn't know I had clamped tight. "Ohhh…"

I wasn't due until next week, but I knew babies didn't always look at the calendar before they arrived.

More pressure. A rush of wetness.

My heart started pounding. A light mist of sweat coated my face. Like it or not, I was going to be a mom.

I was scared to death.

Libby

A person wouldn't need a very sharp knife to cut the tension between Vicky Johnson and her daughter, Angie, behind the Pumpkin Fest pie tables. As Bob and I stood in line waiting for our annual slices of pie, I watched as mother and daughter did a well-orchestrated dance around each other.

To the casual observer, their clumsy waltz may not have been noticeable, but I was still stinging a bit from the quick brush-off Vicky had given me about that recipe project a couple months ago. It was easy for me to read things into her practiced smile and quips, to see past the false frosting that coated her exchanges with Angie in this public place. I'd seen that look in Vicky's eyes myself. Heard the tone in her voice. It could sting like a finger on a hot stove.

I knew it was juvenile of me to take Vicky's rejection so personally. The early flare-up of my depression this fall had clouded many of my hours. I was still waiting to hear from the editor at Prism Publishing. Any high hopes I'd had, had long ago tumbled. My unpublished novel sat inside my computer, a defused bomb. There was nothing to excite me about those words any longer. Apparently nothing about them to excite anyone.

I'd been counting on Vicky's project to bring back the spark to my writing that had dimmed. Instead her dismissal had sent me home reeling. Maybe God didn't want me to write after all.

That day I'd tossed my purse onto the kitchen counter and watched as a tube of lipstick fell from the opening and rolled under the kitchen table. *Let it lie there.* I didn't feel like getting on my knees to retrieve it. Vicky's words had already knocked me flat.

"What do you want? Tell me!" I could talk to God out loud all I wanted. But did it matter? There was no one home.

I went into the living room and plopped myself into what I called my prayer chair. It was the soft seat I'd cried in many long nights after my friend Anne had died. This chair had embraced me through so many tough times. Brian's flirtation with huffing back in junior high. Emily's attempts to grow up by rebelling. Times when Bob and I didn't see eye-to-eye. My weeks and months of depression. Lately I'd spent time here praying over my children's future mates. Brian talked about Katie as if they were already related. Emily had made it clear I should quit asking about her and Mike.

"Mom, there is no me and Mike. Oka-ay?"

Okay.

But not really.

She couldn't stop me from praying. Then again, my track record with praying lately hadn't been good. Not that I hadn't tried. God just didn't seem to be listening.

I'm listening.

Then why doesn't it feel like it?

Are you praying for what you want? Or what I want?

I was hoping we both wanted the same thing.

I shifted in my chair, leaning forward to rest my face in my hands. What *was* this desire I'd felt all my life to put words on paper? To chronicle emotions and make sense of my life by writing it down? If *He* hadn't put it there, I was chasing an elusive mist.

I looked up at the ceiling as if God was hanging out there

waiting for me to speak to Him. What do You *want* from me, Lord?

I want you.

So He *was* there.

You have me.

I want all of you.

What was I supposed to do? Crawl up there to Him? I prayed again. *You have me.* But in all honesty I wasn't sure what that meant. I dipped my head. Closed my eyes. Tried again. *Here's the deal. If You don't want me to write, take this desire away from me. I'm tired of wrestling with it.*

There. If that wasn't giving it up, I didn't know what was.

A long, loud chord from the accordion across the gym brought me back to the Pumpkin Fest. Apparently God had heard my desperate prayer. I'd been having a heck of a time coming up with ideas for my column in the *Banner.*

Bob and I took a giant step forward. As soon as the Pearsons picked up their pie, we'd be next. Looking at Angie Johnson and her engorged stomach, I realized possibly my prayers for Emily and Mike had been answered in a way I hadn't expected. As much as I longed for Emily to return Mike's heart-on-his-sleeve feelings, there were downsides to young love. Just look at Angie.

I watched as she reached out a finger and stroked the Pearson baby's cheek. Did she have any idea what was in store for her in these coming months? After experiencing Vicky's brusque brush-off weeks ago, I had sudden empathy for her daughter. It couldn't be easy for this young woman, practically a child herself, to be having one without her mother's compassion.

I tried to imagine myself in Vicky's shoes. I knew I wouldn't be pleased to have my teenage daughter pregnant. Not at all. But I hoped I'd rise to the occasion and be there for my daughter.

I tried to imagine Emily in the same situation. Of course Emily was a few years older than Angie, important years of maturity Angie didn't yet have. I could see Emily ready to be married. To Mike.

Did you hear that, God?

Bob's hand on the small of my back urged me forward, in contrast to the thought that held my feet to the floor. What had happened to my vow to let God handle Emily's love life? Didn't I think He was big enough? Why did I always try taking these things back from God?

It's because you don't have enough to do.

A hollow space opened inside me as I stepped to the tables to order our pie. I knew my thought was true. I just hadn't had the nerve to actually put it into words. My days were filled with meaningless, make-do work. I hated what I was doing. Or, more to the point, what I *wasn't* doing.

I just didn't know what to do about it.

~

At least it was something to do. With scissors I cut a large corner off a bag of fresh cranberries and poured them into my blender. A little water. A few pulses of the blade. Dump it all in a strainer over the sink. So, okay, maybe those TV kitchen divas wouldn't use a technical term like *dump*. I shook the strainer, watching as the last drops of water dripped away. The good news was, I wasn't about to compete with any of them anytime soon. I picked up a knife and quartered an orange, tossing the tangy smelling chunks into the blender. Within seconds and a cup of sugar, I had the makings for Brian's favorite cranberry sauce.

It was time to make stuffing. I knew the cautions about stuffing the turkey a day ahead of time. Instead, I made my dressing in a separate casserole. I'd baste the spicy bread mix with turkey juices as it cooked tomorrow.

I opened my well-used Betty Crocker cookbook and turned to the gravy-stained page. Nine cups of bread cubes. I pulled a serrated knife from the drawer and started cubing odd bits of partially frozen bread I'd pulled from the freezer. Three hamburger buns left over from summer grilling. A half-loaf of wheat bread I'd discovered behind the buns. Two slices of homemade molasses bread. When had I made *that?* Maybe Thanksgiving was time to be thankful I could clean out my freezer. Goodness knew, I had little else to sing praises about.

Libby, that is not true! Your life is full of friends and family. You have a beautiful house. A husband who loves you.

But nothing to do.

I stabbed the point of my knife into a frozen corn muffin.

I looked at the fifteen-pound turkey lying stiffly in a roasting pan on top of the stove. "I'm *bored!*" As if a turkey cared.

I ripped at the bread with my knife. It wasn't that I was bored about getting Thanksgiving dinner ready for tomorrow. I was talking about my life.

At least this morning had been different. I had a reason to get out of bed. There were people to feed. Tonight Emily would be home from college. Near midnight Brian and Katie would arrive. There was actual *work* to do today. Meaningful, productive work.

I put the stopper in the sink and turned the cold water on full blast. As it ran, I added a cup of salt and stirred it into the icy water with my hand.

Most mornings I spent a good hour or more reading the daily newspaper as if I was the copyeditor. I knew there were people who would envy my life. No alarm to wake me at the crack of dawn. No time clock to punch in by eight in the morning. No boss to answer to. But I'd learned a life of leisure was a life without meaning. What was the purpose of sipping coffee? Slowly turning pages? Trying to avoid thinking about what I was—or *wasn't*—going to find to do once I'd read most every black-and-white page? Some days even the classifieds didn't escape my scrutiny... even though I didn't need a blessed thing.

Maybe what you need is a job.

I'd tossed that idea around more than once. The problem was, in a little town like Brewster, if I got a job simply to fill my time, I'd be taking a position from someone who actually *needed* the money. It didn't seem like a good idea for me to get a job and then spend my time feeling guilty that I'd taken work away from someone else. Bob's income let us live quite nicely, and I was thankful for that. But it left little incentive for me to get out and work. If only I had some grand plan. A deep desire to do... *something*.

You do. Write.

Argh! Stop! I didn't want to write. It was too hard. Too frustrating. Too...too...

I grabbed the thawed turkey and shoved it into the frigid salt water. It felt good to thrust it under the water. To drown my exasperation. To hold it underwater and watch thick bubbles float to the surface and burst. Just like my writing dreams.

Maybe I would make a good Julia Child, after all. *Join Olivia Marsden for her new program, "Cooking as Psychotherapy."*

I let the turkey gurgle. The big bird had two hours to luxuriate in its icy brine-bath before I had to do anything more with it. In the meantime, I would mix together the ingredients for Betty Crocker's stuffing. Over the years I'd pared this Thanksgiving meal down to a science. I did most everything the day before, that way I could enjoy the actual holiday and visit with whatever company we happened to have. This year our table would be smaller than some years. Emily was bringing a college suitemate home. Brian was bringing Katie. I'd already given myself the *talk*.

The conversation where I told myself if Brian liked this young woman as much as he seemed to, I'd better, too. The last thing I wanted was a potential daughter-in-law who hated my guts.

Speaking of which… I plunged my hand into the turkey-water, grubbing around under the slimy skin until I found the bag of giblets hidden there. I'd learned that embarrassing lesson on Bob's and my first Thanksgiving. My mom and Bob's parents had surrounded our table that year. Brian was nothing but a mashed-potato-eating baby at the time. I pulled my perfectly browned turkey from the oven, transferred it to a platter, and brought it to the table proud-as-a-pilgrim. Everything was perfect, just as I'd planned. I handed Bob the long carving knife and fork set we'd gotten as a wedding gift. We posed as my mother took a photo.

"Start there." I pointed to the bulging brown succulent skin. Already my father-in-law was holding out his plate.

Bob carved off a slice. Of skin. And paper. And small portions of liver and gizzard. My mom took another photo of my drop-jawed expression. Then, as I pulled the forgotten turkey giblet bag from the cooked bird, we laughed away the nervousness of perfection and carved the turkey for real.

I hoped Brian's Katie would let go of her veil of perfectionism during this visit. It would be downright stressful, not to mention hard to swallow a good meal, to have her appraising eyes and perfect manners serve as a side dish to our family dinner.

I plucked the innards bag from the water. Funny as it had been the first time, I wouldn't make that mistake again. I'd chop up all but the liver and use the pieces in my gravy broth. As I tucked the bag into the fridge for later, I was reminded that none of our parents were left to join us for holidays. I should be thankful the kids wanted to bring friends home with them. It would be awful if they didn't feel welcome here.

That's why I had to have everything just-so by the time they arrived. I touched a finger to the bread cubes I'd put in a large Tupperware bowl. They were thawed, ready to add dried sage and thyme. Next I rinsed the celery, then chopped the crisp stems, leaves and all. More flavor that way. Quickly I peeled and chopped the onions, keeping my mouth clamped shut. I'd tried every trick in the book to keep onion-induced tears at bay. None were surefire, but I kept checking. Now for the best part, sautéing the vegetables in a thick chicken broth. Here was where Betty Crocker and I parted recipes. She advised butter, but I cut the fat years ago. There hadn't been anyone yet who didn't like my dressing. I opened the cupboard and reached for the chicken base. The space where I usually kept it was empty. Shoot! I'd forgotten to write it on the need-to-get list I kept on the fridge.

I looked at the clock. It was only mid-morning. I had plenty of time to run to the store. I'd stop at the post office and pick up the mail while I was out. It would save me a trip later. But first I needed to get clean sheets on Brian's bed. He'd be on a spare bed down in the basement. Katie would be sleeping in his old room. I wondered if she would notice the basketball trophies he'd won in high school...or just any tiny dust particles I might have missed.

Stop it! She's not even here and you're picking her apart.

As I slipped into my coat, I didn't feel too guilty. Katie was probably doing the same thing to me.

~

The thin, unopened envelope from Prism Publishing sat between the pages of a thick book beside my computer. Just the thought of it there hung over my Thanksgiving table as if it were an albatross hovering over a boat loaded with sardines. Every few seconds the thought of that envelope would swoop through my mind and peck at my thoughts. I should have known a heavy book would do nothing but hide the actual envelope. The makeshift paperweight could do nothing at all to the rampant speculation that dove and spiraled through my mind.

I pushed a bite of sweet potatoes onto my fork and lifted it to my mouth. Try concentrating on sweet potatoes when the end of your life's dream might be sitting in a book in the next room. I wasn't sure if I could swallow.

It could be good news.

Yeah. And I was going to raise a turkey in my backyard for Thanksgiving next year. I needed to forget about that letter and get my head back into the here and now. "Would anyone like anything?"

"Please pass the stuffing." Katie gave me a look I couldn't read. "It's very good."

Well, there she went, trying to be too perfect, again. I handed her the half-empty bowl. "I'm glad you like it. May I pass you anything else, Dear?"

Dear? Dear! Since when do you talk like June Cleaver?

"No. Everything is delicious. You went to so much work."

"Thank you." I filled my mouth with mashed potatoes so I wouldn't say anything I shouldn't. I chewed, trying to stuff away the thought of that thin envelope lurking in the next room.

"I'll have some, too." Sara, Emily's friend, held out her hand for the bowl of stuffing. She seemed as smitten with Katie as the rest of the traitors around the table.

What is wrong with you? Brian brings home a girl with good manners, a young woman who is obviously intelligent and certainly seems to love your son, and you do nothing but dislike her. Some Christian you are.

I felt the weight of conviction press on my shoulders. Busted. Again. I knew the Bible said to pour heaping coals of kindness on my enemy's head. Unfortunately, kindness wasn't exactly what I felt like dumping on the young woman at my table. *Grow up.* I knew Katie wasn't exactly an enemy—

Except for the fact she's stealing Brian's heart.

Oh, so that's it?

Get a grip. You certainly don't want him to be a mama's boy his whole life, do you?

Of course I didn't. I spooned a bite of tart cranberry sauce into my mouth. If I truly wasn't upset that Brian's affections were being absorbed by Katie, then what was it?

Behind the guise of taking a sip from my glass of water, I watched as Katie dabbed at her mouth with her napkin and then picked up her own water glass and swallowed. Sure enough, I'd forgotten that old rule about wiping my mouth first. She must have read the book on manners from cover to cover. She picked up her carefully placed silverware and began eating again. I'd watched enough Dr. Phil to know that qualities in others that screeched like fingernails on a chalkboard were signs of…*something.* For the life of me I couldn't remember what. And it seemed key to figuring out this young woman across the table from me.

"Can I have some more corn?" Sara, Emily's friend, didn't wait for a response, she simply reached across my plate and grabbed the bowl. Now that's how a kid should act. A person felt comfortable around someone who wasn't trying so hard.

Actually, she should have said "may I" and waited for you to pass the bowl.

I should just change my name to "Nitpick."

Before I was tempted to say anything, Sara chimed in around the corn in her mouth. "Are we going to see Mike while we're here?"

Mike? Since when were we allowed to talk about him?

Emily shrugged a shoulder. "Maybe. I suppose we could call him and see if he wants to stop over later."

Maybe? Maybe! Of course we could! I took a small bite of sweet potatoes, hoping they would sugar-coat my words. "That might be nice. I haven't seen Mike for so long. What's he doing these days?"

Sara reached for the cranberry sauce. "He sits by me in Lit class. He is *so* funny." She spooned the red berries onto her plate. "And nice."

I couldn't help but look at Emily. Hadn't we had this conversation before? How many people did it take to tell her what a good guy Mike was? She acknowledged my gaze with a wide-eyed look. *Quiet, Mom.*

Sara forked a small piece of turkey from the platter in front of her. So, okay, maybe good table manners weren't so bad. But as long as she was talking about Mike, let the kid eat. "He used to stop by our dorm room all the time." She put the turkey in her mouth and chewed as she spoke. "But I still see him in class. He said he was going to be in Brewster for Thanksgiving. We should call him when we're done eating."

Fine by me. I pretended not to look at Emily as she murmured a nonchalant, "Sure. Whatever."

Instead of bouncing my head in agreement, an over-eager puppy happy for scraps, I pushed my chair away from the table. "I'm going to start getting the pie ready."

"You didn't make the pie, too? Did you?" Katie again.

She'd caught me. "Don't worry, Katie—" *It's Kate. Kate.* Brian had reminded me twice. "Uh, *Kate.* I had Vicky's Café bake the pies. Pumpkin pie is their specialty. Why try to compete when the experts are living right here? I'll go get it."

I escaped to the kitchen with my dirty plate in hand. *Compete?* Why had I said compete? As if there was something wrong with ordering a pie instead of baking it myself. And why had I thought her question was meant to "catch" me? She was probably just making conversation.

Touchy, aren't we?

Anyone would be touchy when the girl of their son's dreams was getting on a mother's nerves at one table and an unopened letter holding a different dream sat on another.

A small elephant of anxiety shifted onto my chest. It had been a good year or so since I'd felt that heavy weight compress. I'd forgotten just how leaden panic could feel. Instantly the fear-of-fear zinged down my arms.

Breathe.

I filled my lungs.

Again.

There. The pressure was going away just a little. Why now? I didn't need a reccurrence of my panic attacks for dessert.

You're afraid of what's in that letter. You're worried about Brian's feelings for Katie. You wish Emily would have feelings for Mike.

I picked up the knife to slice the pie. I knew all of that. I just didn't want to think about it. Not now. The elephant shifted.

And this is what happens when you try to stuff those things away.

Touché. Dr. Sullivan would be proud of me for recognizing the psychology behind this mild panic attack so quickly. I promised myself I'd dissect these feelings later, over dirty dishes. Proud of my self-diagnosis, I pulled the knife through the soft filling. Half. Quarter. Eight pieces. We could each have a slice, and if Mike stopped over there would be a couple pieces to entice him to stay longer.

I transferred the slices onto six small plates and then spooned white balloons of Cool Whip on each section. If Katie—*Kate*—asked, I'd fess up and say, "Nope, it's not real whipped cream."

Why does it matter so much?

"Do you need some help?" Kate walked into the kitchen carrying a stack of scraped plates. Her reputation as Miss Perfect was intact. She set them on the counter.

"I've got it all covered."

Who, exactly, is trying to be perfect around here?

Vowing to stop my mental carping, I held two of the plates of pie out to her. "Would you mind taking these to the table?"

Are you really wanting her help or just trying to get her away from you?

Sheesh. My conscience was working overtime, considering it was a holiday.

Katie took the two plates in her hands. "I'd really like the recipe for your stuffing. Do you give it out? My mom could sure use it." She gave me a half-smile.

So my cooking was better than her mother's? I half-smiled back. Maybe I could concede one point to her.

Oh, so we're keeping score?

No. We're having a family Thanksgiving dinner. As Katie took the pie slices to the table, I pushed the plastic Cool Whip cover back onto the bowl and put it in the fridge. I covered the two leftover pieces of pie with plastic wrap and put them in the fridge, too. *Lord, help me. I need to change my attitude.*

What was it about that girl that brought my claws out? I reached for the dessert plates.

"Here, I'll get those." Katie's fingers brushed against mine as she picked up two of the plates.

"Oh, I can get them my—" A sudden flashback of the first time Bob had taken me to his parents' house stopped my sentence.

"Could you?" Bob's mom held out a bottle of store-brand salad dressing and pointed to a bowl of lettuce on the counter. When I'd finished tossing the salad she had me pick olives out of a jar with a baby fork. "That's Bob's fork from when he was just starting to eat solid foods," she explained, telling me a story about Bob's dislike of green beans and the precious way he'd line the edge of his plate with them instead of putting them in his mouth.

"He pretended they were *geen-achinces.*" She stirred something on the stove.

I gave her a sideways look.

"Green machines," she quickly interpreted, laughing. "Army trucks or something." She waved a long-handled spoon through the air as she talked. "I hardly ever made green beans because he hated them so much. I wonder if he still dislikes them?"

"Oh, I don't think so," I chimed in, pleased as a girlfriend with inside knowledge of the man we both loved.

His mom gave me a quick smile. "I'm glad you're here." She reached out and squeezed my hand.

So unlike the way I was treating Katie. All I'd done was pick her apart. Think of all the things I didn't like about her. What if this relationship was heading where it seemed to be? If I kept acting the way I was, would I ever spend another holiday with my son?

And whose fault would that be?

Mine.

I pulled my hands away from the plates, holding out one palm toward Katie. An invitation. A peace offering. "If you wouldn't mind getting the rest of these on the table, I'll get some coffee started."

So, okay, it wasn't exactly a warm hug. But it was a start.

"That was great." Brian pushed his empty pie plate toward the center of the table and leaned back in his chair, tilting the two front legs off the floor.

I bit my tongue. The kid was twenty-five. Old enough to know I didn't like his old habit. Leaving soon enough so I could choke back my nagging. I hoped he wouldn't fall. Or break the chair before he left. If I had been Bob's mom, I would turn Brian's habit into a cute story about the time he did fall and needed three stitches on the back of his head. Unfortunately I didn't have her knack for making pleasant stories out of irritations.

While I strangled on what I was determined not to say, Katie reached out and put her hand on Brian's knee. Instantly he put the two front legs of the chair back on the floor and shot me a sheepish look.

Give the girl another point.

If I had still been keeping score, I would have. Instead I mouthed, "Thank you."

She smiled back at me.

A satisfied silence blanketed the table. Stomachs were full. The only thing left was dishes, and it was apparent no one was in a hurry to make the first move.

"Should we call Mike now?" Sara was determined.

"Sure. Whatever." Emily pushed back her chair.

"Just a minute." Brian was sitting up straight now. "I, uh." He glanced at Katie, then took a quick look around the table. It wasn't like Brian to be nervous, and yet I could sense he was. Brian gave Katie a twitching smile. "Uh, there's something I'd...uh, *we'd* like to tell you." He took her hand in his.

Uh-oh. A steady, low drum-beat began to pulse in my ears. It didn't take a genius to know what was coming. All it took was a mom who could read her son like a familiar script. I pasted a pleasant look on my face and folded my hands at the edge of the table as if I were Meryl Streep about to play the part of a lifetime. In my head I rehearsed my next lines while I waited for the director to call the next shot.

"I knew it!" Emily pulled her chair back to the table as if she were waiting for a poker dealer to hand her an ace.

"What?" Sara looked confused.

"They're going to get married." Emily grinned like an over-carved pumpkin. "Isn't that right?" She beamed her smile at Brian and Kate.

"Way to give away the punchline, Em." Brian rolled his eyes in spite of his goofy grin. He threaded his fingers into Katie's and rested their twined hands on the edge of the table. He took a breath. "We're—"

"When is it going to be?" Emily was sitting on her hands, trying to contain her excitement. She leaned forward. "Will it be here? Did you get her a ring?" She turned to Katie. "How did he ask you? Brian can be such a *guy* sometimes. Was it romantic?"

It was a good thing Emily was talking because I couldn't think of a thing to say.

"Sheesh, Emily. Stop already." Brian still knew how to quiet his little sister.

Emily wiggled her fingers as if she could pull words from her brother's mouth. "So…tell." She bit her lips together as she waited for details.

"I will if you give me a chance." Again the goofy grin spread across Brian's face. "I'll be done with my master's program in May. We're thinking we'd like to get married in…"

"…August." Katie was already finishing his sentences.

"Yes!" Emily shot both fists in the air.

Bob pushed his chair away from the table and stood. So did Brian. They shook hands as if they'd just signed a million-dollar business deal. "Congratulations, Son." He clapped him on the back and then pulled him into a quick, manlike shoulder hug. Bob moved to Kate and gave her a kiss on the cheek. Oh, if only I could be so magnanimous.

My cameo in this surreal reality show was next. A Flamenco dancer had started tapping a staccato beat on my heart. Everyone was looking my way. The lines I knew I should have memorized were gone.

As if I was watching the scene unfold in slow-motion through the lens of a large camera, I pulled my chair away from the table and stood. I opened my mouth. Closed it. I fanned my hands out in front of me. From somewhere deep inside my head I heard the stage manager whisper, "*Smile.*" I turned up the corners of my mouth. *Say something.*

"Why...I'm..."

Happy. Overjoyed. Delighted. They were all possibilities. None of them true. I settled for one that was.

"...speechless."

"Oh, Mom, didn't you see it coming?" Emily was standing now, too. "I could tell just by the way they were looking at each other all day that something was up. It's about time is all I can say. My biological bridesmaid clock is ticking."

Leave it to Emily to turn her walk-on role into a scene-stealer. A burst of laughter from the others finally cleared the fuzzy lens that had clouded my view of the unfolding action. I knew exactly what I needed to say now. "Emily! You have no idea if Katie plans to ask you to be a bridesmaid."

"Of course I do. I'm Brian's only sister, and she doesn't have any sisters. It's a no-brainer."

I felt like bopping my brash youngest child on the behind. As critical as I'd been of Katie, I suddenly wondered what she thought of *us*.

Instead of being judgmental, I possibly had some fence-mending to do. As I walked around the table I held my arms open to Brian. "I'm happy for you."

Are you sure?

Yes, I was. If my son was happy, so was his mom. At least she would try to be. I turned to his...fiancée. "Katie."

From behind my back Brian spoke. "Mom, it's *Kate.*"

"Well, see." I smiled at Kate. "Already he's standing up for you. I knew I raised a smart son."

Kate gave me a quick hug. "Thanks," she said, even though I hadn't actually congratulated her.

Maybe she's thanking you for letting her have your son.

The Flamenco dancer stomped. Just once. Hard. Smack in the middle of my heart.

I took a deep breath, trying to loosen the sharp heel of the boot that was stuck in my chest.

An awkward silence hung in the air. They were waiting for me to say something more. I cleared my throat. "I know it's a mother-in-law's job to wear beige and keep her mouth shut. But I want to say one thing before I close it for good."

As if you've ever done that.

For once in my life I would try.

"Kate." At least I'd gotten her name right this time. "I want you to feel free to pick *whomever* you want for your bridesmaids." I glared at Emily. "This is *your* wedding."

I turned to look at my son standing beside me. When had he gotten so tall? So handsome? Old enough to be getting married? And just when had I turned into a possessive, nit-picking shrew? *Lord, forgive me.*

All along, all I'd ever tried to do was to raise Brian to follow his heart. I'd prayed for his future mate for years. No matter that Kate was not my pick. Following his heart was still my wish for him. And if he wanted Katie... Well, then. I knew my closing line.

My throat grew tight. My eyes stung. I would get these words out. I would. I coughed, pushing aside my sudden emotion. "All I ask is that you love Brian as much as I—as much as *we*—do."

Katie was blinking back at me. We were only standing by

our messy dining room table, but the setting felt as sacred as if we were in church. She coughed, much as I had. "I will. I do. I promise."

It was all I could ask of this young woman who would soon be my daughter-in-law. Like it. Or not.

~

Finally, this night was just about over. I pulled back the king-sized blankets and slid into bed. The cool, crisp sheets felt good after a long day in the kitchen. I arranged three pillows behind me and pulled the heavy book onto my lap. I had no interest in the words between the pages, only the envelope tucked inside. It was going to take time for me to get up the nerve to open the letter—if I would do it tonight at all.

I brushed my toes against the soft comfort of my sheets. I knew I could count on the quiet of my bedroom to do some much-needed mulling. The tryptophan in the turkey had done its trick, Bob was dozing in his recliner in the family room. Brian and Katie had driven to Carlton to see a late movie. And Sara, Emily, and Mike were pretending to watch a DVD in the rec room in the basement. Every now and then a loud screech of laughter would penetrate through the floorboards. I hadn't realized Sara had such a high-pitched cackle. Somehow I had the impression her hilarity had nothing to do with the movie.

As I'd emptied the last of the Thanksgiving dishes from the dishwasher, I'd been tempted to call downstairs and tell the kids to pipe down, but the noise hadn't managed to disturb Bob's light snoring one iota. And I knew I had a good hour ahead of me where I would attempt to read, but would, instead, go over the events of the night with a fine-toothed turkey feather. Let the kids have their fun.

By the time I crawled into bed, Mike had already devoured

the two leftover pieces of pumpkin pie. For as long as they'd lasted, I could hardly call them *leftovers*. I smiled as I recalled the way Mike had bounded into our house and wished us all, "*Happy beginning of the Christmas season!*" Leave it to Mike to always look ahead.

He'd walked in just as Brian and Katie were leaving. He shook Brian's hand as if they were long-lost buddies, then did a silly little bow that made us all laugh as he was introduced to Katie. "Pleased to meet you, Madam." Only Mike could get away saying something like that and make it seem perfectly natural.

Katie caught Emily's eye. "I like this guy!"

Well, there was *something* Katie and I had in common.

I wished Emily did, too.

"Mike! Hi!" Sara opened her arms as if she'd been marooned on a desert island and Mike was the first sign of civilization she'd seen in months.

"Miss Sara." Mike couldn't avoid her boisterous hug.

He pulled away from the embrace but didn't move toward Emily. Instead he turned to me. "Mrs. M." He gave me a snappy little salute as if I were the captain of this rag-tag crew.

I couldn't help but laugh and give him a hug. "It's good to see you, Mike. How's school? Did you have a nice Thanksgiving?"

We chatted as Emily shuffled her feet on the sidelines. I couldn't discern the vibe between them or if there was one at all. Had Mike finally taken Emily's friends-only attitude to heart? It seemed so, and for some reason that made me feel unexpectedly sad.

"Let's go downstairs and watch the movie." Sara was bouncing on her toes, eager to stop the chit-chat and get on with the night.

Mike turned to Sara. "Great." Almost as an afterthought he added, "Hey, Em."

"Hey, Mike." She lifted her hand in a halfhearted wave. What was that expression on her face? Indifference? Confusion? A wish to be with someone else? From the few spare moments I'd had to talk to Emily since she'd been home, it didn't sound as if there had been any hot dates recently. Maybe tonight she'd see Mike for the good guy he was. Or maybe not. Already this night hadn't exactly gone as I'd planned. An engagement announcement had never been on my Thanksgiving dinner menu.

Your will, Lord. Not mine. If only I could take my prayer to heart.

Sara led the way to the basement, making sure Mike was right behind her. Emily tagged along as if she were the guest. I'd been trying to decipher the mixed signals coming from the basement for the past hour and a half.

I leaned my head back against the pillows. The announcement of Brian's engagement had sent me into a self-pitying funk. I'd always imagined Brian's wife, my future daughter-in-law, as someone I could take on fun-runs to the mall in Carlton. Emily, his wife, and I would do girly things together. Try on lipstick, spritz perfume, go out to lunch and gab a couple hours away. Somehow I couldn't imagine doing any of this with Katie. Would every future holiday be dampened by my dislike of her?

Stop it!

My feelings toward Katie were ridiculous. I should be happy for Brian; instead, I was doing nothing but focusing on *my* desires.

What about Mine?

Ah, yes, there was that. I needed to put this in God's hands. *Again.* I closed my eyes and murmured a quick prayer. I would let Him deal with my unfounded animosity toward Katie. I would let God handle Brian's future.

Even with my eyes closed, I sensed the weight of the thin

envelope sandwiched in the book on my lap. I tossed in a few words about my future. *What about me, Lord? Do You have any plans for me?*

A lump pushed its way into my throat. It was too late tonight for me to start this familiar lament. It had already been an unexpectedly eventful day. Maybe I should leave opening this letter until tomorrow…*or never.*

Or never. Now that sounded like a plan. At the thought, a fist-sized lump settled in the bottom of my stomach. What would I dream about then?

A muffled shriek of laughter from two floors below penetrated my gloom. I might as well get this over with. My dreams for Brian had already been shattered tonight. Emily was handing Mike to Sara on a silver platter. What did I have to lose? I opened the book on my lap to where the envelope lay.

Another loud burst of laughter. What in the world were those kids doing? Sara, the noisemaker, in particular. I gave my head a shake. I was supposed to be opening an envelope, not dissecting relationships I had no business sticking my nose into. The book was digging into my thigh. I shifted the heavy pages on my lap. I wasn't sure if it was the weight of the book or what I suspected was in the envelope inside that made it so unwieldy.

Just open the letter and get it over with.

Easier said than done. This whole day, all the while I'd acted as if I was engrossed in Thanksgiving preparations and the conversation around the table, the letter hidden in this book had pecked at my mind. I already knew what it must say. If it was good news, if that editor at Prism Publishing had loved my manuscript, I had a strong hunch I would have gotten a phone call, an e-mail, something more than a standard, number-ten business envelope.

Open it. What do you have to lose?

Nothing. Not anymore. Brian's announcement of wedding plans had already sent me reeling. I had surmised he and Katie were serious, but I certainly hadn't expected I'd be feeding my daughter-in-law-to-be today. If anything, I'd hoped Brian would ask Bob and me our opinion about his getting married before he popped the question.

What would you have said?

What indeed? I could hardly point out Katie's impeccable manners, her polite conversation, and her stylish-if-conservative way of dressing as red flags to the relationship. And I highly doubted flat-out declaring, "I just don't like her," would do much to endear me to my only son.

Their announcement had curled into a lead ball in the pit of my stomach that had weighed there the rest of the evening, waiting for me to have a chance to digest the news. I was supposed to be doing that now. If only I could pinpoint my thoughts...

You could try praying some more.

Or maybe the weight was simply too much turkey.

I doubt it.

Why was I so afraid to examine these thoughts? In the past, prayer had often helped me make sense of things that were troubling me. Why couldn't I bow my head and talk to God about Katie? About my feelings for her?

Don't you mean against *her?*

I was ashamed of the way I felt toward this young woman. She had perfect manners. Her speech was polite and measured. She was smart, and she laughed at Brian's dry wit. Mine, too, come to think of it. Any mother would be delighted to welcome Katie into their family. Except me.

Tell Me.

I couldn't. I was embarrassed to confess my childish dislike.

I already know.

Then how could He stand to listen to me whine? How could He put up with my pettiness? If I prayed about this I'd have to admit it all. Who I really was under my polished exterior. Critical. Unkind.

I can handle it.

Could I?

Not tonight. I'd open the envelope, read the verdict, then let my subconscious sort things out overnight. Tomorrow had to be better.

I slid one thumb under the gummed flap of the letter.

"Mom?" There was a soft knock followed by Emily poking her head around the doorframe. "Are you sleeping?"

Quickly, I pushed the envelope into the fold of the book and closed it. "No. What? Come in. I was just reading." *Between the lines of this whole night.* Emily didn't need to know the particulars of the plot I was trying to unravel. "Did Mike leave?"

Emily sat on Bob's side of the bed, slid onto her side and propped her head up on a bent elbow. "No. He's still downstairs with Sara."

"Are you having fun?"

Emily shrugged a shoulder. "Sara is."

I tried to keep my eyebrows from saying, *I figured as much.* I reached out and smoothed my fingers over her slightly mussy hair. It wasn't hard to see that somehow this night hadn't gone exactly as she'd expected either. "Want me to tickle your back?" Back tickles had been Emily's favorite when she was a preteen. She'd requested them less and less as she grew older, and since she'd gone off to college…well, I couldn't remember the last time she'd asked. Maybe she'd gotten too old for my offer.

I needn't have worried. In a blink Emily had unbuttoned her blouse, unhooked her bra, turned on her stomach and lifted her white cotton blouse to bare her smooth back. She turned her face toward me and smiled. "Sure."

I pushed my backrest of pillows closer to her and with the very tips of my fingers I began stroking her back. Up, down, up down. Slow and soft. She closed her eyes and sighed deeply. After a time she turned her head away from me. I could feel her muscles tense as she drew in a breath.

"Mom?"

"Hmmm?"

"Have you ever thought you wanted something and then when you got it, you weren't so sure?"

As if on cue, Sara's high-pitched laughter worked its way through the carpet. I could understand why Emily had found her way upstairs. This had to do with Mike. If my daughter were any more transparent she'd be invisible. But, of course, I didn't dare let on I knew what she was talking about. Even so, I had no trouble adding my own deliberations of the night to her question. There was no doubt I wanted Brian to be happy, but now that he was…I wasn't. I'd wanted to hear from that publisher and now that the answer was lying in my lap I didn't dare look at it.

"Oh, yes," I answered my troubled daughter, sighing myself.

She sighed, again, a different sort of exhalation than before. This one held puzzle and possible heartache, much the same as mine. How could I possibly comfort Emily when I was confused about the course of life myself?

My fingers continued their slow trek around her back, trying to understand how one night could hold so many conflicting emotions. Joy at having my family together. Thankfulness for the plenty of food on our table and the blessings of the past year. Disappointment over Brian's pick of his future mate. Empathy for Emily and the confusing emotions she was dealing with. Disillusionment over the way I kept picking Katie to pieces. I'd thought myself bigger than that. And then there was my dream of writing a novel more-than-likely lying inert at my elbow. The bad seemed to outweigh the good tonight. Some way to end Thanksgiving.

"M?" Emily's sleepy voice broke through my cynical thought.

"What?"

"The letter you just tickled on my back. It was an 'M,' right?"

Instantly I knew she was remembering the old spelling game I used to play to test her on her elementary spelling words, tickling the words, letter-by-letter on her back until she knew them by heart...or by back, anyway. I hadn't intended the wanderings of my fingers to spell anything tonight. But if Emily was playing, so would I.

My mind scanned a mental dictionary trying to come up with an "M" word. I didn't dare spell M-i-k-e. Emily would bolt from the bed for sure. I glanced at the clock. Midnight was too obvious. Thanksgiving was officially over, Christmas on the way.

"E?"

"Yup."

"R...R...Y Merry Christmas!"

I gave her back a soft swat. "Smarty pants."

Smiling, Emily turned over onto her back. She slipped one arm from the sleeve of her shirt. "Will you tickle my arm?" Her eyes pleaded for a few more minutes of this rare treat. What was a mother to do? I moved my fingers to her arm.

"Speaking of 'Merry,'" she said looking at the ceiling. "I know this is a different kind, but weren't you excited when Brian said he and Kate were getting married?" She turned her head to look at me. Her voice held the enthusiasm of a young girl's idea of true love. "I was. She's perfect for Brian. She's so pretty and nice."

Nice? Not the first word I would have used to describe Katie.

Not even the second. My daughter's big heart put me to shame. A vague, noncommittal smile was all I could manage.

"Don't you think so?" She wasn't going to let this drop.

My hand froze, suspended over Emily's arm as my thoughts scrambled to find something to say that would hold enough truth to satisfy Emily and not reveal my real feelings about Katie. "I was so surprised at their announcement. I've hardly had time to think about a wedding." There, that should do it. I started slowly tickling Emily again.

"Oh, I didn't mean their wedding. I meant that Kate is just right for Brian. Don't you think so?"

Why was she pressing this? Did she sense my true feelings? One look at the dreamy expression on her face told me no. All she wanted was confirmation that her brother had found the perfect woman. What was I supposed to say instead?

"I really don't know her very well yet."

Pulling her loose blouse closed, Emily sat up as if she'd been pinched in the rear. "Mom!" She stared at me wide-eyed. "What do you mean you don't know her?" She paused before she dropped her bombshell. "Kate is *exactly* like *you!*"

Her words hit me with the force of mortar fire. A bull's-eye straight to my heart. Speaking of which, mine was thudding as if it were a time bomb, counting down the seconds until explosion. *Kate is exactly like you!* There was no time to duck. Nowhere to hide. *Boom!* I was hit with raw truth. That was why she seemed so familiar. She *was* just like me. Trying too hard. Hiding her true feelings behind a façade of perfection. I could only guess that our surface similarities went deeper. The critical thoughts about Katie that I'd shot off as if they were internal machine gunfire might possibly be heading right back my way from her side of the combat zone. I didn't even want to imagine what Katie might be thinking about me as her future mother-in-law.

I stared at Emily, certain I'd see her assessing the damage. Emily was buttoning her blouse as if she'd had no part in this explosion. Or maybe I should say *implosion*. My carefully erected house-of-cards had fallen in on itself and I was left lying under the rubble suffocating.

"Even Sara said that you and Kate seem so much alike." Emily tugged at the hem of her blouse and then ran her fingers through her hair. "You're both pretty and have cool taste in clothes. And both of you have the same sense of humor. Killer."

Oh, if only she knew… Then again, I was glad she didn't. So far everything Emily had pointed out were good qualities. If she'd been perceptive enough to notice those, surely she'd observed more. I waited for what must be coming.

"I guess it's true what they say about guys marrying women like their moms." She smiled as if this was good news.

Who was this child of mine to be repeating old platitudes as if they were new? As if I'd never heard that old saying a million times.

Then why didn't you realize it?

Why indeed? Maybe I simply hadn't wanted to see myself face-to-face. Maybe I didn't want to look into Katie's young eyes and see all the issues I struggled with over the years staring back at me. What a battlefield I'd left behind…and still faced.

I felt Emily move off the bed. She stood at the edge of the bed, smoothing her blouse with her hands as if she were clueless that a war still raged just a few feet away. "I'm going to go downstairs and tell Sara I'm going to bed." Suddenly she sat back down on the bed, her back to me. "Mom, do you think Mike likes Sara?"

Another loaded question. Would the shooting never stop? It appeared my young daughter was in a skirmish of her own.

"Oh goodness," I said, scrambling for the right words. I had a feeling this was a battle Emily may have already lost. "It's hard not to like Sara. She's so nice." Not much different than what I used to tell Emily about Mike.

Emily traced her finger along the quilting on the bedspread. "Yeah," she said, "I know. It just seems weird."

As hard as I tried, I couldn't hold back. "I thought you wanted Mike for a *friend*."

"I do. I did. I—"

Muffled footsteps. Voices. Sara's extra-loud peal of laughter.

Emily stood up. "I guess I'll go make sure they turned everything off down in the basement."

Or was she making sure Sara and Mike didn't have a moment alone by the door? I didn't have the heart to tell Emily that this time she might have been outmaneuvered by her own battle plan.

I was alone. Again. Finally. My heart heavier, if possible, than it was when I climbed into bed. There was absolutely nothing that could make this night any worse. I flipped open the heavy book and picked up the letter from Prism Publishing. Prism. How appropriate. This night had already exploded into a million tiny fragments. Shards too small to see, but slivers that cut to the quick. Brian's marriage announcement. The unwelcome discovery that Katie and I were practically clones. And now the knowledge that Mike had moved on…taking Emily at her word. Words she seemed to be wishing she could take back. There could be nothing in this letter I hadn't already anticipated. I knew it would say, "Thanks, but no thanks." I might as well read the words and put my imagination out of its misery.

I pushed my thumb under the flap. "Ouch!" I pulled out my thumb and sucked at the cuticle. A paper cut. Why didn't it surprise me?

I tried again, tugging my way through the flap with all the frustration of the night. I pulled the letter from its prison and unfolded it. The old child's taunt played through my mind as I opened the creamy paper. *Sticks and stones may break my bones but words will never hurt me.* Rejection could sting, but I'd get over it.

My eyes scanned the first paragraph. Pretty much what I'd expected.

> I must apologize for taking so long to respond to your manuscript.

Blah. Blah. Feeble excuse. These people had to know there was a living, breathing, high-hoping real person on the other end of a manuscript. *Get to the point.*

> It was with the highest of hopes that I opened your manuscript. My friend, Joan Koller, had spoken so highly of your talent so I was anticipating a great read.

As hard as I tried I couldn't stop the little bubble of renewed hope that began rising in my chest. Maybe...just maybe...

> However, my anticipation didn't last long. I feel I must tell you that if you ever hope to be published you need to go back and learn the craft of writing.

No one had told me there would be a knife in this envelope. That it would stab with the sharpest of points and then twist full-circle. The letter fell to my lap as I cupped one hand protectively over my heart. Surely something inside me was being slashed to shreds.

I leaned my head back against the pillows and tried to absorb what I'd read. I'd expected rejection, but not this. I could understand if my story wasn't what they were looking for. If they'd published something similar recently. Even if she'd preferred to see the story written from another point of view. But how was it possible that Joan Koller had been enthralled with my story, and this...this... I couldn't think of a word to describe this editor in a way that was as hurtful as the words she'd written.

You need to go back and learn the craft of writing. The words were seared in my mind. *You need to go back and learn the craft of writing.* Would I ever think another positive thought from here on out?

Writing that novel had been my lifelong dream. My passion. And now I was left with this. *You need to go back and learn the craft of writing.*

Like a criminal returning to the scene of a horrific crime, I lifted the letter again. Maybe I'd read it wrong. Maybe this strange, off-kilter night had skewed my eyes. No, there it was in black and white. *You need to go back and learn the craft of writing.*

A bizarre sort of mewling started deep in my throat. "Ohhhhh...agghhh..." I was strangling on tears and gasps, trying to inhale and exhale at the same time. Only when Anne died had I felt this sort of desolation. Heard a similar cry. It was the sound of a dream being ripped from my body.

Angie

"Mo–ooommmm!" I bit my teeth together and tried to breathe through the contraction. I hadn't meant to cry out for my mom. She was the last person I wanted here at the hospital.

"It's okay, Angie." Mark patted the top of my hand as if he were dribbling a basketball.

"Don't!" I pulled my hand away. I wanted him beside me and yet I didn't. I'd never seen him so pale or so worried. Looking at the expression on his face made me feel scared. He looked like he wanted his mom as badly as I did. *Didn't.* I meant I didn't want her.

"Here comes another one. Breathe. Huf-huf-huf." The nurse at the Brewster hospital panted at my side.

I tried to follow along but it was hard when all I wanted to do was scream bloody murder. I'd heard having a baby hurt, but I didn't think it would be this bad. *Oooohhhh!*

Ahhh. Finally the contraction let up. I laid my head against the pillow and felt tears dribble down the sides of my cheeks. I didn't want to go through this. It hurt. Bad. And I was scared. What did I know about being a mom? How did I ever get into this mess?

This is what you wanted, remember?

But I didn't. Not any more. I was just a *kid* who did something stupid. Oh, no. Another contraction was coming. *Somebody! Help me!*

I'm here.

"Aaakk…ooooohhh." I didn't have time to think about all the reasons God had to leave me alone. I'd turned my back on Him big time, and now I was paying for it.

I'm here.

A cry of deep pain echoed through the room. I didn't know if it was the contraction that forced out the sound or the thought that God could still love me after what I'd done.

"It *hurts!* Help!"

"You're doing fine." The nurse wiped my forehead with a cool cloth. "Everything is going just like it should. It shouldn't be too much longer now." The nurse didn't look much older than me, but she seemed to know what she was doing a lot better than I did. "We've called Dr. West."

I hoped everyone in the hospital knew what they were doing better than I did. I was supposed to be having this baby in the Carlton hospital. That's where Mark and I had planned to go when the time came. The Brewster hospital didn't deliver babies anymore. *Until tonight.* It had something to do with insurance. If I'd had the nerve to talk about it, I would have asked my dad. He was the insurance expert in Brewster. But I'd been too embarrassed to talk to him about anything having to do with me having a child. And right now I didn't care one bit about some dumb insurance. All I wanted was to have this baby.

"Awwwhhhh…"

I'd about died when my water broke in the bathroom at Pumpkin Fest. It looked like I'd wet my pants. I'd somehow managed to keep my back near the wall and get over to the pie tables. The contractions hadn't been so bad then. My brother, Sam, was there, near the cash box.

"Go find Mark."

"I can't. I have to—" Sam looked up. "Okay."

I didn't even want to imagine what he had seen in my face. I clung to the edge of the table, knowing half the eyes of Brewster were probably watching me.

"Are you okay?" It was my Aunt Ruthie speaking to me from across the table.

I nodded. "Sam's finding Mark. I think I need to go to the hospital. Oh–hhh!" The first hard contraction hit.

"I can drive you." She started untying her apron just as Sam and Mark showed up.

Mark already had the keys to his pickup in his hands. "Can you walk? Should I carry you?"

I gave him a long look. That's all I'd need was to get hauled out of Pumpkin Fest in Mark's arms. As if folks around here didn't have enough to talk about. "My legs still work." At least I hoped they did.

Mark put one arm around my back and held my elbow in the other. "We'll go slow," he said. Either his actions were instinct or he'd watched the same movies I had.

"Ooooo-oooohhh." I bent forward. I thought labor pains would be like bad cramps. They were. Really, *really* bad cramps.

"You don't have time to go slow." Ruthie had ducked under the pumpkin pie table and had her hand on Mark's back, urging him to go faster. "Take her to the Brewster hospital. If there's time to transfer her to Carlton, they will. I don't want you kids delivering this baby in the car."

I didn't either. I trusted Mark to drive, but under these circumstances even that might be pressing our luck. The Brewster hospital was only a few blocks away, not forty miles like the hospital in Carlton.

"Owww....owwww."

"I'll be praying for you." Ruthie quickly touched a hand to my cheek.

"Tell my mom," I whispered through the end of the contraction.

"I will," Ruthie said.

As Mark hurried me toward the door, I looked back at the pie tables. At the line of people whose dessert was being held up by me. If I'd had any hope of getting out of here without anyone knowing what was going on, it was gone. My mom had just stepped out of the kitchen area and was looking right at me.

Without thinking, I mouthed one word. *"Sorry."* I didn't know if it was to apologize for holding up the pie line or for what I'd done to her.

She didn't respond. Maybe she didn't see my mouth move. It was the first time this whole night I'd seen her stand still. Or look at me. One hand reached up and cupped against her heart. Maybe I'd broken it…again.

"The doctor is on her way." The nurse was wiping my forehead. "Breathe."

I was trying to. I'd been trying to ever since I found out I was pregnant.

~

"Here's your little guy." The nurse placed a blue-wrapped bundle into the crook of my elbow. He looked a lot better than he had forty-five minutes ago. I didn't know babies were that red and wet when they were born. He was scrubbed and dry now, soft kitten-like sounds coming from his throat. I had no idea what he meant. But I had a lot to learn about all kinds of stuff having to do with this small person in my lap.

Mark reached out and touched his cheek with the back of his index finger. "Man, I didn't know babies were this small."

"I didn't either." I stared at my baby, then at Mark. He was swallowing nervously, as if he had something caught in his throat. Somehow I'd thought what I didn't know, Mark would. There went that idea.

"So…" Mark bit at the side of his cheek. "Is it still okay if we name him Brett?"

Mark's football hero. The way things were, I didn't think either set of our parents wanted this baby named after anyone on either side of the family. Brett was as good a name as any. "Brett Hoffman," I said out loud. I looked up at Mark and smiled as best I could through the tiredness I was suddenly feeling. I looked down at the baby in my lap. "Hi, Brett." I hoped I sounded more confident than I felt.

⌒

"Really. I can walk." I felt perfectly fine. A little tired, but fine. I didn't want to get wheeled out of the hospital in a wheelchair. I'd had a baby, not a broken leg.

"Hospital policy." The nurse patted the back of the blue, fake-leather chair. "Enjoy the ride. It might be the last chance you get to be pampered for a long time. Believe me," she pushed at her bangs with the back of her hand, "I have three kids. I know."

I huffed a deep breath to let her know I thought this was dumb. Then I sat in the chair. I was going to get pushed to the hospital door, then get on my two perfectly good legs and start my life as a mother. Too weird.

"You take good care of your big little guy." The nurse handed Brett to me. At least I thought it was Brett. She'd bundled him up in so many layers there could have been a seven pound, two ounce ham in those blankets for all I could see of him. "Here you go, Daddy." She handed Mark a plastic bag filled with all sorts of baby things. Even though the hospital no longer officially delivered babies, they'd managed to supply us with baby lotion, shampoo, and diapers. The nurse leaned over the mass of blankets in my lap and spoke in a childlike voice. "Time for you to go see where you live." Who knew if Brett could hear anything under all the wrapping. "Bye, now."

As anxious as I'd been to leave the hospital, suddenly I wanted to climb right back into that uncomfortable bed. What did I know about raising a kid?

Oh, God! It was a two-word prayer. If He was still there for a goof-up like me, I needed Him.

I'm here.

A comforting calm settled on my shoulders as the nurse pushed me down the shiny hallway. Mark slowly walked by my side, carrying our son's first possessions. Diapers and baby lotion were a far cry from the football Mark had been running with the first time I remembered really noticing him. Who knew that in just two short years from that football game we would be married? And have a child. A nervous dread replaced the calm I'd felt just seconds ago. *Help!*

The nurse turned the corner and pushed me into the bright sunlight shining in through the double glass doors of the hospital entrance. I could see Mark's pickup, *our* pickup, parked out front in the blue handicapped zone. This was it. We were on our own now. I wondered if Mark was wishing he could turn back the clock as much as I was.

I stood up carefully. I was still a little weak from the hours I'd been in labor. I'd only spent one night in the hospital. Without insurance to cover my stay, I'd begged Dr. West to let me go home. She agreed only if I promised to rest as much as possible.

"Don't be a martyr. Having a baby is hard work. Let your mom help you."

As if.

Mark stood with his back to the hospital door, ready to push it open as soon as I was ready. I shifted Brett in my arms. Mark might have to stand there all day if he was waiting for me to make the first move.

Instead the door was pulled open from behind him.

"Mom?"

"Angie?"

My heart started thudding in my chest. What was she doing here? I tried to think of something to say. I looked down at the blanket covering Brett's face. My mom's first grandchild was a layer away. Is that why she'd come? Had she forgiven me for what I'd done? For the way I'd changed my life...and hers? I couldn't think of any words to ask those questions.

We simply stared at each other, two statues trying to speak. My mom's mouth opened, then closed. She blinked a few times. Her eyes fell on the soft blue blanket in my arms, then flitted back to me. If she asked to hold my baby I wasn't so sure I could let go. But then this was my mom. If she'd finally forgiven me for the way I'd hurt her, I'd hand Brett over to her in a heartbeat. I needed all the help I could get...especially my mom's.

She found words first. "What do you think you're doing?"

I should have known it would be an accusation. A door slammed shut inside me. I lifted my chin. "I'm going *home*." It felt strange and yet good to call Mark's and my small house on the farm "home." It was the first time that worn-down, old place felt like anything more than a roof over my head. Just now it felt like the only safe place I knew. I held Brett closer to my heart. "Mark is taking us home."

I could feel my mom's eyes on my back as I climbed into the pickup. Mark handed Brett to me. I fumbled with the car seat we'd found at a secondhand store in Carlton. Then I stared straight ahead. I wouldn't give her the satisfaction of even a small glance. Or a glimpse of the tears that were streaming down my face.

She hadn't asked how I was feeling. She didn't ask if my baby was a boy or a girl. She hadn't even asked to see her first grandchild. She didn't ask his name. She didn't care at all. About any of us.

She came.

Yeah, right. She'd probably come to the hospital for something else all together.

Brett squirmed in his cocoon, let out a sharp cry, then wailed the way I wished I could. I moved the covering off his face and we cried together. My hot tears fell on his blue blanket. It was as if he knew there was something wrong. As if we were connected at the heart in some mysterious way.

The way my mom and I *used* to be.

～

"Brett's wet."

Even after four weeks Mark's silly rhyme made me smile. When Mark wasn't working, he and I took turns changing Brett's diapers. I couldn't believe how many he went through in a day. Maybe if we could afford to buy a more expensive kind he wouldn't need changing so much. But we didn't have the money to find out. I pushed myself off the couch. It was my turn to change him.

"Come here." I plucked my little son from his dad's lap. For some reason I always expected Brett to be heavier than he was. He was lighter than a tub full of dishes I was used to clearing off tables at the café. As I raised Brett in the air, I wondered if they'd been busy at the café today for the Thanksgiving buffet. Any other year I would have been there helping. I wasn't concentrating and my arms swung Brett higher than I expected. "Whoops!"

Even though all the stuff I'd read about babies said they didn't really do much of anything but eat and sleep—and wet—until they were weeks older—I could swear he laughed.

"Are you making fun of your mommy?" I lifted him high again.

Maybe we had a genius baby. It felt good to have big dreams for my little boy.

Like your mom had for you?

Yeah, like that. I pushed aside the guilt I felt and carried Brett to Mark's and my bedroom where I would change him on the bed. No fancy changing table for us. But that was okay. Brett seemed to be doing just fine.

I pulled off the miniature sweat pants Mark had put on Brett this morning. He insisted Brett was going to be a football player someday, just like his namesake. I guessed he thought dressing him like one would do the trick. I didn't really care what Brett was when he grew up, as long as he was happy.

I took off his diaper and cleaned him off, then let him lay on the bed and kick his chubby legs around. He might not become a quarterback like Mark was hoping, but if his excitement about kicking kept up, Brett might have a future as a punter.

I smiled as he waved his arms along with his feet. His enthusiasm for life was amazing to watch. I dipped my lips to his soft tummy and snuffled my nose into his sweet-smelling skin. I blew against it gently, wondering if my touch felt as good to him and his did to me.

How could I have ever been afraid to be his mom? How could I have worried I wouldn't know how to love him?

I lifted my head and looked into his wide brown eyes. Two pools of absolute trust stared back. Maybe the books didn't think babies knew much at this age, but I knew for a fact that my baby knew exactly how much I loved him.

Vicky

I blew it! I closed my eyes. I couldn't bear to watch as Mark turned his pickup away from the curb, taking my first grandchild, my son-in-law, and my daughter away from me. I breathed a deep sigh, took a chance, and opened my eyes. They were gone. Around the corner and down the street, maybe turning onto the highway now. As if I'd never set eyes on them at all. As if I'd never said, "What do you think you're doing?" I'd sounded as if my question was a pointed stick, not the surprise of seeing my daughter on the way out of the hospital less than twenty-four hours after she'd had a baby.

How could they send her home already? She had to be tired. And weak. Not to mention she'd turned eighteen only months ago. She was too young to be doing this. I'd had her working with me at the café since she'd been tall enough to reach the tables. She'd never even babysat anyone but her brother, and then not until he was old enough to practically watch himself.

I pushed my fingers through my hair, pulling at the tangled strands as if I could tug my whirling thoughts out of my head. I hadn't intended to see Angie at all on this visit. I'd only wanted to stop at the nurses' station and check on my daughter. With regulations the way they were, I couldn't get any information over the phone when I'd called. I thought if I showed up in person I could wheedle a scrap of news from one of the nurses I was sure to know. I was also hoping for a glimpse of my grandchild in a hospital bassinet.

I wasn't sure how I felt about this baby. I'd thought seeing him, or her, might help crystallize the emotions that had stirred my sleep all night. As upset as I was with Angie, I couldn't stomp down my concern for her. Eighteen years of mothering did that to a mother's heart.

I'd only wanted to ask about Angie. Hear that she was well. I doubted she'd want to see me. I wasn't even so sure I wanted to see her. Not now. In my mind she was still my little girl, not a...*mother*. She'd know someday how this kind of hurt felt. Then again...I said a quick prayer. Hopefully she never would know the hurt of a broken dream.

She already does.

No. This is exactly what she wanted. She'd gotten her dream at the expense of mine. My heart squeezed in on itself, a tight fist crushing any hope I had for her. What kind of life would she have? Married so young. A baby to raise. Mark dropped out of college. Angie never going in the first place. It was too much. I looked longingly at the blue vinyl wheelchair still sitting in the corner of the hospital entrance. I wanted nothing more than to collapse into it. Let someone else take care of me and my mother-load of worries. But what would the coffee crowd at the café say then? As if they weren't already tired of talking about my family.

I filled my lungs with antiseptic air and breathed heavily out. At least I knew Angie was okay. The baby, too. The doctor wouldn't be sending her home if anything was wrong. I'd have to be content with that.

I have learned wherever I am to be content. My old mantra. The Bible words that had been so easy to say until now. Now...when I really needed what they promised. Would I ever be content again?

She looked so tired. And pale. And...defiant.

No. I couldn't think about that. About how it was more than likely *me* who'd caused that stubborn lift of her jaw. If only I could take back my words. Take back these last nine months. Even the few before that. Where had I failed? I hadn't meant to push Angie away. It was just that I no longer knew how to reach out to her. Not with this high wall that stood between us. The wall I'd constructed with my silent bricks of broken dreams.

～

"Have a nice Thanksgiving." I felt as empty as the turkey carcass lying on the counter in the café kitchen. The buffet we'd served had gone smoothly. Afterward Dave, Sam, and I had joined Ruthie, Paul, and their girls out at their farm for our own family celebration. Ruthie had told me she'd invited Angie and Mark. I watched the window all night for a flash of headlights. I listened for a slam of doors. The small cry of a baby. Nothing.

～

"Merry Christmas!" The words rang through the café all month. I smiled. Poured coffee. Smiled some more. I felt as fake as the plastic Christmas tree in the corner of the café. How could I be merry when my daughter was so far from me? When I hadn't yet seen my two-month-old grandson?

I pushed my way into the kitchen to pick up an order and thought of Angie as I'd last seen her, holding her baby as she left the hospital entrance. Mark walking beside her. Two young kids with an infant between them.

I picked up the meatloaf special and was reminded of two other young parents that very first Christmas. From all I'd read, Mary was younger than my Angie. What had her mother thought? She couldn't have been any happier than me and yet look what happened.

December. Dave had gone to see our grandson, but he was

no good at trying to tell me what size Brett's chubby little legs translated to. Angie stopped by Dave's office now and then. She'd told Dave that Mark was helping his dad on the farm and had taken a second job in Carlton. I agonized over gifts. Would Angie accept a gift from me? What could I buy that would say, "Forgive me?"

The distance between us was invisible, but as prickly as the barbed-wire fence that lined the road to the small house where Angie and Mark lived. I knew, I'd driven past it often enough. I prayed I'd have the nerve to turn in. I always drove straight instead.

In the end I filled a new laundry basket to overflowing with wrapped toys and clothes, diapers, and baby food. I included Angie's favorite perfume and a light-blue cotton blouse. A green-and-gold Packers sweatshirt for Mark celebrating his favorite football team went in.

Chicken that I was, I had Dave deliver the package while I waited by the phone, praying for an excited phone call from Angie. A call that never came.

Maybe it was time for me to—

⁓

"Happy New Year!" I said the words but they meant nothing. In years past, we'd closed the café and had a private potluck with our circle of friends. We played charades and silly games until the clock struck twelve. Kisses. Hugs. Friends. Kids. Goofy noisemakers. Snacks. It was right out of a Norman Rockwell painting. Until this year. There was no painter in the world who could find a color to match my dark heart.

Somehow all the holidays had passed…without Angie.

⁓

"Another day, another fifty-cents." Kenny Pearson was holding out a coffee cup, waiting for a refill.

"If you're talking about the price of my coffee, you've been underpaying me for years." I filled his cup, then set the coffeepot on the table for a second. There was no rush today. A January blizzard was blowing just outside the café door. It had kept all my regulars but Kenny away from coffee hour this morning.

"Where is everyone?" He took a loud sip from his cup.

"I'm guessing they're home. Ruthie called from the country and said she didn't dare drive in with the kids. It was a white-out there."

"Bunch of wimps." Kenny couldn't hide the smirk from one side of his mouth. "Either that or I'm nuts for trudging over here from the gas station."

"I'm voting for you." I walked to the counter, poured myself a cup, put the coffeepot back on the warmer, then joined Kenny at his table. I couldn't remember the last time the café had been this quiet. But then, lately, keeping busy had been my specialty. The more I baked and waited tables, cooked and cleaned up, the less time I had to contemplate my life.

When Ruthie had called to say she'd try to make it to the café by lunchtime, I'd spent the empty, early-morning hours making the rolls and pies she usually baked each morning. I didn't care if we'd have day-olds tomorrow as long as I had something to keep me busy. I gave the grill a New Year scrubbing down, then, with still no customers, I took everything out of the large fridge and wiped it down with a mild bleach solution. Thank goodness Kenny had braved the weather or I might have had to resort to actual thinking next.

I pulled out a chair and sat down. Like it or not, Mother Nature had decided to give me a coffee break today. With no customers, there wasn't much left to do. I just hoped Kenny decided to stay a while. I wasn't sure what I would do if I ended up all alone.

I glanced at the clock. Late morning. With any luck this wind would let up and Ruthie would soon be on her way to the café in time for lunch. If I knew the people in Brewster, they were already getting blizzard fever. As soon as things cleared, I could count on the café quickly filling up with retired men and women who needed to talk about the weather...and everything else in town.

Kenny slipped out of his jacket. Good. That meant he'd stay a bit. "So...how's it feel to be a grandma?"

Not that. The one question in the world I didn't know how to answer. Why didn't he leave? Why did he come at all? There wasn't anything I could say. I wavered, my hand over my coffee cup. Kenny had to have heard most of the gossip by now.

He slowly nodded as if he understood all the nuances of my sign language. "Mixed blessing, huh?"

It was an odd thing for plain-talking Kenny to say, but the perfect thing. He had to know all about mixed blessings, what with his son Freddie's problems. I picked up my coffee cup. "I guess." I was positive about the mixed part, not quite as sure about the blessing. But if I allowed myself to think about things at all, I was sure, given time, Angie and I would somehow mend this tear between us. That I would grow to love being called *Grandma*. Given time. How much time would it take before I found the thread that would stitch our family back together? *Oh, Lord...please. Do something.*

"He's a cute little guy." Kenny was looking at the snow gusting past the café windows, but I knew he was talking about Brett.

Every now and then we could catch a glimpse of the vacant store across the street. There wouldn't be many people who would need gas, or coffee, in the next few minutes. There was time to gingerly ask Kenny my question.

"You've seen him?"

"Oh, yeah. A couple times. Angie stopped by to fill her car with gas and I asked for a look."

Good old snoopy Kenny. "How old was he then?"

Kenny rubbed the back of his neck. "Oh man, he was just a squirt. It must have been right after she had him."

What had Angie been doing taking my grandson out into the cold so early?

What choice does she have? You haven't been there to help.

Heavy guilt pressed across my shoulders. I had to say something to lift the weight I felt. "You said you saw him a couple times?"

"Yup. Angie and Mark came into the station to rent a movie for New Year's. Brought the baby with them."

So that's what they'd done to ring in the New Year. I ran a finger around the edge of my cup and wondered if Angie had missed our traditional potluck. Maybe she'd come to town thinking they could drop in. That seeing us with friends around to buffer the meeting would make things easier. Instead of having the party, I'd sat home and watched the ball drop in Times Square, crying in the New Year while Sam slept over at a friend's and Dave dozed next to me on the couch. Again I'd failed. What would it take to knock down this high, thick wall?

With his chin, Kenny motioned to the store across the street. "You heard anything about a business going in over there?" Apparently, he'd had enough of the baby talk.

I wanted to ask so much more.

You should just go see your grandson for yourself.

I knew I should. But how could I after all this hard silence?

Pick up the phone.

As if some mysterious genie had made my thought come to life, the café phone rang. I jumped up as if someone had shocked me. "I'll get that!" As if I expected Kenny might. "Hello!" I spoke much too loud. "Vicky's Café."

"Vicky, it's Ruthie. You busy?"

I felt a weird, sinking sensation inside. Only Ruthie. "No, it's not busy at all." I caught Kenny's eye. Winked. "Kenny's been the only one crazy enough to find his way in. I'm helping him drink our coffee."

Kenny stood up, his hand on his hip, reaching for his billfold. "Just a minute," I said to Ruthie. I covered the receiver with my hand. "It's on me today." I wouldn't make him pay for his coffee; I was too grateful for his conversation.

"No? Okay." He sounded confused. He lifted his hand from his side and held up his ambulance pager. "I just got called. I've gotta get to the hospital and get the ambulance. Man, whoever this is, I hope it's not a car accident. The weather could cause a pile-up I don't even want to think about." He shoved his arms into his jacket. "If this is some dumb kid out bucking snowbanks…" He didn't finish his sentence.

I said a quick, silent prayer as Kenny hurried out of the café. I spoke back into the phone. "Kenny just left. Ambulance run," I explained quietly. We both knew an ambulance run in Brewster more than likely involved someone we knew.

"I wish I were there," Ruthie said unexpectedly.

I looked around the silent café. The two coffee cups were the only dishes that needed washing. "Relax. There's nothing for you to do. The place is empty."

"Well…good. I'm glad you're not running your feet off all alone there. Paul called from the bank and said it was pretty slow. He said if you needed me, he'd drive out here with the four-wheel drive and get me and the—"

"Oh, goodness, no! You stay put. I might as well put the 'Closed' sign up for as busy as it's been. *Not* busy, I mean."

"It's still pretty bad out here. I might have to wait for a snowplow to come by before I make it in."

"Call before you come. The way it's been going I won't need you at all today."

I hung up the phone. Now what would I do? No customers for distraction. Two cups to wash.

Call Angie.

Not now. Someone might come in.

Not in this weather. Call Angie. She needs you.

I could always change the oil in the deep fat fryer. And it wouldn't hurt to sit down and go through my bulging recipe file. Maybe I'd find some new recipes to put on the same-old, same-old menu.

I'd just finished filling the deep fryer with a new batch of oil when the phone rang. I wiped my hands on my apron and glanced out the café kitchen window as I reached for the phone. The wind had gone down some. We might have a crowd for lunch after all. Maybe this was Ruthie, telling me she'd be on her way in.

"Vicky's Café," I said, just in case it wasn't her.

"Mrs. Johnson?" The voice was professional, unfamiliar.

No one but telemarketers called me Mrs. Johnson. For once I had time to listen to their spiel before I said no.

"This is her." My heart made an unexpected, foreboding thump, as if it already knew something I didn't.

"You need to come to the Brewster hospital as quickly as possible. Your daughter is asking for you." Her tone softened. "Please hurry."

I didn't stop to turn off the lights in the café. I didn't lock the front door. I'd always thought it was a case of over-acting when someone in a movie got bad news over the phone and they dropped the receiver and ran, but that's just what I did. I was pushing my arms into my coat as I stumbled out the back door. Fumbling in my pockets for the car keys as I sunk into a mid-calf high snowbank near the front of my car. I jammed the key into the ignition and slammed the gearshift into reverse, then forward.

Be with Angie. Be with Angie. I had no idea what I was running to, but I knew it couldn't be anything good. *Be with Angie,* I prayed again, knowing full-well I should have been there for her all along.

⌐

Keening.

That was the only way to describe the hollow, high-pitched wail coming from the far end of the hospital corridor. A white-clad nurse pointed the way, but I didn't need any directions to find my daughter. I'd never heard Angie make such a sound, and yet I knew it was her. A wounded animal in the wild. I ran to protect my child.

As I rounded the door I grabbed on to the doorframe. When I saw Angie I froze, my feet suddenly two lead weights holding me back, as if not moving forward would somehow hold together my shifting world.

There she sat in a cheap, orange plastic and metal chair, her arms clasped tightly across her stomach as if she was trying to keep her insides from spilling out. She was rocking back and forth, back and forth, the unearthly sound straining from her throat and into the thin air, a siren-song for the wounded.

A young, panicked-looking hospital worker was standing beside Angie, trying to comfort her.

"Angie." My voice was a hoarse whisper. I reached out one hand. "I'm here."

Angie lifted her head from somewhere near her knees and turned to stare at me. Her pupils were two black saucers of sorrow. She blinked dumbly, as if trying to remember why we were both at the hospital. A strangled sob shook her body as she drew in a deep breath. "He's *dead.*"

"*What?*" In an instant I remembered Kenny leaving the café on an ambulance run, hoping against hope it wasn't a car accident in this blizzard. I recalled Dave telling me Mark had taken a second job in Carlton. Forty miles of narrow, two-lane traffic over rolling hills from Brewster to his job. That road was dangerous on a good day. Treacherous in a white-out. Hadn't he known enough to call and say he couldn't make the drive in this weather? Why would he head out in a blizzard when he had a wife and infant son to support?

That's why.

Oh…oh…oh. I should have asked Angie to come back to work. I should have offered to let her bring Brett to the café the same way Ruthie had done when she'd had her baby last spring. Mark wouldn't have needed a second job if I'd reached out to Angie. I should have given them money. I should have—

There were running steps coming down the hall. A voice calling, "Where's Angie?" Then her young, too-young husband, rounded the corner and rushed to Angie's side.

Mark? Here? I'd thought—

"He's *dead.*" The same two words Angie had said to me.

And then I knew. *He* was my grandson. Brett. The baby boy I hadn't known I loved until this instant. The baby child I would never get to hold to my heart in this lifetime. If this lifetime mattered anymore.

I felt a rushing sensation in my head. A dizziness that sent the room adrift.

"No-ooooo-oooo…" Was that me? Angie? Mark?

I stumbled toward the two of them. I knelt down beside my daughter and son-in-law and put my arms around both of them as we cried.

Not like this, Lord. Not like this. This isn't how I wanted my daughter to come back to me.

Libby

There was a palpable pall over all of Brewster as the news of the crib-death of Angie and Mark's ten-week-old son filtered around town. The café was closed. It was as if everyone in town could feel Vicky's pain. The death of a child made my writing woes seem small indeed.

Even the blizzard-like wind that had blown all morning had nothing more to howl about. There was nothing anyone or anything could say. At loose ends—and emotions—I wandered around my house not knowing what I should do to fill the void I felt for Vicky and Dave, Angie and her young husband. I could too well imagine the dreams they'd had for their child, for their life together. Everything had changed in a breath.

I paced, debating if I should stop by Vicky's house and offer my sympathy. I recalled the way she'd rebuffed me earlier when I had tried to follow up on our writing project. There was no sting left in her words. I felt nothing but empathy for her now. But what would I say? What *could* I say that would make this tragedy in some way…better? I shook my head. There was no *better* about it.

As I had so many times in the years following Anne's death, I sat in my prayer chair and pulled my Bible onto my lap. I laid my hands over the navy-blue leather cover as if my open palms could somehow absorb comfort from the words inside. I tried to form my thoughts into meaningful prayer, as if there was something I could mention to God that He didn't already know.

Comfort them.

Hold them close.

Feeble, feeble words. No wonder I would never make it as a writer. No wonder I'd given up that dream.

You haven't.

I have.

I sat there for minutes...an hour? I didn't know. All I did know was that when I heard the side door open, the door leading into my kitchen from the outside, it startled the dickens out of me. Bob wouldn't be home in the middle of the afternoon. No one else in Brewster would simply walk into my house.

"Who's there?" I started to get up, then sat right back down as Emily walked into the living room. What was she doing home? In Brewster? Her college was 200 miles in the other direction. She'd barely been back to school a week since the holiday break. She hadn't planned to come home again until early March, during Spring Break. Not to mention it was a Tuesday. Classes were in session. She had to have been driving right *into* the blizzard to be home now. One look at her face told me not only had she fought the weather, but tears, too. Her eyes looked as if she'd cried all 200 miles.

If she was here now, she couldn't have possibly heard about Angie's baby. And even if she had, Angie hadn't been a close friend of hers. I knew Emily wouldn't drive through a blizzard at hearing the news. A phone call to get the facts, maybe. None of this was adding up.

I tucked my Bible into the side of the chair. "Emily." Now I did stand. "What's wrong?"

"Oh, Mo-*o-m*." She threw her arms around me and burst into tears.

I let her cry as I tried to make sense of this mixed-up afternoon. I rubbed her back, smoothed her hair. Something was terribly wrong. I put my hands on her shoulders, gently easing her away from me.

"Emily, you need to calm down. I can't help you until you tell me what's wrong."

"It's…it's…"

I waited while she tried to catch her breath, imagining all the things that might cause my drama-queen daughter to come undone in a way I'd never seen. Knowing her, she'd flunked her first test ever. A small part of me was already preparing the lecture I'd give her for driving through such awful weather just to fall apart over something so trivial in the whole scheme of life. Especially after knowing what Vicky and Angie were going through right now.

I heard the impatience in my tone. "What's going on?"

She drew in a shuddering breath. "Mom, it's Mike. He has…" She hiccupped more tears. "…cancer."

I'd thought I'd felt emptiness when I'd heard about Angie Hoffman's baby, but this was a kick to my gut I hadn't expected. It felt as though the air had been knocked from my lungs with a karate chop to my chest from a black-belt expert. Only when I'd heard my friend Anne's cancer had returned had I felt a blow like this before.

"*Oh no!*" I had to sit down.

Nodding, Emily wiped at her tears with the backs of both hands. More tears followed. She sniffed, trying to stop them.

"How…? What…? When did he…?" Once again I had no words.

Emily sunk into the corner of the couch. "Sara told me." She burst into tears again. "He couldn't even tell me himself." She looked as empty as I felt. Her eyes brimmed as she spoke. "Mom, he's my best friend. I thought he'd always be there for me. I…

I...I *love* him." She looked at me with tear-filled eyes, and I had no doubt she did.

Now she could say it. Now, when she'd practically handed him to Sara. Now, when he might be dying. When it might be too late.

Oh, God...please, no! I love him, too. I put a hand on either side of my face, as if I needed to hold on to my thoughts to keep them from spinning away. It was as though I had to think to breathe. *Inhale. More. You can do this.*

"Oh, Emily."

"I know." It was all she needed to say.

After a time Emily pushed herself from the couch. I could hear as she pulled ice from the fridge, dropped the cubes into a glass, and filled it with water. "I'm going to go lay down." Even as a toddler a drink of cold water and a nap in her own bed had always made her feel better. She knew what she needed for comfort.

What about you?

I knew what Anne would do. I picked up my Bible. I held the closed book in my lap and stared at it. Nothing. There was nothing inside me. No emotion. No feeling. No hope. Were there words for the way I felt? I doubted it. I turned the pages, not knowing where I should stop. Was there any hope left anywhere?

It seemed as if everything I knew, everything I counted on, had disappeared. Babies weren't supposed to die. Neither was Mike. Emily and Mike were supposed to be together. Brian and Katie weren't. I was supposed to be a writer. None of that was true anymore. None of it.

My hands fell still against the pages as tears slowly filled my eyes. So...there was something left inside me after all. Soon there wouldn't be. As soon as I was done crying I'd be completely empty. A shell of a person.

The tears crept over the edge of my lower lids and rolled down my face. I felt them one-by-one as they dropped onto the back of my hands. Hot. Wet. Liquid pain.

I reached up with one hand to swipe at my face. A tear fell into the void, landed on the open page in my lap. I watched as the tiny drop of hopelessness was absorbed into the Word. There was a small crinkle in the paper that I traced with my finger.

One wrinkled word. *Hope.*

I had none, yet there it was. *Hope.*

I read the words around it. Familiar words I'd forgotten: "For I know the plans I have for you… plans for good and not for evil, to give you a future and a hope."

I sank my face into my hands, pressing the words into the hot tears covering my cheeks.

Lord! Lord! My heart cried as it never had before. *Take it. Take all of it. I can't do it anymore. I can't. It's too much.*

There was no reason to hang on to anything anymore. It was already gone.

They're Yours, Lord. Angie's baby. Emily's love for Mike. Mike. Brian, too.

I drew in a shuddering breath. I'd thought I'd given it all, but I hadn't. There was one thing more.

Take it, Lord. You can have it! My writing, too. If You have no use for it, neither do I. I don't want it anymore if You don't. It's Yours, Lord. My friends. My family. My writing. It's all Yours.

Now.

Now I was empty.

Libby's Letter

There we were, Anne. Vicky Johnson, Angie, Emily, and me. Four lost souls wandering around this little town of Brewster. Empty. Floundering. All of us had experienced a death of our dreams. Oh, we still went through the motions. Vicky opening her café each day, pouring coffee, making pies, acting as if life was moving on. Instead, she told me later, she was treading water, gulping for air, trying to remember if she knew how to swim.

Angie went back to work at the café. She was eighteen and so much more...or less.

Emily went back to college, uncertain about life...and love.

And there I was, climbing out of bed each morning only because the sun was up and I knew it was expected of me. I had no focus. Nothing to do but keep the coffee growers in business. If I truly was not meant to write, what was my purpose? Why did the world make more sense when I wrote things down? Why did the trees seem more colorful when I looked at them through my Crayon box of words? Why did I feel the wind more intensely when I cloaked the winter chill in a wool coat of words? Why? That was the only word I had left. Why?

As I had so many times before, I stopped writing to look at the words on the page. The end of the silver pen was cool as it poked against my cheek. As if Anne herself had reached out with her gift to remind me to continue.

It may have looked to those around me as if life was moving on. Brian and Katie were planning their wedding. Emily was back at college not talking about Mike…or Sara. Bob was busy with his never-ending work at the bank. I was pretending life was something to celebrate. I choked out words when expected. No one knew. They didn't have a clue that a rug had been yanked from under my dream. My life. I was flat on my back. A turtle with no way to right itself.

I put the pen down. I had to stop for a minute. I went to the kitchen and poured myself some coffee. Even though I knew how this story turned out, it was still painful to remember those endless days filled with nothing…not even hope.

I lifted my cup and held it close to my nose. Ah. The heady brew somehow reminded me of Anne. The warmth of the dark liquid seeped through my skin much as her friendship had. So many moments we'd shared with nothing but ceramic coffee cups between her heart and mine.

I walked back to my desk and stood a moment, letting my eyes stop on the photo of Anne and me I still kept on a shelf above my computer. Enough time had passed. I no longer got choked up when I thought of Anne. Instead her memory brought only good things. A smile. A lopsided grin. A sudden warmth in the middle of my chest. Goose bumps of memories running down my arms.

I was ready now to go back to my story. To tell Anne how it ended…

There we were, Anne. Vicky, Angie, Emily, and me. We didn't know we were being drawn into the same circle. That God had a plan to make sense of our dead dreams.

Oh, Anne, quit laughing. I can hear you saying, "But, Libby, that's God's job!"

You always knew that.

But, me? I was still learning…

Vicky

"Are you coming in today?"

"Um ummm." I wiped sleep from the corners of my eyes. Or maybe the residue was dried up tears…if I had any of those left. I could hear the click of a rolling pin through the phone line. More than likely Ruthie was pushing a pie crust into one of her perfect circles. "Sure." But I wasn't.

I looked at the clock. Seven o'clock. The café doors would have been unlocked for a half-hour already. By this time of day I'd usually made a large pan of caramel rolls, fried two dozen Long Johns and frosted them. Poured one pot of coffee and had another pot brewing. Except for these past three weeks.

"Angie's here." I could hear the softness in Ruthie's voice as she said the name of her niece, my daughter. I could also hear her gentle insinuation that if Angie could make it to the café, certainly *I* should be able to.

That's where my daughter and I were different. Angie had lost her child. I'd lost two people. The grandson I'd never taken the time to know and, in some unfathomable way, my daughter. Even though she was still alive, she wasn't the same child I'd raised. I no longer recognized this shell of a girl.

Angie dealt with her loss by not sleeping. Staying busy. Coming to the café early. Staying late. It was easier for me when I simply checked out. Left the café so I didn't have to see Angie and be reminded of what had happened every time I turned around.

Peace came only when I crawled into bed, swallowed a sleeping pill, and drifted through the hours in a dreamless haze.

I knew what I was *supposed* to do, I just didn't know if I had the energy to do it. I slid my legs out from under the covers and sat on the edge of the bed. "I'll try and get there soon."

"We really need you today, Vicky. It's Valentine's Day. We have reservations for dinner starting at five until eight-thirty tonight. There's a lot to do." If Ruthie was trying to make me feel needed, her reminder only did the opposite.

"I'm getting in the shower now," I lied. I felt the weight of responsibility weigh heavy on my shoulders. One more burden to carry around with all the others. I hung up the phone and lay back against the pillows.

There were all sorts of things I *should* be doing. Nothing, not one thing, I wanted to do.

I could feel myself drifting off again. Sleep was my friend.

"Vicky." A gentle shake of my shoulder. "They need you at the café." Dave was leaning over me, dressed for work.

When had he done that? Most days I was at the café before he was even awake. Then I remembered. The baby. The funeral. Everything had changed.

"I'll get there." I turned away from him. I buried my head deeper into the pillow.

I could feel the edge of the bed sag as Dave sat down. His hand rubbed softly across my back. "Vicky." His voice was tender. "It's been almost a month. We're all sad about this. But life goes on."

Ha! Mine didn't. I turned onto my stomach, keeping my face away from him.

He stood up. His voice was firmer now. "The best way to deal with this is to keep busy."

He was a man. Leave it to him to say a thing like that. I pulled the blanket next to my cheek. Snuggled in deeper. I tried to relax but it was hard when I could feel his eyes boring into my back. Two daggers. Maybe if I lay still enough he'd realize he could quit stabbing me. I was already dead.

I could hear him turn, walk toward the bedroom door. In seconds I could return to my sleepy insulation. The door was closing...

A heavy sigh. "Vicky, this café was your dream. Don't let it die. I think we've had enough death in this family to last us for awhile." Then he was gone.

So was sleep. I pushed back the covers, got out of bed, and headed for the shower. If I turned the water hot enough maybe I could forget about the way his words had scalded me.

Angie

"Mom, could you ring up the ticket for the Benders? I've got an order up in the kitchen." I waited a moment to see if she'd heard me. She'd been spacey ever since—Well…she'd just been out of it for awhile. Couldn't she see for herself that Mrs. Bender was tapping her fingernails impatiently on the Lion's mints next to the cash register? And it wasn't like there wasn't anyone else waiting to sit at the table they'd just left. "Mo–om, the *till*."

"Yeah. Okay." She was standing still, staring mindlessly across the café. She put down the two water glasses she was holding and walked toward the counter. Why didn't she just deliver the water to the table on her way? Did I have to tell her that, too? I glanced at the people waiting in the booth. A man and a woman I didn't recognize and a small baby in an infant seat tucked near the wall.

Oh.

I walked by my brother, Sam. "The Benders' table needs cleaning."

He gave me a silly salute. "Aye-aye, Captain."

I rapidly blinked my eyes as I pushed my way into the kitchen. For as long as I could remember it had been all-hands-on-deck on Valentine's night. This year we had everyone: my dad, Sam, Ruthie's husband, Paul, and Mark. It was a good thing because mom was hardly any help at all. And pretty soon, I might not be, either.

You'd think she *was the one who lost a baby.* It wasn't the first time I'd had the thought. But it was the first time I thought what came next. *In a way, she did.* I'd seen her face just now.

I didn't want to think about that. There was a part of me that was still mad at my mom. She'd never even held Brett until he'd di— No! I couldn't think about that day now either.

I could feel the pressure of tears pushing at my throat. As hard as I tried to stay busy, it seemed like my tears never took a break. They were *right there,* sometimes when I least expected them.

I hurried through the kitchen. "I'm going to quick go to the bathroom." I caught Ruthie's eye as she stood next to the grill. I didn't care if she saw my eyes filling. She was used to it by now.

She added a twist of a lemon slice to an order of deep fried shrimp and then picked up the two plates. "I'll take this order out for you." She knew.

I hurried into the bathroom in the back of the kitchen and leaned against the closed door. It was cool in here, not like in the café where the heat of unasked questions and nosy sympathy hovered over every table. I had hoped the busyness of tonight would take the place of my memories. But even a full house didn't stop me from remembering this same night last year. The night my foolish plan was set into motion.

I covered my face with my hands. I didn't have to wait; tears were already running down my face. How naïve I'd been. To think having a baby would keep my life from changing. Instead my thoughtless pregnancy had set in motion a kind of change I never dreamed existed.

I swatted at the toilet paper holder, unrolling a long strip of tissue that I pressed to my face. How incredibly immature I'd been. If there was a class in *Growing Up 101,* I'd already passed it with flying colors. Well, one color—black.

Unrolling more tissue and blowing my nose, I closed the cover on the toilet and sat down. Before I was pregnant I hadn't wanted to leave Brewster. Living here in the safety of this town and all I knew was all I wanted. I shook my head in unbelief at my stupidity. Look what I'd done to try and keep everything the same.

I stared at a torn corner of paper towel lying on the scuffed floor. Maybe if I didn't blink, didn't move, my thoughts would stop, too.

No such luck. When I was expecting Brett I wished I could leave, go off to college like my classmates were. Suddenly registering for classes and moving into a dorm seemed a lot less fearful than being married and having a baby. And now...now when that baby was no more, when I would be free to leave town, go to college, do whatever I wanted as long as Mark agreed, well...there was nothing I wanted to do. I didn't want to stay. I didn't want to go. If truth be told, I wasn't so sure I even wanted to live. But I wasn't going to think about that. I wasn't going to think about any of it.

There was a soft tap on the bathroom door. "Are you all right?"

I flushed the toilet—as if Ruthie didn't know that trick by now—then opened the door. "I just need to wash my hands." I held them out. It looked more like I was pleading for help. I should have known I couldn't fool her.

She leaned over and kissed my cheek. "Hang in there. God's on *your* side."

I'd thought I'd heard them all. All the clichés that were supposed to make me feel better about losing a baby. *You're young, you'll have another baby. God must have needed an angel. Time heals all things.* Ruthie's unexpected advice, "*God's on your side,*" filled my eyes again. Would these tears never stop?

"Come here." She folded me into her arms, patting my back the same way I'd comforted Brett when he had cried.

Why hadn't I known how quickly I would fall in love with my baby?

From the first second I saw Brett I knew my heart had somehow changed. Life wasn't all just about *me* anymore. Now I had a greater purpose. I had a child to raise. To protect. To love.

Oh, sure, I hadn't expected much of the stuff that came with him. Sleepless nights. Dirty diapers. And his cries were a foreign language I hadn't learned. But I'd been trying. It seemed each time I picked him up, each time I looked into his wide eyes, I learned something more. Something about love.

It seemed impossible to imagine that God used my brainless plan and brought Brett into the world. Used him to show me there were so many more important things than friends and fashion, guys and college. Used my tiny son to show me the kind of love my mother must have for me.

The kind of love I have for you.

That, too. How could God love me? After all I'd done? How could my mom? When Brett died it felt as though my heart had ripped right down the middle. As if there was only half of it— half of me—left. Is that how my mom felt about the way our relationship had...ended? Did her heart feel as empty as mine?

A sob pushed its way past my lips. Ruthie held me tighter. If she was worried about the food orders stacked by the grill her arms didn't let on. Or let go.

"I'm so sor–*ry*." I wasn't sure who I was saying *sorry* to. God. Brett. My mom. Mark. My dad. Maybe me...the person I *used* to be. Mostly God.

"He knows." Ruthie whispered near my ear. As usual, she understood what I hadn't said out loud. "He's already forgiven you."

I cried against Ruthie's shoulder as her words settled in my heart. Was it possible? Had I already been forgiven?

I took in a shuddering breath. In the back of my mind, I knew I needed to pull myself together. There were people finishing up their food out in the café, people waiting to have their orders taken, more people waiting to be seated. This was a special night. Valentine's Day. The day of love.

A night when I discovered a new kind of love. God's love.

If He could forgive me, maybe I could forgive myself.

But could my mom ever forgive me?

Libby

"I'll have the tenderloin, medium, please. Hash browns with onions and salad. No toast." I tried to hand the menu to our makeshift waiter, Dave Johnson, but he was concentrating too hard on taking my order to notice the laminated menu. "Oh, and coffee. Decaf tonight."

"Got it." He was writing painstakingly slow. "What kind of potato, again?"

"Make it baked." I couldn't imagine how long it would take him to write what I really wanted. If he asked my advice I'd say "stick to your day job." Selling insurance was definitely his forte.

I laid my menu at the edge of the booth and smiled across the table at Jan Jordan. It had been her idea that the four of us go out to eat tonight. If it had been left up to me, Bob's and my Valentine dinner would have been leftover meatloaf. I'd thought of suggesting we drive to Carlton for a fancy dinner, but knowing Bob made that drive every day for work, I thought it would be enough of a treat to hand him a mushy card and tell him he could stay in Brewster for the night. My instinct had been right.

"Sounds good. I'll have the same." Bob must have felt sorry for Dave having to work so hard tonight. He was making it easy on him. "Oh, but I'll take the Texas Toast."

Great. It might take Dave another five minutes to write down that little "oh." I took a sip of my water. If Vicky or Angie had been waiting on our table I knew my coffee cup would already be full, not to mention refilled.

302

"My turn." Jan turned to Dave. I could hardly wait to see what Dave would do with her order. I'd eaten lunch with her often enough to know this was going to take a while. "I'll have the Shrimp Scampi. But could you leave off the scampi sauce and just steam the shrimp? Tell Ruthie. She knows how I like it. And I'll have a baked potato, no butter. Unless you have rice. Do you have rice?" She blinked up at Dave as if she expected he might offer to make some just for her. Knowing Jan, he might.

I looked past Dave. If only I could flag down Vicky and get my coffee cup filled, I'd be a happy camper. The crowd that had filled the café when we arrived was thinning now. Jan had concocted her plan late-afternoon and by the time she called for reservations the only choice we had was the last one of the night. Bob and I had stopped at Jan and Dan's house for a glass of wine and some cheese and crackers before we headed to the café. As late as it already was, I had the feeling we'd be eating our fancy dinner with the clean-up crew, namely our waiter, his wife, and family.

That is, if Vicky was eating anymore. She had noticed my desperate-for-coffee look and was heading my way. She must have lost ten pounds since I'd last seen her, and even before that she'd been thin. One look told me our earlier idea of writing a recipe book together was nothing but a fanciful dream. There were concentration camp survivors who looked better than she did.

"Are you having a nice time? Is there anything I can get you?" Vicky filled our coffee cups, even though Bob tried to keep her from turning his over and filling it. She was on autopilot.

It would be easy to assume it had been a long and busy night for all of the people working at the café tonight. Easy to dismiss her false conversation as jovial patter. But I knew better. I could see past the mask Vicky was wearing. I'd worn a similar one myself not all that long ago when I went through my bout of clinical depression. It might be easy to fool most of the people, but I didn't consider myself *most*.

The easy out would have been to answer her chatter with more of my own. To let her become part of the background of this night the way most servers at a café were. Wallpaper. Instead I found myself saying softly, "You must be tired."

Her sad eyes locked onto mine. There was more in her eyes than just the work of tonight. She paused and I sensed she was struggling with more than just a reply. No words. Only a tired nod.

I found myself praying for her as she walked away. *Ease her burden.* As Dave took the rest of our order. *Bring healing.* As Jan, Dan, Bob, and I laughed and joked over our dinners. *Comfort her.* As we lingered over angel food cake with strawberry topping and whipped cream. *Hold her close.* More coffee. *Lift her up.* As Sam, Mark, and Paul cleaned the tables around us and Angie pushed the vacuum across the floor. *Hold Angie, too.*

Now that the café was almost ready to close, there was an intimacy present I hadn't noticed during all the daylight meals I'd eaten here. I wondered if Dave and Vicky ever used this place for a romantic getaway. Or if, to them, it was simply *work* to be here. I looked around. If they pulled the shades that covered the big windows facing Brewster's Main Street, kept the overhead lights dimmed and lit a candle or two, why, Vicky's Café had potential.

But another glance at Vicky told me romance was the last thing on her mind tonight. *Bless their marriage, Lord. Let this time of trial bind them closer, not tug them apart.*

"Well, that was good." Dan Jordan pushed at the edge of the booth's table as if he could scoot himself further back to make more room for his full stomach.

I was wishing I had a belt...buttons...something I could loosen. I was stuffed. "It sure was," I agreed.

"Do you guys have time to stop back at our house?" Jan swiped a lipstick across her lips, then dabbed them against a tissue. "We could play *Catch Phrase*." Did this woman never run out of ideas? Or energy?

I knew Bob would come to our rescue. He pointedly looked at his watch. "It's a workday tomorrow. I think I'm going to have to call it a night."

Thank you, Bob. I hoped he could feel my silent praise. Not only was I full, I was feeling a compelling urge to get home and pray for Vicky. "This was fun. Let's do it another time. Soon." There, that should do it.

Dan slid out of the booth. "If you'll excuse me for just a minute, I need to go talk to Dave."

"Oh, no you don't." Bob reached into his back pocket for his wallet. "You're not going to pick up the check for all of us."

Dan held up a hand. "To tell you the truth I forgot we hadn't paid yet. I need to talk to Dave about some business. It'll only take a second." He chuckled. "Keep your money handy."

Jan fluffed her hair with one hand. "He's alwa–ays wor–rking." So even she was getting tired. The fact that her speech was dragging, a lingering side-effect from her Bell's palsy, was a sure sign. It wasn't just middle-aged me.

"Just like my valentine. Always working." I nudged Bob with my shoulder. It would be good to get home. It wasn't *that* late. Maybe I could talk Bob into giving me a back rub—

There it was again. That prod to pray. I put my napkin on the table and pulled my coat onto my shoulders. It was time to go.

"More coffee?" Sam was offering.

"Oh, no—"

"Just half a cup." Jan held her cup out. She looked at Bob and me. "You know Dan. This is going to take longer than he said. And if we don't drink the coffee, Vicky will have to throw it out."

Or sit down and drink it herself. I put my hand over my cup.

"Hey, Bob, good to see you. Thanks for coming out tonight." Paul Bennett, temporary café help, full-time Brewster bank president, and a co-worker with my husband, held out his hand. He nodded at Jan and me. Bob stood as they immediately started talking shop.

Jan leaned across the table and whispered. "I'm going to run to the ladies room."

Was I the *only* person who wanted to get home tonight? If I was tired, I couldn't imagine how Vicky and her family were feeling about now. I was sure they wanted to get home as much as I did. Then again, one look at Vicky restocking silverware and glasses, Angie wiping down the tables a second time, and her young husband, Mark, refilling salt and pepper shakers, I wondered if any of them had anything to get home *to*.

Oh, Lord, be with these young people in this time of lost hope. Unexpectedly my eyes stung. I couldn't help but lump Mike in with my prayers. He did indeed have cancer. A call to his mother confirmed it. I could understand why Mike might have been reluctant to explain the particulars to Sara or Emily. Testicular cancer wasn't something most young men would be glad to talk about. The good news was it had been discovered early. Treatment had already begun and statistics were on his side. But still...

I picked up my coffee cup hoping to wash away the thickening in my throat. Empty. I sipped at the three drops of water left in my glass. *I want to be home.*

You need to pray.

I knew I did. I pushed my arms into the sleeves of my coat. If I could just convince the three other people I was with, we'd be on our way. Already I could sense the warm folds of my sheets, the soft feathers in my pillow. It wouldn't take long to pray myself to sleep tonight.

As I buttoned my coat, Bob and Paul's conversation floated around me. I watched as Dan Jordan tossed a quick look in Vicky's direction then handed something to Dave. Dave looked at it quickly, glanced over his shoulder at Vicky, then slipped the paper, or whatever it was, into his shirt pocket. They shook hands as if they'd sealed a deal.

What was *that* all about?

Suddenly my writer's brain was spinning. What had Dan handed over that was such a secret? If it had been any other two people I might have thought "drug deal." But, I knew better. Dan was in real estate. Dave in insurance. Both of them were on the Brewster Chamber. I had no doubt the two of them had business to talk about, but any insurance policy I'd ever seen had been bigger than that small scrap of...of... *What?*

"Ready to go? I am." Jan stifled a yawn as she pulled her coat from the booth. "Da–an," she called. "Time to go."

Sure. Now. Now when I actually had something to think about. Something to figure out.

〜

I slid my legs between the sheets. With a little help from my electric blanket they were as warm and cozy as I'd imagined.

"'Night." I leaned over to give Bob a kiss. It figured. My valentine was already sleeping.

I turned on my side and pulled the covers over my shoulder, snuggling into the folds. I lay there a minute, then shifted to my back. Now that sleep was mine to claim, my eyes were wide open.

Oh well, more time to pray. But try as I might, my mind wouldn't let go of the exchange I'd seen between Dan and Dave. If I wasn't careful I'd be lying awake all night concocting a mystery plot.

I thought you gave your writing to Me?

That's right. *I did.* I smiled to myself. It felt good to let Him handle that one. Ever since my tearful prayer I'd felt an unusual lightness. The writing monkey that had ridden my back most of my life seemed to have crawled off. It appeared God did want me to give up my dream of writing. And the most surprising thing about it was that I didn't mind at all. Once again, I turned onto my side, then my stomach, my favorite position to fall asleep. Oh, this felt good.

What if I'm calling you back?

To writing?

Yes.

Back? Oh, my. As if in response to the word, I turned onto mine.

Back.

Really?

Yes.

I could have just as well had a cup of coffee because now I was awake for sure.

Vicky

I looked around. The café was clean. The last customers gone. The front door locked. It was good to have this busy night behind me. I'd grab a quick bite with my crew, then blow out the votive candles that were still burning on each table. The short drive home and a quick shower were the only things that stood between me and the refuge of my bed. *Soon,* I promised myself as I bent to straighten the floormat inside the café door. *Soon.*

Only the soft lilt of piano music coming from the stereo speakers broke the quiet. I stood up and stretched against the tight muscles in my back, noticing suddenly that it was *too* quiet. Where was Ruthie? Paul? Angie and Mark? And Sam? We usually ate together after a busy night like this. Had they eaten and I'd somehow missed it? How had they managed to leave without me noticing? Had I been *that* far inside my own world all night? I hoped none of my customers had noticed. Come to think of it, where was my husband? Had he left, too?

I climbed the three steps that led to the main level of the café. "Dave?" He wouldn't have left without me...would he? I pushed my fingers through one side of my tangled hair as I glanced around the café, as if I expected him to be hiding. Then again, why wouldn't he leave? What reason did he have to wait? I untied the apron I'd been wearing and draped it over my arm. I wasn't proud of the way I'd been acting this past month. If I wasn't careful I might lose more than I already had.

"Dave?" *Oh, please be here.*

"I'm right here." With his shoulder he pushed his way through the swinging door that led from the café kitchen carrying two filled salad bowls. He set them on the nearest table, then stood by the table, a funny little smirk on his face. He walked to the wall and turned off the overhead lights. Only candlelight illuminated this familiar space. It looked suddenly...intimate.

A race of fear zipped through my stomach as Dave turned my way. I wasn't ready. I couldn't—I draped my apron over the back of a chair and stood in the middle of the café, my hands on my hips as if this were a showdown. "I thought we were all going to eat together. How come everyone left?"

Only piano music answered my question. I felt an unexplained thrum of...*something*, as Dave walked toward me. Oh. I recognized that look. *Oh no!* How could he look at me like that? I looked away. I knew I looked terrible...and not just because I was tired. A long night at the café couldn't come close to exacting the kind of payment the past weeks had doled out.

As Dave came closer I found myself wrapping my arms around my chest. Other than a casual brush of our bodies as we passed each other in the house, it had been weeks since we'd touched. Ever since Brett's funeral we'd kept our distance. Put it this way, I'd kept *my* distance. Somehow I felt as if the slightest contact, a compassionate hug, a lingering kiss might just be my undoing. It was better if I kept to myself.

Better for who?

I looked again at Dave. He was standing in front of me now. There was anguish around his eyes. Disguised distress I hadn't noticed until now.

You haven't looked.

It was true. I hadn't. My own pain was enough. I didn't have the strength to take on his, too. Or Angie's. Or Mark's.

I do.

Oh... *Oh...* I felt tears creep into the corners of my eyes. *No!* I couldn't start. Not here. Not now. Not ever. I shook my head at Dave. I didn't know if I could offer up what he wanted. It might be best if I didn't even pretend.

In response Dave reached out, took my hand from its grip on my arm, took my other hand in his, too. He simply held my hands and looked into my eyes. Nothing more.

But it was too much.

I blinked furiously at the tears suddenly welling in my eyes. I wanted to take my hand and press it against my heart, but I was afraid to let go. Surely my heart was breaking from the ache I was trying so hard to hold in.

He opened his mouth.

Don't say anything! Don't. Please.

"I love you, Vicky."

How could he? How could he love me after the way I'd turned away from Angie when she'd needed me most? When I'd stayed away from our only grandchild, our *first* grandchild, because of some foolish idea I had that Angie needed to *pay* for her mistake.

Was I happy now that she'd paid the greatest price of all? That we all had?

A gulping sob pushed from my throat. *Oh God. Oh God.*

Dave took me in his arms. Wrapping one arm tightly around my back, he cradled his other hand against the back of my head, holding me close to his chest. A kind of crying I didn't know existed took over. Trembling. Sobbing. Gasping for air. Through it all Dave held me. How could he?

My cry was a lament for all that was lost. For sorrow and forgiveness I didn't deserve.

No one does.

That thought made me cry harder still. I didn't deserve His

forgiveness or Dave's. And yet here it was. Here *I* was. Held tight in loving arms. Proof positive He wouldn't let go.

Too, too much.

Eventually my sobbing slowed. My cry became a whimper. I dared to raise my face from Dave's chest. His shirt was soaked with my tears. I lifted my eyes to his and held his tearful gaze in mine. There was release there. Forgiveness that didn't need words.

"I love you, too." My throat was choked, the words barely audible. It didn't matter. He knew.

He knew.

∽

"Well, that was…different." I wrapped my hands around my coffee cup. "*Nice* different." I smiled tenuously at Dave. There were all sorts of unsaid emotions still between us. But this unexpected meal had been a start toward healing.

Before he'd sat across from me, Dave had grabbed four votive candles from the surrounding tables and placed them in the center of ours. The gentle flames cast a just-big-enough circle around the two of us. As if we were in our own private world tonight. It felt good. Safe. A welcome break from the uncertain world I'd been occupying.

How he and Ruthie had maneuvered behind my back to leave us alone in the café with a two-course meal and dessert at the ready was a mystery. A nice mystery. One I'd let the two of them keep to themselves. It had been a luxury to simply sit and let Dave wait on me. He spooned Thousand Island dressing on my salad. He set a plate of succulent tenderloin, a baked potato, and glazed carrots in front of me with the flair of a big-city maitre d'. He poured coffee when my cup was almost empty, and then produced two pieces of angel food cake and topping as his grand finale.

"I'm impressed." I gave him a look over the top of my coffee cup. "This was a pleasant surprise." I only wished I could have freshened my makeup, changed clothes, and run a brush through my hair. I had to look a fright since the last time I'd glanced in a mirror…sometime around ten in the morning. Even from the start I hadn't looked all that great. And then with my crying jag… Oh, I didn't want to imagine.

You'd never know it, though, by the look in Dave's eyes. I smiled back at him, took a deep breath, sighed contentedly. "I suppose we should think about heading home." Why had I said that? I wasn't so sure I wanted to go there. Not yet. I doubted this magic glow would follow us home. I knew the knife-edge of reality was waiting just outside. It was hard and cold and would pierce this moment in a heartbeat.

"Let's wait a little." Dave had read my mind. "Besides…" He held up a finger, and then he took our two dessert plates from the table and set them on another table an arm's reach from us. He shifted in his chair and pulled an envelope onto the table. He had to have been sitting on it all night. The image made me smile. What else did this man of mine have up his sleeve? *Or under his backside?*

He held the card between his hands, gazing at the soft candlelight. *He got me a card?* Dave and I hadn't exchanged Valentine's Day cards in years. The night was always one of the busiest-of-the-year at the café. We long ago agreed that having to muster up the energy to force some romantic interlude at the end of the evening wasn't something we needed to do to keep our relationship ticking.

It seemed the rules changed this year. But then *everything* had. I was already carrying enough guilt. I wasn't going to add a little thing like not having a card for Dave to the mix. I was going to simply appreciate his thoughtfulness. I reached across the table and touched his hand.

Dave looked up at me, then back to his hands. "I—I…" He took a deep breath and blew it out. "I know things have been bad…*really* bad lately." He paused. Thinking. Searching. He found what he was looking for. His words came in a rush. "I never dreamed that our lives would turn out this way. That Angie would get pregnant and marry so young. That she'd—*we'd*—lose our grand*child*." His voice caught. He blinked rapidly and caught my gaze. "But Vicky, we've lost enough. This has been hard on all of us, but I've watched what it's doing to you. It's like you—" I could hear his feet shuffle under the table. He scrubbed at the side of his face with one hand. "It's like a part of you has died."

I pressed my lips tightly together. I didn't want to start crying again, but I might. How did he know that's exactly how I was feeling? As if a part of me died along with Brett. This man knew me too well.

I raised a hand and rested it against the swelling in my throat.

Dave turned the card in his hands. "Our dreams for our daughter are gone." He stopped.

I put my palm against my mouth. Those words had to be as hard for him to speak as they were for me to hear.

He went on. "Well…*changed*, anyway." Again he stopped to look at me. I gave a slight nod. What he'd said was true. Maybe *not* talking about what had happened was worse than bringing it out into the open.

"It's hard enough watching Angie and Mark deal with this. Do you know they're going to a support group in Carlton?"

I hadn't, but I was glad they were. "That's good," I said softly.

"It is." Dave reached one hand around the candles and held

mine. "They have each other, Vicky. I need *you*. I can't watch you like this anymore. You—*we*—need to move on. And that's why I want to give you this." He tapped the edge of the card against the table, then slid it across the tabletop.

I stared down at the pale pink envelope. At my name written in Dave's loose scrawl. I could hardly imagine what words might be written in a three-dollar card that would help me move on. But I wasn't about to question Dave's sweet gesture. I would try to be happy. I really would. At least I'd pretend I was.

I reached for the card and turned it over. Only the tip of the closure was glued to the paper. I smiled. I knew how much Dave hated licking envelope glue. I broke the seal with my thumb and pulled out the card. It was light pink to match the envelope with an embossed silver heart in the center. Pretty, but no wise words. Those must be inside. I opened the card: *Happy Valentines Day!* The message was preprinted. *Love, Dave* was signed underneath. So much for my worries about what might be written inside. After all the buildup, this was a bit anticlimactic.

I smiled past the vague sense of disappointment I suddenly felt. Even though I hadn't been expecting anything tonight, somehow Dave's short preamble before giving me this card had led me to believe there would be something inside this envelope that would change things. I'd been wrong. "Thank you."

Dave tilted his head and smiled back at me, an expectant look on his face. If he was anticipating wild kisses from this simple card, he didn't know me nearly as well as I thought. "It's nice" was all I could muster for the five words inside the card.

Dave craned his neck to look over the top of the card in my hands. "Shoot! I didn't get it inside the card. Look in the envelope."

I could feel my brow furrow as I picked up the envelope and felt inside. Sure enough, there was something more. A bit thick.

Slightly bigger than a playing card. I pulled it from the envelope. A plain black square surrounded by white trim. It was going to be hard to rally any more enthusiasm than I had up to now.

Dave's head was bobbing like an eager puppy's. "Turn it over."

I followed his instructions, turning over what I now recognized as a Polaroid picture. Candlelight danced over the glossy surface. I tilted the photo to try and make out the dark image.

"A house?"

A nod from Dave confirmed it. I looked again. It was small. Yellow.

"I'm not sure I understa—" And then it dawned on me. "Is this for Angie and Mark?"

"No." He rubbed at the faint stubble on his chin. "I never even thought of that. It's for you."

"Me?" I turned the photo to catch the light, trying to shed more than candlelight on this mysterious gift. I held the photo at an angle, close to the soft light. And then I saw it. Ida Bauer's old house. The house I didn't recognize at first. The house that held my dream. The dream that had died months ago.

No. Dave couldn't possibly think—

I laid one hand against my chest. My heart was thumping as though I'd raced up and down the—I squinted at the photo and counted, one, two, three, four steps leading up to Ida's house at least a hundred times.

He couldn't possibly know how scared this made me. How just the thought of resurrecting my dream sent a lightning bolt of fear zinging through me. I knew what it felt like to have a door slammed on my dreams. I wasn't so sure I even wanted to think about turning the knob on this particular door. "Dave... I..."

He reached out and took one of my hands in his. "Remember how you used to dream about having a different café? One where you could try new recipes? Host parties?" Dave's eyes flicked meaningfully to the photo in my hand. "I talked to Dan Jordan. Kenny, he's Ida's *nephew,* you know, he just lowered the price on her house, and I thought…"

"Oh, Dave." My dream was gone, but one look at his eyes told me his dream for me wasn't. I'd given up, but he hadn't.

I haven't either.

I looked at the photo of the small yellow house. It didn't look like much. Certainly not anything like the fanciful dreams I'd had. They had been stripped away. Reality had taken their place. It would be easy to say no—if it weren't for the look in Dave's eyes. "I just don't—"

He squeezed my hand, then let go. "I just want you to think about it. I didn't give Dan any money. I told him we might be interested. *You* might be interested." He leaned forward across the table. "Are you?"

I wanted to shake my head. To turn this house into a semblance of my former dream would take more time, energy, and elbow grease than I possessed. I wanted to shake my head, but it wouldn't move.

I set the small photo on the table, nudging it closer to the candles with the tip of my finger. From the outside it didn't look like much, but the inside… I hadn't forgotten what those four walls encased. Mottled hand-painted walls that resembled old Europe. Not that I'd ever been there, but I'd certainly walked through those rooms in my dreams. Trailing ivy painted along the corners of the walls. A small crystal chandelier that caught the smallest ray of sunlight and exploded it into a spectrum of color…not unlike this photo was doing to my hibernating dream. Did I dare dream…again?

As I stared down at the photo, I saw beyond the glossy surface.

Way beyond. *Oh, Lord, too many dreams have already died. I can't. I need You to—*

As I cast out my silent plea, one of the four candle flames in the middle of the table flickered and died. A hot cinder broke away and was lifted along with the plume of smoke. It floated for a millisecond. A mere blink. Then it was gone.

But it wasn't. In some odd way the small spark had shifted from the candle to me. I felt a stirring. An ember of golden warmth flickering somewhere near my heart. Hope. My dream. It was there after all.

I raised my eyes to Dave. "I will," I said. "I will think about it."

In truth, I already was.

Angie

I glanced at the clock hanging over my kitchen sink. Two o'clock in the morning and I wasn't even yawning. Mark had been asleep for hours. Lucky for him sleep was an escape. He had to be up early tomorrow to get to his job in Carlton. I was glad that if one of us got the gift of sleep, it was him. That's all we'd need was both of us sitting around noticing Brett wasn't here. I picked up a solid blue puzzle piece and tried to fit it into the jigsaw puzzle I'd been working on the past week. The box cover showed a street scene in Paris with the Eiffel Tower in the background. A place I'd never see except from this farmhouse table.

I sighed. It had been a long night at the café. Valentine's night always was. I'd been hoping the busy night would wear me out completely. I wanted to come home, take a shower, and then tumble into bed, letting exhaustion take the place of my ever-present tears. It hadn't. Slow, tired tears had mingled with the stream of water from the shower. I'd cried more when I found the sweet Valentine's card Mark had propped against the bathroom mirror. I lay beside him until he fell asleep, and then I slipped out of bed and into the kitchen to work on my puzzle. It was the only goal I had right now: Finish the puzzle.

I worked with the piece, turning it one way, then another. There was no way it was going to fit into the small part of the sky I'd already assembled. I put the piece aside and picked up another one. No, the puzzle wasn't ready for that one either.

I fingered through the many small pieces. The easy way would be to put together a building first, then another, then work on the sky. But why would I take the easy route when I was used to doing things the hard way?

I curled my hands into fists and rested my chin on them, staring at the jumble of puzzle pieces on the table. I'd only completed the border and part of a coffee shop. There were so many parts yet to fill in...yet what was the point? I already knew what the picture would look like. A pitiful resemblance of the real thing.

Kind of like my life. Nothing but a sorry story compared to what could have been. College. A marriage. A healthy baby. A career. The only thing I had left out of all that was my marriage. I loved Mark. I truly did. But it didn't take more than my high school diploma and the past few months to understand that what we had right now might be all we ever had.

What was left to hope for? Brett was gone. Mark and I were working three jobs between the two of us just to pay our bills. Why dream of places like Paris when I would never even get out of Brewster? Why try to make the pieces fit when I already knew what my life would look like?

I crossed my arms on the tabletop, right over the partially completed puzzle, put my head down and cried. It wasn't the first time I'd cried my way through a night, and I doubted it would be the last.

⁓

Somehow the night had passed. Then another. And another. Until it was the first week of March. Seven weeks since Brett died. Just barely the length of his short life. How could the days he'd been alive pass so quickly, and the days since his death creep by like slow-moving mud? Easter was late this year—not until April—which meant there was nothing special to plan for at the café until the Easter buffet. There was more than a month of coffee to pour, hamburgers and fries to serve, pies to slice, until something would break the monotony.

I picked up the coffeepots and glanced at my mom straightening the candy in the counter by the cash register. How had she managed to go through this same-old routine every day for the past—I did the math—twenty-some years? How could she stand it? How would I?

"More coffee?" I really didn't need to ask. This group of men would sit here and sip at their cups for at least another half hour as long as I kept pouring. Then they'd get up and leave, and the café would be empty for about forty-five minutes until some of them came back for lunch. Their schedule was as predictable as mine.

Jim Magner pushed his cup to the edge of the table. "Sure, I'll have more."

"Me, too." Kenny Pearson put his cup in line.

Didn't they ever feel like doing something different? Like… like…oh, go *wild* and have *tea* instead? I smiled to myself. They would laugh if I put a tea bag in one of their cups. My life was pretty pathetic if the only thing I had to excite me was playing lame jokes on my customers.

"So what's the lunch special?" Kenny rubbed his stomach. As if he needed to point out how far it stuck out over his belt.

"Turkey melt with fries." I hoped Mark would never look quite that out of shape. But then why would our future be any more exciting than Kenny's? He'd stuck around Brewster his whole life, too.

"Put me down for two. I'll pick them up around noon."

"Two?" Marv Bender reached over and tapped Kenny's belly. "Something you not telling us?"

I felt a familiar icy sensation creep down my arms as I realized they were talking about babies. The one topic that was off-limits around me. Didn't they remember? Had they forgotten so soon? It was a good thing my coffeepots were almost empty. The temptation to dump them over Marv's head was strong.

Kenny pushed Marv's hand away. "Cut it out. Diane and I are done with the kid business. The food is for Pete and me. At the station."

How could Kenny say it just like that? *Done with the kid business.* I wanted to scream at him. *Like you paid some money and came home with a kid. What if that kid got taken away from you? What if it died? Huh? What then?*

I knew I hadn't said anything out loud, and yet Kenny was looking at me as if I had. There was a look in his eyes. A look that said he *knew.* He knew what he'd said. He knew what I was feeling. He'd had a child and things hadn't exactly turned out like he'd planned either.

He pushed himself away from the table. "I gotta get back to work, guys." He pressed his lips together in a sort-of smile, then dug in his pocket and put two dollar bills on the table.

"I'm getting coffee today." Jim Magner reached over and tried to hand the two bills back to Kenny.

He put them back down. "Leave 'em for Angie." His eyes darted my way. "For putting up with us." It seemed there was a lot more he didn't say.

"Thank you," I whispered, surprised at how easily his unlikely apology had melted me to tears.

"Let me." My mom reached around my back and gently took the two coffeepots from my tight fingers. "Why don't you go back into the kitchen. I think Ruthie might need you."

It was a flimsy excuse I was all too ready to grab on to. In the few seconds it took me to walk back to the kitchen, I managed to blink back my tears. Some days it was easier than others. Maybe today would be a good day.

"Need any help?" I pushed through the swinging door leading

into the kitchen. The smell of Smothered Roast Beef, Ruthie's special recipe, made my stomach clench. Ever since Brett died, I hadn't had much of an appetite for anything, especially breakfast.

Or life.

There was that, too. I purposely didn't look at Ruthie as I wiped at the crumbs on the counter. I didn't want her to guess my thoughts. She tried so hard to understand. But how could she, when she had her baby to hug and I didn't?

"Can you start chopping the stuff for lunch salads?" Ruthie stirred something on the stove.

"Sure." I washed my hands and then opened the door of the cooler and pulled a mix of lettuce and vegetables from the shelves. Mom and Ruthie were big into serving healthy food. They wouldn't dream of serving a salad of just plain old lettuce. Well, not *old* lettuce, but they agreed it was the other stuff…carrots and cucumbers, tomatoes, and even broccoli sometimes, that made Vicky's salads special. I had to give my mom and Ruthie credit. For living in a little town, they still tried to do things in a big way. They weren't like so many people in this town who sort of gave up. Who acted as though there wasn't anything more in the world but the few blocks that made up Brewster. As if just because we lived in a small town we couldn't have interesting lives.

Aren't you thinking that right now?

I paused with my knife over a cucumber. Busted. I glanced at Ruthie out of the corner of my eye. I knew enough of her past to know that she, too, had wrestled with the idea of living a small-town life. She'd lived in Brewster from the time I could remember, until I was maybe in junior high, running the town's small radio station until it closed, helping my mom when things were busy at the café. She'd even lived with us for a time. Ruthie had been a combination aunt and big sister to me. Then she'd moved to

Minneapolis. It could have been New York considering how far away from Brewster it had seemed to me.

I pushed my knife through the cucumber as I recalled those days. I'd missed her. I remembered how she'd let me sit close beside her on the couch while we'd look through fashion magazines. Together we wondered what kind of life a person would have to have to wear those sorts of clothes. Not the kind of life anyone we knew had, that was for sure. Sometimes Ruthie would coax me off the couch to do my exaggerated imitation of a fancy model walk. Head high, mouth in a pout, one hand on my hip, practically tripping over my growing feet. Then we'd laugh.

I'd been shocked when Ruthie announced she was moving. And sad. Never once had it occurred to me that she wasn't happy in Brewster. That she didn't love what she was doing. Or love living near me. For the first time in my life I started wondering what life might be like if I lived somewhere else. And it scared me. Why would I want to leave my family? My friends? I loved Brewster. At least I thought I did. Was I missing something?

And then Ruthie was back. Back *home* where she belonged. She was the same, but different. More…more… I didn't have a word for it back then, but now I knew. It was *content*. Somehow during her time away she'd found…something. Something I needed now.

Using the blade of the knife, I scooped the chopped cucumber into a large metal bowl. Next I ripped open a bag of prechopped carrots and dumped them into the bowl, mixing the cool vegetables with my hands. Tomatoes were next. They'd gotten so expensive we'd stopped using them for a while, but the price had dropped and they were back in the salad mix again.

I reached for a serrated knife and began slicing. Across the middle. Turn the half on its side. Divide the half into slices, then turn the slices into cubes. I'd watched my mom do it for so many years that her method had turned into mine. I started on a second tomato. There was odd comfort in my routine. In having something to do that needed doing. In not having to think and analyze, in not having to *feel* anything but the cool moistness under my fingers. Not having to worry if a customer would say something that would bring back my tears. Or wonder what Brett would be doing right now if he were still alive. *Chop the tomatoes.* It didn't seem like much, but today it was enough.

"Did your mom talk to you yet?"

Ruthie's question startled me out of the chopping zone I'd been in. "Huh?"

"Your mom," Ruthie reminded, as if I'd forgotten who mom was. "Did she *talk* to you yet?"

"Well…yeah." I wasn't sure what Ruthie meant. My mom and Ruthie jabbered to each other all the time. I'd learned a long time ago that there wasn't much my mom didn't tell her sister. It didn't bother me. I told the same stuff to Ruthie I told Mom. Sometimes I told Ruthie more. Now that I was working at the café full-time, some days it was more like a junior high slumber party back in the kitchen than a café. Ruthie had to have noticed that things between my mom and me had been…better.

The thick wall that had been between us had cracked big time the day Brett died. When I saw my mom standing in the hospital doorway I knew the stuff I'd let come between us had been stupid. My stubbornness, my embarrassment, my "I'm old enough to know everything" attitude had crumpled. I wasn't old enough to have my baby die. I'd never be that old. I'd never be old enough not to need my mom.

She'd held out her arms and there it was. The love I'd been missing. The love Brett would never know.

The days after that were still a blur, parts missing that I didn't ever want to remember. But the image I couldn't forget was the way my mom and dad were there for me. Not pushing. Not trying to

force Mark and me to do things their way. Instead they were just…
there. At our house. At the funeral home. At the funeral. We didn't
talk more than we had to. There was nothing to say. But there was a
power in their presence I didn't know I needed until they were there.

I still wasn't sure how the café kept running during that time.
Ruthie must have done most of it on her own. Maybe Sam pitched
in after school. I wasn't sure I'd ever have the words to ask. The
day of the funeral the café had been closed. There was no need
to put a sign on the door. Everyone knew why. The shades pulled
tight during the day said it all.

And suddenly one whole week had passed. I'd lived through
it, even when there were times I didn't think I wanted to. I didn't
talk to Mom or Ruthie about coming back to work. I just did. It
was better to be busy than to sit at home and remember.

There was an awkwardness at first. As if everyone in town was
tiptoeing when they were near me. As if I might break at the light
tap of a spoon stirring sugar into coffee. But as close as my mom
had stood by me, there was still something between us that kept
the wall upright.

I gave my head a shake. How long had I been standing here
remembering? Ruthie was sampling the soup simmering on the
stovetop as she looked at me over the top of her spoon. Her simple
question, "Has your mom talked to you, yet?" hung in the air.

What did Ruthie want to hear? That I knew there were things
that would never be said? That somehow *knowing* made it okay?
Because if that's what Ruthie thought, she was wrong. Brett dying
would never be okay. The space he'd left between my mom and
me was a vast hole. A hole so cavernous I doubted there was a
cement in this world big enough or strong enough to fill it. We
were just going to have to learn to live with an open wound. Learn
to make the words we spoke to each other somehow jump across
what we couldn't say.

Did Ruthie want to hear all that? Right before the lunch rush wasn't great timing for a conversation like that. I shrugged one shoulder. Cut to the chase. "You *know* we've talked."

Ruthie grinned. "So…what do you think? Should she do it?"

Do what? I'd already told her mom and I were back on speaking terms. Maybe she wanted to hear it from me. "We… she…already has."

"She bought it? Yes-sss!" Ruthie made a fist and pumped it by her side. Then she put down the spoon she was holding and did a goofy-sort of dance as she came over to hug me. "Aren't you excited?"

My arms hung limply around Ruthie. Of course I was happy my mom and I were talking again. But if anyone should be dancing over that it should be me. None of this was making any sense. I pulled away from her hug. "Are we talking about the same thing?"

"The house! You said she bought it, right?" Ruthie grabbed me again. "This is going to be so much fun."

"Okay," I said stepping back from her embrace. "I have no idea what you're talking about."

"I thought they'd never leave." Hands filled with coffee cups, my mom backed her way through the swinging door into the kitchen. "It's a wonder those guys get any work done the way they sit here some days. What…?" She stood still, looking between Ruthie and me.

"That's what we'd like to know." Ruthie held one hand on her hip like a question mark. "What?"

Mom walked to the counter and set the dirty cups near the dishwasher. "What, *what?*"

Ruthie and I spoke over each other.

"You bought the house, and you didn't tell me."

"What's this about buying a house?"

Mom gave Ruthie a long look. "I haven't *bought* it, yet. And if

I do I was going to *surprise* her." She looked at me. "It was going to be a surprise."

"Well," I said holding out my hands, "it is. Does anyone want to tell me what you're talking about?"

"Better, yet," Mom said a slow smile spreading across her face, "I'll *show* you. But it's going to have to wait until after lunch. I'll call Dan Jordan and see if I can get the key." There was a sparkle in her eyes I hadn't seen in ages.

As I turned back to my salad prep I wanted to ask, "*What key?*" but it seemed "what" was all any of us had said the past few minutes...and I still didn't have any answers. I decided to let Mom reveal her surprise in her own good time.

Easier said than done. One customer came in for lunch, then another, and another. I found myself sharing secret, questioning smiles with my mom. She'd slightly shake her head at me and take an order. Lift her eyebrows in a *just-you-wait* tease and fill another coffee cup. There were no hints as to what the afternoon lull might hold.

I placed an order of hamburgers and fries in front of one customer, got the ketchup she needed, then rang up the two to-go lunch specials for Kenny. I couldn't help but watch the clock. How long until these people would be through with lunch? I found myself hoping the people in Brewster weren't all that hungry today. That the ones who were would eat fast.

How long had it been since I'd had anything to look forward to? Since any of us had? I doubted whatever surprise Mom had to show me would change much of anything, and yet I couldn't help but hope.

"Hope." Now there was a word I hadn't thought of in a long... too long...time.

Hope.

Libby

So, okay, this would make it official. I quickly glanced down either side of my street and then raised my hand and knocked on the front door. I was now the certified "nosy neighbor" of Ninth Street. I listened for someone to call, "Come in." When all I heard was silence, I turned the knob and stuck my head inside the door, "Knock knock. *Hello-o!* I've got cookies." My voice echoed in the empty entryway. As I stepped across the threshold, I told myself at least *cookies* were a good excuse to be here. I wiped my feet on a cotton throw rug in front of the door and peeked around. "Anyone home?" I knew someone was here, I'd seen her unlock the door over two hours ago.

Off and on for the past three days I'd watched Vicky Johnson, her husband, Dave, and their two kids, Angie and Sam, parade in and out of Ida's old house. I'd just about convinced myself they were moving out of their spacious house three blocks over and into my former neighbor's cracker-box of a house, until I realized they weren't hauling anything *in*, only stuff out. Now and then Vicky's sister, Ruthie, stopped by...and stayed...sometimes for several hours. Not that I was watching.

You're as bad as Ida used to be.

And it had never hurt our neighborhood one iota to have Ida's eagle eye on us all. Someone had to take her place.

And that would be you?

I glanced around the empty space. Yes, there was no denying

329

it, at least for right now, that would be nosy old *me*. I might as well play the part. "Yoo-hoo, is anyone here?"

Yoo-hoo? Who said "yoo-hoo" any more? Once again, that would be me. I peeked around the short wall to my right. No one in the kitchen. I was already standing in the living room. It was empty, too. Did I dare look around any more? How about the hallway straight ahead? I took one step off the throw rug.

A voice from somewhere in the house floated my way. "Is someone here?"

I snapped my foot back on the rug. I was starting to feel like Goldilocks...the little snoop. "It's Libby. Olivia Marsden. From across the street."

Vicky came around the corner from the small hallway wiping her hands on the sides of her jeans. "Oh, hi!" She gave me a lopsided grin. "You're my first caller." She laughed. "Oh, sorry. Whenever I'm here I find myself talking like I'm in a time warp." She waved a hand around the small living room. "Doesn't this house just take you...somewhere?"

My eyes followed her hand. I'd been so intent on looking for a person in the house that I hadn't noticed the house itself. Buttery dappled gold walls. Painted vines, green and brown, trailing around the room. A small crystal chandelier in the center of the ceiling. Instantly I was transported to another time. I wasn't sure exactly *when*, but it certainly wasn't now. No wonder I'd been saying things like "yoo-hoo."

"This is amazing."

"Isn't it?" Vicky was standing with her hands on her hips. "I couldn't believe it either, the first time I saw it."

"And to think I lived across the street from Ida all these years and I never noticed. I guess the few times I stopped by I always went to her kitchen door."

Vicky turned to look at me. "Well, in your defense, it was a little harder to notice the details when all of Ida's furniture was still in here. She had a lot of stuff in this little house."

"So that's what you've been hauling out." So what if she knew I'd been watching? If the slow, steady traffic down our street was any indication, I was sure I wasn't the only person in town who was curious.

"Yeah. Ida's family is going to have an auction sale when the weather gets nicer. We've been storing most of the stuff in the garage out back." She motioned vaguely toward the backyard. "Some of it is down in the basement."

One mystery solved. There was an awkward pause as I scrambled through my brain trying to figure out how to politely grill Vicky for the rest of the story. TV detectives had an advantage, they had a script. I didn't. But I did have cookies.

"Here. I almost forgot why I came." *You big fibber!* I held the paper plate of molasses crinkles out to Vicky. "I wanted to welcome you to the neighborhood."

And find out what in the heck you're doing over here.

"Thank you." Vicky took the plate from my hands. "I'd offer you coffee, but I don't have any. Or," she chuckled as she waved a hand around the empty room, "chairs, either, for that matter. Guess that's not saying much for what's supposed to be Brewster's newest restaurant."

Newest restaurant? This was turning into more of a mystery than when I started. I was going to have to do my best *Columbo* impression. I acted nonchalant. "Did you say restaurant?"

"You haven't heard?" Vicky lifted the plastic wrap over the cookies, broke off a small bite, and popped it into her mouth. "I'm disappointed. What's happening to the grapevine in this town?"

I shrugged a shoulder. "Don't worry too much. It just goes to show how little I get out these days."

"Hey, these are good." Vicky was holding a whole cookie now.

She waved it in the air. "You know, usually *I'm* the one feeding people. This is a nice treat for a change. Thanks."

Before I could think about it, I found myself saying, "If you need a break we could walk across the street to my house. I've got a pot of coffee going." My plan had been to drop the cookies off, find out what was going on over here, then head home and enjoy a fresh cup of coffee and a cookie by myself.

Vicky looked at her wristwatch. "One cup and then I need to get back at it." She handed the plate of cookies back to me and bent to pick up her jacket that was lying on the floor. "So you really haven't heard a word about this place?" She pushed her arms into the jacket sleeves and opened the door. She waited as I stepped around her, then followed me outside.

"No, I haven't heard. But I'd like to." Why did I feel as if I were the one who had just opened some sort of door?

~

"And you're planning to do this all by yourself?" I filled Vicky's cup for the second time.

She swallowed a bite of cookie and took a quick sip of her coffee. "I have to. Ruthie and Angie are running the café. Dave has his business to tend to. And Sam is in school. They'll help when they can, but for now I'm sort of dividing my time between the café and..." she motioned with the side of her head, "the house." One side of her mouth turned up. "I've gotta think of a name to call that place. It's starting to take on a life of its own." She formed quote marks in the air with her fingers. "Somehow *The House* doesn't quite do it for me."

I smiled. "Me either."

Vicky pointed the crumbled edge of a cookie at me. "You're a writer. Maybe you can come up with a name. I'll give you free coffee for life!"

"Now that's tempting. I'll have to think about it," I said as I sipped my coffee, determined to change the course of this conversation. I didn't want to go there. To that writer place. Ever since I'd turned it all over to God I'd felt a refreshing lightness to my days. As if that particular monkey had, once-and-for-all, climbed off my back and returned to the jungle where he belonged. It had only been in the past few weeks that I'd felt an odd tug, a strange sort of pull to return to my web of words.

As if something is missing?

I tried not to think about it, but I knew it was true. I did miss the mulling. The forming of thoughts as if they would be *read* by someone. It had all started the night I watched Dan Jordan hand over what I now knew was a photo of Ida's house to Vicky's husband, Dave. The mystery was solved, but in the intervening weeks my mind had run amok with story ideas.

Back.

There it was again. The word I'd been trying to ignore.

I'm calling you back.

Vicky interrupted my thoughts by pushing back her chair. "I really need to get to work over there. Thanks, this was just what I needed." She stood and took a final sip of her coffee. "Stop by again. Any time. You don't even need to bring cookies. I could use the moral support."

"Could you use some help?" The words surprised me as much as they seemed to surprise Vicky. *You'll do anything to run away from writing, won't you?*

Vicky looked at me with wide eyes for a second. Then she blinked. "Absolutely not. I wouldn't dream of asking you to help with my project."

"You didn't ask. I did." What was I saying?

I work in mysterious ways.

"Really, I'd love to pitch in. I have nothing better to do." Who was this person who was so generously offering my precious time?

Precious time? You haven't done much of anything for months. You're lazy. You—

STOP! I wasn't going to go *there* either. Those self-defeating thoughts from the days of my depression were never far away.

"Honest, I'd love to help." Apparently I'd given myself over to the alien that had inhabited my body.

Vicky picked up her coffee cup and downed another sip. I could hear her swallow. Was she trying to think of a reason to refuse my offer? I could feel my cheeks burning. I didn't blush easily, but if I was as red-faced as I felt, Vicky might take one look at me and call 9-1-1 just to get me off her hands. This was *her* project, not mine. I'd been too pushy. She didn't want my help. The help I suddenly wanted to give more than anything.

And now that she doesn't want you, what will you do with your precious time?

Stop it! I'd find something.

Something having to do with binoculars and peering across the street? You need a life.

Lord, I prayed, *please. Give me something to do.*

Vicky cleared her throat. I could already feel disappointment rising in my chest. This is what I got for being a snoop in the first place.

"I couldn't pay you."

"What?"

"I couldn't afford to pay you. For helping." She pushed a strand of hair behind one ear. "The only reason I can afford to do this project at all is because the main café is paid for. When my parents died…" She scratched the back of her hand. "Well, maybe you don't remember that. It was a long time ago."

Not for the first time I wished I were Anne. She would reach out and pull Vicky into a tight embrace. Instead all I could do was say, "I do remember." Give me some credit, I did look straight into her eyes.

Vicky's eyes glistened as she met my steady gaze. "Maybe this idea is…foolish. But—" She looked out my kitchen window and across the street. "I just… We all…needed *something*."

Just like I did.

I pulled in a slow breath through my nose. I could do this. I'd already proven that by walking across the street in the first place. Somehow this next step seemed farther.

Anne's voice urged me. *You can do this, Libby. Take the first step. It'll be fine.*

I took a step forward and opened my arms.

Who knew what I might embrace?

~

Within two days I had a new routine. A reason to get out of bed, fill a thermos with steaming coffee, grab two mugs, and head across the street.

"Today I want to scrub down these bedroom walls." Vicky had her hands wrapped around the thick ceramic coffee mug I'd handed her. She motioned with the mug, as if circling the small bedroom where we were standing. "I still can't believe these walls were never painted over. It's incredible."

It really was. This room was detailed with a delicate mural. Two women and three small children having a picnic…somewhere that definitely wasn't Brewster…in a time that no longer existed. "Do you think we dare put a wet rag on that?"

"I wondered the same thing. I tested a corner of the detailing in the living room. It seems to stand up. We won't *scrub* those women, we'll just *dab* at 'em." Vicky checked the bottom of her mug and then set it on the wide oak windowsill. "You're sure you're not getting tired of this?"

I took a long swallow and set my mug by Vicky's. "Positive. Let's do it."

By mid-morning I was in a sweat. Wetting and rewetting the old towel I was using as a rag. Ringing it out. Bending up and down. Sharing a ladder with Vicky as we took turns washing the walls near the ceiling or kneeling to clean near the trim boards. We'd scrubbed down the bathroom and the one other bedroom the day before. Easy conversation punctuated comfortable silence. Light snow was falling through the early-spring sun trying to shine just outside the large window. The low hum of the furnace made the house feel familiar and cozy. And activity felt good in contrast to the many days I had sat at home, staring at my computer, looking out the window, hoping against hope that God would show me why He'd put me here. So many days I struggled, but today I was content with my simple task.

Vicky's back was to me as she circled her wet rag against the wall. "I used to think I had life figured out."

"I'm listening." If Vicky had a secret to share, I was all ears.

"I said *used* to." Vicky turned and dunked her rag in the basin of warm water. She wrung it out and continued her work.

A deep sigh from Vicky broke through my thoughts. "Now all I'm trying to do is understand if it was *wrong* for me to have so many dreams for my daughter."

She didn't have to say more. I dipped my rag into the water and watched as clean water replaced the years of dust I'd rubbed into it.

Kind of like all those dreams I'd had. They had amounted to nothing but dust. Mere imaginings that were being replaced with who knew what. I twisted the cloth between my fingers. Why did I think that wringing dirty water back into the tub made the cloth I was holding clean again?

I will wash you whiter than snow. I'd never been good about recalling Bible verses, but somewhere in that Bible of mine

I knew there was a verse about being washed white as snow. About taking away the dingy old stuff of life and replacing it with something better. I only had to look out the window at the early spring flurries to see just how clean and white snow was. I glanced outside. Blinding, actually. So bright that for a moment I couldn't see.

I squinted my eyes against the intense light and waited while the world came back into focus. Was there some message in the glare? Even if I couldn't see for a second, I knew it was still snowing. Was something happening in my life that I simply couldn't see? I sure hoped so. If only I knew what my purpose was. If I knew any of this meant anything it might make my days easier.

"If only I could see a future for Angie." Once again Vicky's words broke through my musing. The fact that her thoughts were so similar to mine was uncanny.

She seemed not to mind that I hadn't answered her question about the rightness of dreaming. She had no idea my mind had spun so far so quickly. Besides, I had no answers, only questions of my own. "Umm," I murmured, letting her know I'd heard.

"I mean here she is, barely eighteen, and she's been pregnant and married. And now Brett is gone." Vicky put the rag she was holding onto the floor and sat back on her bent legs for a moment. It wasn't hard to feel her discouragement. Slowly she turned around and sat with her back to the wall.

I took my cue from her. I stopped my scrubbing and sat on the thin, old carpet, facing her across the small room. With one finger I mindlessly traced the faint pattern in the faded carpet. "Young people are resilient."

Tell her.

No, I can't. I don't share that part of my story. "I'm sure she'll be fine." A platitude if ever I heard one.

Vicky bent her knees and wrapped her arms around them.

"Oh, I know. But if *I'm* feeling hopeless, I can't imagine how Angie feels. I only wanted the best for her, and now it seems as if her future is already mapped out."

Tell her.

I ran a finger slowly down the leg of my worn jeans, wondering if I dared. I was learning when God prompted it was best to follow His lead. But I'd never been one to share my failures openly. If you could call an unplanned pregnancy that resulted in Brian a failure.

Tell her.

I stared at the carpet and spoke softly. "I was pregnant before I got married." Had I ever said that out loud before?

"What?"

I glanced up at Vicky and gave a small nod. I still wasn't so sure I wanted to get into this. "I was nineteen. Barely."

"You?" Her mouth wasn't quite hanging open, but it might as well have been. I knew what she was thinking before she said it. "But—but…you're a banker's wife. Your life is supposed to be…*perfect.*"

I laughed. Not loud, but laughter all the same. "Ah yes, and I was a banker's daughter before that. I have the silver spoon I was born with tucked away somewhere."

I could almost see Vicky's brain working overtime trying to figure out what to say next. Maybe I could help her out. "I know I don't fit the image of an unwed, pregnant teen. Not now. It's been…what? Twenty-five…twenty-six years? I'm sure there are a few old ladies in Brewster who still count on their fingers when they see me… or Brian." I knew who those people were. I didn't need them to judge me. I'd done enough of that myself.

I brushed a strand of hair from my eyes. "I guess what I'm trying to tell you is that Angie can have a future—a good one. Dumb mistakes don't have to stay that way." I wouldn't have said what I said next earlier in my life, but now I knew it was true. "God has a way of using even our mess-ups for good."

"But how?" Vicky was sitting cross-legged now, leaning forward.

"It wasn't easy. I was so embarrassed. Mortified, really." I pressed a hand to my cheek. I could still recall how ashamed I'd felt. "I wasn't what you'd call *religious*, but I knew what I'd done wasn't right. I dropped out of college and Bob and I got married. I worked some crummy part-time jobs until Bob graduated. You know, not too many people are anxious to hire a pregnant teen for anything more than minimum wage."

Vicky raised an eyebrow. "I know."

I'd seen some of the young people Vicky had had work part-time for her over the years. She had to know the pitfalls of hiring young employees. Another reason, no doubt, she was so concerned for her daughter.

"About all we had when Bob graduated was a job offer at the bank in Brewster. You might not remember, but my dad used to be president of the bank here. He died when I was in high school, but my mom was still a stockholder and she put in a good word for her new son-in-law. When we moved back, we didn't have anything more than an old saggy couch the Salvation Army wouldn't even take."

One side of Vicky's mouth turned up. "I think Angie and Mark have that couch."

I pressed my lips together in a wry smile. "It won't hurt them. They'll learn to value the little things that make life better. Things like a new chair. An end table. A decent lamp. Things they took for granted when they lived at home."

Vicky rolled her hand in a gesture that said "tell me more." "How'd you survive?"

"Hard work. Bob worked at the bank and did some odd jobs

on the side. I worked off and on, too. We didn't take vacations. We didn't drive new cars. But...you know what?" I smiled at Vicky.

"What?"

"I couldn't see it at the time, but I look back now and realize those were some of the best years of our lives."

Vicky uncrossed her legs and leaned her head back against the wall while she took in a deep breath. "I know what you mean. I've been so busy worrying about Angie...and being mad at her...I forgot."

"And you know..." I paused. I wanted to be certain she heard this. "I went back to college just a few years ago and got my degree. Angie still has the whole world in front of her. Maybe she can't see that right now."

"Blind but now I see?" Vicky quoted the familiar line from the hymn.

"Something like that. They're both young. You need to encourage her...and Mark. Don't let their own discouragement defeat them. Or yours. They can have a wonderful life right here in Brewster." I pointed a hand to myself. "Look at me."

I left out the part about my struggle with depression and my angst over what to do with my writing. In talking to Vicky, I realized I might have that same anguish no matter where I lived or how old I was. Still, all in all, life had been good to me. I would simply have to trust that God was using my time for His good.

I am.

Funny how simply sharing my story put my life in perspective. Those times I'd thought were so awful had led me into God's arms. Had led me here. Right here. Where life felt suddenly, subtly, very good.

"Thank you." Vicky spoke into the quiet. "I needed to hear that."

Now you know why you're here.

One of those unexpected lumps filled my throat. There was nowhere else I wanted to be other than on this floor, in this old house, right now. I knew the moment would evaporate soon, so I filed it in my heart so I could remember how right life felt when I was in God's will.

"I think it's time for a break." Vicky pushed herself to her knees and then stood up.

I looked up at her from my spot on the floor. "Didn't we just have one?"

She gave me a lopsided smile. "I mean a different kind of break." She put the palms of her hands on the small of her back and leaned into the pressure. Watching her made me want to do the same thing, I just wasn't sure I could pick myself off the floor to do it.

Vicky looked at her watch. "If you don't mind being left alone for a few minutes, I might quick run over to the café." She pressed a hand against her chest and blinked rapidly. "I have a kid I need to hug."

I knew that feeling. "Go on. As long as I'm down here, I'm going to finish this section. Then, except for the closet, we'll be done with this room."

"I'll bring you back a surprise."

I knew the kind of surprises in store at Vicky's Café. As long as I was being offered a bribe I'd take advantage. "A Long John, preferably." Normally I wouldn't beg for food, and certainly not a calorie-laden, deep-fried roll, but since when had I been acting like myself lately?

"You got it." Vicky put her arms over her head and stretched. "I won't be long. When you're done with this wall, you stop, okay? I don't want to work my free labor to death."

"Get!" I waved her away.

I waited until I heard the door close and then forced myself to get back into gear. Why was it always so much harder to get going after a rest? My lower back ached as I crawled over to the water-filled tub. My muscles would loosen as soon as I got busy. I dunked my rag into the water. Ick, it was ice cold. Oh well, I only had the smallest section of wall left...from the doorframe of the small closet into the corner. A foot-wide section at most. I made quick work of it. There. Done.

I stood in the middle of the room and surveyed our morning's work. Like Vicky, I pressed my hands into my back and stretched. It felt good to have done something I could measure with my eyes. If I hurried, I could wipe down the walls of the small closet and have a surprise for Vicky myself. Another room *all* done.

I dumped the cold water down the bathtub drain, took a quick bathroom break, then refilled the plastic tub with hot water and Mr. Clean. I carried the concoction back to the small bedroom and got to work. I made quick work of the bottom two-thirds of the closet. There was no hanging rod, only four old-fashioned hooks that would bring good money on eBay and two painted wooden shelves. I pulled the ladder as far into the closet as I could get and climbed one rung. It was an easy couple minutes as I wiped down the short expanse of wall and the lower shelf. The last bit would be harder.

I tried to maneuver the ladder into a better position to reach the top shelf, but there was none. The shelf was cut back a few inches so a person could reach a hand under the doorframe and still make use of the shelf. But taking into account the awkward angle, combined with the height of the shelf, I doubted short little Ida Bauer had ever used it.

I was tempted to swipe the edge of the shelf and call it good. How much dust could collect in such an unlikely spot, anyway? And who would ever see it? I stepped off the ladder and rinsed my rag for the last time. Well, maybe not *last*. My good conscience got the better of me. I would know that shelf hadn't been cleaned… and it would bother me. I wrung out the rag and climbed the ladder. I ducked my head under the doorframe. There wasn't enough space to watch what I was doing. I had no choice but to angle my arm and wipe blindly.

I swept a cloud of ancient particles into my face. Oh good grief, I hadn't bargained for *this* in my volunteer job. I sneezed, a stubborn streak rising in me. I was determined to get all the old grime out of there. All of it.

I climbed down and rinsed the rag, then mounted my perch again. I ducked my head and pushed my shoulder under the doorframe, reaching with a cocked elbow into the farthest corner of the closet. I pushed, then pulled the rag. *"Ack!"* There was something in there!

I yanked my hand out of the dark recess, slamming my knuckles against the edge of the frame. *Ouch!* Visions of bats and dead mice ran through my mind and down my back. *Ick!* I didn't want to reach back up there, but I could hardly let some old, dead animal hide in a room that was going to be used for eating.

I took a deep breath as I formed the wet rag into a sort of all-purpose catcher's mitt. With any luck I could snag the beast and not have to touch it. I wasn't sure just what I'd *do* with it… besides scream and drop it in the middle of the floor. But I'd deal with that later.

I took a deep breath and pushed my arm into the void. There was a scream hanging on my tongue, just waiting for release. My brave front failed me. Instead of capturing the unknown blob in my mitt-like rag, I made a quick swipe over the surface of the shelf and jumped backward off the ladder as a dusty lump of… *something*… fell to the floor.

"Awwckk!" I wasn't sure what I was screaming at, but it felt like the right thing to do.

I kept my distance, waiting for the thing to move, wiggle, anything but just lay there. It didn't take but a second or two for me to realize a dust-covered book wouldn't be attacking me anytime soon. A small giggle replaced my waiting scream. This would be a good joke for one of those blooper shows.

I put down my rag and knelt next to the small book. Even without the covering of dust it was obviously old. The edges of the deep-blue cover were frayed, the cut edges of the pages yellowed. I bent low and blew a cloud of dust off the cover. Oh, my. There might be scientists who would like to capture this old dirt and study it. How *ancient* was this thing?

As I reached out and picked it up, the dust on the book made it almost slippery. I lifted the damp rag near my knees and carefully wiped off the layers of powdery grime. There, that was better. The old cloth binding had held up well.

There was no marking on the cover. No title or author. Simply faded blue cloth. Fine particles of dust fell from the inner pages as I opened the cover.

Edith Grace McKenna

The hand-written name was in an old-style cursive kids these days would never learn. Even in my years-ago elementary schooling we'd only been taught the basics, not the fine lines and flourishes of this confident hand. I turned the page.

March, 1902.

Dear Diary,

Tonight I met the man I'm going to marry!

Oh, my. Goose bumps raced down my arms as sudden warmth filled my chest. The dead animal I'd been imagining was a journal filled with life. A life that would be long over by now, but still alive on these pages.

I turned one page, then the next, and the next. Not reading, only scanning and questioning. How had the book ended up in this small house? On that high shelf? Who put it there? How long ago? Who was the young woman who had written those infatuated words? Was her heart broken or did she marry him?

I wanted nothing more than to pour myself a cup of coffee, push my back against a corner, and read every word of the fountain-penned diary. It wasn't thick, but there were more pages than I could read in a few minutes. Besides, from the sound of that first sentence, I knew I wanted to savor what came next. It was the power of *story* that tugged at me. What *happened?*

See what words can do? You're a writer. Write.

And then I *knew.* This was it! The idea for Vicky's recipe book that had eluded both of us until now.

I hugged the small book to my chest. Tears filled my eyes as a bubble of joy broke in my throat.

"What's so funny?" I hadn't heard Vicky return but there she was in the bedroom doorway.

I waved a hand toward the closet. "That." I pointed to the ladder. "And that." I nodded at the wet rag. "And that." Finally I held out the faded book. "And this."

Vicky's eyebrows puzzled together as she slowly shook her head "You've been working too hard."

"Oh, no," I said, finally getting to my feet, clinging to the small book as if it were part of me. "I'm only getting started."

Vicky

"Be careful. Don't scrape the walls. Oooohhh…" I cringed as Dave and Paul, Ruthie's husband, tried for a second time to angle the rectangular old table through the front door. I wasn't one bit worried about the table, it was already nicked and scratched. It had built-in character. A quality I didn't want added to my newly washed walls.

"Lift your end higher, Dad." Sam was right behind them with a simple curved-back oak chair in each hand.

"There. Got it." Paul back-stepped his way into the living room. "Where do you want this?"

I pointed to the far end of the room. "Set it there, about three feet out from the wall. Good. Thanks."

Sam lined up the chairs in the short hallway. As soon as all the tables were in place, the chairs would be positioned around them. The guys didn't wait for more instructions; already they were headed back outside, into the dusk. There were two pickups out there that needed unloading. Moving the tables and chairs into the restaurant was the last major project before the opening… besides thinking of a name for the place.

I'd been wracking my brain for weeks and still hadn't come up with anything I liked. It seemed everyone in town had an opinion, and they felt free to share their ideas whether I wanted their input or not.

"The Attic." That suggestion from Marv one afternoon when he stopped by Vicky's to buy a candy bar. "I had to climb up there one time. Ida thought she might have a squirrel's nest. I think she just wanted some company."

Kenny thought it was great I'd bought his aunt's little house. "Just call it 'Ida's.' Everyone in town is going to call it that anyway, you know." He sipped his coffee as if it were all decided.

The trouble was, none of the names grabbed me. They were meaningless names that had nothing to do with my dream. I had to think of something...and soon. The *Brewster Banner* planned to do a feature on my new business in the paper two weeks from now. I certainly didn't want my charming new restaurant to be tagged with the name "No Name."

I felt a wash of worry as I picked up a damp rag and wiped off the surface of the table, bending and cleaning the table legs, too. *Have I forgotten anything?* These past weeks, in between scrubbing down walls with Libby, shampooing the wildly patterned, faded carpets, and supervising the local carpenter who'd brought the dated kitchen up to code, I'd spent hours and hours searching for tables and chairs that would transform this quiet old house into the quaint restaurant of my dreams.

I never dreamed the people of Brewster had so many pieces of ancient furniture in their basements and backyard sheds. They were willing to part with most of it for mere pennies...well, *dollars*, but not that many of them. Some of the pieces had been handed over to me with nothing more than a "Good luck. I'm glad to be rid of it." All it had taken was a small ad in the *Brewster Banner*.

> Spring cleaning? Let Vicky Johnson help.
> I need old tables, chairs, a floor lamp...or three.
> Call Vicky's Café and leave a message.

That want ad and some well-placed conversational tidbits as Angie and Ruthie poured coffee at the café was all it took for the phone to start ringing. I quickly learned offering up old furniture was a good way for folks to find out why I wanted it.

More than a few times I heard, "The missus says she's got two old chairs if you want 'em." There'd be a long pause as a slow breath was taken in and breathed out. "She says to ask what you're planning to do with 'em." As if it was only *the missus* who wanted to know.

Secret agents these folks weren't. But I didn't care who knew about the plans I had for Ida's old house. I considered it free preadvertising.

As it was, I was going to need all the help I could get from the people of Brewster to make this whimsical dream of mine come true.

I directed Paul and Dave where to set each of the smaller tables they carried in next. A table for two tucked near the doorway. A card-table sized one near by. I sent Sam into the small bedroom I called "the nook" with his small table. A few more trips and they'd be done.

I hoped Angie would stop by as soon as the café closed to check out her and Mark's handiwork. I'd hired the two of them to refinish the pieces in the worst shape. They'd painted all of the tables a creamy white, not bothering with sanding out any nicks. I planned to use tablecloths to tie the look together. Besides, I kind of liked being able to see the history of these well-used pieces. It fit the old-world charm of the house. The chairs I'd had Angie and Mark strip to the bare wood. A light walnut stain and two coats of tung oil matched up the odd assortment of furniture surprisingly well.

"Where do you want these?"

I turned to see Dave, Paul, and Sam each holding a floor lamp as if they were going to perform some sort of unusual, very long baton routine. I welcomed the chance to laugh. We hadn't done much of that this past year. "Put that one over there." I pointed Sam into the far corner of the living room. I pointed next to Paul. "That one can go right here." There was an outlet near the doorway. "And you," I directed Dave, "can put yours in the first bedroom. Uh...the lunch nook." As if it already had been transformed.

"Anything else?" Paul was swiping his hands against his jeans.

"No, I think that's it for now. Thanks." I reached out a hand and gave his upper arm a quick pat. I snared Sam as he came near and pulled him close. "Thank you, too."

He ducked his head as I kissed his cheek. "No problem."

Dave was brushing his hands together as he walked into the room. "You ready to head home?"

I shook my head. "You guys head out. I've got a few things to do yet."

As Dave walked past he stopped and gave me a quick hug. "It's shaping up."

It was. I felt the warmth of his words and his hug. Our hard work, the work *all* of us had done, was almost over.

Or just beginning.

A satisfied smile covered my face as I watched *my* guys climb into their trucks to head home. Whether the work was almost done, or just starting, either way, it felt good to have a reason to get up in the morning. A new place to go. A different sort of schedule to think about. Soon, very soon, this new addition to Brewster would be ready to open its doors.

But first there were all kinds of finishing touches that needed doing. I reached out and turned the switch on the floor lamp nearest me. I crossed the room to turn on the other one. Two circles of yellow lamplight fell across the bare tables and chairs, softly illuminating corners the small chandelier overhead couldn't reach. I went into the kitchen and brought out the stack of newly edged tablecloths Mark had picked up from a seamstress in Carlton on his way home from work yesterday.

I set the stack on the table-for-two and unfurled one with a loud *crack* of the large rectangular cloth. A lift of my hands sent it floating across the table. I watched as it settled into place, a woven garden of gold, orange, green, and brown. Muted cotton foliage that blended perfectly with the painted vines on the walls.

I covered the remaining tables in their new garments, then stood back and imagined what the room would look like once I had a few pictures hung and candles on each table. The etiquette gurus might say it wasn't proper to burn candles during the day, that they should be lit in the evening or only on special occasions. I had one word for that advice: "*Phooey.*" Every time the doors of this dream of mine were open would be special enough for me.

"Wow, this looks nice." I hadn't heard Ruthie come in.

"You just missed Paul," I said, feeling a vague sense of disappointment. I'd been hoping for Angie. I kept hoping that one of these times, if she and I were alone together, I'd somehow find the words that would mend the unsettled space between us. I didn't know what those words were exactly. I'd been praying that when the time was right I'd find them. But it wouldn't be tonight. Angie wasn't here; Ruthie was. "Paul said he was going to go pick up the girls and head home."

Ruthie looked at her watch. "Good. His mother was watching them tonight. I'm sure she's ready to call it a night."

"You must be, too."

Ruthie slipped out of her coat and draped it over the back of a nearby chair. "I told Paul I was going to come over here after work and help you. The sooner we get this place put together, the sooner we can get our lives back again."

The words slipped from my mouth. "I'm not so sure I want that life back again."

Ruthie eyed me with a look I knew. "Then make it a better one."

Of the two of us, she'd always been the more outspoken. Quick to state her feelings whether I wanted to hear them or not. Sometimes her blunt words hurt, but there was always truth in them. And she was just as quick to apologize or ask forgiveness when she thought she might have offended. There was no offense tonight.

"I'm trying," I answered. "But Angie…" Quick tears pushed into my eyes. I'd been running on mere fumes this whole week, working toward our goal of quietly opening the doors of this new restaurant next weekend. Time to practice before we announced the opening in the local paper. "I'm sorry," I said, brushing at the tears with the back of my hand. "I'm tired."

"We all are." Ruthie stepped close and wrapped her arms around me in a tight hug. She was the older sister, but so often in the past, I'd been the one to take on the role of advisor and comforter. It was nice letting Ruthie share my burden. Tonight she was not only my sister, she was the mother I'd lost much too early.

How much is Angie missing you now?

As if Ruthie read my thoughts she said, "You need to talk to Angie."

"I've tried." My voice was muffled against Ruthie's shoulder. "The words won't come."

Ruthie gave me a squeeze then loosened her arms. "Then I'll pray you find the words."

"I can't."

She put her hands on each of my shoulders and looked me

straight in the eyes. "Maybe *you* can't, but God can. Now," she said, letting go of me, "what can I do?"

It was so like Ruthie to jump from the profound to reality. I wasn't as good at making abrupt transitions. With one hand I rubbed the back of my neck, leaning hard into the welcomed pressure. I'd spent the entire day here and planned on heading home to bed as soon as I saw what the new tablecloths looked like on the tables. But it was nice to have some company, and the more I got done tonight meant there would be that much less to do tomorrow.

"Would you mind helping me finish putting the tablecloths on the tables in the other rooms?"

Before I finished the sentence, Ruthie was picking up the stack of tablecloths and was heading toward the adjacent room. If she was going to be that cooperative...

"There's some pictures I could use some help hanging, too."

"I told Paul I might be late. Let's get it done."

We made quick work of the tablecloths. The warm colors of the cloths added a layer of coziness. What had at first felt like just another cold jumble of rooms filled with hard-surfaced tables was now warm and inviting. We opened two boxes of clean-lined hurricane-style candle holders, wiped them off with a soft cloth, and put one in the middle of each table. We placed a large votive candle inside each lamp.

Ruthie stood at the edge of the living room and surveyed our work. "I'd eat here."

I laughed. "Too bad you won't get to very often."

We'd already spent many hours deciding how we were going to cover the work that needed doing in both places. I wasn't completely oblivious to the fact that this fanciful dream of mine might not fly in Brewster. Most of my regular customers were set in their ways. They liked their coffee fast, hot, and free flowing. Leisurely dining was not in their dictionary. This was one of the reasons I'd decided to open this restaurant only for lunch Thursday through Saturday, with special reservations-only dinners every other Saturday night. On the weekends I was hoping to import some people from Carlton who might be up for a little adventure. Goodness knew, the folks from Brewster drove to Carlton often enough. The road went both ways, and we could use some of their big-city business here.

I could also use any extra food at Vicky's during the week. I didn't want to open a fridge full of spoiled food every Thursday. That would cut into a bottom line I already knew would be slim. Even though I wasn't doing this to make money, I did hope to break even. Eventually. In the meantime I was praying that this place would be a new beginning...for all of us.

I blew a puff of air from my mouth. "You know, I think all that's left is to hang those pictures." I waved a hand at the short stack of framed old-style prints leaning against the hallway wall.

"Let's do it." Ruthie bent to pick up the hammer and container of nails I'd brought from home.

I didn't plan to decorate much. The walls of this old house were artwork in themselves. There were only four walls, two in the living room and one in each of the two "nook" rooms, that could use a painting.

Ruthie put the hammer and nails on a nearby table, picked up one of the paintings and held it against the wall. "What do you think? This one...here?"

I eyeballed the picture. "A little to the left and an inch lower." I took another step back. "I think."

"It's good. Put your finger on the spot." Ruthie tilted the frame as my index finger marked where the nail would go. She set the picture down and picked up the hammer. "So everything turned out okay with the city council?"

"Didn't I tell you?" With me spending my days here, and Ruthie at the café, our usual tell-every-little-detail conversations had a few missing links. "It turns out Brewster doesn't have a zoning ordinance. So it's okay to have a restaurant in the middle of a residential area. About the only thing they were worried about was the parking, but with my limited hours and limited seating, they didn't think it would be an issue. As long as the neighbors don't complain, I'm fine."

Speaking of neighbors, my gaze drifted out the front window and across the street. As I watched, the garage door raised and Libby's navy-blue Lincoln glided inside. If I remembered right, she was returning from her out-of-town conference tonight. She'd probably be up late unpacking. I couldn't wait to hear all about it. As we worked together the past weeks she'd shared with me her nervousness about going to her first writer's conference.

What was it she said?

"Watching you make your dream a reality with this house gave me the courage to pursue mine, again." Whatever her exact words were, I felt I had as much of a stake in her future as she had in mine. She'd been such a help getting this house in shape. I knew Libby would be pleasantly surprised to see the finishing touches in place. I had no doubt she'd be here in the morning, hot coffee ready to pour. If I were lucky, I'd have nothing more to do than sit at one of these tables and visit with her.

"Anything else?" Ruthie had walked slowly through the house, checking the finished product. "Should we call it a night?" She yawned. "Sorry." She covered her mouth with her hand as she yawned again. "I'm really not that tired."

"Yes, you are." After all our years of working together I could read my sister like a book. I, on the other hand, had picked up a second wind somewhere between hanging pictures three and four. "You go home. I'll be right behind you. I just want to sit a minute and think if there's anything I've forgotten to do."

I didn't have to tell her twice.

"See you tomorrow." Ruthie pressed her cheek next to mine. "I'm proud of you."

Looking over the finished room, I was too. As I heard the door latch click shut, I turned off the overhead light, pulled out a chair, and sat down in the intimate circle of light glowing through the sheer silk shade of the floor lamp. I looked over the room pretending I was my first customer. What sort of feeling did this place give me? Who would I invite to eat here with me? Most importantly, what was for lunch?

My dream-like imagining vanished. *The menu!* How could I have forgotten about that? For years I'd collected recipes for this someday dream...but *someday* was now... and I needed something to serve that first customer—pronto!

I went into the kitchen and grabbed the notepad I kept near the phone. A pen, too. I returned to the living room—now the *Main Dining Room* in this renovated house—and started jotting down menu ideas. After years of dreaming, it wasn't hard to quickly fill two pages with ideas. Beef Medallions in a Merlot-Mushroom Sauce. Cranberry-Covered Chicken Breasts.

I didn't plan to have a printed menu...simply a handwritten offering on antique gold paper I'd found at an office supply store in Carlton. I'd plan my menus around what was fresh and in season each week.

I nibbled on the end of the pen as I concocted dishes in my head. Combinations of food I never dared try at plain old Vicky's seemed perfect for...for...what? I needed a name for this place as much as I needed a menu.

A light tap at the front door made me jump. Before I could get there, it was followed by a whisper, as if I might be sleeping.

"Are you still here?" Libby poked her head around the front door. "I saw lights and your car. Oh…*my*." She stepped all the way in. "Vicky, this is…it's beautiful. I never imagined it would look like…" She floated her hand in a generous circle, "…this."

I knew my grin matched hers. "Welcome home." I hurried to the door and gave her a hug. She'd been gone less than a week, and I suddenly realized how much I missed her company during the long days of working on this house by myself.

At her insistence, I gave her a very quick tour of the house and then tugged at her hand. "Come. Sit." She could see for herself what I'd accomplished in her absence. I, on the other hand, had no idea what she'd been up to. I motioned for Libby to sit in the chair I'd been in. She could have full view of the renovated room. I'd sit next to her and soak up the ambiance.

She took a seat, setting a yellow file folder of papers on the table in front of her. I smiled to myself. So she'd brought show-and-tell from her writer's conference. Did any of us ever outgrow the need for approval?

Libby turned her head, taking it all in. "It looks like you could open for business tomorrow."

I laughed. "I could if there was food in the fridge. If the dishes to serve the food weren't in boxes and in need of washing. And…" This was the topic of the night. "I had a name for this place." I didn't even want to ask if she'd thought of any ideas. Libby had done more than enough for me…without pay, although I did intend to treat her to as many lunches as she cared to eat here. I waved a hand across my face. "Oh, I'm tired of talking… thinking…about this place." I leaned forward on my elbows, cupping my hands beneath my chin. "Let's talk about you and your trip. The conference—was it everything you thought it would be?"

For a moment she didn't speak. Her mouth worked silently.

Her eyes darted and blinked. It was as though there was so much inside her that the thoughts were scuffling to see which would burst out of her first. She sighed, sat back, and then grinned. "It was like trying to take a sip of water from a fire hose."

No wonder she was a writer. I had no trouble at all envisioning Libby trying to take in as much information as she could in the few days of her first writer's conference.

I leaned forward even further. In the days while we'd scrubbed walls and shampooed carpets, Libby had confided her writing dreams to me. I had to ask. "So…? Did they say anything about your novel?"

Now it was her turn to quickly wave a hand through the air. "Oh, no one ever sells a novel at a conference. All you get is a chance to pitch it to see if there is any interest."

She'd told me all about "pitching." About the one or two sentences a writer had to use to hook an editor. She'd even practiced her pitch on me as we'd hung honeycombed shades and filmy side-curtains over the windows.

"So…" I riffled my fingers through the air, trying to coax information from her.

She lifted one shoulder as if it was nothing. "I have a few requests to see the first few chapters."

"Great!" I reached out a hand and squeezed her arm.

"I'm not getting my hopes up. I talked to enough people at the conference to know the reality is that getting a novel published is difficult. It more than likely will never happen. I'll follow up but—" She paused as she pulled the thin folder on the table into her hands. "This is what I'm really excited about." She tapped her hand against the yellow file folder and smiled as if it was holding a big surprise.

"What?"

She started to open the file, then closed it. "Remember that book I found in the closet? The diary?"

I hadn't thought much about the dusty old book, but of course I remembered, mainly because of Libby's hilarious recounting of the way she'd found it. A dead animal it wasn't; a good story it was. I'd told her she was welcome to keep it. "Yeah...so?"

"So..." Now she did open the file. "I think I have a name for your restaurant."

I leaned my head closer, trying to catch a glimpse of the papers under her hands. She spread her fingers over the top page. "Just a minute. I need to tell you a story first."

"I should have figured a writer would have a story." One side of my mouth turned up.

So did hers. "Just listen. I think you'll like this."

I crossed my arms and sat back in my chair. From working with her the past few weeks I knew Libby was good at this.

"Before I left for the conference I read through the diary." As she talked, Libby ran her thumb through the small sheaf of pages in front of her. "The first few pages of the diary were a lot more interesting than the rest of the entries. It turns out Edith wasn't that great about writing down details." She smiled. "Frankly, I think love took over, and then life. The entries were pretty spotty. But she did marry the guy—the one she mentioned on the first page."

"Well, that's nice." As a storyteller I could understand why Libby might find this fact fascinating, but for the life of me I couldn't see where she was headed.

She pushed at her hair as if rearranging ideas. "I couldn't let it go. The idea of a diary, I mean. It just kept nagging at me as if there was something I was missing. And then on the plane, on the way to the conference, it came to me." Her voice rose and she leaned forward in her seat. "We could write the recipe book in the same format." Her tone held an enthusiasm I couldn't catch.

I didn't want to appear dense, but I had to say it. "I don't get it."

"Like a diary." She took a deep breath. Was she searching for words? Or patience over my lack of understanding? "Remember we talked about incorporating the history of Brewster in with the recipes?"

Gosh, how long ago had that been? So much had happened in-between. "Vaguely."

Libby thrust her hands between her knees as though she could hardly sit still. "In the diary I found out that the man Edith married ended up being a city judge in Brewster. He was the one who built this house for his new bride. She was from Minneapolis and, I'm guessing, wasn't thrilled about moving to a little town in North Dakota." With one hand she lifted the paper in front of her and turned it my way. "I filled in the blanks. I'm going to have to do some research about the history of Brewster. We can tie in recipes between the entries."

I bent my head trying to quickly absorb all she'd said. I looked up. "Slow down. I'm not following this."

She took a deep breath. "I'm sorry, this always happens when I get excited. Here." She handed me the top two pages. "It might be better if you just read what I wrote."

I took the two hand-lettered pages into my hands and glanced at them. I looked up. Libby was leaning so far my way she practically obstructed my view.

"Sorry," she said again. "I'm going to go get a drink of water. You read."

I couldn't help but smile at her anxiety. "I think that might work better."

She pointed to the page in my hand. "Read it."

As Libby got up from the table I turned the paper so that it caught the soft glow of the floor lamp and began to read...

March, 1902
Minneapolis, Minnesota

Dear Diary,

Tonight I met the man I'm going to marry! My sister, Cassie, my friend, Clara, and I attended the concert at church tonight. It was all perfectly innocent. We certainly did not go there looking to meet men. However, the men's quartet performed two numbers, and I couldn't help but notice the extremely handsome dark-haired fellow on the right. I was dying to meet him. But since our parents weren't at the concert, there was no one to introduce us. Not that I would have had the nerve to ask Father to do so anyway.

Well...there were refreshments served in the church basement after the program, and as I was walking into the fellowship hall, whispering to Clara, wondering how I ever would meet this gentleman, my shoe caught the doorjamb and I tripped right into George. That's his name. George.

He caught my elbow and I just knew...it was meant to be.

He invited us to sit with him and his friends. We had the most delightful time. He is extremely smart. A law student! Studying in St. Paul. He has asked to call on me during the Easter break.

The church ladies outdid themselves. Never have I tasted a more delicious lunch.

Hurry Easter, hurry!

Love,

Edith

(Vicky: We can insert Cookie recipe here.)

I'd been so quickly caught up in Libby's story that the sudden surprise of something so mundane as the suggestion of a cookie recipe caused me to shake my head and blink. But I knew just the recipe. The delicious Molasses Crinkles Libby had brought to this house the day she'd walked across the street and offered her help.

I was starting to understand what Libby had in mind. I could feel my heart pick up an excited rhythm as my eyes flicked back to the page.

> January, 1903
> St. Paul, Minnesota
>
> It is with great anticipation that I look forward to my graduation from law school in May. While the years here have been a challenge, I find myself anxious to go into business for myself:
>
> George M. McKenna, Attorney at Law
>
> I like the sound of that!
> My friend J.J. Murphy has started a partnership arrangement forming the State Bank of Brewster in Brewster, N.D. He has informed me that they have great need for an attorney in town. I had always thought that my work would be in Minneapolis, however it sounds as if there is much opportunity in the Dakotas. I will travel to Brewster next week to see for myself.
>
> George

Oh...Libby planned to have both the judge *and* his wife tell this story. I was liking this more and more. I could already imagine the men of Brewster being interested in the history part of this book, the women, the recipes…and Libby's story. I turned my eyes to the pages, again.

October, 1903
Mower County, Minnesota

Dearest Diary,

It seems this year shall last forever! I am enjoying my teaching position with the Mower County School District. The ladies of the county gave me such a lovely welcome tea. They served the most delicious spiced breads. I must get the recipes and serve them to George.

Being so far from George is much harder than I ever imagined it would be. He has written me the sweetest letters. Sigh. But for the life of me, I cannot imagine what he finds so appealing in that little town of Brewster. In North Dakota, no less! I hope he comes to his senses soon and returns to the city for good. I shall persuade him at the Christmas break. I think I shall go mad until I see him again at Christmastime.

Love,
Edith Grace

(Vicky: We can insert Spiced Bread recipe here.)
Now I knew exactly what Libby had planned. I liked it—a lot! I wanted to read more…

November, 1903
Brewster, North Dakota

What a hunt! J.J. and I went out hunting prairie chickens this A.M.—had more than enough in one hour. I am convinced this area of the country is home to half the game birds on this earth. J.J.'s sister fixed a couple of our prairie chickens for supper. She served it with brown rice and a chokecherry concoction over the birds—whatever it was, it was GOOD!

On the work front, my practice of law continues to grow as more people move to town each week. I am convinced this town has a great future, and I look forward to being a part of it.

I am planning to ask Edith to marry me when I return to Minneapolis for the holidays. I am more than ready to settle down, and I feel I have a good life to offer Edith here on the plains of North Dakota. If she loves this countryside half as much as I do, we shall be very happy here.

George

What? There was no more? I turned the paper over. I wanted to read the rest of the story. I knew exactly which chicken recipe would follow George's entry, but I didn't know how their lives unfolded.

It's fiction, Vicky. It really didn't happen.

But it seemed as if it had. Right here in Brewster. In this very house.

At my elbow Libby softly cleared her throat. "Are you done? What do you think?"

For a moment I was speechless. What did I think? I loved it! But more than that, I wanted to know what happened to those two people. How did they end up in this house? What happened when they moved to Brewster?

It's fiction. Remember?

I had to keep reminding myself of that. I gazed at the two pages in my hand. The story felt so real.

That's why God called Libby to write.

Of course. It was her *gift*. Just as cooking and serving people was mine. Butterfly wings brushed along the surface of my arms as I looked up at Libby. "It's... It's..." No wonder Libby was the writer. There were no words in my vocabulary to tell her what I was thinking.

She sat on the edge of her chair. "Good? Bad?" She grimaced as if fearing the worst.

"Wonderful!" I tried to find another word. A better one. "*Stellar!*" Now there was a perfect word I'd grabbed from my son.

Libby sighed deeply. "Oh, good." She lifted crossed fingers. "I was hoping you'd like it. Sometimes writers get so close to their work it's hard to be objective."

"When can I read the rest of it?"

Libby pushed herself further into the chair. "Now that's the perfect compliment. Wanting to read more." She was smiling as she shuffled through the papers still in the file folder. "I've got the story line plotted out. Some notes about the recipes jotted down. I'm going to have to go to the library and go through some old issues of the *Banner* so I can get the town history right. But first...do you want to hear the name I thought of for you?"

Did I? Of course I did. I'd been so caught up in Libby's story I'd forgotten. "Tell me." I closed my eyes, waiting to hear her idea.

I could hear her take in a breath. Pause. Was she praying I'd like it? If she wasn't, I was. This house needed a name.

"The Judge's Chambers."

Oh, yes. I could see it. *Feel it.* The *judge.* Quiet confidence. A subdued elegance. Authority. And *chambers.* The coziness of a comfortable home. Only then did I open my eyes.

"That's it."

I didn't need to say more.

⌒

"Are you ready for tomorrow?" Libby was squatting at the edge of the main dining room making sure the tablecloth edges were in perfect alignment. She'd already checked that the pictures on the walls were straight and that the greenery on the silk trees I'd purchased to liven a few corners was fluffed to the max.

Tomorrow. It had taken forever to get here, and yet no time at all.

My eyes fell on the small plaque that had been hanging by the front door when I bought this house. *God bless our home.* There was no reason to take it down. God's blessing was always welcome. But it made me think of something…*someone*…who wasn't here: Ida. I wished she could be here tomorrow. To serve as a guest-of-honor, of sorts. She'd nixed my idea pretty quickly…

"Ida?"

She was lying in her bed at the nursing home under a light-blue knitted afghan. I wasn't sure if her eyes were simply closed, or if she was sound asleep, dreaming of other times. One of the aides had told me to go ahead and wake her if she was sleeping. It seemed most of her time these days was spent dreaming.

"Ida?" I lightly rubbed my fingers on the shoulder of her polyester dress. "Are you awake? It's Vicky."

Her eyes struggled to open, to leave that dreamy place she'd been. She blinked at me. "Wicky?"

I sat in the wheelchair that was pushed next to the bed. "Can you wake up and visit with me? I have something I want to ask you."

She turned onto her side and then pushed herself up on her elbow. The position didn't look one bit comfortable, but she seemed steady enough. "I von't take my house back if dat's vhy you're here."

I wasn't sure, but I thought I could catch a gleam in her watery eyes. A twinkle to let me know she was teasing. She'd been delighted when Dave and I had visited with her about purchasing her small home and turning it into a specialty restaurant.

"You can't have it back." I leaned forward, wishing I could take her hand in mine. This dear woman had worked her way into my heart over the years. She'd taught me to make pie crusts from scratch. She'd helped out in our booth at Pumpkin Fest more years than I could count. And up to a year ago, she'd been as reliable as the sun when it came to showing up for coffee time at the café. She'd even manned the cash register a few times when things were especially busy. She was honorary aunt, grandma, and very good friend.

I reached out and put my hand on the afghan over her leg. "If it weren't for you keeping that house in such good shape all these years, it wouldn't have nearly the character it does now. I was hoping Dave could pick you up tomorrow and bring you to the grand opening. I'd like you to see what we've done, and I'd like people to see you. It'll be a fun time."

She wobbled a bit on her elbow, then eased herself back onto the bed, her head nearly flat on the thin pillow. "Acht." She waved a fragile hand in the air the way I'd seen her do a thousand times over the years when she thought something was foolish. "My fun times are here." She touched her head, then laid the same hand over her heart. "I vant to rememper my house da vay it vas."

I'd had a feeling she would say something like that. "You're sure? I'd love to have you there more than anything."

She reached out her hand, and I took it in mine. "Oh, childt, your memories in dat house are chust beginning. Make dem goodt vuns. You haff my blessing."

I knew then that's what I'd come for. I could feel tired tears from the past weeks of work, the past year of worry, fill my eyes. "Thank you." It was nearly a whisper, but I knew she'd heard, if not with her ears...then with her heart.

Now I stared at the small plaque. It would remind me of God's blessings on this house and on Ida. I looked around the house-turned-restaurant, pretending to think, but I knew there was absolutely nothing more we could do in this house that would make it more ready for our grand opening tomorrow at lunchtime.

My parent's fine china was hand-washed and ready. The mix-and-match dishes I'd collected over the years were waiting, too. The kitchen floor was waxed, the fridge was full, tomorrow's menus hand-printed. Even Libby was going to be wearing an apron. I wondered what the gossips in Brewster would make of the banker's wife pouring coffee. Somehow the folks around here didn't think of Ruthie in the same gravy boat as Olivia. Oh well, it was only for tomorrow they'd get to wag their tongues. After the weekend Libby planned to put the finishing touches on the recipe book we were collaborating on.

I sighed and ran both hands through my hair. It was hard to believe that life could look so different after the dark, dark months of the past year. "Everything's ready," I said finally.

Libby stood with one hand on the doorknob. "Then I guess I'll go home and get a good night's sleep. Tomorrow will be here soon enough."

"It will." I waved her out the door. "Thanks. See you tomorrow."

I stood in the doorway and watched as she crossed the street.

The sun was setting, a brilliant orange against a blue spring sky. The end of one day. The end of something else entirely...at least I hoped it was.

I glanced at my watch, then went inside to get my coat and keys. Hopefully I'd timed this right. There was one door left to close before this one could open. One thing more no one could help with. No one but me.

And Me.

I needed to talk to Angie.

Angie

"Is there anything else I can get you?" I put the register ticket on the table.

"So what's for lunch?" Lydia Glass was trying to satisfy more than her curiosity. Three other pairs of ears at her table were waiting to hear my answer.

It was six-thirty at night, and I didn't even have to wonder if she was asking about the lunch special here tomorrow. I knew she was talking about what would be served at my mom's new restaurant. I lifted the picked-over plates from their table and said for maybe the twenty-fourth time tonight, "I know it's not hamburgers and fries."

They chuckled politely but I could tell my flip answer wasn't what they wanted to hear. The truth was, I didn't know what Mom planned to serve tomorrow. While that hard place between us had softened since Brett died, there was still an invisible ridge that kept us from truly connecting. And while Mom had been so busy working to open her new place, Ruthie and I had put in extra time at Vicky's. None of our schedules left much time for chatting. As if I would ever be able to say to my mom what I needed to.

With my back I pushed through the swinging door into the kitchen carrying the dirty dishes.

"What's it look like out there?" Ruthie was at the grill frying two hamburgers. As she spoke she lowered a basket of fries into the hot oil and put two buttered bun tops on the grill to toast.

"Busy," I said, quickly scraping the dirty dishes and placing them in the countertop dishwasher. "Another table just filled up."

Ruthie caught my eye. "We should have had our new help come in tonight."

We should have. After weeks of advertising in the *Banner*, we'd finally managed to hire two part-time people to fill in at the café. They'd been training this past week during the day, but Wednesday evenings were usually slow, and Ruthie and I had our routine fine-tuned. I tossed the dirty silverware into a tub of warm water to soak. "Who knew?"

Ruthie flipped the hamburgers and pressed at them with a metal spatula. "I should have guessed. Anything new in this town brings out people like ants in the spring."

At least it was something different. I didn't mind being busy. It kept me from thinking too much. About Brett. About my mom. "I'd better get back out there."

"Wait one second." Ruthie held up a finger. "I'll get this order ready and save you a trip." She quickly plated the hamburgers, shook the oil from the fry basket, and divided the fries between the two plates. "There you go."

I pushed my way back into the café. Not only had one table filled, now there were two more. I was glad for the business, but wondering how late we'd end up staying open. I set the hamburger order on the table and went to get water for the new customers. An already long day was getting longer. Ruthie had opened the café this morning baking pies and rolls before I arrived for the breakfast shift. She'd taken a several-hour break just after lunch. Usually, she went home and played with her little girls while her daycare help did some cleaning for her. But today I knew she'd taken her break at my mom's new restaurant. If you could call that a break.

I envied Ruthie's easy way with my mom. The couple times I'd stopped by the little house to offer help, Mom had said, "You've already done more than enough." As if the few tables Mark and I had painted while we filled in late-night hours when we couldn't sleep anyway was too much.

Tomorrow would be the first time I'd really spend some time at the house. The plan was for Ruthie and our new waitresses to run Vicky's tomorrow, while Mom and I, with some help from Olivia Marsden, would handle the grand opening of The Judge's Chambers. All the lunch reservations had been snapped up a week ago. If things weren't too wild here, Ruthie hoped to sneak away for the afternoon open house. Free coffee and dessert tasting were sure to fill that little space to the max.

I pretended I wasn't all that excited about the new restaurant, but the truth was…I was. It wasn't hard to see how having something new to think about had energized my mom. I was hoping some of that same enthusiasm would rub off on me. *Someday.* About something. As it was, my life stretched out in front of me like a dusty country road with no end in sight. If only one day someone would open the door of this café and somehow make my life different. I could only hope.

"May I take your order?" How many more times in my life would I repeat that?

I heard a familiar *whoosh* as the front door of the cafe opened. Not *more* customers.

You just said you wanted *someone to come in and make things different.*

I sighed. As if that would ever really happen. Although the sign in the window said we were open until eight, if there were customers we stayed open until they were gone. How long would I be here tonight? I dared a glance. Apparently my dad, Sam, and Mark thought they needed to eat supper here, too. At least I could make them clear their own plates while I cleaned up after other customers.

I turned back to the table I was waiting on. Before I could take their order, once more the door swished and I found myself turning. I felt a small stab of disappointment as Marv Bender walked in.

Same old, same old.

~

CLOSED. With a sigh I flipped the sign in the café window. Things had finally quieted down forty-five minutes ago. I'd told Ruthie to go on home. She had her kids waiting for her, and I didn't mind staying alone to finish cleaning up.

I pushed the vacuum across the café carpet, cleaning a carpet that had already been swept after the dinner hour. Mark had offered to stay and help me clean up. He didn't like being alone in our empty house any more than I did. When I told him I didn't have that much left to do, he said he was going to go back to the farm and help his dad work on a piece of machinery. I knew exactly what he meant. He'd do *anything* to keep from feeling, from thinking. Exactly why I vacuumed a carpet twice.

It had been kind of nice having Dad and Sam and Mark here for supper. For the first time in almost a year there was some kind of vibe that made all of us being in the same room together seem almost normal. *Almost.* But even in the noisy busyness of the café I could feel the vacant spot where Brett should have been. The empty spot in the booth where my mom would have sat beside my dad if she ever took time to sit down. I blew a breath of air out of my mouth as I switched off the vacuum cleaner. I was just going to have to get used to that unfilled space.

"Angie?"

"Ack! What? Who!" I jumped as my mom's voice filled the

sudden silence left by the now quiet vacuum. I put a hand on my thumping heart. "You scared me."

"I'm sorry." Mom walked into the café from the kitchen door. She must have come in through the back. "I didn't mean to. I saw the lights still on. I thought maybe you needed some help."

"No," I said, bending to wrap the vacuum cleaner cord around the holder, my heart still pounding. "I'm just finishing up."

Why was she here tonight? The new restaurant would be opening tomorrow. If there wasn't anything else to do to get ready, she could use the sleep. I knew for certain her nights had been as late as mine these past months. Every night after I closed the café I'd driven by that little house and saw *her* lights on, felt the tug to slow down, pull to the curb, walk in, and…*what*?

How did a person speak words of regret and sorrow that hadn't been invented?

Mom was walking toward the cash register. "Did you get the deposit ready?" She knew my routine. She should, it was hers.

"I was just going to do that."

"I'll do it." She paused with her hands on the till.

What was she thinking? Did she feel the heavy stretch of space between us, too? The silence that wasn't quiet at all?

"Were you busy tonight?" The tinny bell on the register rang as the drawer popped open. Before I could say anything she looked into the full drawer. "*Oh*. You were. I should have been here to help."

"That's okay." I pushed the vacuum cleaner into a small closet built behind the corner booth. A rope of unsettled quiet pulled and tugged between us, longing to be filled with words I couldn't say.

I could hear my mom counting ones into stacks of twenty-five. Sorting checks into a different pile. I closed the closet door, then looked around for something more to do. The salt and pepper shakers had been filled and wiped off. The ketchup bottles were full and in the fridge for the night. All that was left was to turn off the lights and lock the door.

It was just Mom and me…and the unsettled vibe between us. All of a sudden I was anxious to climb into my car and drive home. The radio would fill in for things I'd never say. "Are we done? Can I turn off the lights?"

Mom tucked the money pouch under the M&M's. One of us would run it over to the bank in the morning. "Done." She ran her fingers through her hair as she walked to the booth nearest the kitchen door where I was standing and plopped into it. "I'm tired."

I wished I was. I switched off the lights over the cash register area and waited for Mom to stand up. When she simply sat there, I switched off the rest of the lights anyway. There was enough light that filtered through the shades from the street outside. We both knew this restaurant like the back of our hands. Neither of us would trip on our way out.

There was something about being in the café in the dark that made it feel different. The soft light from the street, the faint smell of coffee, the lingering smells from the grill combined into a blanket of familiar comfort. I'd practically grown up in this café. It was as much *home* to me as my parents' house was.

But I didn't plan to sleep here. "You ready to go?"

"I just need to sit a minute." My mom slouched against the back of the booth. "It feels good to not have anything to do sometimes."

I remembered that feeling from the last day of school. No homework every night. No having to be out of bed at the buzz of an alarm clock every morning. I guessed turning off the lights of the café gave mom a similar good feeling. Nothing to do until morning.

Which would be here soon enough. "I suppose…" I leaned against the swinging door leading into the kitchen, opening it part way. I didn't want to leave my mom sitting alone in the dark. I knew how that felt all too well. I wished she'd get up. It was too weird to watch her just sit there. My mom rarely sat still.

"Thanks for helping tonight, Angie."

More weirdness. I *worked* here after all. "No problem. You ready?" Again I pushed on the swinging door.

"I guess." She pushed herself away from the back of the booth and rested her arms on the tabletop. In the dim light I could see her open her mouth, then close it. As if she was trying to say the same words I couldn't speak. She tried again.

No, not now…

She sighed heavily. "Angie." She patted the table with her hand. "Sit with me a minute."

My heart started pumping overtime. I didn't want to talk. Not now. Maybe not ever. We'd never talked about…about any of it. There was too much to say. Too much I simply couldn't say. It was so much easier to keep my words inside.

Is it?

No, it wasn't. But I wasn't sure it was possible to say the things that needed saying. Not yet. I knew someday I was going to have to ask my mom if she could ever forgive me for the way I'd changed our family. But not now. Not tonight. It was too soon after Brett—I knew I couldn't talk. All I would do is cry.

Already tears were pushing their way past my throat and into my eyes. I walked through the faint darkness and slid into the booth across from my mom. We'd sat in this same booth, in these same spots, maybe a thousand times before, but never had there been so much filling the space between us.

I stared down at my hands. I was glad the lights were off.

Maybe in the dark I could push the words out. Get them out on the table. Out of my heart. Maybe then I would begin to heal.

I took a slow, deep breath. If I just said them fast, maybe I could say the words before the tears caught up. I closed my eyes and opened my mouth.

"Forgive me?"

My eyes flew open. I hadn't spoken. My mom had. She'd said the very two words I'd been trying to say for months. "What?"

"Angie." Mom reached through the darkness and took my hands in hers. "I've wanted to say this for...so long but..." Her voice sounded as thick as my throat felt. "But..." She squeezed my hand as if gathering courage to go on. "I have no excuse. I've been a terrible mother to you these past months, and I need to ask your forgiveness."

My forgiveness? What was she talking about? It was *me* who should be asking *her*. I was the one who purposely got pregnant. Who'd run off and gotten married without even inviting my family. Who'd had a baby too young. Who'd had a baby die. I was the person who had ripped apart my parents' dreams for me. Who had ruined not only my life, but theirs. If anyone needed to ask for forgiveness, it was me.

You've already been forgiven.

A soft cry worked its way from my throat. A kittenlike whimper. "Oh, Mom...*m-o-m*... I'm *so* sorry. For...*every*thing." Hot tears poured down my face.

"Oh, Angie, so am I." There was no accusation in her voice. No hint of her disappointment in me. Only genuine sorrow that made me cry harder.

I looked across the table. In the dim light I could see tears glistening in my mom's eyes. "Can you ever forgive me, Mom?"

"An-*gie*." The word was half-cry, half-laugh. "It's me who

needs *your* forgiveness. You're a…child. A child who needed her mother, and I wasn't there for you."

"But I wouldn't let you be." Only now that I'd said the words did I understand how badly I'd needed her…*wanted* her. A sob hiccupped its way through my tears. "I'm sorry."

My mom slid out from her side of the booth and slipped in beside me. I could feel the welcome warmth of her body as she put her arms around me and pulled me close. With the palm of her hand she cupped the back of my head and held it next to her cheek. "I've been working on this apology for a long time, Angie. Too long. Let me take the blame for this. Please."

How could my mom be held accountable for my foolish mistakes? It wasn't right. It wasn't fair.

"Please?"

I felt as her hand gently maneuvered my head forward then back. Forward. Back. An answer to her question. She thought I was giving her forgiveness when actually she was giving it to me.

"Oh, Mom." I wrapped my arms around her, laughing through my tears. I couldn't believe how good it felt to simply let my mother hold me. To let her take the responsibility for something I'd started. If this was what being a parent involved, I might not be ready for that responsibility for a long time.

Her hand slowly stroked the back of my hair. The café furnace started with its usual clunk, then fell to a familiar hum as my world shifted into place. Not quite where it had been before all… *this*, but back to a place that felt something like home.

"I love you, Angie. I always have. I always will."

This time I nodded my head into her shoulder all by myself. "Me, too."

My mom held me close, the same way she had when I was little and needed comforting after a bad dream. There was no space between us anymore. None. How could something so intangible have weighed so heavy for so long and then evaporated like mist? It was a riddle I didn't need answered. Not tonight. Not ever. Not as long as things were okay between us again.

Mom gave me a tight squeeze. She gently cupped my face in her warm hands and lifted it close to hers. I could see tears glisten in her eyes. "Tomorrow," she said softly. "I can't wait for tomorrow."

And suddenly, for the first time in ages, I couldn't either.

Libby

"Here's your room key, Ms. Marsden. The bellman will show you to your room. Registration for the conference is just down the hall to your left."

I reached for the plastic key card and turned to follow the bellman. For right now I wasn't going to risk even a glance to my left. If I caught so much as a glimpse of anyone attending the conference who looked one iota more confident than me—which wouldn't take much—I might turn around and go home.

As I stepped past the bellman and into my hotel room, the low thrum of anxiety I'd felt since Bob dropped me off at the airport in Carlton edged up a notch. This was the first time in my life I'd ever been in a hotel room without Bob.

It's about time.

Maybe it was, but right now I was wishing, *hard,* for the security blanket of a husband.

The bellman stood by the door. "Is there anything I can get for you?"

He might get the wrong impression if I requested a roommate. "No. Nothing. I'm fine. It's very nice. Thank you." My self pep-talk wasn't working.

"Ice?"

"No. I'll be going to dinner in a bit." As if he cared. He'd shown me how to adjust the room temperature and pointed out the coffeepot, after he'd put my brick of a suitcase on a stand and whisked open the drapes of my tenth-floor room. The view was dazzling…and dizzying, considering I was all alone. "Thank you," I said again.

"Enjoy your stay." His eyes flicked to the purse on my shoulder.

A *tip!* Of course. He was waiting for a tip. Bob always handled that awkward task when we traveled. I could feel warmth creeping from my chest into my cheeks as I rummaged for two ones and pushed them into his hand.

"Thank you very much." With a smile he stepped out and closed the door.

I stood by the large window and gazed out at the skyscrapers that made up the city skyline. I was a far cry from Brewster.

What are you doing here? This is ridiculous. A waste of money. Coming to a writer's conference won't make you a writer. You'll never get pub—

STOP!

I turned from the window and walked to my suitcase. My shaking hands fumbled with the combination lock until it sprung open. I grabbed my makeup case and went into the bathroom. I wasn't going to let negative thinking send me packing. I was here. Bob had encouraged me. My friends, Jan, Katie, and Vicky, too. Even Brian and Emily had each called before I left, cheering me on. I'd be disappointing more than myself if I left now.

Me, too.

I looked at my travel-tired face in the harsh light of the bathroom mirror and forced a grim smile. It was only by the grace of God that I was here in the first place. The impulsive way I'd registered for the conference over a year ago was long gone. Too much had happened in between. Brian and Kate's engagement. Mike's cancer. Angie Hoffman's baby. The callous rejection letter. I'd given up writing entirely. For months. And yet here I was. Most people wouldn't call this trip a miracle, but if they knew how scared and filled with doubt I was, they might change their minds.

I opened the wrapper on the small bar of soap and washed my hands. *Lord, You've got to walk with me here or I'm not going to set foot outside this room.*

I didn't hear anything. Instead I felt a calm hand of assurance guiding mine as I refreshed my makeup.

You can do this.

I could.

I would.

As I stepped into the hall, I pulled on the hotel room door, making sure I heard it lock. As often as I'd traveled with Bob on business, I'd never once given thought to what countless businesswomen did every week. I felt vulnerable all alone.

But you aren't.

I lifted my chin and headed toward the elevators. I needed all the reminding I could get. I'd come to this conference bolstered only by the confidence of the people around me. I certainly had none of my own.

In the year since I missed last year's conference, I'd been well aware that if I skipped this year's meeting I would be giving in to defeat. I'd spent weeks praying about whether to come. There had been a point this past year when I felt certain the writing door was closed and barred. In utter frustration I'd given my dream to God. *Take it! It's Yours. I don't want it anymore!* And that's when He'd given it back. When I gave it all to Him.

It was still His. I was only here doing His work.

I stood at the bank of elevators. They were certainly slow. *Maybe you should go back to your room and call room service.*

Maybe I should. The meetings didn't officially start until tomorrow. There was only registration and dinner-on-your-own tonight. The spotty airline schedule out of North Dakota was the only reason I was here early. I'd prayed I would feel a *part* of this group, not *apart*. But if most of the group wasn't here yet, it might be too early to expect answered prayer.

"Excuse me." A woman reached around me and pushed the "down" button.

"Oh, sorry." I laughed nervously, realizing I'd been so caught up in my thoughts I hadn't pushed the call button. "I guess I was daydreaming."

She smiled as she adjusted the large cloth bag in her hand. "Occupational hazard with me. But then, that's what I get paid for." She pointed a finger to her chest. "I'm a writer. Conference starts tomorrow."

"Me, too." I cleared my throat. "I mean, I'm here for the writer's conference, too." The elevator doors swooshed open, and I motioned her in ahead of me.

"Welcome." She held out her hand. "I'm Mary Ann. Have you been here before?"

I hoped she hadn't felt the sudden clamminess of my hand. "No. This is my first time."

It didn't take her long to tell me how *much* I was going to *love* the conference. How these would be some of the *most* interesting people I would ever meet. The *best* workshops ever. I hoped she was right and that some of her enthusiasm would rub off on me.

The elevator stopped at the lobby floor and before I could step out Mary Ann was surrounded by women squealing and hugging. Obviously old friends. Alumni from other conferences like this. A quick image of the first day of junior high came to mind. If it wouldn't have been so obvious, I would have scooted right back up to the safety of my room. I'd never been a squealer. Or been part of a group that was. They hadn't even walked off yet and I was feeling invisible. I closed my eyes and sighed. I only had three more days to get through and I could go home.

"Come here." I felt a tug on my arm. Mary Ann was pulling me into her circle. "This is Olivia." She caught my eye. "Right?"

I nodded, hoping I didn't look as dazed as I felt. "You can call me Libby."

And that's when I thought of Anne. She'd been the one to change my name. Change me. Somehow, after all these years, she was still at work. She wasn't here, but she might as well have been for the way I suddenly felt included.

                              ~

"Go on," Mary Ann nudged me with her elbow. "That's what they're here for."

I swallowed hard, mentally rehearsing my words as I crossed the short distance to where the editor stood. It would be easier to ask a stranger for a kidney donation than this. "Are you interested in women's contemporary fiction?"

My question didn't faze him in the slightest. "Yes."

"Okay then." Now I would simply cut open my chest and hand over my heart.

I could feel my eyes rolling back in my head as if I could read this from a script. I silently thanked Mary Ann and her friends who had forced me to practice my pitch on them last night.

"My book is about the friendship between two women. One is having trouble with her kids. One has…" Oh, gosh. Did I dare say this to a man? A complete stranger? I'd have to, it was the crux of the story. "…breast cancer." I pushed the rest of the words out. As soon as I said them and he said, "no, thanks" I could turn and run. "It's about the power of friendship to get you through hard times."

I wished it would be appropriate to bend at the waist, put my hands on my knees, and gasp for air. My heart was pumping so hard I felt as though I'd run a marathon.

The man pressed his lips together and dipped his head as if thinking. How many ways were there to say no?

Long seconds ticked by. Maybe I could help him out. I'd just say, "Thank you for listening" and move on. I opened my mouth.

He reached a hand into his breast pocket and pulled out a business card. "Here," he said, holding out the white rectangle between his index and middle finger. "E-mail me three chapters."

I took the card into my hand. Did I say thanks already? If not, I'd say it again. "Thanks." Twice couldn't hurt. If he wanted, I'd say it a hundred times.

I walked back to where Mary Ann was standing. No, I wasn't walking…I was floating. A Thanksgiving-parade balloon thankful to be tethered by my new friend.

"See? What'd I tell you? It wasn't so hard, was it?"

No, it hadn't been. It had only taken twenty-eight years of dreaming and writing and giving up and writing some more.

And praying.

And praying.

⁓

Three weeks and five "*send its*" later, my balloon of excitement hadn't so much popped, as it had simply developed a slow, steady leak. Within the week of returning from the writer's conference, I'd followed up on all my leads. E-mailing two submissions, snail-mailing three. I'd had to call Emily at college and have her talk me through the process of sending an attachment along with an e-mail. Leave it to my kid to pull me into the new millennium. With a trembling finger I'd pushed the "send" icon, a last-ditch launch of my dream into cyberspace.

My own e-mail was returned to me within a millisecond. *This message could not be sent. You need to specify a recipient for the message.* I blew out the breath I didn't know I was holding and carefully typed in the address from the business card I'd been hoarding. Midas and his gold. Then I took a deep breath, looked the e-mail over one last time, said a prayer, and sent it off.

It was a good thing my internet provider didn't charge by the number of times I checked my inbox. I was getting in pretty good shape between helping Vicky and running back and forth across the street to check my e-mail. Vicky was just as anxious and I was to see if I would get a quick response.

By the end of the first week, Vicky and I had both curbed our enthusiasm. I was beginning to feel that pinprick of deflated dreams. Starting to question the inflated hopes I'd carried home from the conference. I'd been so sure at least one editor would be beating down the door of my e-mail account to get a glimpse at my brilliant writing within the hour...or at least the week.

By the time an e-mail arrived from the very first editor who'd held out his card to me, I'd learned not to get my hopes up.

I'd like to read the rest of your manuscript. Please e-mail it at your soonest convenience.

Soonest convenience? Was that correct grammar? Did I care?

I thanked my lucky stars I'd spent all those dull days editing my story. I e-mailed the entire 400-plus page document within the hour.

As I crossed the street to Ida's house, I reminded myself of the agent who'd asked to read the full manuscript...and of her turn-down. Been there. Done that. Still, Vicky and I spent the afternoon washing china by hand and speculating what it would be like to be interviewed by Oprah.

That smidgen of hope carried me through the grand opening of The Judge's Chambers. A day when the North Dakota spring breeze was balmy and the folks in Brewster were generous in their praise of Vicky's dream. Angie, Vicky, and I worked together serving the crowd as if we'd been choreographed...as opposed to the rag-tag confusion anyone outside the kitchen couldn't see. There was an easiness between Vicky and her daughter that brought a lump to my throat.

Mid-afternoon Angie and I danced around each other near the kitchen entry. As I hurried to get more coffee, she paused with a tray of cheesecake bites in her hands to see which way I was going. When we finally arranged ourselves so we wouldn't trip over each other, Angie tilted her head in the direction of her mom, who was greeting people like long-lost relatives as they came in the front door. "Isn't this the *coolest?* It doesn't even seem like Brewster."

It didn't...but it did. I knew the laughter and community spirit that filled this small space would be hard to duplicate anywhere else.

Just then Vicky looked our way. Her grin was wide as her gaze held Angie's eye. Even weeks later, my eyes stung when I recalled the look that passed between them. Love pure and simple. And something more. The satisfied look of a dream being fulfilled.

If only that look would sustain me through the discouragement I was feeling now. Three more weeks had passed with no reply from the editor. My manuscript could just as well be floating in some sort of cyberspace limbo for all I knew. Not that I was watching the calendar, but even the summer birds outside my window didn't seem to be singing quite as blissfully.

It seemed I might have to quit dreaming. Again.

Or find something else to dream about.

∽

The cookbook project was almost complete. It was surprising

how fast the storyline had come together once Vicky caught on to my idea. It hadn't taken her long to pull recipes from her files to fill in the food-related part of the book. Over the course of spring, I armed myself with highlights of Brewster's history and a few obscure tidbits pulled from old issues of the *Banner* and wrote up a storm. The book was at a print shop in Carlton now. I was confident *The Judge's Chambers Cookbook* would be a steady seller in Vicky's new restaurant. Even I had been caught up in the old-world charm of the characters I'd created.

Now, weeks later, my pathetic balloon of writing hope was left with only the barest gasp of air. I had no doubt that by the end of summer it would be as flat as a pancake.·

I pulled damp clothes from the washer and piled them into the laundry basket at my feet. It was a perfect day for hanging clothes on the line. A light breeze was blowing. The cool of the morning would soon give way to late-morning July heat. What wasn't so perfect were the thoughts that swished through my brain like an extra wash cycle.

Brian and Katie were busy making wedding plans for next summer. Well, put it this way, Katie was making plans and telling the rest of us, including Brian, about them. Her method struck me as a little old-school, but as long as Brian was fine with it, who was I to speak up? I was proud of the way I'd managed to keep my mouth shut. My only suggestion had been that they consider having a small reception back here in Brewster sometime after their wedding in Katie's hometown. So far I hadn't heard *aye* or *nay*.

Emily was staying on campus for the summer. Between the two classes she was taking and her part-time job, she hadn't had a chance to make it home for so much as a lunch at The Judge's Chambers with me. "Soon," she promised. I knew Mike was also on campus this summer. His treatments had caused him to drop a couple classes last semester, and he was using these months to catch up. I had no idea if Emily's summer plans had anything at all to do with Mike's. I knew better than to assume anything these days.

As I balanced the heavy basket of clothes on my hip, I grabbed the clothespin holder and tossed it into the basket. I was well aware of the fact that *this* might be my lot in life.

Now that the cookbook was written I had nothing more to work on other than my columns for the *Banner*. And really, now that the kids were long gone from home, my live-in material for the column was growing slim.

With my shoulder I pushed my way out the door and into the backyard. Even the two birds singing their little hearts out on my clothesline didn't do much for my soggy spirit. The birds took flight as I neared the line and eased my basket of clothes onto the ground. How I wished my life was as simple as theirs. That I could fly away to some place new anytime the notion struck… and when I got there it would be worth crowing about. I'd always thought my life would hold something more than simply being a wife, or a mom. Something…exciting. Something to do with writing. I could see now that it wouldn't. I was going to have to quit wishing for what I didn't have and start praying that God would make what I did have enough.

Lord. It was the only prayer I could muster. He knew what was in my heart.

I pulled one of Bob's cotton shirts from the basket and clipped it to the line. I bent to reach for another. In the distance I could hear my feathered friends take up their wild trilling again. No. Wait. That was the phone.

I lurched toward the back door. There was absolutely no reason in the world for us to have an answering machine. I was physically incapable of letting a ringing phone go unanswered, even if I had to slide through wet grass and leap a flight of steps to do it. I jammed my knuckle against the screen door latch and still managed to answer the phone in the middle of the third ring.

"Hello." I turned the receiver away from my mouth. No need to force whoever was calling to listen to my out-of-shape wheezing.

"I'm calling for Olivia Marsden."

Salesman. Only people who didn't know me well called me Olivia anymore. I'd almost broken my neck for a stranger I didn't want to talk to. Might be great fodder for my column though. "You're talking to her." I'd make quick work of this.

"This is Eric Jameson from Apex Publishing. Is this a good time for you?"

It took a fraction of a second for his words to register. Apex Publishing. Eric Jameson. The first editor I'd met at the writer's conference. *An editor.* The editor. *My* editor. The one I'd pinned my hopes on like a game of "Pin-the-Tail-on-the-Editor." I'd thought my blindfolded e-mail had struck far from the mark, yet here he was on the other end of the line. The editor who had requested my full manuscript.

Was this a good time for me?

"Ye-ess." I could hear the hesitation in my answer. If he wanted to tell me no thanks, an e-mail would suffice. However if he had something else to say...

"I'm calling with what I know will be good news." He paused as if waiting for some sort of response from me.

Dead silence.

Then he continued, "I've shared your manuscript with several readers here at Apex. I presented it at the Publishing Committee meeting yesterday afternoon, and we all agree this is a story we'd like to publish."

There was a weird echo in my ear, as if I were holding a seashell to my head and listening to his words come from some faraway island. Just possibly *I* was the person on the island. I'd been lost. Adrift for years. Here was my life-ring, floating to me through this phone line. A sudden lump pushed its way into my throat. Tears stung my eyes.

"Ms. Marsden? Are you still there?"

"Yes." The word was nothing but a croak.

"I thought maybe we got cut off."

"No. No, I'm here. I'm…just…stunned." I blinked rapidly as I stared at the sunny day outside. It looked so different than I remembered from a minute ago. The trees were greener. The sky bluer. "Is all." None of it made sense. His words. Mine. "I mean, I wasn't expecting this. I'd given—" No, he didn't need to hear that part. One tear ran down my cheek as laughter followed. "I was out in the backyard hanging clothes." As if he needed to hear *that.*

This Eric person, my new best friend, laughed along. "Then it must be a nice day there."

"It's a *gorgeous* day!" It was. The best day ever. I ran my fingers through one side of my hair. "Could you tell me what you said again? I want to make sure I heard you right before I start screaming."

Again he laughed. "We'd like to publish *After Anne.* It's a wonderful story. We'd also like to see a proposal for a follow-up story. Authors tend to build readership over time, so we like to have another book in the works."

Another book? My legs felt rubbery. I pulled out a kitchen chair and sat down. "That's…great. You don't know how long I've waited to hear those words."

"Well, soon other people will be able to read your words." I could hear papers shuffling through the phone line. "There are some details we'll need to go over a bit later. I'll be sending you a contract in the mail. You don't have an agent, do you?"

An agent? I almost hooted into the phone. As if. I doubted the species even existed in the state of North Dakota. "No, I don't."

"You might want to look into getting one, although for a first book deal our offer is pretty standard across the board."

Yeah, I'd do that. *Look into getting an agent.* Oh my, wait till I told that to Anne.

Anne. I missed her with sudden fierceness. Without her this wouldn't have happened. She should be here to share this with me.

She knows.

Tears of a different kind filled my eyes. I blinked them away as Eric cleared his throat into the phone. He spoke. "I just want to clarify some things. Did you co-write this story?"

"Co-write it?" I could hear the puzzlement in my voice.

"Yes." The sound of more papers being shuffled. "There are chapters titled "Olivia," and then there are chapters headed by "Anne." I assumed this might be a partnership."

"Oh. No." It had never occurred to me someone would think Anne had written her part of this story. I mean, she'd died. How could she? I'd written it all.

"It's not true then?"

"Well...yes. I mean...no. Not all of it. Not most of it. I did have a friend who died. It's about friendship." Hadn't I said as much in my cover letter? I'd written that letter so long ago. Surely I'd made the intent of my novel clear. But then again, how would I begin to explain?

How could someone who hadn't lived through our friendship begin to understand the bond Anne and I had? If that person hadn't heard the thoughts and feelings Anne and I had shared, how would they know there was a way to communicate without words? Even if Anne hadn't written her parts, I knew what she'd say. Some things we hadn't talked about, but it didn't take much imagination for me to know how Anne would have felt.

My manuscript was a novel. I had license to fill in the blanks, change a fact here and there to make the story flow better. She'd been the one to tell me, "Put it in the book." The story of friendship she knew I was destined to write.

Our friendship was true. And Anne's faith. Later, mine. Anne would understand…but would this editor?

A quick stab of panic shot through me. What if I'd gotten this far only to have my unconventional telling of this story ruin my chances? I couldn't very well bring Anne back from the dead to rewrite her side of things. If her story was going to be told, it was up to me.

And Me.

Oh, yes. I had no doubt God had a hand in all this.

The editor cleared his throat. "It's a powerful story."

What could I say? "Thank you."

"Is there going to be a problem with the family of…" He paused as if realizing for the first time my best friend had really died. "…Anne? I mean—" He sounded confused. "It just reads so *real*. Will they be comfortable with it?"

I took a deep breath. It was up to me to stand up for this story. Stand up for Anne. For the friend she'd been. For what she'd taught me. "It'll be fine," I said, knowing it would. Anne's husband, Kevin, knew how close Anne and I had been. If nothing else, this story would be a gift to their daughter, Janey. The daughter Anne never got to see grow up. I hoped, too, it would be a gift to many others…the way Anne's friendship had been to me.

As I hung up the phone, the editor's good-bye rang in my mind. "Congratulations, Olivia. We look forward to working with you."

I stood and stared at the receiver for a moment. Had what I imagined really just happened? I reached out and put my hand on the phone. Yup, it was damp and warm. Proof that I'd been gripping onto it just moments ago. Hearing the words I'd dreamed of for so long.

We want to publish your story. A tingle as light as the downy feathers on a baby bird ran down my arms.

I reached for the phone. Who should I call first? Bob? I looked at the clock on the wall. He had a meeting with his loan officers every week at this time. His secretary would only take a message if I called now. I wanted to give him this memo in person even though I knew what he'd say: "I always knew it would happen one of these days."

What about Jan? Or my friend in Carlton, Katie Jeffries? Maybe the two of them could meet me for lunch at The Judge's Chambers in a few hours. I picked up the phone. Should I tell them on the phone or wait until lunch? Their excited cries, *I knew it! I knew it!* would be a fine side-dish to whatever Vicky was serving today. And yet something held me back from pressing the numbers. My hand fell to my side.

I looked out the window. Maybe I should just dash across the street and share my news with Vicky. I knew she was over there. I didn't even have to cross the street to imagine her tight hug and encouraging words. *What did I tell you? I knew you'd do it!*

It seemed everyone expected this but me.

I knew.

So…there was someone else I needed to talk to first. I turned my back on the phone and walked out into the backyard. A breeze lightly tousled my hair as I went down the steps and stood on the morning-damp grass. After a bit I sat on the bottom step, leaned back on my elbows and tilted my face to the sky. Closing my eyes I let the warmth of the summer sun caress my skin as if God Himself had reached down and cupped my face in His hands.

I replayed the phone call of minutes ago in my mind, as if I were retelling it to God.

As if I didn't arrange it all.

I smiled, then whispered, "Thank You."

Answered prayer was so incredibly sweet. Before I opened my eyes, before I hung up the rest of the clothes in the basket, before I called Bob, Brian, or Emily, or any of my friends, I had one more thing to say. "Tell Anne, okay?"

One year later...

Angie

"Are you sure you don't mind if I leave?" I looked around at the stack of dirty dishes on The Judge's Chambers' kitchen counter. Thursday lunches were always busy. It was as if women from Carlton just waited for the end of the week so they could get out of town. "It's still kind of a mess around here."

"Get! Go!" My mom swished a dish towel at me. "Sometimes it's kind of nice to be here by myself."

I put the extra cloth napkins we hadn't used today in a drawer and then grabbed my purse sitting on the floor by the back door. I knew what Mom meant about liking to be here alone. I'd grown to love this old house and what Mom had done with it. It was a peaceful place...even when it was busy like today. The way our customers lingered over coffee and dessert, I had a feeling they felt that way, too.

I dug in my purse and pulled out my car keys. "See you tomorrow. Oh, that's right, I won't." I ran over and gave Mom a hug.

As she hugged me back she started talking. "Now you remember not to overcook the prime rib, right? And don't forget to put the potatoes in. And the salad should—"

"Mom." I stepped back and gave her a look out of the corner of my eye. She knew I knew how to cook this dinner. "I've done it before. And besides, Mark will be here helping. Maybe I can con Sam into coming in, too."

"Oh, *now* I feel better. I'm already worried about leaving your brother at home alone. I just hope the house is still standing when your Dad and I get back." She laughed as she pulled dirty silverware from the stack of dishes and dunked them in soapy water.

For the first time in forever, my mom and Dad were going away for a long weekend in Minneapolis. Ruthie was going to be in charge of Vicky's Café for the weekend, and Mark and I were going to manage The Judge's Chambers together.

When Mark wasn't busy on the farm with his dad, he often came by The Chambers and pitched in. It turned out he had a knack for cooking that none of us knew, not even him...until my mom handed him a recipe one busy day and said, "If you can read, you can cook." And he could.

I had a wild dream that someday Mark and I would buy this place from my mom. Maybe we could start a whole chain of specialty restaurants. It was a dream for now. And dreams had been in short supply until recently. It was good to let my mind fly toward fantastic possibilities again. There were too many things that weren't possible for me anymore, but I was learning there were far more things that were.

"Sam will like this." Mom wrapped a piece of foil over the leftover manicotti we'd served for lunch and tucked it into the fridge. "You'd better get going."

"I'm going." I jiggled my cars keys and opened the back door of the small house. "Have fun in Minneapolis. Drive careful. Call when you get there."

"That's supposed to be my line." I could hear the bubble of laughter in Mom's throat. "But I will. Now go. You'll be late."

I wouldn't be late. I had plenty of time. I climbed into my car and turned it toward the familiar road to Carlton. I had a rare forty minutes to do nothing but sing along to the radio. I cranked up the volume and tapped at the steering wheel. There had been a time when I doubted I'd ever enjoy music again. But slowly that had changed.

There were so many ways I'd changed since…Brett. Ways I knew now were far ahead of the normal learning curve of growing up.

I glanced in the rearview mirror, then set the cruise control on my old car. One of the few extras this car had. No use wishing for things I couldn't have right now. There was a lot my headstrong foolishness had caused me to miss. But I knew now, even after all that had happened, everything would be okay.

I pushed at my blinker and tapped on the brake, merging onto the highway that would take me to Carlton. I'd learned that God could take my stupid mistakes…*our* stupid mistakes, and turn them into something good. I certainly didn't regret marrying Mark. I just wished we hadn't married so early. We were growing up together and sometimes that was hard.

I looked out the window at the long road ahead of me and pushed the resume button on the steering wheel. I had miles to go before I'd be in Carlton. Plenty more time to remember this bittersweet anniversary. The date I couldn't help remembering every month Brett didn't turn another month older.

It was on this same date, six months after Brett died, that I woke late one night to find Mark's side of the bed empty. Usually it was me who couldn't sleep. I slipped out of bed and walked into our small living room. Mark was sitting on the couch holding a picture of the three of us between his hands, his head bent over the photo. Over his shoulder I could see us. Mark, Brett, me. Smiling in that too-brief window of time we'd had together.

Sometimes I loved looking at that picture, other times I didn't. Tonight it brought comfort.

"Hey," I said softly to let Mark know I was there.

He didn't look up. Instead he just stared at the picture. "I miss him." He lifted his wet eyes.

My eyes filled with tears, too. "I know."

Mark put the picture in his lap and lifted his arm, silently inviting me to sit close. I snuggled under his arm and put my head against his chest. There was nothing to say, only sorrow and love to share between us.

Mark took in a deep breath. Blew it out. "I went to a store today after work. At the mall in Carlton. I wanted..." He paused. Breathed deep, again. "I wanted to get you something to remember him—"

"I don't need—"

Mark put a soft finger to my lips. "I was looking at a locket. I was going to put our pictures in it for you. For us. So we'd always remember." He blew a puff of air from his mouth. "But when the salesman started explaining how it was twenty-four carat gold..." Once again Mark stopped to take in a shaky breath. "I held it in my hand and it just seemed like...like...*junk*. It wasn't him."

He pulled me close and held me tight. His voice was full when he finally spoke again. "I figured it out. It wasn't *jewelry* I needed. It's...you. As long as we have each other we'll have Brett." He raised his hand and laid his fingers against my cheek. "Promise me something?" he asked. "Don't ever leave."

I lifted my chin and looked at him through my tears. Somehow the two words I would say held more promise than the two I'd said in city hall the day we got married. "I won't."

Billboards along the side of the road announced that I was nearing Carlton and I tapped at the brake as I neared my exit. There was a hole in my heart...and Mark's too... that would never completely heal. But in a strange way the raw edges had begun to mend. Even if we hadn't gotten married so young, there were no guarantees that life's realities wouldn't come soon enough. One of my friends' parents had died of a heart attack last month. Mike Anderson, who was barely older than me, had cancer. Sometimes I found myself giving thanks that God had taught me what He did over this past year.

I had a hard-won perspective on life most kids my age didn't. For one thing, I was more compassionate to people who were grieving. Funny, it was as if I had a sixth sense for sorrow. I could tell right away when someone came in the café carrying along their hollow heart of sadness. I'd been given a gift along with my grief. I tried to use it gently.

There was much I'd missed, but also much I'd gained. Would I trade any of it?

Of course I would. I wouldn't wish the pain Mark and I...my whole family...had gone through on anyone. Then again, that very pain had brought us so much closer. Who knew?

I did.

I smiled to myself as I pulled into the parking lot. I reached across the seat and grabbed my backpack. *Oooff.* College textbooks were *heavy*. Good thing I only had two of them to lug around this semester. Good thing, too, that my parents and Mark's were helping both of us through college. We couldn't afford it on our own, but we try to pay them back by getting good grades. Part-time classes and a full-time job made for an extra-full-time life.

"Hey, Angie." My new friend Patti was waiting for me on the sidewalk. "Ready for class?"

"Ready," I said as I fell into step beside her.

I shifted my backpack over my shoulder. I was ready for class and so much more. I was ready for life.

Vicky

"May Your hand of comfort rest on us who mourn." Pastor Ammon stepped near the casket and laid his hand on the dark wood. "Into this earth we commit the body of our dear friend, Ida Bauer."

I dabbed at my eyes with a soggy tissue. I'd thought I'd done all my crying at the church, yet here I was at the cemetery starting all over again. Out of the corner of my eye I could see Libby wiping her eyes, too. Her dry-eyed daughter, Emily, had a hand resting on her mother's waist.

We had all known this would happen someday, and yet it took us by surprise. What wasn't surprising was the beautiful fall day God had arranged for Ida's funeral. I could almost hear what she'd be saying if she were here: "Chust vunnerful vedter. You folks shouldtn't be shtanding aroundt feeling sadt. I'm home now. You shouldt be, too."

I couldn't help but smile through my tears. Ida had lived a good, long life. Even though she never had children, she left her legacy of friendship standing outside around her casket on a gorgeous Saturday morning. I could see her nephew, Kenny, wiping at his cheeks with the back of his hand. His wife, Diane, was blinking rapidly as she tried to keep their young son, Freddie, from toddling off. Jan Jordan was between Diane and Libby. How she could look so good while crying was a mystery.

And even more of a mystery was how a woman Ida's age had managed to have so many younger friends. Those of us standing here were a testimony to her. I knew we all had our special memories of this precious woman.

As Pastor Ammon opened his Bible and began to read, I remembered the time, shortly after I'd purchased the café, that Ida had volunteered to teach me to make pie crust.

"Don't overvork the dough. Roll it tin," she said, pressing against my hands with hers so I'd learn just the right pressure to make pie crusts. Crusts that would hold up to the creamy filling she would teach me to make next. I didn't know her lessons would be the start of our friendship.

How many times had she sat in her favorite booth at the café, sipping coffee and visiting with anyone, local or stranger, who happened to pass by her table? She'd made everyone feel welcome in Vicky's Café and taught me by example. Many a time she'd linger long after the coffee rush had passed, helping me clear off tables as if she had nothing better to do than listen to me jabber about how hard it was to run a small town café. How many Pumpkin Fests had she helped me serve pie? She'd served up her love of people along with the whipped cream.

I recalled the several visits Libby and I had made together to visit Ida in the rest home over the past two years. At first Libby told Ida it was research for the recipe book. Ida had been proud as a fluffy meringue to share her stories of the early days with us. But as the recipe book went to print and Ida's health declined, our visits continued. We all knew Ida's time on this earth was nearing its end. If she was ever going to share her memories, we'd better listen. I was glad we had.

How many people would miss her quiet presence around Brewster? I had a hunch almost everyone.

"Let us pray." Pastor Ammon bent his head and so did I. I would miss my dear teacher and friend. Tears ran down my cheeks as the pastor prayed thanks for Ida's loving spirit.

"Amen." The pastor gently smiled as his eyes traveled around our small group. "Ida is home. Let's rejoice with her."

The September sunshine cut through the crisp morning air like a warm hug. There was much rejoicing to do today. For Ida's life…and back at The Judge's Chambers. I knew Ida would understand if I hurried off this morning. We were expecting quite a crowd in just a few hours.

I wiggled my fingers at Libby. "See you soon," I mouthed.

"Okay. What do you want me to do?" I tied an apron around my waist. There was no use trying to touch up my tear-streaked face now. I would sneak a chance to freshen up just before the crowd arrived.

"Mark and Dad set up the buffet table in the main room." Angie stopped filling cherry tomatoes while she marked off what had been done on her fingers. "The cake table is next to it. I told them to put the tablecloths on, too. Sam was supposed to arrange the forks and napkins there, and then set out the punch bowl and cups on the front porch outside, but I haven't had a chance to check if it's done. Maybe you could do that?"

That was it? Check on what had already been done without me?

I looked around the small Chambers kitchen. Mark, Sam, and Dave were up to their elbows in cream cheese-and-olive filling. It was taking all three of them to cut the crusts from the loaves of bread and then spread the creamy filling on the slices. Once that was done, the sandwiches would be cut into finger-sized portions. They'd made no bones what they thought about that last night when we were going over the details of today.

"Why waste good bread by spreading it with *cream cheese?*"

Sam wrinkled his nose as he unwrapped a brick of the white stuff.

"And olives." Mark looked up from the cutting board where he was busy chopping green olives and pimentos into fine bits.

Dave couldn't resist chiming in with his testosterone-loaded two cents. "And what kind of a sandwich is it if you can eat it in one bite?"

"Yeah." Sam and Mark were his chorus.

I smiled. We'd been through this before. "You don't have to eat the sandwiches, you just have to make them."

It was good to see they were following instructions this morning. I opened the fridge. There were already two trays of finger sandwiches covered with a damp cloth on the shelves. Sesame Salmon Bites were marinating in a large bowl. They would get broiled as the guests arrived. Pineapple juice and ginger ale were chilling, ready to turn into punch soon. I could smell the Merlot Meatballs in the large slow-cooker on the counter. There wasn't much for me to do.

I closed the fridge. "I guess I'll go check that everything is ready." I was talking to no one.

I walked into what used to be Ida's living room. I'd described to her in detail what I'd done to this house during one of my recent visits. How we'd scrubbed it next-to-new, added a small front porch, and remodeled the kitchen. I also told her again how grateful I was for the loving care she'd taken of this house over the years. Most days I could feel her still here, welcoming guests as if they were old friends.

Come in. Come in. Shtep quickly so da fliess don't come in. Dere. Now you chust sit andt let me get you somes coffees.

I had a hunch Ida would be peeking in on the celebration today from her window in heaven.

In the past year this little house had hosted countless lunches between friends, special Saturday dinners, anniversary parties, birthday parties...fortieth, eightieth, and numbers in between. Several graduation parties. Even a small wedding. Who could have imagined in our little town my shattered dream could turn into all this?

I could hear God chuckling as I walked through the room.

Ida knew all about today, too. I'd told her what I planned to do for the wedding reception two weeks ago, before she took a turn toward her next life. I ran my hand over the thick white tablecloths on one of the tables. There were fresh apricot-colored roses surrounded by polished greenery tightly tucked into antique vases on each of the tables. A dozen long-stemmed, saffron-tinted roses spilled from a vase on the buffet. I bent to smell the soft, sweet fragrance. I never thought I'd have time to do that on a busy day like today. But it seemed Angie had everything under control.

I walked to the picture window and looked out. Fall was slowly arriving in our small North Dakota town. Green leaves were trading places with orange and gold ones as I watched...a bit the way Angie was trading places with me lately. I used to be the one in charge. But, like the leaves, I'd learned letting go could lead to something better.

One-by-one leaves drifted to the grass. That, too, I noticed was starting to change color. Nothing stays the same.

Summer was gone. So was Ida. And Brett. Along with most of my dreams. I rubbed at the tears pricking the corners of my eyes. It puzzled me how I could lose so much so fast and yet today, feel so filled.

I blinked at the changing world outside. There was so much I missed when I was trying to plan out my life. I'd been blind to the ways Angie needed me even when it seemed she didn't. I'd been so busy lamenting all the reasons why my dreams would never come true that I didn't see how running the café and serving people was what gave me my greatest joy. I simply didn't see the many ways God was working in my life because I was too busy making my own plans.

It was only when my routine life was yanked from under me, and when I understood I didn't have an iota of control over any of it, that I realized I'd never been in charge in the first place. It was only then that I learned I could live with my loss.

My *loss*.

I shook my head against the wonder of it all. Out of my loss had come...this. I turned from the window and looked at the walls that had sheltered me through this past year. How could this small house hold so much more than my dreams?

The Judge's Chambers Cookbook was bound, printed, and selling as well as the sweets on the dessert tray.

Angie and Mark were at college, working hard to make a good life for themselves. Hopefully they'd have another child someday. For now, they had growing to do together. I planned to help in whatever way I could, but it was their life to live...not mine.

Sam was a senior this fall. Out for football. Off with his friends. Willing to pitch in whenever asked. Sometimes he didn't even wait to be asked. It seemed he liked hanging around with us, especially Angie and Mark. Mark was the big brother Sam never had. It was as if Sam was afraid he was going to miss out on something important if he wasn't in the thick of things. The *thick* of our family, that is. He'd be going off to college a year from now. At least that's what he said. I was laying low, trying to let him hear God's plan instead of mine.

I was listening, too. Between the two cafés, there was always *something* going on. Ruthie's girls were growing fast, and she was more than willing to let our part-time help take on more hours at Vicky's. Angie stepped in and filled Ruthie's shoes and mine wherever filling was needed. Sometimes I worried Angie was trying to do too much, but she was young and eager to try new things. I'd forgotten what that was like. Watching Angie was helping me remember.

Libby lunched at The Chambers at least once a week. Sometimes she came early and sipped coffee in the kitchen while Angie and I organized for the day. Some days she waited until the last car had driven away.

"Any leftovers?" she'd ask as we were putting food away in the kitchen.

Those days I usually shooed Angie back to Vicky's. Libby would help me clean up, and then we'd sit together over dessert and coffee in the warm quiet of Ida's house and talk about anything and everything. Memories. Dreams. The mysteries of life.

Against all odds, both our dreams had come true. This restaurant. Her book. Yet there were so many things we hadn't figured out. More riddles I would bring up the next time we talked.

I didn't understand life. And yet I knew God had His hand in it all. Maybe someday I'd figure it out. But not today. I straightened the polished silver dessert forks on the cake table, moved the vase of roses two inches to the left, and then I bent and pushed my nose into the plush cool center of the bouquet and breathed deep.

Today was for celebrating dreams...broken, mended, made new. I planned to do just that.

Libby

"Okay, everybody!" I clapped my hands as if I were a demented wedding-reception planner. I had a feeling Katie might be thinking I was exactly that. Oh, well, *someone* had to get this motley crew moving. "It's time to go. *Now!*"

Brian hooked me with a tuxedoed arm and kissed my cheek. "It's going to be fine, Mom. Chill."

Oh sure, now that he was an "old" married-man-of-a-month, he thought he could sweet talk me. He was right. He could. He'd always had me wrapped around his little finger, and his index finger, and that handsome, young face of his. But I'd learned I could do some finagling of my own with my son.

"I'm going to head on over and check on things. I'll take Katie with me. You and your dad make sure Emily gets there on time." I looked at the clock on the piano. "She's got fifteen minutes to finish whatever she's doing in that bathroom and that's *all*." I pointed a finger at him. "You're in charge."

He grinned. "Whoa-aaa! Tough duty." He hadn't been gone from home *that* long. He had to remember how his sister monopolized the bathroom ever since she'd been tall enough to see her reflection in the mirror. That and a can of hair spray could make our whole family late for church.

"Fifteen minutes." I grabbed the sequined evening bag I'd filled with a lipstick and two tissues. Once we got to the reception at The Chambers, if I really needed anything I could sneak back across the street and grab it.

"Katie?" *Kate*, I mentally corrected. I crooked my finger at my new daughter-in-law. "At least two people in this family can be on time."

She looked up from the couch where she was paging through a photo album of Brian's baby pictures. She closed the album and put it on the end table as she stood. She glanced at Brian. I could see his faint nod as he encouraged her to leave with me. Alone.

She took a deep breath. For courage? Other than a time or two in the kitchen, we'd never spent more than a few seconds with only each other for company. I was trying to change that. "Ready?"

"I'm ready." She brushed at the lap of her pale green dress, smoothing imaginary wrinkles.

We'd had a discussion over what Brian and Katie should wear today. Brian hadn't been at all excited about renting another tux only a month after his wedding, but some wheedling from his sister changed his mind. Katie, on the other hand, had met Emily in Minneapolis for a girls-only shopping spree. The fact that they included me still brought a lump to my throat. I grabbed another tissue and stuffed it into my purse for good measure and then picked up the car keys. "Meet you at the church," I said to Brian and Bob.

Katie turned to Brian. "Don't be late." I couldn't tell if she was warning him or on my side.

We walked out to the car. It wouldn't take long to get to the church. Nothing was too far away in Brewster. With the weather as nice as it was, Katie and I could have walked to the church, but we would need to hurry back to the reception where people would be waiting.

In August Katie and Brian had a full-blown, *Brides* magazine type of wedding in her hometown. That was followed by a stuffy hotel reception that finally relaxed when Mike Anderson somehow took over for the disc jockey and got everyone on their feet for a funky version of the Hokey Pokey. Even though I'd sworn off the Hokey Pokey years ago, I'd ended up dancing and laughing until my stomach hurt.

I didn't even want to imagine what Mike might do today in his own hometown.

"This is sure different than our wedding." Katie was staring out the car window. She sounded young. Wistful. Not nearly as sure of herself as I'd first thought when I met her. Was she nervous about meeting many of Brian's friends, so many people from Brewster, at the reception this afternoon?

I had an urge to reach out and rub the back of her hand with my fingers. Instead I gripped the steering wheel. "You'll be fine. No one expects you to know who everyone is, and Brian will make sure you don't get stranded with anyone for too long."

"Thanks," she said, throwing a quick glance my way.

I was developing a timid affection for my new daughter-in-law. She wasn't a syrupy-sweet kind of gal. But then neither was I. Sometimes it was hard to tell if we were bonding or simply being overly polite. I planned to keep working at it until I tipped the scales toward love. Or *affection*, anyway.

It had taken Emily's observation about how similar Katie and I were to rip away the unkind microscope I'd been viewing her through. No one could hold up under that kind of lens. Anne had taught me that sometimes I had to be the one to open my heart first. It wasn't always easy to unravel the twisted mess of my emotions when it came to my son's wife. I could wish her different…but then she wouldn't be the young woman Brian loved. God knew I was still winding that yarn ball now and then.

You could help her the way Anne helped you.

I felt a wave of unexpected compassion for this young woman. I knew how miserable my inner nit-picking had made me. The years of depression it had caused. If we truly were so much alike, Katie probably beat herself up with words as much as I used to. Maybe I could help her skirt past the many miserable days, months, and years I'd suffered through.

I kept my eyes open, but said a silent prayer. *Lord, help me grow to love Katie. Show me how to be her...friend. The kind of friend Anne was to me. Help me to see Katie through Brian's eyes. And Yours. Anne's, too.*

And then, as we pulled up to the church, it hit me. No wonder I kept calling Kate, *Katie*. It was the same thing Anne had done to me. Changed me from uptight Olivia, into *Libby* through-and-through. She saw right through my *I'm-fine-by-myself* façade, and pulled me kicking and screaming into the friend she knew I could be.

It seemed maybe God was nudging me to do the same with my daughter-in-law.

I had to start somewhere and what better place than in front of a church. I reached across the seat and took Katie's hand into mine. It was ice cold.

"Are you nervous?"

She nodded. "A little."

"Don't be," I said, rubbing her hand between mine until there was some warmth there. "Everyone here is a friend." Even me.

I sat alone in the front pew trying to hold my restless hands in my lap. Katie's nervousness had rubbed off on me. I had no reason to be anxious. This wedding was supposed to be a celebration. They'd kept it small on purpose, saying only God and a few family members needed to hear their vows. There would be more people at the reception and by then all nerves should be long gone. I could only hope.

I glanced over my shoulder. What was the holdup? I knew Emily was here. I'd adjusted her necklace and given her a kiss before I'd been seated. I smiled at the couple sitting behind me, acting as though I knew perfectly well why this wedding wasn't running on time. The woman was rummaging in her purse for something. Ah, a tissue…already.

Thank goodness I wasn't a crier. The only reason I carried tissues was to hand off to other people.

There were a handful of familiar faces across the aisle from me. I smiled and looked past them to the back of the church. There stood Brian and Bob, both handsome in tuxedo-black, Katie in pale-green and pearls between them, holding a small bouquet of white baby roses.

As I turned to face the front of the church the organ music changed. I recognized the first notes of "Jesu, Joy of Man's Desiring," the same song Bob and I had at our small wedding.

Pastor Ammon stepped to the middle of the altar area and nodded to the back of the church. He'd already put in a full day's work. What would it be like to perform a funeral in the morning and a wedding in the afternoon? I didn't have time to ponder the complexities of his job now. I had a wedding to watch.

I twisted around, watching as Bob stepped aside to let Brian and Katie start their measured walk down the aisle. Tears filled my eyes by the time my son and his bride reached my pew.

They took their places at the front of the church. The music swelled; Pastor Ammon nodded at me. I stood and turned, watching as Emily threaded her hand onto her dad's arm. She looked up and then stood on her tiptoes and gave him a kiss right through her shimmering veil.

Lipstick stain was my first thought. *Love* was my second.

As they began their slow walk down the carpeted aisle, Bob

was blinking as though he had bugs in both eyes. I looked to the front of the church. So was Mike.

At the short rehearsal last night Pastor Ammon had instructed us all...

"*Mom*...all you have to do is stand up and turn when I nod. *Dad*...you walk your lovely daughter down the aisle and stop when you get to the first pew. *Mike*...you wait patiently for your bride until *Dad* agrees to give her away in marriage. Got that?"

We'd nodded. How hard could it be?

Too hard for Mike. Bob and Emily were barely halfway down the aisle when Mike broke rank and half-ran to meet them. The old me might have been tempted to step into the aisle and tug him back to his place. The new me laughed out loud as the teary-eyed threesome walked to the front of the church. When they reached my pew, tissue-to-my-eye, I stepped out to join them.

This was a day for celebration, and I wasn't going to miss a second of it.

~

I signed the FedEx delivery slip then exchanged the clip pad for the medium-sized box the delivery man was holding. I knew what was inside. There was no need to tear it open. Not yet. I'd been writing and waiting almost thirty years for this. I could wait just a little bit more.

I set the box on my kitchen table, slipped my arms into my coat, pulled a hat onto my head, and then stepped outside onto our backyard steps. I sat down on the top step and watched as my breath made small pillows in the late-morning October air.

So much had happened in one year; it was hard to take it all in. No wonder I had to sit out on the back step in the cold to clear my head. I'd spent *forever* praying for most of it, and then it was as if someone had pressed the fast-forward button on my life and it happened all at once. Brian and Katie's wedding announcement last Thanksgiving had been just the start. Mike's diagnosis with cancer had eventually propelled Emily and him together like two strong magnets. If anyone wanted to pull them apart now, I dared them to try. Even when I had my doubts about those two, I'd somehow known they'd end up together. But God could have spared me some sleepless nights and prayers and clued me in a little earlier. As it was, I didn't know they were seeing each other *that way* until… I smiled at the memory of Emily showing up on our doorstep almost six months ago…

"What are you doing home?" I had said when I opened the door and saw her standing there in a parka and mittens on a weekday evening. In a split second I remembered the day she'd come home unexpectedly when Mike had been diagnosed with cancer. One look at her face told me this visit was different. "Don't you have class this week?" My mind was working overtime. It wasn't spring break, was it? Why had she rung the doorbell instead of barging in like she always did? Why was she standing out there in the cold? I stepped aside as if she were company.

Instead she stayed out on the step. Grinning. "I have two surprises for you. Where's Dad?" She looked over my shoulder into the living room.

"Bob," I called. "Come here." I could hear as he muted the TV and pushed himself out of the chair.

Emily stood with both hands behind her back, an impish grin on her face. If dandelions had been in season I might have expected her to pull a bouquet from back there. "Mom. Dad." She passed her smile between our puzzled faces. "Ta-da!" She held her mittened right hand out to her side as if she was the prize presenter on *The Price Is Right*. Mike stepped out from the shadows where he'd apparently been lurking. He was wearing an old-fashioned fedora on his head and what looked to be an old tweed topcoat from the fifties…and the Salvation Army.

Okaayyy. I didn't get it. I was happy to see him, and I hoped my face reflected that fact. I was happy they were standing there together. But weren't they both missing class to be here? For what? I knew they'd been *hanging out* as Emily referred to what she did with most everyone. So…?

"Hi, Mike," I said, wiggling my fingers his way. He looked great. His treatments had been over for some time. His tests now negative. "How are you?" It seemed the polite thing to say instead of "*What?*"

"Mom. Dad." Emily was bouncing on her toes. Repeating herself. She exchanged a glance with Mike.

I felt an odd twinge of nervousness. Something was about to happen. I just didn't know what.

Mike took over. "Mr. and Mrs. Marsden?"

Uh oh.

Leave it to Mike. He dipped to one knee. "I've asked Emily to marry me."

"And I said yes!" She pulled off her mitten and held out her left hand. The white-gold ring sported the tiniest, shiniest diamond I'd ever seen.

Mike was back on both feet now. "I know it's not very big, but I wanted to spend my money on *quality*." He put an arm around my daughter. "Like Emily."

And Mike.

Answered prayer was sweet. So were my memories of that night. I was thrilled to have Mike for a son-in-law, but couldn't help the finger of concern that wondered if my daughter might be widowed young. I'd learned, like so many other things, to give it to God. There was so *much* I couldn't handle, *nothing* He couldn't.

I rubbed my hands together. It was almost as cold out here this morning as it had been on the doorstep that night.

I should go inside where it was warm and open the box. But once I opened that box everything would change. With one dream-come-true I'd have to start dreaming of something different. I'd never even considered another dream. And yet there was a part of me that knew, in spite of all this, nothing would change. My day-to-day life would stay the same. Bob would go to work. The kids would go about their lives. I'd get up and sit in front of my computer. How could things change so much and still stay the same? It was another mystery of life to ponder with Vicky over coffee. But that would come later today. Right now I simply wanted to savor what was waiting for me inside.

My book. My thoughts on paper for the whole world to read. Was I ready for that?

As if the world will read your book.

STOP! I wasn't going to let those sorts of thoughts spoil this moment.

Yes. I was ready for that. So there. I'd come a long way from those days of self-doubt. Knowing someone thought my writing was worth reading was part of it. Knowing I was doing what God wanted me to meant more.

A small flock of sparrows swooped through the backyard. I wasn't sure if sparrows migrated for the winter or not. If they did, they'd better get a move on. By the chill in the air, winter wasn't far off. If they didn't, they were welcome to camp out on my clothesline for a few months.

I smiled as I recalled the day a little more than a year ago when I'd vaulted these same steps to answer the call that told me my book would be published. No wonder I'd gravitated to my backyard today. Full circle. Even the birds were back to celebrate.

As I'd done that day, I tilted my face to the sky and said the same words. I meant them just as much…maybe more. "Thank You."

Now. Now I was ready to open the box. I pushed myself off the step and went into the house. I might as well make an occasion of this. I hung up my coat, dumped the dregs of coffee left in the pot, and started a fresh new pot.

The smell of brewing coffee filled the kitchen as I tore the cardboard strip from the top of the box. I'd imagined this moment a thousand times. I thought I knew what it would feel like.

I pulled the thick book from the box. All my imagining hadn't come close.

With my foot I pushed at a kitchen chair. I sat down. I didn't know…I'd never dreamed…

Here it was.

My dream. In my hands.

I ran my fingertips over the shiny cover. Over the illustration of writing paper and a silver pen. Over the title: *After Anne.* Over my name.

My name.

On the cover of a book.

I sat in my kitchen and simply looked at it, trying to take it in. I remembered the long days when I'd questioned God, questioned my purpose. Here it was. Finally. If the wait hadn't been so long… if it hadn't been so hard…would it be half as satisfying now?

I doubted it.

My hands fingered the glossy cover. I held the words I'd kept inside for so long. It had been worth the wait.

I whispered again, "Thank You."

Five years later...

Libby

It was getting to be a familiar sight. Once a year. Like clock-work.

"Hi!" I waved to the FedEx driver as he climbed down from his truck. As usual, I'd been at my computer, dreaming up imaginary things for my characters to do. Only chance had me gazing out the window today as he'd pulled to the curb.

"Another book?"

"Yeah," I said as I signed for the FedEx box. "Another one."

We exchanged clipboard for package. "How many is this?"

I held the box to my chest. "Five."

"Oh, man." He tucked the pen behind his ear. "I couldn't even write *one.*"

I nodded. I understood. There was a time when I didn't think I could write one either.

"What's this one about?"

I smiled to myself. The FedEx man was interested in my books. Go figure. Even though I'd been writing full-time for five years now, it was still hard to believe God let me do this every day.

"It's about *purpose,*" I said.

He waved a hand toward his truck. "Guess I'm gonna have to read that one, too."

"You've read my books?"

He kicked at the sidewalk. "Sure. You gave me a copy of that *After Anne* book when my wife had…breast cancer." He shrugged a shoulder. "You're the only writer I know."

I get that a lot in North Dakota. I'd expected it somewhat, but what I hadn't expected was the mail I received from readers all over the world. God had used my simple stories in amazing ways.

I walked back into my house and did what I'd done with each of my books. I started a fresh pot of coffee and listened to it brew as I pulled my latest book from the box. Number five. The last book in this series.

Once more I ran my fingers over the shiny cover. The title. My name.

My dream had been fulfilled…and so much more. I'd dreamed of writing one book. Just one. Never two. Three. Certainly not five.

When the coffee was done brewing, I poured myself a cup. I sipped while I read through the acknowledgments. The names of my family and friends. My editor. My agent. The people who cheered me on each day. That was all the further I'd read. I knew what was between these covers. I'd spent most of the previous year with these fictional people. People who were as real to me as my family.

I closed the book and held it tightly between my hands, savoring the joy of purposeful work.

Thank You.

I walked to my bookshelf and ran my fingers across the other titles on my shelf. *After Anne,* my book about friendship. *Finding Ruth,* the book that detailed my struggle to find contentment. *Becoming Olivia,* the story of my triumph over clinical depression. *Always Jan.* I'd turned fifty while I wrote that book about aging. And now I had the final book of my journey to add to this shelf. Only I knew just how true these stories really were.

And Me.

Yes…and You, Lord.

There was only one thing more I needed to do.

I set the book aside, walked to my desk, and pulled out the notebook I'd been writing in these past many years. I picked up the silver pen. The one Anne had given me. *Write on,* she'd had engraved on its side. *Write on.*

I would.

I walked back to the kitchen and refilled my cup. Sitting down, I took a sip of coffee and started writing…

> *My latest book was delivered today. One of the books you always knew I'd write. A few years ago I sent a copy of* After Anne *to your daughter, Janey. Maybe someday when she's old enough, she'll read it and know what true friendship is all about.*
>
> *When I'm done here, I'll stick this notebook on a shelf somewhere near my books. A place where I'll always be able to find it. I don't need it to remind me, but you never know, maybe someday someone will want to know the whole story. The story of what your friendship did to me.*

I sat back and stared out the window at the gray autumn sky. The clouds were swirling, dancing in the wind. The kind of day that was perfect for writing. I put pen to paper.

> *So there you have it, Anne. The whole story. From the night we met at that cold football game to now.*
>
> *The end?*
>
> *Only God knows what's yet to be written.*
>
> *Keep the coffee hot and a soft chair waiting. I'll*

*see you, again...someday. I can't wait to tell you all
that happens between now and then.*

I pressed the silver pen to my lips and reread the last line.
Tears filled my eyes as I imagined Anne sitting by an empty chair.
The one waiting for me.

I didn't want to let go of this story. But it was time. There were
only three words left to write. I took a trembling breath, put my
pen to the paper.

I whispered as I wrote.

"With love,"

Libby

A Final Word from Roxy
and Conversation Questions

Most of us will never be called to serve God from some grand, public stage. Our "stage" will be our living rooms and kitchens, our backyards, maybe the garage, or even a computer keyboard.

All my life I felt as if writing was the gift God gave me...but how could I use it from where I lived? For many years I sat in my cozy house in rural North Dakota thinking I couldn't possibly be a writer when I lived in the middle of nowhere. Oh my, did God ever have a surprise for me! But it took stepping out in faith, using the gift He'd given, to find out just what His plans were.

The point isn't *where* we serve Him...the point is *are* we serving Him? Are we doing our best? Are we using our talents? Are we listening for His leading? Are we giving our all? Or are we ignoring His direction and doing things our way?

No matter where God has placed us, no matter what our circumstances, or no matter the messes we've made in our lives, He's given us gifts and work to do. We need to seek His purpose and His will for our lives. No matter what God has called us to do...big or small, it's never too late. Everything is for His glory.

Are you doing the work He's called you to do?

Conversation questions

1. Do you think everyone has a purpose in life? Do you know what your purpose is?

2. Are things like where you live, how much money you make, your level of education legitimate reasons to keep you from your dream?

3. Discuss the purpose of waiting to see a dream fulfilled. Would you rather achieve several smaller dreams or one big one? Why? Are some *dreams fulfilled* more satisfying than others? Share some examples.

4. Do you have an "impossible" dream? Brainstorm ways it might be possible after all. Is God bigger than the obstacles?

5. Think of Angie. What did fear do to keep her from her purpose? What are other things that keep us from achieving our goals?

6. What difficult circumstances has God used to help you grow? Talk about the ways difficulties can propel us from our comfort zones into something more.

7. What happens to someone when a dream dies?

8. Do we sometimes need to change our dreams? If so, how do we do that?

9. What happens when a long-held dream is achieved? Is it possible to have no goals or dreams?

10. If you've read the other books in the Coming Home to Brewster series, talk about the different friendships Libby has formed throughout the series. Do we have friends for the different seasons of our lives? What are some of the important friendships in your life? How have they ministered to you? How have they helped you find your purpose?

Other fine books in the
Coming Home to Brewster series...

AFTER ANNE
Newcomer Anne and aloof Olivia's unlikely friendship blossoms in the midst of misunderstandings, illness, and new life. Will Olivia, drawn to Anne's deep faith, turn to God when her life is threatened?

FINDING RUTH
Ruthie dreamed of success in the big city. But when her big chance comes, will it be worth the price? Will she have to say goodbye to Paul Bennett, her first love, a second time?

BECOMING OLIVIA
In this third novel in the Coming Home to Brewster series, Libby Marsden discovers that sometimes God works through unexpected circumstances to help us become who we're meant to be.

ALWAYS JAN
Jan Jordan is having a birthday she's been dreading since she learned to count. Kenny Pearson never really grew up. Ida Bauer's husband is gone and so are most of her friends—and she has to face it—soon she will be, too. What does she have to offer?

This book deals with aging in ways that will have you smiling, nodding in recognition, and learning about the joys God brings with the gift of years.

About Roxanne Henke

Roxanne Sayler Henke lives in rural North Dakota with her husband, Lorren, and their dog, Gunner. They have two very cool young adult daughters, Rachael and Tegan. As a family they enjoy spending time at their lake cabin in northern Minnesota. Roxanne has a degree in behavioral and social science from the University of Mary and for many years was a newspaper humor columnist. She has also written and recorded radio commercials, written for and performed in a comedy duo, and cowritten school lyceums.

Fans of Roxanne Henke are discovering the wonderful fiction
of Susan Meissner and the praise continues to pour in
from readers and reviewers everywhere....

Why the Sky Is Blue

Tracy Farnsworth, reviewer for roundtablereviews.com says: "Bring out the Kleenex, you are certain to need them. Susan Meissner's debut novel is...an impressive debut and one that leaves me hungry for more."

A book group leader in Tennessee reports: "...it was one of [our] favorites out of all the ones we have read...We discussed in depth, the characters, and how you made them so real. One woman said you had a gift for allowing the reader to identify with each one, rather than with just one or two. A few shared how they had cried as certain parts of your story touched their hearts in various personal ways...We are a diverse group of readers. Quite a range in ages and in tastes. Only a few books have been as well received by this bunch as was *Why the Sky Is Blue*."

Roxanne Henke, author of *After Anne, Becoming Olivia,* and *Always, Jan* says: "*Why the Sky is Blue* was so real it broke my heart, then, somehow, mended it. I loved this book!"

A Minnesotan says: "Wow! What a brutally honest, beautifully expressed, compelling book! I simply could not put it down. I will definitely recommend it to many, since I work in my local public library. This book is so personal, that I thought I was reading a diary or personal letter..."

Jill Elizabeth Nelson, Romantictimes.com reviewer says, "Meissner crafts a gripping novel of lives torn apart by tragedy but healed by the light of sacrificial love."

A Window to the World

A high school teacher in Minnesota says: "I just finished *A Window to the World*—it was amazing! I could hardly put it down and snuck it to school to finish the last couple chapters because I just couldn't wait...There is so much in this novel! You really made each character come to life and filled the events with meaning at every turn...Thank you for writing one of the most entertaining and thought-provoking books I have ever read."

A teenager in cyberspace says, "I am only 14 years old but I bought your book and I couldn't put it down....I just wanted to tell you that your book doesn't only have an impact on grownups but also on teens. It really made me understand how bad things that happen to us is also a way that God is shaping us even though we may not realize it till later."

Sara Mills, reviewer at www.christianfictionreviewer.com says: "POWERFUL. I can sum this book in a single word… When I finished the last page, all I could think was, WOW. The book was beautiful… The threads of happiness and joy blend with the threads of sorrow to make something that is stronger than either could be alone…I highly recommend this book, and applaud Susan Meissner for writing so eloquently what is almost impossible to put into words."

The Remedy for Regret

Kelli Standish, reviewer at focusonfiction.net says: "…This timeless story, and Susan Meissner's lilting, lyrical prose, entranced me from the first page…The plot moves well, and climaxes with a …scene that is so powerful and laden with such an unmistakable sense of the Divine it had me in tears. And the message of the story is so poignant and gentle, you feel as though you've been hugged. Bottom line? Meissner's incredible gift with words has never shone truer than in *Remedy for Regret,* and this book is a must for any discerning reader's library."

Marilyn in Iowa says, "You did it again! I have read all three of your books—just finished *The Remedy for Regret* and love it!!! Can't wait for number four!!!!